TÁCNBORA BOOK ONE

EXILE AND PAGANS

This is a work of historical fiction. While inspired by real events and historical figures, many characters, places, and dialogues have been fictionalised for narrative purposes. Any resemblance to actual persons, living or dead, outside the scope of known historical figures, is purely coincidental.

Cover design by Charlotte Mouncey www.bookstyle.co.uk
Typeset in Adobe Garamond Pro 11.8 pt on 14pt

First published in 2026 by Larbok Creative.
ISBN: 978-1-0683723-1-5

LARBOK CREATIVE

Dedicated to my mother Ellen (Nellie) with special memories of a wonderful Christmas Eve in Droichead Nua, Co Kildare, after which town Colm-Bruide's sword is named.

TÁCNBORA BOOK ONE

EXILE AND PAGANS

AIDAN K. MORRISSEY

"Gæða sceal wið gode, gælda sceal wið lafe;
æghwæþres sceal endebyrdnes wyrcean."

["Good must be matched with good, and evil with reparation;
every deed must find its due reward."]

— *Beowulf,* lines 1055–1057

Main Characters:

Ecclesiastical Figures and Hy Residents

Columba (Colm Cille):	Irish bishop and missionary who founded the monastery on Hy. Exiled from Ireland after the Battle of Cúl Dreimhne.
Cobthach:	Columba's cousin and one of the twelve disciples who travelled with him to Iona. Father of Finn (fictional).
Baithéne:	Brother of Cobthach and one of Columba's disciples. Succeeded Columba as Abbot of Iona.
Tochannu:	Columba's cantor and a senior member of the Hy community.
Grilán:	The monk responsible for ringing the bells.
Ernán:	Uncle of Columba. Steward or caretaker of the land and supplies.
Scandal mac Bresail:	The infirmarer, responsible for the sick.
Lugaid:	Almoner, distributor of charity and alms.
Rus & Fichna:	Twin brothers in charge of training novices.
Finnian:	A goatherd on Iona. Teacher of herbal lore. Father of Darragh.
Máire:	Finnian's wife. Herbalist and midwife and mother of Darragh.

The House of Cobthach

Findlugán (Finn)	(Fictional) Son of Cobthach. Trained as both monk and warrior. Married Morag, father of Colm-Bruide. Later becomes Tácnbora (Standard Bearer).
Colm-Bruide mac Findlugán:	(Fictional) Son of Finn and Morag. Raised among the Picts.

The Kings and Nobility of Dál Riata

King Diarmait mac Cerbaill	High King of Ireland, defeated at the Battle of Cúl Dreimhne.
King Conall mac Comgaill:	King of Dál Riata. Patron of Columba and Iona.
Queen Sabhdha:	Wife of Conall mac Comgaill. Strong influence at court, teacher of Finn.
Connad:	Son of Conall and Sabhdha. Trains with Finn and Eochaid.
Áedán mac Gabráin:	Succeeds Conall as King of Dál Riata. Father of Eochaid, Domangart, and Eochaid Find.
Eochaid:	Youngest son of Áedán. Later becomes King.
Domangart & Eochaid Find:	Older sons of Áedán.

The Picts and Their Allies

King Bruide mac Maelchon:	King of the Picts. Father of Morag.
Morag:	(Fictional) Daughter of King Bruide. Marries Finn, mother of Colm-Bruide.

The Kingdoms of Northumbria

Hering, son of Hussa:	Pretender to the throne of Bernicia.
King Æthelfrith:	Historical King of Bernicia and Deira. Father of Oswald.
Queen Acha:	Second wife of Æthelfrith. Mother of Oswald.
Prince Oswald:	Future king and saint.

Place Names and Modern Equivalents

Historical Name	*Modern Equivalent*
Daire	Derry / Londonderry, Ireland
Hy	Iona, Scotland
Muile	Mull, Scotland
An t-Òban	Oban, Scotland
Dún Att	Dunadd Fort, Argyll
Abhainn Nis	River Ness, Scotland
Hinba	Possibly Jura or Eileach an Naoimh
Bebbanburg	Bamburgh, Northumberland
Pictland	Ancient Scotland (North of the Forth)
Dál Riata	Irish/Gaelic kingdom in western Scotland and northeastern Ireland.

6TH/7TH CENTURY IRELAND SCOTLAND AND ENGLAND

Prologue

Ad Gefrin, Kingdom of Northumbria: 641 AD

All men must die. Some fall gloriously in battle, others waste away in the grip of disease. The fortunate slip quietly from the world, wrapped in blankets and surrounded by those who love them. But no man, especially a great man, should die alone.

Oswald, King of Northumbria, stood motionless, gazing down at the still form stretched upon the straw pallet. The old man's beard, once streaked with fire, had faded to grey. His face, worn by years and weather, held no pain now, only peace.

A tear traced a slow path down Oswald's cheek. 'Oh, Finn,' he whispered, voice thick with grief, 'my truest friend. You've guided kings and saints, fought in the shadows for peace while others claimed the glory. Why were you alone at the end?'

He knelt beside the bed, trembling. 'Why now, when our enemies gather? When your wisdom and guidance are more vital than ever? Why have you been taken from us at the very moment we can least afford to lose you?'

His voice broke on the final word, and silence filled the space where once a legend had breathed.

Riverbank mud, streaked with dried blood, clung to the dead man's forehead and cheeks. Oswald knelt beside the lifeless body, his trembling hands gently brushing away the tangled blades of grass and fallen leaves caught in the old man's silver hair.

He had been a humble man of God, an acolyte and cousin to Saint Columba, companion of the blesséd Bishop Aidan of Lindisfarne. A healer of souls and a quiet force in the shadows of kings. He had carried saints to safety, whispered comfort to the dying, and when the times demanded it, sent warriors, princes, and tyrants, without hesitation, to their graves.

By day, he fed the hungry. By night, he prayed with the weary. His voice had once calmed storms in the hearts of men but created fear in his and God's enemies.

Yet on this bright autumn morning, no voice had come to soothe his own end. No hand had eased his passing. He had died alone.

His once-fiery hair had long since faded to iron-grey. But on that day, already slipping into legend and song, the cowled old priest had reached once more for *Fidelis* the sword of his youth and the goat-headed staff of his office. He stood, not as a relic of the past, but as a warrior of the present. It was said he cut down at least five East Anglian raiders leaving their lifeless forms in the great hall.

They had come in the night, a horde of pagan marauders descending like a storm.

The settlement was engulfed. Flames devoured timber and thatch; screams pierced the darkness and then fell silent. Infants lay motionless in crimson-stained cribs. Children, maimed and broken, crouched in corners, lifeless eyes staring through smoke. Women were dragged from their homes, their cries muffled, their bodies brutalised, their throats slit. Their remains littered the streets like discarded cloth. The old men, too frail to flee or fight, were lined up before the hall and beheaded one by one.

In the end, only the crackle of fire and the slow seep of

blood through splintered floorboards remained. Smoke curled skyward, thick with ash and the stench of flesh.

But before the Great Hall fell, before the raiders breached the upper terrace, the old priest had acted. He had taken Oswald, his siblings, and their mother by the hand, leading them silently through the shadowed trees and thick bramble that edged the riverbank. He whispered prayers as they crouched beneath the undergrowth, the prince's face pressed into his mother's cloak.

Then the old man had risen, staff in hand, sword at his side, and walked back up the hill.

To delay them. To draw their fury away. If necessary to die in the attempt to save the Queen and her children.

Oswald climbed a tree, a mighty oak, the same tree under which the priest's lifeless body had been found this morning. From its high branches, he watched his world unravel. Eyes stinging with grief, he stared down at the ruins of his childhood, a once vibrant and joyful settlement reduced to an abattoir.

Bodies lay strewn across scorched earth. Faces frozen in terror. Limbs twisted into shapes no living body could take. Blood pooled thick in the soil, sinking deep into the dry cracks like water into thirsting ground. His fingers dug into bark. His chest tightened with each shallow breath.

When he finally climbed down, silence wrapped the place in a suffocating shroud, a silence more terrible than the screams that had come before.

Finn rejoined the royal family at the treeline, they crossed the river in silence, fording its shallow width under cover of trees. They headed north, towards sanctuary in Dál Riata and the protection of its Irish king.

In exile, Oswald was forged in fire.

He learned the craft of kingship beside Finn, theory by day, battle by dusk. Together they fought against Pictish raiders and ambitious Irish pretenders. Blood marked their blades and hands, but through it, Oswald was shaped, not only into a warrior, but into a ruler worthy of loyalty.

And Finn, the old man now lying lifeless, had been the chisel and the shield.

He never spoke English, not in the decades he lived among Oswald's people. No one could remember a single moment he had tried. With Oswald, he spoke only the soft, lilting Irish of his homeland, a language the young king had learned in exile, and now clung to with reverence. When Finn prayed, it was always in Latin, the tongue of Church, of saints, and, some say, of heaven.

Every night, Finn sat at the king's table, though he ate little. After the meal, while others lingered or laughed, he would gather the untouched bread and meat from plates and kitchens and carry them into the homes of the settlement's sick and poor.

He fed the frail, tended the dying, laid gentle hands upon fevered brows. And as they ate, he sang. Quiet, haunting songs in Irish, love ballads, hymns, laments, warrior chants, no one understood the words. But none needed to.

The melody itself was enough.

Calloused hands paused mid-labour. Mothers' shoulders softened as sick children slept at last in their arms. Old men, knotted with pain, sighed as something, pain, or perhaps, time disappeared for a moment.

'Rath Dé ort,' he would whisper as he left each home. *May the grace of God be upon you.*

That phrase, those three words, were the only Irish most of them ever learned. And in reply, they offered their own.

'May God protect you too, Father.'

Once, Oswald had asked him, 'Why don't you speak to my people in their own tongue?'

Finn had shrugged. 'I've enough to say in Latin and Irish. I've no time to be misunderstood in this crude language you teach your children. If I had my way, the whole world would speak Irish.'

The king never raised the matter again.

Oswald owed him everything.

This warrior-priest, this stubborn, holy contradiction, had prepared him for kingship. He had negotiated the alliances that made Oswald's rise possible, forged the path that led to the crushing of the pagan Cadwallon, and cleared the way for Oswald to unite Bernicia and Deira. Now he sat as the most powerful overlord in the land.

And it was because of the man now lying still in front of him.

He thought of Finn in his prime, standing tall in the shield wall, or riding into battle, sword aloft, hair blazing like fire under the sun. He saw him smiling, laughing, banner raised high as he rode ahead of the king. The royal standard snapping in the wind behind him, unflinching, unwavering, just like the man himself.

The body before him bore little resemblance to that memory. Frail. Stilled. But even now, something of that power lingered.

His given name was long forgotten, known only to a handful of elders. It no longer mattered.

He had been many things, monk, warrior, mentor, husband, father and grandfather.

But to the world, and to Oswald, he would always be known simply as:

'TÁCNBORA', THE STANDARD BEARER.

The story of his life.

Part One

EXILE

It is better for each man that he avenge
his friend than to mourn him much.
Beowulf [Unknown]

Chapter 1

Province of Uladh, Ireland 556 AD

Do gach bó a buinín, agus don leabhar a chóip féin.

(To every cow belongs her calf, therefore to every book belongs its copy.)

King Diarmait mac Cerbail -High King of Ireland.

The child screamed hoarsely, his small fists pounding against the wooden frame of the bed where his mother lay. His cheeks were wet with tears and mucus, his voice raw from hours of crying out a single, desperate word, *Mama.* But the woman beside him made no comforting move. Niamh tossed and moaned, her skin slick with sweat, limbs twitching with fever. Her eyes, when they opened, stared through shadows, seeing only ghosts.

'Cobthach...' she whispered, her lips cracked and bleeding. 'Cobthach, please...'

But her husband could not hear her.

Far across the hills, Cobthach sat alone beneath a tree, his face buried in his hands, his monk's cowl soaked with blood that was not his own. Around him lay the ruin of the day's slaughter, limbs twisted in death, the air still thick with the iron tang of spilled life. He wept not only for the fallen, but for the ones he could not protect. For the woman he loved, now fading in a dark room. For Finn his son, too young to understand, too fragile to be left behind in such a cruel world.

In Daire, the wind howled through the monastery, rattling shutters and stirring ashes. Finn wailed into the cold night, his small body shivering, arms reaching again and again for a mother who could no longer hold him.

Would either of them live long enough to see Cobthach's return?

Before him, the pride of Connacht lay strewn around the hillside. The cool evening breeze could not dilute the stench of death. Bodies counted by the thousand, decapitated, dismembered, disembowelled. Mercifully dead, or piteously, painfully dying. Screams resounded across the once green valley and verdant meadows. The keening Banshees would be busy tonight.

Blood pooled in natural hollows, streams of the crimson life force ran down the incline slowly coagulating like cooling volcanic magma. High above, majestic white-tailed eagles circled, biding their time, whilst new battles and skirmishes broke out below. The eagles watched as magpies fought ravens, rooks ganged up on jackdaws and red-legged chough vied viciously for meat with hooded crows. The eagles cared nothing for these scavenging corvids. When they were ready, they swooped, razor sharp beaks and clenched claws prepared to rip their share of the carrion feast the day had provided for them. Caws, screeches and calls became intermingled with the screams of dying.

Such a contrast with the morning. Hordes of farmers, fishermen, and fresh-faced youths, followed the warriors of their King. Diarmait mac Cerbaill, High King of Ireland, rode proudly at the vanguard. As the mists cleared, and the autumn sun rose from beyond the rolling hills, a sea of banners fluttered throughout the throng. Maroon and white, green and gold, blue and yellow, green and red, black and white; all the clans of Connacht were represented. A display of might and power, designed to strike fear into anyone who dared confront the King with the hope of obtaining bloodless surrender.

At the top of the hill, a coalition of warriors from the clans of the northern Uí Néill encircled Abbot Columba. Despite inferior numbers no sign of concern lined the rugged bearded faces of the men who'd come here to exact revenge.

'You see, Father Abbot, that Druid is talking continuously into Diarmait's ear. He's even got a Raven on his arm, cawing the Morrigan's support for his words. The constant chattering must be like a buzzing fly... I'll enjoy swatting that one.' It was Cormaic, the leader of the coalition army who spoke.

'I doubt he'll be anywhere near when the fighting starts, Cormaic. He'll hide behind Diarmait when the time comes, and Diarmait himself will stay well clear. He'll have reason enough for allowing the pagan to counsel him. He was crowned under pagan law but feigns Christianity when it suits him. I have found to my cost, that my cousin Diarmait, is a coward. He is not a man to sully his hands with blood. He prefers to send mercenaries and heavily armed warriors to kill young men supposedly safe in the sanctuary of God's holy church.'

'Pagans have no time for the one true God, Father, and Diarmait has no time for God if the Christian faith gets in the way of what he wants.'

'You're right, Cormaic. Today he will be taught a lesson. God will ensure our victory. He should not have killed Curnan, should not have had his men, armed with axe, spear and sword threaten and cut me and he should not have boasted about it later. Are the men ready?'

'We, here, are all ready. The rest are preparing their arrival by sea. The great Niall himself would have been proud of the raiding boats. Five hundred more clansmen will arrive when they hear the signal that the battle is commencing.'

'Good. Curnan's father made a wise choice placing you in charge of this campaign,' said Columba. 'However, before battle we must deal with this approaching messenger.' He pointed to the nobleman riding up on horseback.

'The mighty Diarmait, High King of Tara, son of Cerbaill, son of Fergus, son of Conall, son of Niall of the Nine Hostages, commands you to return to the lands from whence you came. The omens and law are against you. If you retreat now, no further repercussions will follow. However, if you refuse to leave, the might of the southern Uí Néill and the Connachti will destroy you and make widows of your wives.'

Cormaic threw his head back and laughed.

'Tell your mighty High King, that I speak in this matter for King Áed, the father of Curnan, and for his Holiness Abbot Columba of Daire, son of Fedhlimdh, son of Fergus, son of Conall, son of Niall of the Nine Hostages. The armies of the Cenél Conaill and Cenél nEógain, gathered here today on this hillside, care nought for pagan omens, dreamed up by demented druids, and their false gods. Just as your, so-called King, cares nothing for the laws of the one true God and his holy church.' He pointed towards the tent being erected for Diarmait to shelter in and watch the forthcoming battle. 'The lad, Curnan, like your King, and Abbot Columba was also a grandson of Fergus mac Conall, grandson of the great Niall. Curnan's death, at the command of Diarmait, was in violation of the sacred laws of sanctuary. The men who murdered him also threatened Abbot Columba and cut his face with a knife. We are here to demonstrate that God's laws of the Church are more important than the laws of any earthly King, and Diarmait will learn that lesson. He will pay dearly with the blood of those whom he has forced to be here, on this day.'

He picked up a spear, threw it over the head of the messenger. 'Tell your King that any man who passes that spear will not be returning to his home.'

The messenger remained unmoved. 'You speak brave words for a man who commands a force less than one third the size of our armies in the valley.'

'We have God on our side. Each man here has ten avenging angels surrounding him giving him all their power and strength. We are not afraid.'

'If you are certain, that is the message you wish me to convey, I will do so. Who shall I say gave me this message?'

'Cormaic, son of... who knows? I am Cormaic the Bastard,' he laughed; 'a name that Diarmait will never forget after today.'

The messenger galloped away, the sun on his back, he glanced and spat at the spear as he passed.

Less than an hour later the warriors of Diarmait lined in formation with the enforced volunteers behind them. Cormaic and Columba had chosen this place well. The attacking force had to come uphill across rock filled terrain which would not allow them to form any sort of sustainable shield wall, nor could they launch any cavalry attack. Hand to hand combat was the only alternative, at least for the Connachti.

The defenders had had days to prepare, and they had prepared well. Boulders and wooden stakes had been collected and placed strategically, forming a defensive wall difficult to penetrate. The northern warriors retreated behind this wall now. Cormaic had thrown the spear, not only as a warning to Diarmait but also as a marker for his own warriors, who were now gathering in six rows of one hundred and fifty beside their piles of weapons. With spears in hand, they began a rhythmic pounding on their shields. A thunderous roar matching the percussion, echoed from hill to hill, a signal which also reminded the forces below they were marching into hell.

Columba knelt, holding his book of psalms which he raised in the air. He was joined by his cousins, Baithéne and Cobthach, constant companions from the Abbey. They prayed for victory and the safekeeping of the soldiers who had come here at the Abbot's request. Cobthach also prayed for Finn and Niamh, his young child and wife.

Banners billowed in the wind, Connacht's kingly colours, blue, black and white flowed freely, the throng began to sing as they moved confidently forward. An upbeat marching song, calling on their gods to ensure victory. A song quickly learned and, for those standing on the hill, never to be forgotten.

The raven-haired Morrigan is with us,
Victory cannot be denied,
The mighty Lugh, and Badb Catha fight
With us, side by side.

Our weapons forged by Goibhniu,
Provide our strength and might.
The enemies of Connacht will die,
Or flee, before day turns into night.

As the first rank of warriors reached the spear marker, the first volley of spears hit them, then the second, the third, on and on, a continuous stream of death. It only needed a small percentage of these to find their target and the advancing warriors were cut down. The singing stopped under the relentless volleys. The peasant force, armed only with farming implements or axes, tried to pick up the shields of the fallen warriors for some protection, to little avail.

No banners flew. Tainted and tarnished with mud and blood, the symbols of Connacht now carpeted swathes of this bloody hillside of certain death.

'Keep advancing, no surrender,' Diarmait shouted from the safety of his tent.

Clambering uphill, over corpses with bloodied grass and broken banners underfoot was making progress difficult. Still, they pushed forward, greater numbers meaningless in this bloodbath.

Suddenly it became even worse for the Connachti.

From behind them, an alarming cry of 'At them Uí Néills, for God and Uladh!' Those with the strength to look behind saw hundreds of heavily armed warriors arriving from the sea. Farmers and fishermen with only pitchforks, scythes, axes, and spears recovered from the grass or pulled from the dead, were no match for ferociously wielded swords. Wheat farmers against fierce warriors, piscators with fishing spears and tridents could not defend against pikes, swords and axes.

With the new arrivals carving into the rear, and the shield bearing warriors all dead, Cormaic and his men left the protection of the now obsolete defensive wall and pressed down the hill, crushing Diarmait's conscripted army from both sides, leaving them nowhere to run, other than into impaling spikes already crimson from the blood of their fallen companions.

It was a speedy slaughter. There was no thunderous clash of shield wall hitting shield wall. No swearing and urging of strong experienced warriors for men to push harder. Just one-sided carnage. Cormaic's prophecy that any southerner who crossed the spear line would not return was fulfilled. Northern Uí Neill soldiers, surrounding Diarmait to prevent his escape. They began jeering.

'Be silent,' the deep tones of Abbot Columba's voice boomed from somewhere up the hill.

He arrived to see Diarmait sitting on the ground, tears flowing freely down his face. The Druid sat beside him, the crow still on his arm.

'Three thousand arrived with me this morning, and now none of them remain,' Diarmait lamented.

'You were warned Diarmait, you only have yourself to blame,' replied Columba.

'Kill me now, just be done with it.'

'No,' said Columba. 'You must live with what you have brought about today. You wronged me and the Church when your men murdered Curnan. You wronged the Cenél Conaill and Cenél nEógain by depriving them of their prince and future king.'

'But he killed the son of a nobleman.'

'It was a sporting accident, if you allow games to be played without rules, giving a hefty wooden camán and ball in the hands of young, unyielding, boisterous men, someone will always get hurt. You could have asked for the honour price, not assassinate the boy.'

'The dead boy's father would not be satisfied with the Lóg n-enech, of a few dozen milk cows. What good is milk when your only son is gone?'

'Then blame him for this.'

'No, Columba. I blame you. We are kin, and you have done this? I see you are carrying the stolen book you were ordered to return. I judged you fairly in that matter, but still, you disobey my ruling. Curnan's death was a mere excuse for this battle. I will ensure that you are punished for this act of massacre.'

'I will answer to God for what has happened, and He alone will judge me. You, Prince Curnan and I share common ancestry. It takes more than blood to make kinship mean anything. Curnan was your blood kin. That didn't stop you.'

'Curnan and his conniving father had eyes on my throne! The nobleman was eliminating a potential rival to that crown. '

'So that is your true motivation for killing the boy and now three thousand men? Fear and greed. I will not grant your wish to die today, for the souls of those men lying out there will weigh heavily upon you. You're waking and sleeping hours will be filled with the sights of this massacre until one cold, frost-filled morning, a son of Suibne will take your life on the bank of the River Boyne. I doubt we will meet again in this life. Goodbye cousin.'

Cormaic raised his sword. 'But someone else will die today.' He sliced the tempered metal into the neck of the druid. The raven tried to fly but was tethered to the man's wrist. Cormaic deftly removed its head. 'If you are but a simple raven, I apologise. If, however, you are indeed The Morrigan, then I am happy to have destroyed such a powerful pagan pretence of a god.'

Columba sat on the hilltop, with Baithéne and Cobthach, Cormaic and Cathall, leader of the sea forces who came to attack the rear of the Connachti. The sun was setting behind the sea, the sky a bright crimson, scattered clouds diffusing the light.

'It seems all the bloodied souls are making their way to heaven together,' said Cobthach, breaking the silence.

'What tales will you tell your son about this day Cobthach?' asked Cathall.

'The truth. This was not a battle to weave into greatness by clever words. The most skilful of the filidh could not change this from the massacre it was. How many casualties did we sustain?'

'One dead and fifteen injured,' replied Cormaic 'and the death was a man slipping in blood and falling on his own sword.'

'Let us away home,' said Columba, 'Although the day has been successful, it has not been good. Too many souls have been sent to their celestial destinies, leaving families and loved ones to mourn and try to cope with the loss of breadwinners. Also, I have much work to do, I believe my time to do it here is limited.'

'What are you saying, Columba? Are you going to die?' asked Baithéne.

'God does not tell, even me, the date of my death, my friend. However, I believe he may have other plans for me.'

Chapter 2

Is tre chert noco n-étar colainn.
(It is through justice that the body is not torn apart.)
– Old Irish Proverb

Returning from the battlefield, Columba entered the monastery, the solemn chanting of monks greeted him, their voices thick with grief. The scent of incense, meant to purify, couldn't mask the stench of war that clung to his robe.

Then, from the darkened corridor, a new sound, thin, reedy, insistent. An infant's cry.

He turned the corner and saw a nurse seated on a low stool, Finn half-asleep in her lap. The child's head rested heavily against her shoulder, soft tufts of red hair clinging to his brow. His eyes fluttered open at the sound of footsteps, wide and unfocused, and he whimpered softly. One small hand clutched at the fabric of her cloak, the other twitching with dreamy, aimless movements.

'He will be a strong one,' Columba murmured. 'A warrior or a scholar, perhaps both.'

The nurse did not look up. 'If he lives that long, I have brought him here to pray for him.'

A monk approached with Cobthach, and Baithéne and urged Columba, into the quiet of the sacristy.

'I bear grave and sad news,' he said, his tone muted. 'Cobthach, your wife, Niamh, is much worse and has the plague. She is being nursed by some of the other wives, but she has been calling out for you.'

'I must go to her immediately. What about Finn? Is my son well?'

'You need not worry for him. He is presently with my own nurse. We are offering prayers for him and Niamh.'

Columba took Cobthach's arm. 'I'll come with you,' he said; 'Baithéne will join me to keep vigil while you take care of Finn.'

'But I must be with Niamh, she needs me.'

'Go to her and say what you need, but at this moment Finn needs you more.'

Niamh. Beautiful, resilient, courageous, Niamh, seemed to have shrunk to half her normal size. Her vibrant, flowing red hair looked rusty and matted against the pillow soaked with sweat. Her eyes, those penetrating green eyes, looked opaque and unseeing. Cobthach stumbled to her bedside and knelt. She reacted to the touch of his hand on her face and turned her head towards him.

'Cobthach,' she struggled with his name. 'Finn… take care of Finn.'

'We both will, my love. Once you're well.'

A smile broadened her lips a little. 'Bring him to me. Get him.'

'No Niamh, I want to stay with you.'

'Finn…, get…,' she exhaled loudly, 'get…Finn.'

Cobthach turned to Columba, who nodded, 'I am here with Baithéne, we will care for her until you return. Do as you have been asked and bring your son to his mother.'

As Cobthach left, Columba went to his friend's bedside, tears rolled down his cheeks. She tried to smile as he approached. 'Take care of them both, Colm,' she said using the shortened form of Colmcille his name in Irish. 'Cobthach needs you even more than Finn does at this moment, but Finn…' her voice faded to nothing.

'Niamh, don't worry yourself. Finn will grow into a fine man and will live a long, fulfilling life. One that will make you proud as you look down on him from Heaven.'

She blinked twice, closed her eyes, inhaled a gentle breath and sighed.

Columba prayed as Cobthach returned, a young crying toddler in his arms.

'Hush now little one,' Columba said, taking the boy from Cobthach; 'your Mammy has gone to be an angel in heaven with God, but she'll always be looking out for you.'

Finn whimpered unaware of the silence settling over the room. His mother's body lay still, her lips parted in a final breath.

Cobthach, tears flowing freely, stared at his son. 'She wanted to see you,' he whispered. 'She wanted to hold you one last time.'

Finn let out a tiny sigh and nestled against Columba's robes. The infant would never remember this moment, but Cobthach would. He would remember forever.

Cobthach fell to his knees beside the bed and sobbed, 'Why did I leave you? If I hadn't gone to Cúl Dreimhne, I could have saved you, I could have saved you.'

'No, Cobthach, it would have made no difference.' Baithéne put his arm around his brother's shoulder 'It was her time to go, and she goes knowing that she was dearly loved by all who knew her, she was a beautiful soul and has left you with a fine son.'

When spring arrived, and the scent of blossom filled the air, Columba was walking amongst his favourite budding oak trees, a messenger hurried along the pathway behind him. Columba heard his footsteps and heavy breathing and surprised the messenger when he turned.

'Holy Abbot, Holy Abbot, I have important information.'

Columba prepared hurriedly for a long journey. More than a hundred miles, from his beloved Daire to the monastery in Tailtin to the south. 'They've charged me with raising an army in a matter secular and not spiritual, resulting in the deaths of 3,000 souls,' he said to Baithéne. 'King Diarmait must be behind this, only he has the power to request a synod to be convened at such short notice. He is calling for my excommunication or even execution and doesn't want me there to defend myself.'

Normally, he would have walked, if he had time, but the sessions were to begin in two days. He ordered a horse to be saddled and readied for him.

'Let us come with you Colm,' Baithéne and Cobthach said.

'This is something I must face alone. Cobthach, Finn needs you here. Baithéne, dear friend and cousin, I do not wish you to become sullied with any sin I may have committed. If things do not go my way, I want you to carry on my work here in Daire and our other churches and communities.'

'How will you get there on time?'

'It is not my first time to travel to Tailtin. Although I have always walked before, taking several weeks, calling into our monasteries on the way. Tonight, I will ride to Domhnach Fainre, eat, rest and change my horse. Tomorrow I will go to Ard Mhacha then to Dún a Rí and finally onto Kells. It will be a long and hard ride but with fresh horses and alternating between a canter and a trot it is achievable. After a rest and change of clothes I will leave Kells after Lauds and walk to the synod. I should arrive in Tailtin in time for Terce, my prayer schedule will not be interrupted and, hopefully, my presence will surprise them.

The journey was hard but uneventful. Columba arrived at Kells in time to celebrate Compline, the monks were delighted by the presence of their Abbot and mentor.

He bade farewell to his hosts for the night and took a leisurely stroll on the bright spring day, across the hills and valleys where sheep and cattle grazed. He talked with farmers, their wives and children. The walk would normally take about two hours, but he had three to kill. He didn't want to arrive too early.

He arrived too late. The synod was in a hurry, beginning immediately after Lauds, just as Columba was leaving Kells and a vote had already been taken. Excommunication. His crime? The taking up of arms and creating political unrest.

As he walked towards the convening priests, he spotted one friendly face. His friend and teacher, Bishop Brendan of Birr, approached him and hugged him in welcome.

'How dare you embrace an excommunicate?' asked the synod leader.

'You would do as I do,' replied Brendan; 'if you opened your eyes to see what I can see. As Columba entered these chambers, a pillar of fire preceded him, even now an angelic host surrounds him. This man is destined to bring souls to the Christian faith. God himself has ordained this, who are we to go against the will of God. I have argued long that he should not be excommunicated without at least hearing from him. Never has such a punishment of an Abbot, been meted out *in abstentia.*'

'I have seen no fire nor angelic host and the decision has been made. I see no reason to change that.'

'But as he is here now before us, let us hear what he has to say.' Brendan was determined and the faces of the synod with few exceptions showed they agreed.

'Very well, but beware, Colmcille of the Cenél Conaill, for

you should no longer use your holy Latin name of Columba, we know you to be of both an excitable and vindictive character. You are too passionate about the disputes of your kin and are not averse to getting involved, as you did at Cúl Dreimhne. You directly caused the death of thousands of Pagans, preventing them from being brought into the Church.'

'Dear brothers in Christ,' Columba began.

'You are excommunicate we are not your brothers.'

Columba, ever composed, ignored the interruption. He stood tall in his worn woollen robe, his voice calm, clear.

'Dear brothers in Christ,' he repeated, 'I admit to being passionate, passionate about my faith, my ministry, and my God. But I am also a man of justice. Diarmait mac Cerbaill is of my kin, yes, we share a grandfather, as I did with Curnan mac Aedo, but my anger was not of blood. My fury arose from a violation of sacred trust. Curnan sought sanctuary within my church. I gave it to him, as is the duty of all servants of God. Diarmait's men dragged him away, sword and spear bared, slashing at me, spilling blood on the threshold of Christ's house. They murdered him in front of women and children.'

He touched his cheek where a pale scar traced the memory of that day. 'I bear this mark not for revenge, but for righteousness.'

One of the bishops leaned forward. 'Are you certain, Columba, that your rage was not provoked by more… personal motives? The matter of the Psalter, for instance?'

Columba met the man's gaze. 'Do you believe I would raise men to battle over a book?' He held up his hand, calm but firm. 'One which I still possess, not out of pride, but as a testament to my labour. I worked for months, in silence and solitude. I used my own ink, my own parchment, my own hand. Which part of that effort belonged to Bishop Finian?'

'You are of the Uí Néill,' another bishop said, voice edged with reproach. 'Your kin have gone to war for far less.'

Columba's mouth tightened. 'Diarmait was wrong in his judgment. He likened a Psalter to a calf and its mother. A copy is not theft. Knowledge cannot be bound by ownership. But even that, grievous though it was, would not have driven me to arms. It was Curnan's murder that demanded justice.'

'Curb your ire, Columba,' said another bishop.

'I stand here, not in anger, but in sorrow,' Columba said, lowering his voice. 'But I ask you this: do you judge me by God's law, or Diarmait's? He who mocks our faith with druids at his side and keeps one foot planted in the old ways? Did he come to you alone, or with his pagan seer to whisper fear and favour?'

There was silence. The room, heavy with incense and judgment, gave no answer.

'Enough,' the presiding bishop said. 'You are dismissed. We will send for you when our deliberations are complete. You may take food in the refectory.'

The day turned to dusk, and dusk into a long, watchful night. At last, as Columba prayed alone in the chapel, Brendan entered, face drawn.

'They are ready to speak with you, Colm. Come.'

They walked in silence through the cloister. In the chamber, the seven bishops sat in quiet gravity. The presider stood.

'This was not an easy decision. Our hearts are divided. But we have chosen a path forward. The excommunication will be lifted, under one condition. You must leave Ireland and take up the path of *peregrinatio pro Christo*, exile for the sake of Christ.'

Columba caught his breath. Exile. Not punishment, but a calling. A cross laid upon his shoulders.

'You are to win back as many souls to Christ as perished at Cúl Dreimhne, three thousand. That shall be both your penance and your mission.'

He bowed his head. 'I will do as you command. But I will not forsake my homeland forever. If God wills it, I shall return.'

The presider hesitated, then nodded. 'Go in peace. May your zeal be a light to the isles.'

Columba left Tailtin with his heart torn in two. He stopped at every monastery on the journey home, embracing the brethren who had once followed him, who now watched him walk a lonelier road. Word of his exile spread, and already the tale began to grow, of a monk being cast out, not in shame, but in devotion.

He would cross the sea. He would take the Word to distant shores. And perhaps, one day, the path would lead home again. Although he swore that the man who would return would not be the one who had departed.

Chapter 3

Tairngir do Dia is ní bága do farraige.
(Trust in God and do not fear the sea.)
— Old Irish Saying

A shaved head and grey cowl, an expertly woven dove embroidered on one sleeve, Finn looked like the twelve other monks aboard this small currach. Faithfull followers of Abbot Columba, joining the revered man of God into exile. Only Finn's stature set him apart. At six years of age, he appeared tiny as he sat next to his identically dressed father holding onto his hand. In the years since his mother's death Finn, had grown into a clever and willing student, mature beyond his tender years.

It appeared the whole province of Uladh thronged the harbour and shoreline to bid sorrowful farewell to their religious leader and inspiration. Now in his forty-third year, Columba did not want to leave his beloved homeland. Daire, the city of oaks where, he believed on every leaf a white angel sits, listening to the monks singing God's praises, was where his heart was happiest. He had founded his first Abbey here and the city grew up around it. He loved to walk in the oak groves which he held sacred, forbidding any tree from being cut down. If one was toppled in a storm a novena was invoked.

The fallen tree was to lie untouched for the requisite nine days before monks could use saw and axe to divide its precious wood between the city's poor and the Abbey.

As the boat cast off, the tall, imposing Abbot, wearing the blue cowl of his rank over his white tunic, stood at the prow. Staring at the embroidered dove on Columba's back, Finn was growing impatient, waiting to perform the duty he had been assigned.

'Uncle Colm, Uncle Colm, are you ready yet?' Finn, shortly to celebrate his seventh birthday, held the caged bird tightly to his chest.'

Columba, catching sight of his mother and sisters on the dock, tried in vain to force back tears running in rivulets down his cheeks, soaking his tunic. How a child's voice can lift the spirits. He smiled. 'Yes please, Finn, but watch your step.'

Carefully opening the cage, enveloping the dove in his large, caring hands, Columba turned towards the shore. Raising his arms aloft he gently released the feathered symbol of peace. On graceful wings it soared high into the azure sky, circling before deciding in which direction its freedom would take him.

In a deep, melodious voice that could be heard across valleys Columba sang.

Sweet white dove your home is here,
As my heart will remain forever,
Fly to me, if troubles come,
I'll abandon Daire, never.

God has called from across the sea,
His Word I must obey,
When I pray, my first and last will always be,
Of the people and angelic oaks of my beloved Daire.

Finn gripped his father's hand tightly as the currach drifted farther from the shore. The crowds were still visible, but their voices faded into the wind. He had tried to be excited at this great adventure, but the further they sailed, the more his stomach ached.

Taking Finn's hand, Columba walked to the stern of the boat and held the steering oar tightly, never glancing back.

'Come young brother, keep me company and pray with me as we start this great adventure together,'

'Uncle Colm, why are we going, if it makes you so sad?'

'There are many reasons Finn, some, easy to explain. I can tell you stories to fill the hours of our journey. Other reasons, your father and I will tell you about as you continue your education together with us, and others, in Dál Riata.'

Finn's small fingers tightened around Columba's hand as the shore faded. 'Will we ever come back?'

Columba looked down at him, his face unreadable. 'I don't know, Finn.'

'You said you'd never abandon Daire.'

'In my heart, I never will,' Columba replied.

Finn swallowed. He had thought of exile as a journey, but now it felt like something else; something being taken from him.

'What about my mother's grave?' he said. 'Will she be lonely?'

Columba inhaled sharply. He knelt beside the boy and cupped his cheek. 'Your mother will never be alone, Finn. She is with God. No matter how far we go, she is with us too.'

Finn's fingers curled into the fabric of Columba's robe. He wanted to believe. Columba gently rested a hand on the boy's shoulder. 'I know it is hard. But where we are going, you will learn many things. You will grow strong. And one day, Finn, you will understand why we had to go.'

Finn nodded, but a single tear slipped down his cheek as he turned back. His homeland faded into the mist.

'Are there really pagans where we're going?' Finn said.

'Not everywhere. The place we are traveling to is like another part of Ireland, ruled by Irish Kings, who are my cousins. We will have to travel to find pagans, but we'll be doing that a lot.'

'Can I come with you to visit them?'

'When you can read and write better, have learned the scriptures and the Pictish and Saxon languages, you'll travel with me, with others, or alone. Your fate is to be a guardian of souls and defender of the righteous.'

The boat stayed in sight of the shore for several hours. The monks, with saddened hearts but in high spirits, sang as they rowed. Although heading to exile, they were happy to follow their Abbot, helping him on his enforced mission.

As the Irish coastline moved further away, a favourable wind meant the small sail could be hoisted and the crew could relax their straining, aching muscles. Finn distributed milk and bread and his uncle, Baithéne, led the prayers.

May God bless and protect us as we journey to do His work. Bless this food and may it nourish our souls as well as our bodies.

Amen.

Columba did not eat. He raised his eyes to heaven and remained in quiet contemplation. Even Finn knew it was best not to disturb him at such times.

After, what seemed to Finn to be forever, Columba turned to the young acolyte.

'I promised you, that I would tell you why we are making this journey,' he said; 'away from the most beautiful country and city God blessed the world with. To do this, I must tell you about my sins of pride and anger, for those are the true causes of our plight.' He paused momentarily. 'Let me start with the day I caused the death of three thousand men. Men with wives, children, mothers, who would never return to the arms of their loved ones or the warming hearths of their homes.'

'Are you talking about the battle of Cúl Dreimhne?' Finn asked.

'Yes, Finn. I am.'

'I've heard that you went to war over who owned a book, is that right?'

'I hope not Finn, but my pride-fuelled anger over that matter may have made my actions and feelings towards King Diarmait more severe than might otherwise have been the case. He made, what I believe was, an unfair judgment against me. I had laboured long hours, foregoing sleep and food to make a copy of a psalter, a book of psalms. Diarmait sided with Abbot Finnian, who laid claim to my book because he owned the original.' Columba's eyes narrowed, and he took several deep breaths before continuing. 'I pleaded my case, but the King decided a copy of a book is like a calf to its mother.' His voice hardened as he spoke. 'That cannot be, but that story is for another time, another journey. In truth, I sought the arms and assistance of my fellow northern Uí Néills, to punish Diarmait for violating the church's sacred law of sanctuary.'

'What's sanctuary?'

'Sanctuary, Finn, is a demonstration of Christ's infinite mercy. Anyone who feels afraid of punishment and is being sought by others can ask the Church to shelter them and keep them safe from those who wish them harm.'

'What happened?'

'A young man, named Curnan, accidently killed the son of a nobleman in the Court of King Diarmait, during a boisterous game of iomáint. He came to me, in fear for his own life, fleeing Diarmait's soldiers. He asked me for sanctuary, and I happily granted it, for he was the son of King Áed, my dear cousin and friend.'

Again, he paused, his gaze struggled to move away from the disappearing rocky Irish coastline. 'Sanctuary should have ensured Curnan's safety whilst the honour price was negotiated between Diarmait and King Áed. However, Diarmait and the dead boy's father are not true Christians. Diarmait pretended to be when it suited him, but he always had a druid by his side. Soldiers came to Daire and, although I stood in front of the boy, they sliced my face, seized Curnan and murdered him in front of me. I will bear this facial scar of that attack forever, but it was the brazen disregard for God's law that scarred my heart and hardened me to punish Diarmait.'

'I thought you got that scar in the battle.'

'No, Finn. I went to Cúl Dreimhne with your father and your uncle Baithéne, not to fight but to pray. Cormaic, the commander of the army gathered in my name, led the battle.'

'Is that the Cormaic who told me the story of how he killed a pagan god by chopping off her head?'

'Yes, Finn, the same Cormaic. He likes to tell that story, but it never happened the way he normally tells it. Cormaic is a great narrator, almost as good as he is a soldier but, like all bards, he is inclined to make things sound better than they were in reality.'

'You mean a lie?'

'Not exactly, Finn. A story doesn't have to be true to be a good and entertaining tale. A lie is something not true and designed to deceive or hurt the person hearing it or another. Believe what you read in the Bible but don't always believe the stories told by storytellers.'

'Are you a storyteller, Uncle Colm? Should I always believe you?'

Columba laughed. 'Think of me as a history-teller, Finn. I'll tell you exactly what I saw happen and I will not try to change what I saw to make the story more interesting. Now do you want me to tell you the story of the Battle of Cúl Dreimhne or not?'

'Sorry, Uncle Colm. Yes, please.'

With a smile on his face, Columba began.

'We arrived at the site of the battle the night before. Cormaic and his men had been there for days, preparing a fine defensive position at the top of a steep hill. Boulders and wooden stakes were placed strategically forming a defensive wall difficult to penetrate.'

Finn's eyes widened as the famous orator began a tale he had always wanted to hear. His father refused to talk about that day.

'Pits, with spikes in the bottom, were dug at intervals down the hill. 'We'll make them come to us,' Cormaic said. 'Diarmait is no warrior and lacks the wit to control a battle. There's only one, narrow approach to our position and we're ready.' I had trust in Cormaic and total faith in God. I did not sleep that night but stayed awake praying with your father and uncle.'

'What happened in the morning?'

'A heavy mist blew in from the sea overnight,' Columba continued; 'From the top of the hill it was impossible to see beyond halfway down. The sounds of Diarmait's army filtered through the mist, but we could not see them, nor they us. We prayed for fair weather, and the sun began to burn through the mist. When it had cleared enough, we saw a magnificent sight. Diarmait had brought with him an army of thousands. He had equipped them with many banners, and they sang. Oh, Finn, how they sang, some of the finest voices I've ever heard. But their words were in adoration of pagan gods, calling upon them to defeat their foes, in this case, us.'

Columba sang the pagan marching song, the words still etched into his heart.

'That song still haunts me, Columba,' said Cobthach; 'why are you teaching my son that?'

'It's an important part of that dreadful day, the day that sealed our fate.'

'Is it not a sin to sing a pagan song about gods? Uncle Colm?'

'It is not a sin, Finn, to learn about the beliefs of others. We call non-believers in Christ and the one true God, "pagans." However, they are really believers in other gods and are just as fervent in their beliefs as we are. We are missionaries, our duty is to teach.'

'But how can we teach, and convince the non-believers to trust in Christ?'

'There are different ways. There is the way of the Romans and in many ways the Roman Catholic Church, the followers of the teachings of St. Peter. When the Romans were in Britain, Gaul and the other countries, they sent their legions to defeat the peoples of the conquered lands, convincing them that a greater army meant a greater God. This was not an effective way to change minds, as it created resentment and hatred. Eventually, it stirred rebellion. In Britain, the Romans never defeated the Picts in the north and had to build a great wall to keep them out.'

'Does that mean the Picts' gods are mightier?'

'It was not the gods who were mightier, but the Picts were better at fighting the Romans, than most.'

Baithéne frowned. 'You make it sound as if their gods are equal to ours.'

'No,' Columba said firmly. 'However, their faith is just as strong. That is why we must not mock them but guide them.'

'Guide them? Or destroy their beliefs?' Finn asked.

Columba smiled. 'That is for them to decide, Finn. We offer them the truth and a choice. Whether they accept it or not, is between them and God.'

Finn's brow furrowed. 'How can we teach the pagans if they think their gods are real?'

Columba smiled. 'We show them the truth. Not by force, but through faith and patience.'

Baithéne snorted. 'Faith and patience do little when a man has an axe in his hand.'

Finn glanced at his father, who remained silent. 'Father, if we know their gods aren't real,' the boy pressed, 'why don't we just destroy their idols?'

Cobthach hesitated. 'Because belief is not a thing that can be burned away, Finn. It clings to a man's soul like blood to iron.'

Baithéne crossed his arms. 'The Romans forced the world to believe in Christ through war. And their empire spread far because of it.'

Columba's expression darkened. 'And where is that empire now?'

The silence stretched between them.

Finn's mind raced. *If the Roman way had failed, and talking to pagans would not always work, what was left?*

'Will we need an army if we are to fight the Picts?'

'We will not be fighting the Picts , Finn. Our Church deals with things differently.'

'But we follow the Pope and the Roman Catholic faith.'

Columba couldn't help himself. He laughed, Finn looked crestfallen.

'Oh Finn, your teachers have done a great job with you, and you have listened and learned, but not everything is straightforward. Yes, we believe that the Pope, as a descendant of St. Peter, the rock on which His church was built, is the leader of our Church. But we, in our Celtic church, follow Christ in accordance with the teachings of St. John. There are differences in the way we worship, the way we preach and the way we live our lives.'

'What differences?'

'You will learn more as your education continues Finn, but some of the differences are, monks in the Roman Church cannot marry or have children, like your mother and father. They prefer to enclose people in Churches, we prefer to preach outside, reserving church for certain occasions. Christ held his sermons in the open, we do the same. There are other differences but, as I say, you will learn these as time goes on. It is important though that you know we are the same church with the same beliefs, but a different way of following those beliefs.'

Finn was thoughtful. 'I think I understand, Uncle Colm. But can I hear more about the battle now?'

'Of course, but first let us sing a hymn. This was the hymn we sang before the battle. Our song was very different from theirs. "Be my eyes O dear Lord of my soul." Come, let's sing it now together.'

Columba vocalised the first note, the others joined in with melodious monastic voices.

Be my eyes, O dear Lord of my soul,
Be my strength, and my courage, making me whole
Fill my thoughts with your glory both day and night
When darkness descendeth, please be my light.

Today be my armour, my sword for the fray;
My shield and my breastplate, throughout this long day;
Thy wisdom please guide me, give power to my arm,
Thy guidance before me, protect me from harm…

The hymn continued for four more verses, at the end all sang 'Amen' together.

'This song of prayer asks God for strength, not only before

a battle but whenever we need help, guidance and the courage to do what's right.'

'Was the battle right?'

'At the time, I believed so, but now, two years later, I regret the slaughter, the needless loss of life.' He sighed. 'It is necessary for us to examine our consciences, to decide if what we have done is right or if our passion and rage have taken control of us. In the heat of battle, I believed with everything I am that I was doing the right thing, but innocent soldiers, farmers and slaves paid the price, not Diarmait or his nobleman who incited the fight. They deserved God's vengeance, but they made others stand and die in their place.' He looked directly at Finn and with emphasis on every syllable he said, 'The time is coming Finn, when you will have to decide, for yourself and others, whether to fight or talk. I hope by learning about this battle it will help with those future decisions.'

'Why would I ever have to make a decision like that?'

Columba studied the boy carefully. 'In time, you will see. God has set out a plan for you. You will be more than a monk, Finn. You will be a protector. A standard-bearer not only in war, but in faith.'

Finn frowned. 'But I don't want to go to war.'

'You may not have a choice, son,' Cobthach said.

Finn's stomach knotted. 'But I'm not strong like you.'

Columba smiled. 'Strength is not only in the arm, Finn. It is in the mind, in the heart. You will be strong in ways even I cannot foresee.'

Finn looked down at his hands again. Small, weak hands. The way Columba spoke it seemed they would one day carry something great.

Chapter 4

'I care not when I sleep tonight, If I waken ever.'
— St. Colmcille (Columba)

The wind and seas remained kind and the small group made steady progress. By mid-afternoon the horizon began to take shape, land rising above the grey waters.

Columba continued instructing Finn on the battle at Cúl Dreimhne and Finn kept asking questions.

'But isn't King Diarmait also of the Uí Néills?'

'He is King of the southern Uí Néills, he's also my cousin. We share a common grandfather, Fergus mac Conall, who was a grandson of the mighty King Niall. There's great rivalry between the clans of the north and south, but, thanks be to God, bloodshed is infrequent. On this occasion, Diarmait exceeded the boundaries of kinship and blood and murdered the heir to the northern Crown. Even worse, he did this in the sacred grounds of my church, drew my blood and showed open defiance to God's law.'

'You seem to have many cousins, Uncle Colm.'

'No more than you, Finn, you are my cousin, as I am yours and all my cousins are your cousins. We have the warrior blood of King Niall of the Nine Hostages, scourge of the Bretons,

Britons and Romans, running through our veins. I have decided to use his strength for the furtherance of God's work; in time you will have to decide which path you will take.'

'I will follow the way of you and my father.'

'Will you little brother? We will speak of this many times in the future before you are as old as me. They may not be easy conversations. Now on with the story, within two hours we will make landfall and will need to find somewhere to sleep.'

Finn was confused, but he wanted to hear about the battle so made no comment.

'The things I saw that day, Finn, and the cries I heard, I cannot take out of my soul.' After a pause lasting a few minutes, he continued; 'There must have been thirty thousand spears on the battlefield before it became even worse for the attackers.'

'How could it have been worse?' asked Finn.

'Because Cormaic is a great tactician in the art of war. Half of our forces had arrived by sea and awaited the first cries from the battlefield to march on Diarmait's army from the rear. Within three hours, three thousand bodies lay dead or dying.' A chill came into his voice, like water slowly freezing. 'War is not glorious, Finn. It assails your hearing, you want to shut the noise out. It fills your nostrils with the stench of blood, death and dying, your eyes see unforgettable horrors that return to you forever, whether you are awake or asleep. Avoid war, if you can, Finn, only kill in God's defence and even then, if there is no other way. I believe the Banshee cry was heard throughout Ireland that night.'

'I think I heard a Banshee the night my mother died.' Finn seemed downcast.

'You were too young to have remembered anything that night, Finn.'

'But I still hear an awful wailing and keening sound whenever anyone talks about my mother. It is not a sound I enjoy, and

I've stopped asking about her because of it.'

Columba placed his arm around the young boy's shoulders. 'It was a terrible loss to us all. Your mother was one of the finest women I have ever met. You have her eyes, and if your head wasn't shaved, you'd also have her hair, as red as a dawning sky. Your father misses her more than the rest of us, but he, and we, have you to remind us of her. Now come, we must prepare to beach this boat.'

Once ashore, Columba called Baithéne and Cobthach to his side. Finn followed his father.

'I'm sorry Finn, you need to stay here. Help Brother Ernán to build a fire to keep us warm tonight. I need to go with your father and Baithéne to see if this land is a suitable place for us to build our new home. If all is well, I'll take you fishing tomorrow.'

By the time the three monks reached the top of the hill, the sun was lowering in the sky. It was partially hidden behind a distant blue outline, a far-off mountain. Columba was dismayed.

'We need to move on tomorrow. I cannot live here.'

'What's wrong Colm?' asked Baithéne.

'Those distant hills are draining my will to go on,' Columba replied. 'Our beloved land is still within our sights. Erin's hills will forever be in my heart and mind's eye, I cannot have them physically visible in the morning when I wake. My heart would break, my soul would be burdened seeing that beautiful island every day. All our thoughts and energies must now look forward. We need to move further away. We'll set sail in the morning at dawn. Let's join our companions, take supper and try to sleep. God will tell us when we find the right place.'

As the eastern sun lit up the distant Irish hills, the monks and their Abbot took to the currach moving northward stopping at islands, if the Irish coastline was visible, they'd move on. Eight nights had passed since leaving the oaks. Lashed by storms and half-blinded by rain, they followed Columba's prayers more than the stars. But on this morning, when the mist lifted just enough to show land ahead, they rowed with every last ounce of strength they had. Their bodies were broken, their strength was failing. The beach was nothing more than a sliver of rock and shingle, lashed by rain and wind that seemed to come from every direction at once. Now, half-frozen, and feeling more than a little lost, the monks huddled under their winter cowls, as Columba surveyed the land with narrowed eyes. Looking west, even his keen eye could not catch a glimpse of home.

As the boat touched the shore, Finn hesitated. This wasn't Ireland. The land smelled different, the wind carried a sharper edge, and the sky seemed too vast, too unfamiliar.

His father jumped down first, followed by Columba, and the others. Finn gripped the edge of the boat. His heart pounding.

'What are you waiting for, Finn?' Cobthach called.

'I… I don't know. This island feels different to the others we have stopped at.'

He didn't expect the words, but he felt them. Ireland had always been beneath his feet. His mother had walked on Irish soil, he visited her grave every day. Now, stepping onto this land felt like leaving a part of her behind.

Then, he saw them, a herd of goats, wild and free, moving along a ridge above the shore. Their bleating, sharp and unmusical, struck something in him. More beautiful than any hymn, it called him home in a way the land did not.

His hesitation vanished. Without thinking, he leapt from the boat and sprinted toward them, arms flailing with joy.

'Father look, Uncle Colm, uncle Baithéne look, there are goats here, hundreds of them.'

Columba smiled. 'And so, the boy forgets exile in the company of goats.'

'That's the way of children. And perhaps, the way of healing,' said Cobthach.

In the Abbey at Daire, Finn's favourite job was caring for the goats and sheep. He had feared he would never again get to play amongst the mischievous providers of milk and flesh for the monks' sustenance. He ran towards them greeting them, as he had with the flock in Ireland, but here, unlike at home, they scattered in alarm.

As he ran, behind him, the monks, exhausted from their journey, were struggling to lift sacks and tools onto the beach, but the sight of the young boy chasing goats, lightened their hearts making them forget their weariness for a few moments and laugh.

These might be the signs I have prayed for,' said Columba.

Finn returned. The hood of his cowl held tightly in the hand of a tall shepherd, dressed in goat and sheep skin.

'I assume this belongs to you, holy father,' he said looking towards Columba. 'He's after scaring the milk out of my goats, so he has.' His stern words couldn't mask the laughter in his eyes. 'If I hadn't caught a-hold of him he'd be clear away to the other end of the island and maybe into the sea to drown.'

'I'm a good swimmer, I wouldn't drown,' Finn said, bravado trying to mask his embarrassment.

'Oh yes, and what about the sea monsters? You wouldn't make much of a meal for one of them but a tasty snack twixt *bricfeasta* and *nunchin*, now that's a different tale.'

'There are no monsters, Saint Patrick got rid of them all.' Finn's defiance caused his face to change colour, blue and reddish hues crossed his tightened features.

'Now, now, Finn don't be too sure,' said Columba; 'St. Patrick drove the snakes from Ireland, and we are no longer there. It's just possible they learned to swim and ended up on this side of the water. With all the salmon and other fish in these parts they may well have grown to a size capable of crunching on your bones. This man may have just saved your life. You must thank him.'

'Ah, Finn is it? Well now wouldn't that be my own name. Finnian, my friends call me.' He released the struggling boy who fell to the ground.

'Well, my name is not Finnian, it's Finnl…'

'Finn that's enough.' Cobthach knew his son. This was an argument which might continue to beyond humour. 'Now thank Finnian, so we can talk about this island.'

'Thank you Finnian.' Finn had perfected inserting annoyance and irritability into the simplest of sentences. Now they oozed from every extended syllable.

'It's my pleasure, boy,' said Finnian, 'perhaps you could help me round up my flock later.'

Finn tried but failed to obscure the pleasure that this idea brought him.

'I'm not sure we'll be staying,' he said. You'll have to ask my father.'

Columba had been listening closely. 'You know this land, Finnian.'

'Aye, I've been herding here long enough to know every stone by name and every storm by its clouds. We now call it Hy, though some still whisper its older names Ioua, or Innis nan Druidhneach, the Isle of the Druids.'

Columba raised an eyebrow. 'An ancient place of worship?'

Finnian nodded, eyes glinting. 'And of learning. Long before the armies of Rome came and built their wall, even before our Lord, Jesus Christ, died to save us, the old ones came here to dream. They read the stars, spoke with birds and trees, carved signs in stone. Some say the ground still remembers. Thin places, I call them. Where one world brushes another. You'll feel it, in time.'

'Then we have not landed by accident,' said Columba, looking out across the barren hills. 'God has guided our exile well.'

Finn stared up at the island's wild ridges and crooked stones. The goats were climbing again, sure-footed and proud. A strange warmth bloomed in his chest. Maybe this strange place wasn't so strange after all.

'Finnian, come sit with us,' Columba said; 'I'm afraid our meagre food stocks are low, but we can offer you some bread and perhaps a little wine.'

'Is it Holy Communion you're offering me and this not a Sunday or great feast day?' Finnian said. 'By the looks of you, you're all in need of a good feed. My croft is just a short walk over the brow of that hill, and I'm heading that way now as I'm sure that's where I'll find my goats after young Finn here sent them scurrying away looking for sanctuary. Can you run, Finn?' he asked.

'Not quite as fast as a goat it would seem, but nearly.'

'Good. Now how's about you run ahead and tell the woman of the house, we have guests. You'll know who she is, she's the only one around with two legs, well apart from the chickens and geese I suppose. However, I'm sure we won't find you talking to a goose when we arrive behind you.'

Columba liked this shepherd, and they walked together towards the hill. 'Who owns this island, Finnian?' he asked.

'We're in the lands of the Cenél Loairn in the realm of High King Conall mac Comgaill of the Dál Riata Uí Néills,' Finnian replied. 'It's just a small island with a few free families enjoying the efforts of keeping loved ones alive and fed, paying our dues to our lords and selling our meat or fish on the big island of Muile, or at an t-Òban on the mainland.'

'What do you think of King Conall?'

'Ach, sure he's a fair man, we don't have much need to be in contact wi' him in these parts or he, us. My eldest son is a soldier in his army at Dún Att and he likes the King right enough. Though that young cousin of his, Áedán, who some say will be our next king, seems a bit strange so he does.'

'Áedán may or may not be your next king, only God can decide that, but he is a special kind of person in need of constant spiritual and physical guidance.'

'So, you know Áedán, then?'

'I do. Conall is a close cousin of mine and Áedán stayed with me for two years at my Abbey in Ireland. He was brought there by his father, King Gabráin, who was concerned for him. '

'Well, it's lucky for me I didn't talk treachery or sedition when you asked me my thoughts on the King.'

'I wasn't trying to catch you out, Finnian. I have always liked Conall. We've been friends since childhood, and he has been asking me to visit him for many years. I wanted to know what others think of him, that's all.'

'We like him well enough. I hear he's in Dún Att the now, so you'll be making your way there I suppose, for a short while?'

'Maybe not so short Finnian, I am here to bring the word of God, to those in need of it, and to continue my missionary work on this side of the sea. I'm hoping Conall will let me build a church in a suitable place, from which I and my fellow monks can teach the true religion.'

'Well, you could do worse than base your church here, on Hy. There's plenty of room for prayer and solitude if it's needed, and we are a friendly folk.' He laughed.

'Why are you laughing? Are you being ironic, do you think this would not be a good place?'

'No, it's not that. I think after you've seen it you'll agree, it's perfect. I had a thought as I was speaking, how wonderful it would be able to praise God on Hy.'

Columba tried to hide his mirth.

'When must you arrive at Dún Att?' continued Finnian

'There is no set time, I haven't told Conall we're coming, so we'll arrive when we arrive, and not before or after.'

'Conall, is not one who is renowned for liking surprises. We'll need to get word to him. Let's say you will arrive there in four days' time. That'll give me the chance to show you the small isle we call home and meet some of my neighbours.'

As they reached the top of the hill, smoke rose from a large outdoor cooking fire. Finn was laughing and playing with some goats.

'It seems the boy has learned the local goat accent and is making friends,' said Finnian.

'Finn's a good boy and outstanding student, but he needs to spend time away from the religious life, he is maturing too quickly, he needs to be a child for a while. He'll have to forge his own way through life and closeted with us is too restrictive and not good for him.'

Cobthach had heard the conversation and joined in. 'But Columba, you yourself spent your time almost since your birth being cared for in the church. It did you no harm.'

'Finn is not me, Cobthach, and he is not you.' Columba slammed his crook on the ground. 'Before my birth, my mother and father had a vision, the same vision on the same night. An angel informed them that their, soon to be born son, would be important to the church. That is why they named me, Colmcille, 'Dove of the Church.' As far as I know neither you nor the greatly missed, Niamh, had such a vision before Finn's birth.'

His voice softened. 'In the time Baithéne and I looked after her, whilst you cared for your infant son, not once did she ask us to take Finn into the church. She pleaded with us to take care of him and you, which we would do out of love for you both anyway, but never did she envisage a life in a cloistered monastery for the son she so longed for in life.'

Finnian and his cheerful wife, Máire, were clearly no strangers to entertaining large groups of people. A table, big enough for everyone to sit around comfortably, was taken out of a barn by the monks under Finnian's supervision. Stools and chairs were also brought out. Cold mutton and goats' meat were in plentiful supply as was milk and mead. Bread was distributed and the monks ate heartily.

'I'm afraid we've no fish today,' said Máire. 'I wasn't expecting company so haven't been down to the fishermen on the coast. It's not far, from one end of the island to the other, is only three miles and I've a wee donkey to make the journey easier, but today is my bread making day so you've fresh bread at least.'

'You have provided us with a wonderful, veritable feast, Máire, and we thank you.' Columba spoke for them all as the hungry brethren were busy taking in the delights of the best food they had eaten since leaving Daire.

'We'll have to find you all places to stay tonight, Finnian tells me you're headed for the stone castle at Dún Att, to meet with the High King himself. Well, you'll need to be rested and nourished afore you make that journey. We can take three here, the others will stay with neighbours, though some of them are a hilly walk away.'

'Bless you, Máire but we have become used to sleeping in the open over the last eight days.'

'Yes, and can't I just see that? Have you taken a look at yourselves? What kind of Dál Riata welcome would it be if we left you outside and for you to arrive before the King in this bedraggled state. We'll feed you and clean your clothes before you make that journey. It'll take us a little while to organise your transport, so you'll be our guests for two or three days.'

After the meal, Finnian and Columba departed to look around the island. Finnian provided sturdy ponies for the trip and the two set off in amiable conversation. The sea glistened under the high sun, and the wind carried the faint tang of salt and peat. Hills rolled softly inland, dotted with heather and gorse, and birds cried above as they rode through ancient sheep paths. As they climbed toward a small rise overlooking the eastern shore, Finnian gestured with his staff.

'There,' he said, pointing to a moss-covered ring of standing stones. 'They say this circle is older than memory, raised before the island bore its name. Long ago, the druids gathered here at sunrise, sunset and by moonlight, chanting to the old powers. Some say the land still remembers, if you know how to listen.'

Columba's eyes followed the line of stones, simple and weathered, yet each seemed to hum with quiet power.

'This is one of the thin places,' said Finnian.

Columba raised an eyebrow. 'You believe that?'

'Not just me. Most of the islanders do, any who have spent time near here. This is a place where the veil between worlds is worn thin. Where you can hear God, or the gods, more clearly.'

Columba dismounted, walking slowly toward the circle. The wind dipped and rose again like God's breath on his shoulders.

'The Lord is truly in this place,' he murmured. 'It seems that Hy is indeed a threshold. We are meant to be here. Perhaps this island is not exile but a calling.'

They stood for a while in reverent silence before continuing the ride.

It was mid-afternoon when they returned, and they were not alone. Several carts followed them, their drivers taunting the speed of the others. This was a happy community.

Columba dismounted. 'My brothers, I think we have found our new home. From this day forward we must look to the north, the east and the south and no longer think of the west, for there lies only the pain of memory. These generous people are welcoming us into their homes, let us be thankful to them and to God, we'll all sleep well tonight.'

It was decided that Columba together with the monks, Diarmait, his assistant, and Ernán, his uncle, would stay with Finnian. The others were divided into the carts to go and stay with one or other of the neighbours.

'Can't I stay here with the goats?' Finn pleaded.

'You already smell like a goat, Finn, we can't present you to the King smelling like that, he might suspect you are really a goat and turn you out into a field.'

'Well at least I'd be happy.' His eyes told his father exactly what he was thinking. 'Uncle Colm, you said I would have to find what I am to be in life. I've decided. A goatherd. I can't be bothered with kings and such things. Leave me here with the goats, that's enough for me.'

Cobthach, scooped the young boy up in his arms and placed him, wriggling, in one of the carts, before climbing up together with Baithéne. 'A goatherd is a fine thing to aspire to, but that is not a decision you'll be making today.'

'I want to be a goatherd, tell Uncle Colm, I want to be a goatherd.'

As the carts drove off, those who remained continued to hear Finn's voice fading into the distance for several minutes. The words could not be deciphered but the meaning was abundantly clear. Goats were his passion.

In the cart, after a while to cool down, Finn tugged at his father's sleeve, he wasn't sure if he was asleep or in contemplation. If Columba was like this he would never disturb him, but his father was another thing entirely.

'Does Uncle Colm know all the kings of Ireland and Dál Riata?'

'I'm not sure he knows them all, but he is closely related to most of them,' replied Cobthach; 'if God had not called him to do His bidding, your uncle could himself have been King of Tara and High King of all of Ireland.'

'I think Ireland would have been a happier, more peaceful place if he was.'

Cobthach smiled. 'I think you're probably right, Finn. However, the Irish do like a good fight, and, at times, your cousin is no exception. He is a capable swordsman and tactical genius.'

'He gave me a wooden sword once, when I was little, but told me not to play with it.'

Finn could brighten any mood. 'I might be wrong Finn, but I think that might have been a crucifix, not a sword.'

'But he told me that it would serve me well in the battles that I would face in the future.'

'If he predicted that, then it most certainly will. Our holy Abbot is renowned for being able to see things in the future. Have I told you of the time Columba went to visit the monastery at Clonmacnoise?'

'No,' replied Finn, turning one short syllable into a very long one.

'It was many years ago now. Not long after the foundation of the Abbey in Daire. Columba had become famous throughout Ireland as an exceptionally holy priest. It is said, like Jesus Christ, he once turned water into wine and had healed the sick by his prayers.

'Did he really turn water into wine?'

'I've never asked him, Finn. If you have the courage perhaps you could ask him.'

'I couldn't do that, as much as I love him and believe he loves me, he does scare me sometimes.'

'You should never be afraid of him, Finn, but you must always respect him and his way of doing things. We are lucky to be living with, and learning from, a man who is especially favoured by God. We are surely sharing our lives with a saint. Now, shall I continue with the story?'

'Is it just a story or is it true?'

Finn jumped at the sound of Baithéne's laughter.

'So, you do listen sometimes Finn,' said his uncle; 'I heard, Columba tell you the difference whilst we were sailing. You'll do well to remember that. Always be wary about stories that are not witnessed and confirmed by someone you trust. However, this story is true, I was there and can confirm it.'

Cobthach continued. 'A huge crowd had gathered to greet him, amongst them was a young man who was being raised in the monastery for he was abandoned as a child. He couldn't speak properly, and it was very difficult to get him to wash or wear clean clothes. He shied away from people, preferring to keep himself to himself, but he had heard of Columba, and he believed that if he could just touch the cloak of the holy man things would be better for him.'

'Had he received a vision, like Columba does?'

'I don't know, Finn. So many questions?'

'I'm trying to get all the details. Details matter.' Finn shrugged his shoulders wondering what was wrong with asking questions. Perhaps that was something he could talk to Columba about.

'Right, now where was I?'

'At the part where you don't know if the boy had a vision or not.' Finn sometimes found it difficult to let things go.

Cobthach shook his head. 'If he had received a vision or not we cannot say. All we know is that as Columba walked in procession, he was surrounded by the huge throng. To keep him from being obstructed, five men walked beside carrying a wooden canopy.'

'I was one of them,' said Baithéne.

'Don't interrupt him Uncle Baithéne. He doesn't like it.' Finn said, exchanging winks with his uncle.

'I've never found it so difficult to tell a story. Now, be quiet both of you.'

Finn put his hand to his mouth to stifle a snigger.

Cobthach ignored him. 'Concealing himself as well as he could, he approached from behind, that he might touch, unperceived, the hem of Columba's cloak. However, nothing ever escapes Columba, whether he can see it with his eyes or not. Stopping suddenly, and putting his hand behind him, Columba seized the boy and pulled him round to face him.'

Pausing to emphasise his next words he continued, 'The crowd, were afraid that Columba would hurt the boy. They didn't know him you see, only his reputation. They cried out. 'Please holy father let him go, let him go. He is witless and the poor unfortunate lad meant no harm.' Columba raised his hand to silence the crowd. He told the boy to open his mouth and put out his tongue. The young man, did so, trembling with fear. Columba gently extended his hand and carefully blessed the boy's tongue. 'Though this boy appears to you now, both contemptible and worthless,' he announced; 'do not continue to hold him in disdain. For from this hour, he will please you in both his manner and his words. As time passes, slowly, day by day, he shall impress with his conduct. He will grow in wisdom, prudence and the virtues of the soul. His tongue shall receive from God, the gift of eloquence, his mind, the gift of understanding. He will become great among you.'

He released the boy who, for the first time in his life, spoke clearly. 'Bless you, holy father, for you have released me from a cage. I have listened to your words, and I promise to learn and be guided by your life.' Before that moment, he had walked in a crooked way, now he stood tall and straight and strode into the crowd who were in awe of what they had witnessed.'

'Is it alright if I ask a question now, father?'

'If you must.'

'Did the prophecy come true, did he become great in his community?'

‘Not just in his community, Finn.’ It was Baithéne who answered; ‘he is now the Abbot of the monastery at Clonal.’

‘We’re arriving at my house now, brothers.’ It was the cart driver who spoke for the first time since they had set off. ‘I hadn’t realised just who your Abbot was until I heard your story. This is a blessed day, that’s for sure, a blessed day. Now come and meet my family, they’ll enjoy having some new faces around.’

‘Thank you,’ said Baithéne; ‘we’ll surely sleep well tonight and tomorrow we can prepare for our meeting with your King.’

Chapter 5

'...you have wine, which the Lord Jesus has lent,
to perform his mysteries.'
– St. Adomnan of Iona: 'The Life of St. Colmcille or Columba'

Two days later, the group of fourteen together with Finnian, sailed from Hy to Creag an Iubhair on the larger island, of Muile. It seemed that their arrival was anticipated.

'God has blessed us with your presence, Father,' a fisherman, mending his nets, called out as they walked along the quay.

'It's like they know who he is,' said Finn.

'They may not know his name, but they know the blue cowl, and the silver crucifix and what it signifies. That is enough.'

'Or maybe our host for the past two nights has been spreading the word through the fishing community.'

'That too is possible, Finn, that too is possible.'

The locals found them accommodation for the night, and, the following morning, arranged for more boats to take them to the small fishing village of An t-Òban on the mainland. They confirmed that a messenger was sent to King Conall to advise him of their impending visit.

'As he is in Dún Att it's better to go to the mainland. If he had been in his crannog at Dalruadhain, it would be far easier to go by boat,' Finnian had said.

Arriving on the mainland the following morning a group of soldiers were waiting to greet them with horses for the journey.

'Holy father, my Lord, King Conall, apologises that he is not here to greet you personally.' A tall soldier bowed as he greeted Columba. 'There were matters of great importance which required his presence at Dún Att so he charged me with bringing you and your companions to him. He will meet you when we arrive.'

'Thank you,' replied Columba: 'and by which name do we call you?'

'I'm Darragh. The King thought it appropriate that I should meet you, given the association of my name with your Abbey.'

'Indeed so, Darragh. That is exactly the kind of thing King Conall would do. He is ever attentive.'

The young soldier called over the men leading the horses. Finn believed he recognised the soldier's features. His face was beardless but there was something about his demeanour, his height and stature.

'Are you Finnian's son?' he asked.

'Indeed, I am young man. How did you guess?'

'It wasn't a guess, you have his hands, and I'll never forget those since he held me by the neck.'

'Now, Finn,' said Columba; 'don't tell lies, he held you by the hood of your cowl, not your neck.'

'It's not a lie, Uncle Colm, you said it wasn't a lie if it was to make a story sound better.'

'So, you're a storyteller now are you, Finn? We'll have to talk about this later. I'm going to need you to tell me the truth, not stories, if I am to place my trust in you.'

'What do you mean?'

'Sometimes, Finn, you are too old for your years. We will

talk about this another time. The King awaits.' He turned and mounted the grey horse Darragh was holding, abruptly blocking Finn's next question.

The others were all given their horses with the smallest one reserved for Finn, who despite his age, was no stranger to horse riding. All the monks were accomplished horse riders, but many, including Columba, preferred to walk whilst carrying out their ministries. It's easy to ignore people and ride past on horseback, walking removes that temptation. Today, it was better to ride. This journey could be achieved in a day on horseback, to walk would have taken at least two.

Darragh rode beside Finn for much of the journey and told him of some of the mischievous games he and his brothers used to play on their father, hiding his goats or taking the chicken eggs from the nests before he got up and pretending the hens had stopped laying.

Despite travelling, Columba always insisted that the monks prayed at the required times. In this he, like most Abbots, followed the teachings of St. Benedict and set out the eight daily prayer sessions. On this journey, they had said the offices of Terce on the boat. As they rode towards Dún Att, it was Sext which was next in the order of the day. At around midday Columba called a halt and the group all dismounted. Baithéne took out the folded altar and set it down on a rock. Columba recited a prayer he had written for the monks in his abbeys and priories to use at this time. As he started, all, soldiers, monks and it appeared, even the horses, fell into silence.

As we walk in your footsteps, O Lord of light, fill our souls with thy grace, our hearts with thy voice. As your son died on the cross to save us from sin may you give us the strength and courage to spread thy joy. May we join you in Heaven when our time here is done and share in thy son's resurrection. Through Jesus Christ thy son.

Amen.

Even travelling, the formality of the offices needed to be kept. Led by Ernán, Columba's uncle, the monks sang in unison 'O God, make speed to save us; O Lord, make haste to help us.' This was followed by *Gloria in excelsis Deo.* Sext is one of the shortest offices, with only 3 psalms to be sung. Psalm 122 began with '*I rejoiced with those who said to me, 'Let us go to the house of the Lord.*' and ended with the final lines of Psalm 124; '*Our help is in the name of the Lord, the Maker of heaven and earth.*' The soldiers, joined in as best they could.

'Do you pray like this every day?' Darragh asked Finn.

'Oh yes, seven times a day, starting at sunrise and ending before we go to bed,' he replied; 'and once more during the night. Sext is short with only 3 psalms, sometimes we have 7 or 10. Columba says it gives us a sense of unity and brotherhood. I think we have that anyway, but if God says we must, we cannot argue. Our lives in the monastery are based around these gatherings.'

'It must be hard, for someone as young as you.'

'Sometimes, but I've always had my goats to tend to and help me when it feels hard to get up in the morning.'

'In that you are like my father, he tells me something similar.'

'I'm not sure I want to be like your father.'

'You could do a lot worse, he's a good man, who cares about God and his family, not forgetting his goats. You could learn a lot from him. The King calls upon him if we are going into battle as he's a wonderful healer. On Hy everyone goes to him if injured or feeling sick.'

Conversation was interrupted as the travellers crested a hill and the vast purple expanse of Moine Mhòr stretched out in front of them. Many harriers were flying, low and slow, looking for grouse or voles, whilst Kestrels hovered above, swooping to the ground when sighting their next meal. Finn had enjoyed watching the harriers and merlin on walks with his father across

Ballynahone Bog, when they travelled from Daire to other monasteries.

'This is just like home,' Finn said to no one in particular.

'This is home now, son,' his father replied; 'we just need to get you some goats.'

The seemingly impenetrable fortress of Dún Att stood high above the marshy moor, its commanding presence both daunting and awe-inspiring. Jagged stone walls, blackened with age and moss, encircled a towering rock outcrop that seemed to be rooted in the earth. Layers of fortification climbed the hill in concentric defiance of time and weather, each one narrower and steeper than the last. From below, it looked less a fortress and more a crown of stone carved by the gods.

The air was crisp, filled with the tang of peat smoke and damp heather. As the company of riders crested the rise, a lone scout galloped ahead, his crimson cloak snapping in the wind, signalling their approach.

The lower gate creaked open, revealing the first ring of walls and the bustle of soldiers in formation. Bronze helmets caught the early light, and spear tips glinted like distant stars. At a barked command, two lines of guards emerged from either side of the gate and formed a guard of honour. Their chant rang out in thick Irish:

'Glóir do Dhia ar an Ard agus cosnaigh a sheirbhíseach Colm Cille.'

'Glory be to God on High and protect His servant, the dove of the Church.'

The cadence of their prayer echoed off the stone, amplifying as the riders passed between them. Columba rode to the front, his companions falling behind with quiet reverence. The soldiers who had accompanied them from the coast dropped to the rear, their duty ending at the gate.

Each layer of the fortress revealed another facet of its people. Women carried woven baskets filled with smoked fish and flatbread; blacksmiths paused in their hammering to lower their heads in respect; children peered from behind rough-woven cloaks, whispering at the sight of the famed Abbot. Chickens scattered in front of the riders as they passed into the heart of the citadel.

The final gate opened onto a courtyard built against the great stone of the Dún itself, where smoke drifted from a central hearth and the scent of roasting meat mingled with that of crushed pine needles underfoot. There, waiting with arms folded, stood King Conall mac Comgaill. A bear of a man, his beard was streaked with grey and his eyes burned with the wary pride of a ruler whose hospitality was honour but not without scrutiny. He wore a tunic dyed a deep rust red beneath a heavy sheepskin mantle, and his sword hung easily at his hip.

Finn, wide-eyed, swallowed. 'He doesn't seem happy to see us,' he whispered.

Cobthach leaned closer. 'Don't worry, Finn. He is a good friend of Columba. We are safe here.'

Columba dismounted, brushing dust from his cloak. Before a word was spoken, the King strode forward, and without hesitation, drew the Abbot into a crushing embrace.

'Finally, the great Abbot leaves his comforts in Daire and deigns to visit his poor cousin on this side of the water,' he boomed.

Columba managed a smile, muffled in the King's shoulder. 'Your poor cousin who commands a fortress strong enough to repel Pict and Roman alike? I see humility still does not dwell at Dún Att.'

Laughter broke the tension. Soldiers relaxed their grips on spear hafts. The King released Columba, eyes shining. 'Come. Eat. Speak. I've had the finest deer slaughtered and my best brewer woken early. Tonight, we honour your arrival. Tomorrow, we talk of matters less pleasant.'

Colomba continued, 'Conall, you know well the reasons for my being here,' he said. 'The synod at Tailtin was angry I defended the church against Diarmait and I am here to continue God's work away from my beloved homeland.'

'Ah, Colm, I don't care about reasons. Diarmait deserved to get his ærs kicked, and you were just the man to do it. It's great to see you, cousin. It's been too long. Remember, this is your homeland too. We are one nation, united by kinship and faith. Ask me anything and if it is within my power it will be granted.' He placed his hand on Columba's shoulder. 'This is a truly blessed day. But let's leave all that for now, plenty of time for reminiscing the past and planning the future after you've rested. Áedán will show you to your accommodation. Get ready to feast, you're skinnier than a hungry squirrel, we need to build you up.'

'I eat all that I need to, my tastes are simple. How is your wife, the beautiful, Sabhdha?'

'She is busy preparing the servants for tonight. She will join us then. And yes, she is as beautiful as the day we wed. Now go, get yourselves washed and ready.'

The hall of Dún Att was warm with life. The scent of roasting boar, deer and herbs hung heavy in the smoky air, mingling with the tang of sweat and spilt ale. Long trestle tables were already filling with warriors and councillors. Hounds lazed near the hearth, their ears twitching with the clatter of knives and chatter of tongues. Above, the smoke from the central fire curled into the rafters, escaping through a hole in the thatch.

Columba paused at the entrance, eyes adjusting to the dim light after the glare of the courtyard. His gaze swept the space, settling first on Áedán mac Gabráin, seated beside King Conall at the head table. Áedán's angular features were made more severe by the flickering shadows; his dark eyes held a sharpness, alert and restless.

Columba remembered the boy well, sharp-tongued, uncertain, often bristling with unspoken resentments. He had spent two years under Columba's guidance at Daire after his father, King Gabráin, expressed doubt about Áedán's readiness to inherit the throne. 'Too quick to rage,' Gabráin had said. 'Too long to forgive. The crown will go to Conall first.'

Áedán had chafed under the abbot's rules, questioned everything, and refused silence in prayer. But Columba had persisted, and slowly, through scripture and sword-practice alike, they had learned to tolerate, even trust, one another.

'Well met, cousin,' Áedán called, rising to greet him. His smile was genuine, but there was always a challenge in his tone. 'I trust your crossing was not too grim. I've missed your stern lectures and pious riddles.'

Columba returned the smile with calm grace. 'And I yours, Áedán. Especially your cheerful defiance. It always did make for lively debates.'

Áedán gestured toward a bench beside him. 'Come now, sit. I want to hear the truth of Cúl Dreimhne. The bards will tell it as a triumph of saints and thunderbolts, but they won't speak without silver, and even then, they lie like drunkards in a windstorm.'

'Truth,' Columba said, settling beside him, 'is rarely sung. And rarer still when silver and gold dictate the verse.'

Laughter rolled across the high beams.

A small boy emerged from Áedán's shadow, wiry, sharp-eyed, perhaps ten or eleven. He stood stiffly beside his father, frowning with exaggerated seriousness.

'This is my son, Eochaid,' Áedán said. 'A fierce one. He's convinced himself that priests can't fight.'

Eochaid took a pace forward and looked Finn over. 'He's dressed like one of you,' he said, nodding at Columba. 'Doesn't look like he could hold a blade.'

Finn squared his shoulders. 'I've held one. I've trained with it. Want to see?'

Áedán chuckled. 'See? Already rivals. Maybe it'll keep them sharp.'

Columba raised a hand. 'Do not mistake cloth for cowardice, Eochaid. I have seen many men fall to those who prayed more than they boasted. You and he will one day stand side by side on a battlefield, perhaps even lead armies. But greatness will be judged not by who strikes first, but by who fights for something greater than himself.'

The boy blinked, caught between pride and thoughtfulness.

'One day,' Columba continued, 'you and Finn, and Connad, your cousin, will be warriors, not just for your people, but for justice and peace. May you learn from one another. May you trust each other when blood runs thick and the sky darkens with omens.'

Columba's eyes rested on Eochaid for a long, measured moment. 'He will need to be sharp,' the abbot said quietly.

Áedán's mirth faded. 'What are you saying, Colm?'

'That this one, your youngest, will sit upon your throne one day.'

A silence fell. Eochaid blinked, uncertain whether he should be proud or afraid.

Áedán's brow furrowed. 'And what of my eldest? Domangart is already commanding men. Eochaid Find has fought in more battles than this boy has years.'

Columba's voice remained calm, but the weight behind it was unshakable. 'Domangart and Eochaid Find will die in battle. Their blood will bless the soil of a distant land. And when the smoke clears, it is this Eochaid who will be left to lead.'

Áedán's face darkened, jaw clenching. 'You prophesy the death of my sons like you're forecasting the weather.'

'I name only what is shown to me,' Columba replied. 'I do

not rejoice in it. But the Lord's will is not altered by grief or denial.'

Eochaid moved uneasily, suddenly aware of the intensity in his father's gaze, and the finality in Columba's words.

Áedán turned away, muttering something under his breath. 'Let's hope your visions are as cloudy as the Hebridean sky.'

'Would that they were,' Columba said, almost to himself.

Finn looked at Eochaid with new eyes, the edge of rivalry giving way to a flicker of respect and perhaps fear. He then turned toward Columba, eyes wide. His respect for the abbot had deepened ever since hearing the tale of the miracle at Clonmacnoise and now here he was, speaking prophecies into the smoky air of a king's hall. Were these just words to curry favour, or did he truly see what lay ahead?

Finn wasn't sure. But he knew one thing: he wanted to hear more.

The following morning began for Finn as most others had: with the hush of first light, the breath of cold air before dawn, and the murmur of monks assembling in the small chapel nestled within Dún Att's inner wall. The scent of damp stone and beeswax candles filled the sacred space as the cantation of psalms rose in steady rhythm, wrapping the fortress in a quiet veil of prayer.

But something was different.

After prayers, Columba beckoned Finn aside. The boy approached, bleary-eyed but alert, always ready for instruction.

'Finn,' Columba said gently, resting a hand on the boy's shoulder. 'For the rest of our time here, I release you from the obligation to attend prayers.'

Finn blinked. 'But why? Did I do something wrong?'

A chuckle rumbled in Columba's throat. 'No, child. Quite the opposite. You've done much that is right. But I see in you the weight of duty pressing too early, too firmly. You've studied, trained, and carried burdens beyond your years. It's time you tasted freedom, the kind of joy that shapes a boy before the world insists he becomes a man.'

Finn furrowed his brow. 'But… what should I do instead?'

'Find Eochaid and Connad, the boys you met last night. Let them show you what fills their days. Climb, run, chase goats if they let you. Laugh. These are holy things too, though spoken of less in our scriptures. Let the land and its people speak to you.'

Finn hesitated. 'May I still come to prayers? Sometimes?'

'Of course,' said Columba, smiling. 'But I suspect you'll be too busy or too tired to rise. And that, my lad, would be no sin.'

Finn grinned, gave a hurried nod, and ran off, his sandals slapping the packed earth of the fortress yard.

Columba watched him go, his smile lingering, then turned toward the path that climbed the hill behind the inner ramparts. He walked slowly, letting the cool air bite his cheeks. The fort stirred to life below; soldiers drilling, kitchen fires smoking, hounds barking at the morning stir. But up here, near the summit of the Dún, there was silence.

He reached the inauguration stone, a slab of ancient, weathered rock that bore the imprint of a human foot, worn smooth by centuries of kings pressing their bare flesh into its hollow. Here, each new king of Dál Riata stood barefoot, linking his body to the land itself, declaring his sacred bond to the earth and its people.

Columba removed his sandals and placed his own foot beside the print, not in imitation, but in reflection.

Beyond the stone, the land opened out before him. To the west, the boglands of Moine Mhòr, the 'Great Moss' shimmered in the early light, a vast sprawl of golden grasses and silver water-veins stretching toward the sea. To the north and east, forested hills gave way to rugged peaks. Smoke curled from scattered homesteads below. The world felt ancient here, rooted and humming with a power too quiet for speech.

This was the heart of Dál Riata. A seat of strength, hidden in difficult terrain, protected by nature's own defences. No invading army could march easily across the great bog. No fleet could land undetected. The people are safe here, not just by sword, but by the will of the land itself.

Columba folded his arms and lifted his face to the wind.

'Lord,' he whispered, 'you place your hand upon the earth in many ways. May this stone, this land, this boy, may they all serve your purpose.'

He stood there for some time, wrapped in thought and wind, a lone figure in the high places, neither king nor soldier, but something other. A man whose power came not from dominion, but from faith.

Below, Finn was enjoying a lesson in swordsmanship with Eochaid and Connad, Darragh was their instructor. Finn surprised himself at how much he enjoyed this and was enthusiastically swinging his wooden sword at Darragh, when Baithéne walked up.

'Finn, have you seen Columba?'

'I saw him after Vespers, he went walking up the hill. Look, there he is at the very top.'

'Please can you go to him and tell him that King Conall would like to see him. A merchant is arriving from Gaul and Conall thinks it important for Columba to meet him.'

'Yes, uncle,' said Finn, handing his sword to Eochaid. He began to run up the steep hill. The embankment was arduous and Finn had slowed to a panting walk by the time he got to the top. He saw Columba.

Finn froze.

Columba stood rigid, his eyes locked on something far beyond the horizon.

A cold shiver crawled up Finn's spine. The air felt heavier, thick with something unseen.

Then: light.

Not the golden glow of the sun, something sharper, whiter, painful to look at.

Columba's face twisted in anguish.

Finn couldn't catch his breath. What is he seeing?

Columba suddenly gasped. His hands clenched, his voice hoarse. 'A fire of sulphur is pouring down from the heavens at this very moment. A city under Rome. But not of Rome. A city cursed by its own faith.'

Finn stumbled backwards. The hairs on his arms standing on end.

'Uncle Colm, what are you talking about?'

Columba blinked, the light around him fading. His voice was quieter now. 'A terrible vengeance has been exacted. Women are running, clutching their children. Men are screaming. The church doors are barred. There is no escape. No mercy. 'It's like Cúl Dreimhne all over again."

Finn's heart pounded. 'But how do you know?'

Columba turned, his piercing eyes locking onto Finn's. 'Because I see it.'

Finn wanted to run, to escape, those words frightened him.

'What if you're wrong?' he asked, swallowing hard

Columba sighed. 'We shall see when the news arrives. But Finn… my visions, as vivid as this, have never been wrong before.'

Finn's legs felt weak. He had heard the stories of Columba's visions but had never witnessed one.

He wasn't sure he wanted to. Ever again.

'Now, Finn, what is it that brought you here?'

'Baithéne says, King Conall is expecting a trader from Gaul and believes you should meet him.'

‘I must go down, it’s time for Terce and I will be ready for greeting guests after that.’

‘May I join you and the others in prayer?’ asked Finn.

‘Oh, Finn, your break from the monastic way hasn’t lasted long, has it?’

‘It’s not that. I’m having fun learning to fight with a sword, but why can’t I do both?’

Columba smiled, it seemed that again, his visions were proving to be true. ‘Perhaps you are a person who can do both, in time we shall see. You don’t need to ask if you can join us in prayer, you are a part of our family and are always welcome. The bell will always be rung and you can stop and join us or you can carry on what you’re doing. I only want that you don’t feel obliged.’

‘My obligation would be to God.’

‘How have you become so old and wise?’

‘I have you, my father and the others as guides and you are all very wise… and very old.’

Columba wasn’t sure if that was a joke but laughed anyway.

The group of monks remained at Dún Att for seven days. In that short span, bonds had deepened, and the fortress had come to feel almost like home. On the final evening, Columba and King Conall sat together in the high chamber overlooking the darkening glen. A low fire burned between them, its light casting flickering shadows across their weathered faces.

Conall poured a second cup of heather mead and passed it to Columba without comment. They had eaten well, roasted venison, oat cakes, and soft cheese, and now the air hung with the quiet comfort of two old friends.

‘I wish you would stay longer, Colm,’ Conall said at last, his voice low and genuine. ‘Your company, and that of your congregation, has been a gift. I’ve missed this part of Ireland.’

Columba smiled. ‘That’s kind of you to say, cousin. I had

two matters to raise with you before we depart, but I believe you've already guessed the first.'

'Hy,' said Conall, nodding. 'The island. You want it.'

'I believe it may serve as a new beginning,' Columba said, choosing his words carefully.

'Then let it be yours.' Conall leaned back in his carved chair, fingers laced across his belly. 'The land technically belongs to the Cenél Loairn, but I'll handle the politics. You'll have no trouble. I'll send men and materials to help you build. A priory. A home. A fortress of faith, if that's what God demands.'

Columba inclined his head. 'Praise be to God.'

Conall's tone grew heavier. 'The Picts need guidance, Colm. Their ways are… dark. Some of the stories I've heard, blood sacrifices, bone charms, night rituals under stone circles…'

'No stranger than our own forefathers once were,' Columba interrupted gently.

Conall frowned. 'You mean the druids?'

'I mean us, cousin. Before Patrick. Before Christ.' He folded his arms. 'We have short memories when it suits us. Fear shapes belief, and when men are afraid, they turn to what they know.'

'I've heard Picts offer men to their gods,' Conall muttered, his voice taut.

'Do you believe every tale from a wandering bard or drunken warrior?' Columba asked. 'The Picts are a proud and clever people. They want outsiders to be afraid of them. Stories help them quicker and more effectively than swords ever could.'

Conall chuckled. 'I tell tales myself, to Eochaid and Connad. Of the headless horseman who rides the fortress paths after sundown. Keeps them from wandering.'

'Exactly,' said Columba, smiling. 'Fear works. But it's not faith. The Picts may frighten us with their gods, but ours…'

'Demands faith,' Conall finished.

'And love,' Columba added. 'You cannot frighten men into heaven.'

Conall was silent, his fingers drumming against the polished wood of his chair.

'So, you'd let them carry on as they are? Let them defy the Gospel?'

Columba's expression hardened. 'No. But I would answer fear with something greater. Not the sword, not fire. Something deeper. A gentler strength.'

Conall's eyes narrowed. 'And if they reject it?'

Columba met his gaze with unwavering calm. 'Then we pray for them. And hope, one day, they'll pray for us in return.'

A long silence followed. The fire cracked and hissed.

Conall finally exhaled and muttered, 'You always were stubborn, Colm.'

Columba's mouth curved in amusement. 'So were you.'

Conall refilled his cup. 'You said you had two questions. What's the second?'

'In a way, it concerns Eochaid and Connad.' Columba's tone grew more measured. 'But first, I must thank you, for your hospitality, for the land, for everything. You've been generous far beyond expectation. I would have asked only permission to build on Hy. You have gifted it.'

Conall raised his hand to wave off the praise.

'It's a rock with poor soil and wind that never stops blowing. Good only for sheep and goats, and perhaps for monks with too much prayer and not enough sleep,' he said, grinning.

'Finnian will keep the goats and sheep and be responsible for the produce of the island.'

'Finnian? He's the one robbing his overlord. I doubt the man's ever counted a goat for paying tax that ended up in his stew, or that of his neighbours.'

Columba chuckled. 'He's more honest than most.'

'That's not saying much,' said Conall with mock gravity. 'But you're right, Finnian's heart is good. The island's flocks will continue to do well under his care.'

Columba's face sobered. 'That brings me to my second request. I would like Finn to stay here with you for a time. Not just as my ward, but as a guest of your house.'

Conall tilted his head. 'Not taking him back to Hy with you?'

'Not yet. He's... exceptional. You've seen it. He's beginning to outgrow the cloister walls. He needs more than scripture. He needs the world, its politics, its swords, its sorrows. He has a path to walk, and I believe it runs through Dún Att.'

Conall nodded. 'He's young. But sharp. And strange. He has the eyes of someone twice his years.'

'He listens. He learns. He remembers everything. And more importantly, he questions. That is rare, and holy.'

Conall looked thoughtful. 'He, Eochaid, and Connad have taken to each other. That's a bond I'd like to encourage. They need him as much as he needs them. Connad has too much fire; Eochaid, too little. Finn may be the balance between them.'

'I think so too,' Columba said.

'Then let him stay,' said Conall. 'With us, at Dún Att, at court, in the saddle. Wherever we ride, he will ride with us. And when you call for him, we'll send him back. A little taller. A little wilder. And a lot wiser.'

Columba nodded, satisfaction in his eyes.

A new chapter was beginning.

Finn froze, the words landing like stones in his stomach. 'You... want me to stay here?' he asked, his voice shaking.

Columba nodded solemnly. 'It will be good for you, Finn. You must learn from both worlds, faith and the sword. A servant of God must also know the hearts of men. Here, you'll begin to understand both.'

'But…' Finn hesitated, eyes darting between Columba and his father. 'I've always been with you. With my father. I've never…'

'You are not being left alone,' Columba said gently. 'This place is safe. You'll be among friends. Eochaid and Connad will be your brothers in all but blood. The priest here is a good man and will help with your prayers if you need it.'

Finn turned to his father. Cobthach's face was unreadable, calm but distant. Was he agreeing? Did he even want this?

'Am I…' Finn swallowed hard. 'Am I being sent away?'

Cobthach lowered himself to one knee until they were eye to eye. His hands, calloused from years of toil and prayer alike, gripped Finn's shoulders with a steady strength.

'No, my son,' he said quietly. 'You're being given a choice.'

The silence that followed was thick with meaning. Not an exile, but a way to grow.

Finn looked down at the dusty ground beneath his feet. His thoughts drifted to the chapel at Daire, the soothing cadence of psalms echoing in stone halls, the comforting scent of beeswax and old books, the rhythm of the scriptorium. That world felt clean, ordered, eternal. He thought of Hy and Finnian's goats, of the promise of a new life.

But he also felt the rush of wind as he sparred with Eochaid and Connad in the courtyard, the sting of sweat, the laughter, the thrill of testing his limits. The roughness of life outside the cloister stirred something in him, something fresh and new.

He looked back up at Columba, at the man who had been his teacher, his protector, his second father.

Perhaps he was right. Perhaps this was not a parting but a beginning.

Finn straightened his back, pushing away the twist in his gut. 'I will stay,' he said. Then, after a pause: 'If that is what you both wish.'

Columba stepped forward and placed a hand over Finn's heart. 'What I wish,' he said softly, 'is that you grow into the man God is calling you to be. And sometimes, that means letting go of our comforts, even those we love.'

Finn nodded, blinking against the burn in his eyes.

'When will you go?' he asked.

'Tomorrow. At first light.'

'Will I see you again soon?'

Columba smiled, though his eyes were heavy with meaning. 'You will always see me, Finn. In the morning prayers. In the wind through the glens. In the sound of the birds at dawn over the moor. And you will return to us, to the windy shores of Hy, often and when the time is right.'

Cobthach pulled Finn into a brief but strong embrace. 'Make me proud, son.'

'I'll try.'

'No,' his father whispered. 'Don't try. Do.'

As the torchlight flickered along the hall's stone walls and the sounds of the fortress began to fade into night, Finn remained standing torn between two worlds, and yet, for the first time, beginning to understand he might belong to both.

Chapter 6

Neart agus gliceas a dhéanann an laoch.
(Strength and cunning make the warrior.)
— Old Irish Proverb

Dún Att stood like a sentinel at the top of a forbidding hill, its stone walls darkened by time, shaped by fierce winds and relentless rain. Encircled by marshland and thick mist, the fortress seemed to rise from the earth like a relic of some older, grimmer age. On many mornings, the fog clung low to the reeds and rough grasses like a ghostly shroud, casting an eerie pall across the land.

This was a place made for warriors, harsh, unforgiving, and utterly without softness. And those who trained within its walls were expected to become the same.

Within the ramparts, Finn's new life had begun in earnest. Each day, he trained beside his royal cousins, Eochaid and Connad, under the watchful eye of the arms master, Darragh. The days started early and ended late, with hard hours of physical exertion: drills, combat forms, weapons practice, and strength building. There was no leniency, no excuses.

Darragh, a grizzled veteran with a voice like gravel and a stare that could cut steel, pushed them hard.

'Strength and guile,' he repeated like a mantra, pacing before them, wooden staff tapping against his palm. 'If you're weak and your enemy is strong, you will die. You must be quicker than him in mind and arm, you must out-think him. Use his own strength against him. Strength and guile!'

The boys groaned as they were handed axes to chop down a row of trees. The wood was tough, knotted with age.

'I'm not sure how being skilful at chopping trees helps in a battle,' muttered Finn, wiping sweat from his brow.

'Something to do with strength and guile, I suppose,' Connad added, grinning. Eochaid burst out laughing, and soon all three were chuckling despite their aching arms.

Darragh didn't mind the levity, not when it came from comrades-in-arms. He'd seen enough war to know that the best soldiers laughed together before they bled together.

At first, they trained with wooden weapons, lightweight, harmless mock-ups that stung more than hurt. Each boy had to build strength, control, and precision. There would be no glory in accidents or wasted energy in battle.

In time, each of them found a rhythm. Eochaid, tall and broad-shouldered, relied on power, his strikes heavy and crushing. Connad, lean and wiry, moved like a shadow, quick, unpredictable, and endlessly clever. Finn was somewhere in between. He lacked Eochaid's brute force and Connad's instinctive speed, but what he did possess was harder to define: a quiet tenacity, a fire that refused to die, even when he stumbled.

He tried harder. Learned faster. Failure soon forgotten and overcome. Darragh noticed.

The weapons changed with their progress. Training swords, heavier and blunted, replaced the wooden ones. Spears were introduced. Bows followed. Each tool of war demanded a different kind of discipline. Darragh made sure they learned them all.

‘Strength and guile!’ he barked, ushering them toward the practice yard.

The yard was stark and unforgiving, much like the man himself. Enclosed by stone walls, it offered no distraction from the task at hand. Straw dummies lined one side, their leather faces slashed from hundreds of strikes. The dirt floor had long been compacted by the footfalls of countless warriors.

Weapons lined the racks: swords, spears, and shields, each meticulously cleaned and maintained by the boys themselves under Darragh’s stern supervision. There was no honour in using a weapon you hadn’t cared for.

‘Eochaid, Finn, swords. Connad, you’re with me,’ Darragh ordered, crossing his arms.

Eochaid moved forward, lifting his blunted training blade and rolling his shoulder.

Finn mirrored him, adjusting his stance. They circled, feet crunching the dirt, swords held steady.

‘Strength and guile,’ they shouted in unison.

Finn struck first, his blade angling toward Eochaid’s side. The prince deflected it smoothly and launched a counterthrust that nearly caught Finn’s shoulder. The swords clattered with each blow, metal ringing like bells against the stone walls.

‘Faster, Finn!’ Darragh growled. ‘Hesitation will get you killed!’

Finn set his jaw and lunged again, this time feinting left and pivoting right. The sudden shift caught Eochaid off guard. The prince stumbled, just a step, but it was enough. Finn’s blade tapped his ribs.

Darragh grunted with approval. ‘Better.’

Across the yard, Connad danced around the older man’s strikes. Darragh moved like a bear, heavy but controlled. Connad was all reflexes, darting and parrying with a quickness that reminded Darragh of his own youth.

'Good,' Darragh said, breath steady even as Connad ducked a wide sweep. 'But don't think speed alone will save you. One mistake, and you're meat for the crows.'

There was no winner that day, and there never was in training. That was not the point. Victory here was not about besting your opponent, it was about preparing for the day, when failure would mean death.

And though they joked and jostled each other, between drills, each of the three boys understood: every bruise earned, every blow endured, brought them one step closer to the men they would need to become.

War would not wait for their youth to end.

After an hour of swordplay, Darragh called for a change. Time for the spear.

The weapon of the common soldier, yes, but also one of the most versatile tools in battle. He handed each boy a long wooden shaft tipped with a blunted metal point. 'Keep your enemies at a distance. Control the fight,' he instructed, his tone sharp and measured.

The boys practiced thrusting and sweeping motions, the spears whistling through the air. Darragh demonstrated techniques to disarm and unbalance an opponent, his movements fluid and precise, refined by years on real battlefields. He circled them as they worked, correcting posture, footwork, the angle of a thrust.

Eochaid, with his raw power and growing height, excelled at the weapon, each thrust driving deep into the straw dummies, sending clouds of chaff into the air. His strikes came down like hammer blows.

Connad, however, found the spear unwieldy, its reach throwing off his rhythm. He winced each time his aim faltered.

'Focus on your footwork, Connad,' Darragh advised, his voice losing none of its edge. 'The spear isn't just about the arms. Your whole body must move with it.'

Finn, determined to prove himself, attacked the dummy with fierce intensity. His strikes lacked Eochaid's brute force but were quick, controlled, and relentless, a barrage of movements that left his straw opponent shredded. Darragh's approval was evident in a rare smile and a curt nod.

By midday, their tunics clung to them with sweat, their muscles burning with exertion. The moorland breeze offered little relief. Darragh allowed them a brief rest before moving on.

'The bow now,' he announced. 'A good archer can change the tide of battle without stepping foot into the fray.'

He led them to a row of targets set against the far stone wall. The boys took up bows, each carefully selecting a handful of arrows from a shared quiver.

Eochaid was the first to shoot. His arrow struck just outside the centre. He grunted, already nocking another with determined efficiency.

Connad, ever the strategist, took his time aiming. His first arrow landed near the centre, drawing an approving grunt from Darragh.

Finn, however, struggled with the unfamiliar weapon. His arrows veered wide, one even sailing past the target entirely to clatter against the far wall. Frustration flickered in his face, but he didn't step away.

'Don't rush,' Darragh said, coming to his side. 'Breathe. Let the arrow find its mark. A still hand and a calm mind.'

Finn breathed in deeply, narrowed his eyes, held his breath and released the string. The arrow flew true, not a perfect shot, but it struck the outer ring of the target with a satisfying thud. Better. Darragh said nothing, but the faint curl of his lip said enough.

As the sun dipped lower in the sky, casting amber light across the courtyard, Darragh raised his hand. 'That's enough for today. Tomorrow, we begin sparring in battle dress. You'll need your wits, and every ounce of strength. Rest well.'

The boys staggered back toward the hall, weapons slung over shoulders, spirits high despite the ache in their limbs. The routine was demanding, an hour of conditioning, an hour with the sword, rest, then spear and bow, always the same, yet never repetitive.

In the stone corridors of Dún Att, the echo of their laughter rang out.

Inside the great hall, firelight bathed the high rafters in golden warmth. At the long oak table, platters of roasted meat, fresh bread, and root vegetables awaited them. Their stomachs growled louder than their boasts.

'Eochaid,' Finn said with a smirk, reaching for a slab of roast venison, 'I almost had you with the sword today.'

Eochaid chuckled, tearing off a piece of bread. 'Almost isn't good enough, little cousin. You'll need more than fancy footwork.'

Connad leaned in with a crooked grin. 'One day, I'll best both of you. Wait and see. Just don't ask me to do it with a spear.'

Their laughter mixed with the crackle of the hearth and the bustle of servants clearing empty jugs and bowls. For all their lineage and burdens, prince, heir, monk-in-training. here they were only boys. Young warriors in the making, bound by friendship, rivalry, and the thrill of purpose.

Outside, the wind howled through the glens. But within the walls of Dún Att, there was warmth, and camaraderie, and the bright flame of youth not yet dimmed by the darkness to come.

As night fell, the castle grew quiet, its occupants retiring to their chambers. The marshland beyond the walls was shrouded in darkness, the stillness broken only by the occasional call of a night bird or the distant croak of a frog. In their shared chamber, Eochaid, Connad, and Finn lay on their straw-stuffed mattresses, their minds drifting to dreams of the battles they would one day fight.

'Do you think we'll ever see real war?' Connad asked, his voice more of a whisper.

Eochaid turned to face his cousin, his expression serious. 'We live in very troubled times. It's not a matter of if, but when. We must be ready.'

Finn nodded in agreement, his determination shining even in the dim light. 'And when the time comes, we'll fight side by side. For our people. For our land.'

'And for God, Finn. You'll perhaps be fighting as a monk.'

'Whoever I'm fighting for, we'll be together.'

The promise hung in the air, binding them. Outside, the wind howled over the marshes, a reminder of the unforgiving world beyond the castle walls. But within the fortress, the three young warriors found strength in their bond, ready to face whatever trials the future would bring.

Each time Finn returned to the familiar shores of Hy, it felt a little different. The sea was the same, the salt sharp in his nose, the wind tugging at his cloak like an impatient hound. But he was changing, and the island seemed to change with him.

In the years that had passed since he joined the royal household to train at Dún Att, he came every year to his monastic island home. Each visit lasted a few months, long enough to pray with the brothers, to speak quietly with Colm, to sit beside his father in the evenings and feel part of something larger than war drills and sword forms. But this time, something had changed.

Now in his thirteenth year, taller, broader of shoulder, Finn stood confidently in the boat as it scraped the pebbled shore, the messenger's pouch slung across his chest. He was no longer just visiting as a boy returning to his cradle; he had come bearing news, carrying trust.

Above the landing beach, the monastery sat cradled against the curve of the land. From the water, he could see the changes, nothing dramatic, but steady. The wooden chapel, its white-harled walls glowing in the pale afternoon light, now bore a simple, elegant cross at its peak. New buildings, still of timber and turf, had been added, another monk's cell, a small scriptorium, neatly fenced gardens.

He stepped off the boat with the same deliberate care he used dismounting a horse, his feet already sure on the path that led to the gate. A few monks paused their work to greet him with nods and quiet blessings.

Near the vegetable garden, Cobthach knelt, pressing seeds into the black soil. His back was bent with the effort of many seasons, but his hands still moved with strength and precision. He didn't look up until something caused him to turn.

He saw the boy first, then the man he was becoming.

Finn stood at the garden's edge, silhouetted against the sun. Seemingly a child no longer. His frame had broadened, his stance steady and sure. His once round face now cut with sharper angles, and the sword at his hip looking as though it belonged there. But his eyes, his mother's eyes, still held that same spark of mischief and warmth.

Cobthach let out a sharp breath, as if struck. The basket in his hands slipped, rolling into the dirt, scattering seeds across the ground. 'Finn.' His voice soft. Then, louder. 'Finn!'

He surged forward, crossing the space between them in three strides. Finn hardly had time to react before his father's arms crushed him in a fierce embrace. 'My God, look at you!'

Cobthach pulled back, gripping Finn's shoulders with both hands reassuring himself that this was real. His weathered fingers traced the fabric of Finn's tunic, noting the fine weave. 'You're as tall as me now!'

Finn lowered his hood and laughed,. 'Father, it's good to see you. It's only been nine months since I was last here, You seem surprised.'

Cobthach barked a rough, joyful laugh. He clapped a hand to Finn's cheek, shaking his head in disbelief. 'Nine months?

The changes in you make it feel longer. You've grown strong, like an oak. Your mother would burst with pride.'

Finn swallowed. 'I hope so.'

'You've finally grown into that sword, then?'

'Nearly,' Finn replied, glancing down at the blade hanging from his belt. 'It feels less like I'm borrowing it.'

Cobthach gave a short, proud nod. 'You look strong. Dún Att is treating you well.'

'It is. I brought a letter from King Conall, for Uncle Colm.'

'We'll get to that, but first…' Cobthach reached out, cupping the back of Finn's head in one rough palm, '… welcome home.'

Finn breathed softly and let the feeling settle over him. Yes. For all its storms and silence, its harsh work and holy duties, Hy was still home.

Cobthach pulled him close again, briefly pressing his forehead against his son's. A father's quiet blessing.

'And to see you! Though I'd hardly recognize you with those broad shoulders, that warrior's stride and those flowing locks of hair. Your mother's hair, the colour of burning peat embers.' His eyes glazed over for a moment, drawn into the distance. Remembering. 'Dún Att has served you well, Finn.'

As they walked together along the edge of the gardens, the smell of fresh earth and salt air mingled in the breeze, Cobthach's face grew thoughtful. 'Your mother always believed you were destined for great things,' he said softly. 'And I see now that she was right. Tell me, what brings you back to Hy at this time? I wasn't expecting you for another month.'

Finn paused, his expression shifting to seriousness. 'I need to speak with Colm. Is he here?'

Cobthach nodded. 'He's in his study on the far side of the complex. He spends much of his time there these days, writing, praying. You'll find him easily enough.'

Finn clasped his father's arm. 'Thank you, Father. We'll speak more later, I promise.'

Cobthach clasped his son's arm once more, eyeing the boy's belt with a furrowed brow. 'Just remember, Finn, a monastery is no place for weapons. Even for a future King's Guard, there are places where steel should not follow.'

Finn stood taller, as if reciting something he had been taught many times. 'Queen Sabhdha says that, like Eochaid and Connad, I am a prince and will soon be among the King's Guard of Dál Riata. As such, I should always wear my sword to show my station. But I will, as is right, leave this and all other weapons outside of a holy place or the Great Hall of Kings and Lords, unless I am there to protect them.'

'Good. Queen Sabhdha's trained you well, but don't let her do all the thinking for you.'

'I don't, but she does try and teach a lot.'

Cobthach chuckled. 'Aye, I'm starting to gather that.'

'Make sure you remember to leave your sword outside the chapel,' Cobthach said, though the trace of a smile softened the warning. 'It's good to see you, boy. I think you've enjoyed your time with the King and his family. And what fine clothes you're wearing.'

'Queen Sabhdha says…'

'Queen Sabhdha says, Queen Sabhdha says,' Cobthach interrupted with a laugh. "Does anyone else get to speak in Conall's court?'

'Occasionally,' Finn admitted with a grin. 'But the King is always busy. We spend more time with the Queen. She's a good teacher. Kind. Wise.'

'How long are you staying with us?'

'You know very well, Father, that's not my decision. Uncle Colm and King Conall decide between them. They say when I'm sixteen I can start making my own choices. Until then, I must do as I'm told.'

'You're already talking like a royal,' Cobthach said, shaking his head. 'Now go and find the Abbot. Lord knows how, but he's probably expecting you.'

Finn turned and began walking toward the monastery gate. Cobthach watched him go, pride and love mingling in his gaze. Once his son disappeared from view, he knelt again in the damp soil, his rough hands pressing into the earth.

'Lord, forgive me for the sin of pride,' he murmured. 'But how can I not be proud?'

The wind stirred the grasses around him, and his breath caught in his throat.

He closed his eyes. 'Niamh… can you see him?'

His fingers gripped the soil tighter. 'Our boy is strong. He is good. He has your fire, your heart,' he chuckled; '…and your hair.'

His voice dropped to a whisper. 'I wish you could see him, my love. I wish you could tell me what to do.'

The wind gusted, sharp with the salt of the sea.

Cobthach let out a slow breath, loosening his grip on the earth. Finally, he bowed his head.

'Lord, let me be enough for him.'

A smile lingered on his lips, soft and reverent, a father's quiet joy, wrapped in humble gratitude and whispered hope.

Finn paused at the monastery gates and held his breath. From the boat he had noticed small changes, the contours of the shoreline, the distant white gleam of the church. But now, standing at the entrance, he saw it all with fresh eyes. Everything had changed from the time he and his fellow exiles had landed and he had chased Finnian's goats.

The wild, windswept fields were gone. In their place stood ordered gardens, low stone walls, and neatly laid paths of crushed shell and gravel. A deep ditch and earthwork embankment encircled the monastic enclosure, giving it the feel of a small fortress as much as a sanctuary. What had once been little more than clustered huts was now a settlement of purpose.

The simple timber chapel they had first built had been replaced. White-harled and gleaming against the dull grey sky, the church rose with new authority. A wooden bell tower stood tall beside it, and above the arched doorway, a dark iron cross stretched upward, stark and solemn. Finn should have felt pride. Instead, a knot tightened in his chest.

This had once been his refuge, a place of peace, of quiet ritual and familiarity. But now it seemed like something else entirely. Larger. Grander. Stricter.

Perhaps this is what growing older means: to return to the places of your youth and find them changed… or to discover that it is you who no longer fits within them.

He walked along the stone-lined path toward the priory, his boots crunching on the gravel. On either side rose buildings he didn't recognise, new cells with clay-daubed walls, a long refectory hall with smoke curling from its vents, and further back, what he guessed must be a scriptorium, its narrow windows shaded by hides to protect the delicate vellum within.

The air was full of life and labour. Hammers rang from the smithy, sharp and rhythmic. The scent of baking bread drifted from stone ovens. Chanting rolled gently from the church, layered voices harmonising in prayer. Monks passed in silence, robed figures carrying timber, scrolls, baskets of herbs. This was no longer a cluster of exiles. It was a thriving monastic city.

When he had first left for Dún Att, there had been thirteen monks. Now there must be close to two hundred. He marvelled at the transformation, and at the determination it must have taken to shape something so complete from a barren, windswept island.

In the centre of the complex, rising on top of a low mound,

stood a large circular building unlike anything he remembered. Its walls were thick, its thatched roof high and conical. Finn paused, curious. A chapter house? A meeting hall? Something about its placement, central, elevated, suggested it held a special significance.

He stood there a moment longer, absorbing it all. This place had grown without him. Yet part of him still hoped it might welcome him back.

As Finn rounded a corner near the new central building, the chanting from the church behind him faded, replaced by the clatter of cartwheels and the low murmur of voices. A young monk, perhaps not much older than Finn himself, emerged from a side building, carrying a basket of linen and robes.

The monk stopped abruptly when he saw Finn. His eyes flicked to the boy's finely woven tunic, the small decorative brooch at his shoulder, and elegant but empty sword sheath at his hip. He bowed his head respectfully.

'My lord,' the monk said in a quiet, formal tone. 'Forgive me, I did not see you coming. May I help you find someone? One of the brothers, perhaps? Or the Abbot?'

Finn blinked, caught off guard. The deference in the monk's voice was unfamiliar, almost uncomfortable.

'I… thank you,' Finn replied. 'I'm looking for the Abbot Columba. Is he in his study?'

'He is,' the monk nodded. 'Shall I announce you?'

A smile tugged at the corner of Finn's mouth. 'No need. He'll know me when he sees me.'

The monk hesitated, clearly unsure whether to challenge or obey, then gave a respectful nod and stepped aside. As Finn passed, the monk turned to watch him go, his expression puzzled.

Finn couldn't help but grin to himself. So much had changed. He was no longer the boy the monks remembered, some didn't know him at all.

He continued down the path toward Columba's study, the white harled walls of the church gleaming behind him, and the scent of sea salt and heather thick in the air.

Finn found Columba in his study atop the rise the monks now called *Tòrr an Aba,* Abbot's Hill. The hut was modest, round and thatched, but positioned to command a full view of the monastery and the sea beyond. Inside, the scent of vellum, beeswax and peat smoke hung in the air. Columba sat hunched over his desk, quill in hand, the soft scratching of ink on parchment the only sound.

Finn knocked gently on the doorframe.

'That knock sounds suspiciously like a visitor who's spent too long in royal courts,' Columba called, without turning.

Finn smiled. 'I hoped I was more than a visitor.'

Columba stood slowly, the familiar warmth in his eyes chasing away any lingering stiffness in his frame. He crossed the room in two strides and embraced Finn tightly. 'Welcome home, young cousin. How are you? The moors have given you shoulders, and Dún Att seems to have given you purpose. We've missed you here.'

'I'm very well, Uncle Colm. Thank you. I bring a message from King Conall. The trader from Gaul should arrive in the coming weeks. His ship carries Communion wine, and the King says it's time you began trading directly for the abbey's needs.' Finn then opened his pouch and handed Columba the private letter bearing the seal of King Conall.

Columba nodded thoughtfully, then tilted his head. 'Thank you, Finn. You've delivered the message with the bearing of a nobleman. But now, go and change. Two new tunics and cowls have been prepared for you. While you may dress as Queen Sabhdha pleases in court, here you must keep to the Rule of St Benedict.'

Finn hesitated. 'How long am I staying?'

Columba raised an eyebrow. 'Already thinking of leaving? Has the sea air lost its charm? Or have we grown too plain for your royal tastes?'

Finn's cheeks flushed. 'No, Uncle Colm. Please don't think that of me. It's just… my father asked. I wanted to be able to tell him.'

Columba chuckled, resting a hand on Finn's shoulder. 'Good. Never lose that honesty. St Benedict may frown on idle chatter, but even he allows for a little laughter to renew the soul. You'll stay two seasons. We have much to teach you… and perhaps even more to learn from you. But let all that wait. After the Gaulish merchant arrives, there will be talk enough.'

He turned back to his desk and picked up a wax tablet. 'After Nones, join me in the round house. I'll talk you through the changes to the abbey, our small miracle rising from rock and prayer.'

As Finn turned to go, Columba called after him, 'And Finn… welcome home. Truly.'

Finn quickly re-adapted to the rhythm of monastic life. The fine clothes of court were folded away, stored carefully for his return journey. In their place, he donned the simple garments worn by all within the abbey's walls.

There was no vanity in a monk's attire. Even this was an act of obedience. The Rule of St Benedict stated only that monks should be clothed modestly and practically, with two tunics and two cowls, to allow for washing and warmth. At Hy, the tunics were plain undyed linen, while the cowls were made of coarse brown wool, cheap, local, and sturdy. For the travelling brothers or Columba's acolytes, like Finn, a grey cowl marked them out, often adorned with a small, embroidered dove to signify their calling.

Rather than explaining this all at once, Finn was reminded of the symbolism gradually. As he folded his new cowl over his shoulders, he remembered Baithéne's words from the past: 'We wear these so the wind may pass through us like it does the grass. We are not here to resist the world, but to bend with it, and grow in its soil.'

Properly clothed, Finn joined the brothers for the service of Nones. Though he had tried to maintain the daily hours of prayer at Dún Att, he could never quite remember which psalms belonged to which day. Improvisation had filled the gaps, and he hoped God would understand. Perhaps he should confess it, he thought. He would ask his father later.

Today was Tuesday. The words of Psalms 125, 126, and 127 flowed easily from memory. Finn especially liked Psalm 127, which praised children as a reward from God. 'Like arrows in the hands of a warrior,' he sang with surprising strength, 'are children born in one's youth.' He liked the image. Being an arrow.

He sang with such energy that Cobthach turned to raise an eyebrow at him. Finn grinned and kept singing. Around them, a few monks exchanged small smiles. They had missed this spark of joy. As more families prepared to settle within and near the monastery, it was this spirit they hoped would one day fill the community: a joyful, unguarded presence.

After the prayers, Finn joined his father in the round chamber with a wide oaken table at its centre. Fourteen chairs encircled it. Gradually, the others arrived: Columba and the twelve original disciples who had first travelled from Daire to this wild island, building the abbey from windswept soil and salt-kissed stone.

Columba began with a prayer. Then, he sat back, unusually relaxed. 'This is the first time since we set foot on Hy that the original company has met alone,' he said. 'We began as pilgrims. Now we are stewards.'

He looked around, his gaze settling on Finn. 'Even though you are still young, Finn, you are part of this family. You may spend only part of each year here, but you are woven into the fabric of this place. One day, you may take your seat at this table. For now, listen. Learn. Ask questions when you must. Never be afraid to speak, for God often chooses the youngest voice to carry the clearest truth.'

Finn tilted his head at that but said nothing.

Columba continued. 'Every brother here has his role. Baithéne is now Prior. He speaks for me in my absence. We read together what St Benedict warns about Priors, and Baithéne assures me it won't be a problem.'

Baithéne chuckled. 'Our holy guide warns that some Priors become puffed-up with pride, imagining themselves equal to their Abbot. Pride leads to envy, quarrels, and broken obedience. In short, a disaster.'

Laughter circled the room.

Finn leaned forward. 'Does it really say that?'

'It does,' Baithéne said. 'And it also says that children who forget their psalms should be whipped.'

More laughter. Finn stood up, mock indignant. 'No! It doesn't! I've never even seen a whip!'

Baithéne grinned. 'Well, perhaps that part we leave aside in the Celtic Church. Just as we ignore the rule about making novices knock for days at the door before entry.'

Finn smirked. 'In any case, I never forget my psalms.'

Cobthach raised a hand. 'Careful, lad. Humility is a virtue Benedict insists upon. Perhaps the Abbot will reconsider the whip after all?'

Columba held up his hand, still smiling. 'Enough. Finn, your father is right. Humility. Patience. Obedience. Respect. Compassion. These are not ideas, they are habits. And they are what make a monk. I believe you already carry many of them.

But the rest must be learned.'

He continued explaining roles: Ernán as Steward, Cobthach as Guest Master, Diarmait as personal servant, Eochaid as Cellarer responsible for provisions, the inseparable Rus and Fichna to guide novices, Lugaid the Almoner, Scandal mac Bresail the Infirmarer, Tochannu the Cantor, Carnan the Chamberlain, and Grillán as Keeper of the Hours, responsible for calling each office of prayer.

'If you have questions, Finn, ask the one best placed to answer. I cannot know all. Nor can your father. But you are welcome in my study each day while you're here.'

Then he looked to Eochaid. 'Brother Cellarer, have you brought the mead?'

A jug appeared and was poured.

Columba raised his cup. 'Let us drink in moderation and lift our voices. Let us sing the hymn we sang at sea, when we came here with only hope and God's promise.'

And so, they did.

The following morning, Finn, dressed in his newly acquired tunic, he didn't need the cowl as it was a bright and pleasant spring morning, went to join his father in the fields. Spring was here. The first opportunity to plant the soil carefully prepared in the autumn. Back-breaking work that Finn had missed by remaining at Dún Att.

'I can help you until Terce,' he said as he dropped to his knees beside his father; 'what are you planting?'

Cobthach held out his hand. 'You tell me.'

Finn looked at the flat, round, brown seeds and smiled. 'Parsnips, my favourite,' he said.

'You're right, Finn but that was an easy one. Let's finish these drills and I'll have a tougher question for you.'

Father and son worked amicably side by side. Finn, as

always, asking questions and Cobthach patiently answering them. When the parsnips were done, Cobthach rose from his knees, placed his hands on his hips and leaned backwards, stretching the muscles in his lower back.

'Are you unwell, father?'

'No, just a little stiff, it's a problem with old age.' He laughed. 'Now let's see how good you are with the next seeds.' He walked over to a small pouch he had left beside the next drills and poured a few seeds into his hand.

Finn rushed to his side. 'Too easy; you haven't removed the spines. Carrots.'

'Correct, but which colour?'

'Like you, we'll know when they grow. Some will be white for use in medical potions and some will be purple for eating. You've tried to trick me on that one before.'

'You never need telling twice, Finn, you're a good student.'

The Terce bell rang. 'Thank you, father. After Terce I must go to Uncle Colm, he says he has plans for me. See you later.'

Cobthach followed his son, who ran everywhere, at a steady walking pace. 'You'll convert every pagan in Pictland in a week, if you carry on at that pace,' he said but no one was around to hear.

Columba always stayed longer in his prayers than the other monks, and Finn fidgeted around waiting for the Holy Man. He was in Columba's day room, the desk as usual covered in manuscripts and letters. Finn was doing well at reading, it was, along with writing, a focus of his education while in the royal court. Those, and the development of battle skills. He enjoyed all three equally. His studies were in both Irish and Latin and he was becoming highly proficient in the languages his life centred around. His eyes fell on a manuscript in the centre of the table. He was able to make out the words at the top. *'REGULA S.P.N. BENEDICT'* The Rule of St. Benedict.

‘Surely uncle Colm knows that by heart,’ he said.

‘It doesn’t hurt to remind oneself of the finer details,’ a voice replied from the entranceway; ‘Have you seen anything of interest amongst my private papers?’

‘I didn’t touch anything, Uncle Colm, I promise. I was bored waiting for you.’

‘You should fill your spare time, with prayer, Finn. What did I tell you only yesterday about patience? We have no tolerance for boredom, even for those as young as you. But worry not, for I have a task that will keep you busy.’

‘What’s that?’

‘Well now, let’s see if I can find the passage in that manuscript you were so interested in before shall I?’

‘But I…’

Columba raised his hand to prevent any further discussion. He picked up the manuscript and flicked through the pages, until he found the place he was searching for. ‘Here it is, now let’s see if you can read it, Finn.’

Finn approached the table, the light in this room was strong as the doorway was big and open and the glass-less windows were also large.

Looking at where Columba was pointing he began to read, falteringly.

‘Before everything and above everything, care of the sick is to be had…’

‘Well done Finn, your reading of Latin is getting better. That’s enough for now. So, what do you think my task is for you?’

‘You… you want me to take care of someone who is sick? Who is it? Is it my father? He didn’t look too well this morning after planting the seeds. Is he sick?’

‘No, Finn. As far as I am aware, your father is healthy. No, it’s more important than that. A new brother will soon be arriving from Ireland, a man who is very efficient at apothecary. I'm going to need you to help him whilst you are here. We will need to set up a herb garden, I'll need you to go to Finnian and speak to him about his medicines and obtain as much knowledge about herbs as he can give you.'

'Finnian, you mean Finnian with the goats?'

'I don't know of any other by that name, do you?'

'You want me to learn about herbs and sickness?'

Columba nodded. 'You will benefit from this knowledge, Finn. Healing is a gift, just as battle is a skill. You will have need of both.'

'But, Uncle Colm, I am just getting good at swordsmanship. Darragh said I am improving every day.'

Columba's gaze was steady. 'A sword takes life. A healer restores it. Tell me, which is the greater skill?'

Finn hesitated. He wanted to say the sword, but the weight of Columba's words pressed against him.

'What if… what if I am meant to fight?'

Columba smiled. 'Perhaps you are, one day. But strength without wisdom is dangerous. Learn to heal first, Finn. Then, you may choose whether to wound.'

Finn swallowed. He wasn't sure he liked that answer. 'No, but…'

'No buts, Finn. Again, think back to the meeting yesterday. I talked about obedience did I not? I said you already had this quality, did I not?'

'Yes uncle Colm. Sorry.'

'Now, after the trading ship has arrived, you are to go to Finnian's house, where he and Máire will teach you and you will write what they tell you and bring it back here. Conall tells me you are very capable at writing. You are to stay with them for 4 weeks and this will be repeated whenever you are back with us.'

Finn looked down at his hands. Calloused from swordplay, bruised from sparring. A warrior's hands. He looked at Columba's hands. Worn from writing, gentle in their strength. Two paths. One day, he would have to choose.

Finn straightened his shoulders. 'I'll do it.'

Columba's lips curled into a smile. 'Oh? No complaints?'

Finn smirked. 'Well… I'd rather be fighting.'

Columba laughed. 'And that is exactly why you must learn to heal first. Also, don't forget, you'll be able to help Finnian take care of his goats, and you'll be responsible for bringing some back here to start our own herd.'

This cheered Finn up greatly.

'Now go and practice your writing in the Scriptorium, I'm sure Tochannu will find you something suitable to copy.'

'But copying text doesn't help, you can be illiterate to copy text, in Dún Att we have to write what is said to us.'

'Welcome back, Finn. Now, go to Tochannu.'

Chapter 7

Is fír dom rád.
(It is truth I speak.)
– Old Irish expression used in storytelling and oath-swearing

The Gallic ship anchored in deep water. The trader and some of the crew rowed across to the landing area. He was greeted by Cobthach, as Master of Guests, and escorted to the newly completed guest quarters where, in accordance with the Rule, their feet were washed and welcome prayers were said.

Columba greeted the Gaul warmly. 'Welcome, Camulus. Are your quarters comfortable? You are the first guest to stay in the new house.'

'More than comfortable, Abbot, thank you. It's as good or better than any monastery I've stayed in throughout Europe, and better than at some royal palaces too I can tell you.'

'You are too kind, my friend, and perhaps exaggerating just a little?'

Camulus laughed. 'Don't worry Abbot, I'm not trying to flatter in order to exact a higher price from you. The price negotiations have all been done. King Conall insists that he pay for all your needs here at the monastery.'

'That is a kind, Christian gesture.'

'Aye, as maybe, but he did say to tell you not to take advantage and feed half the people in the Kingdom.'

Now it was Columba's turn to laugh. 'That's an old joke between us, tell him he has no need to worry on that score. Now, Camulus, let me introduce you to Brother Eochaid, he is our Cellarer and will inform you of our needs. Have you brought us anything on this trip?'

'Oh yes, I have wine, also malachite and Verdigris for green colouring, orpiment for yellow and ultramarine for blue. If you need, I also have Tyrian blue.'

'We do need the Tyrian, we have requested our own from the Abbey in Daire but they are in short supply. We will soon be able to make our own here, on the island. I have sent several novices out this morning to check on the sea snails here about,' Eochaid replied; 'and perhaps if we can make enough, we can export it through you, Camulus?'

'I think we'll be able to use all we produce Brother Eochaid.' Columba seemed a little nervous.

'I also bring olive oil and ceramic bowls,' Camulus continued. 'I have wood for your building works, bronze and iron. Also, I have a gift for you Abbot from your friend the Abbott of Tours, who remembers your visit with great fondness. It is a thurible of silver and incense to burn within it.'

'Such generosity,' said Columba. All these items are most welcome. Do you bring that other great gift I always need?'

'What is that?'

'News, Camulus, news. Do you bear any news from Rome, or other religious houses?'

'Have you heard of the fate of Scylletium? The city on the southern coast.'

'Is that not the Roman city used by the blasphemous Arianists?'

'Abbot, there is no such thing any more as a 'Roman City.' Rome has been reduced to a Duchy and a mere puppet of Byzantium. But yes it is, or I should say was, that city.'

'Why 'was' that city?' Columba's anxiety grew.

'It has been completely annihilated.'

Finn edged closer, his pulse quickening. Camulus had his full attention now.

The Gaul continued. 'Battles are raging in Italy between Byzantium and the Lombards. The Lombards are slowly gaining ground and with each victory push further ahead.'

'Yes, but surely, that is in the north of the country not in Calabria.'

'Indeed Abbot, but the Lombards, who also follow the religion of the heretic Arius, seem intent on controlling the whole country and the Duke of Rome grew paranoid. For many reasons, he turned his attention to Scylletium, a city he hated for its blasphemy. He convinced the young Byzantine co-emperor, Theodosius, that the Calabrian city might be a gateway for the Lombards to send troops by sea from the north. They could launch attacks from there, and try to squeeze the Byzantine territory between two, well sustained, Arian heretical armies.

Finn looked up at Columba 'Who were they, Uncle Colm? What did they believe that was so terrible?'

'Later, Finn.' Columba put his hand on Finn's shoulder. 'Please, Camulus, continue.'

'With the blessings of Theodosius, Rome sent an army, two full legions, equipped with a hundred catapults or more. The city was well guarded and a long siege was to be avoided. Byzantine ships sailed to the Ionian sea to blockade the harbour. The land forces surrounded the city, killing or harrying anyone outside the gates to get inside. The city leaders came out to negotiate surrender, their decapitated bodies returned on their horses. Their heads were placed on long pikes, hammered into the ground, sightless eyes looking towards the city of peace they had, until minutes before, governed.'

He paused, looking at the faces of his enraptured audience. 'With no negotiation, no surrender accepted and no escape possible, there was no hope.

'Roman soldiers formed a seemingly impenetrable shield wall outside of the gate, barring it completely. No one was to be allowed to leave. I visited Scylletium many times as a young sailor learning my trade. Its position, nestling beside the Calabrian coast was like a cultural crossroads. Trade brought merchants, like my father. They came from Africa and all around the Mediterranean. The city's churches were magnificent. Adorned with mosaics depicting Christ as the Logos.'

'What's the Logos?' asked Finn

Columba raised his hand. 'Finn, I told you keep your questions for later. You like writing what you are told not what you copy, so write down your questions if there are too many to remember.'

'Ugh!' groaned Finn. There was no way he was going to the scriptorium for writing equipment, he didn't want to miss this tale, even though he was struggling to understand some of the things being said. He had already stored 'Arianism' for later, now he added 'Logos' to the list in his head.

Camulus continued.

'Arianism grew, despite decrees and bullying from Rome. Scholars and theologians from the Christian world came, fostering an environment of intellectual and spiritual exchange. Bishop Eliodoro encouraged open debate. He understood the beliefs of Rome but couldn't adhere to them. The community thrived and the citizens of Scylletium learned to live with the religious shadow cast over them. They hoped that they would be left alone, to worship God, the same God adored in Rome, but under the teachings of, and particularly in the manner of,

Arius of Alexander. Their prayers were not answered as politics entered the fray. The Byzantium Emperor decided he could deflect from his lost battles in the north and try and teach the Arian Lombards a lesson.'

'How often the innocent are made to suffer by the power hungry,' Columba said.

Finn was about to say something about not interrupting. A stern look from Columba made the words freeze in his throat.

'Very true Abbot, so very true. The order was given, and the Roman catapults unleashed their fury upon the city. The once-peaceful place was engulfed in chaos and death as fiery missiles arced through the sky, setting buildings alight and scattering defenders. The Roman artillerists, worked in relentless unison, each shot striking with precision. Flames erupted on impact, consuming rooftops and spreading rapidly through the narrow streets. Thick black smoke billowed into the air, choking defenders as they scrambled to contain the inferno. The crackle of burning wood mixed with the terrified cries of citizens trying to flee. Roman soldiers worked tirelessly, feeding their siege engines with fuel and fire, each volley intensifying the destruction. Watchtowers collapsed in blazing ruin, their timbers reduced to ash. The city's defenders struggled to rally, their resolve flickering like the flames that surrounded them. Scylletium burned, and with every fiery strike, the city's fate grew darker. The air was thick with the acrid scent of smoke, the skies, above the town, aglow with an eerie orange hue as the homes, churches and markets, burned'

Camulus coughed. Finn thought that even the retelling of the story was enough to make the Gaul feel the thick smoke. Or maybe it was a storyteller's trick, to keep the story alive and the audience listening.

'What had once been a bustling city, with its intricate marble streets and vibrant markets, was now engulfed in pain and death. The cries inside the walls became screams as sulphurous balls of flame rained down. A soldier who witnessed it told me everything. He said it was like Pompeii reborn, sulphurous fire raining from the sky, devouring the city in an unholy storm. Volley after volley, flames surged, turning stone to ash and flesh to char.

'Gradually the screams diminished, the blazes grew in intensity until finally the commanders stopped the catapults. The attack began suddenly, like a storm breaking upon the sea. Soldiers broke their shield wall and marched through the gates. Their orders were clear: To stamp out the heresy by any means necessary. The city's defenders, armed with little more than swords and shields, were no match for the imperial forces.

'The rhythmic thumping of soldiers' boots on the marble walkways mingled with the cries of mothers shielding their children as they fled their burning homes. Priests, clutching sacred texts and relics ran towards the Basilica whispering prayers to God for deliverance. In the great basilica, the survivors gathered.

'The imposing figure of Bishop Eliodoro stood resolute before the magnificent marble altar, crozier in hand. He had shepherded his flock through years of persecution, his sermons a source of hope and resilience. Now, as the city burned, his face was calm, though his eyes betrayed the weight of despair. His crimson robes were illuminated by the flickering glow of the all-consuming fires filtering from outside. His voice steady despite the chaos. "Do not fear. Even in the face of death, we are not forsaken. Our faith is our shield, and our God is just."

'Around him, hundreds of terrified citizens knelt, seeking shelter from the relentless Roman onslaught that had turned Scylletium into a smouldering ruin. Mothers clutched their children, men stood protectively before their families, and priests murmured prayers in trembling voices. Their whispered pleas echoed off the stone walls, mingling with the distant clash of steel and the anguished cries of the dying.

'Bishop Eliodoro raised his hands, calling for silence amidst the chaos. His deep voice filled the Basilica, steady and unwavering despite the fear that thickened the air. "Do not be afraid," he said, his voice a beacon of calm in the storm. "In this hour, we commend our souls to the hands of the Lord. We shall face what is to come with faith and courage." The crowd bowed their heads as he led them in prayer, a final act of defiance against the violence that drew ever closer.

'The heavy oak doors of the Basilica burst open with a thunderous crash, and a cold wind swept through the sanctuary, carrying the scent of ash and blood. Roman soldiers poured into the sacred space, their bronze helmets glinting in the firelight, their swords stained with the lives they had already taken. At their head marched the Roman legate, his expression a mask of cold determination. His eyes scanned the room, lingering briefly on the bishop before hardening with grim resolve.

'Bishop Eliodoro did not flinch. Leaning on his crozier he knelt slowly, laying his staff of office on the ground he clasped the simple wooden cross chained around his neck in prayer. He raised his eyes to the large golden crucifix suspended from the ceiling. This symbol seen in all Catholic churches, symbolised Christ's sacrifice to mankind for the Church of Rome, but his obedience and subordination to God for the Arianist. Eliodoro obeyed God all his life and he accepted his fate as Christ had done. Christ suffered some doubt asking the Supreme Being why he had been forsaken. Eliodoro knew he hadn't been forsaken but chosen. For a fleeting moment, the chaos seemed to freeze, the world balanced on a razor's edge between life and death. The legate strode forward with measured steps, his sword gleaming in his hand. He stopped in front of the bishop, towering over the kneeling man.

"In the name of the father, the son and holy spirit" the legate said, knowing these words would offend the holy man.

"God forgive him, he knows not what he is doing," the Bishop responded, mirroring the words of Christ.

'The legate raised his weapon high and vertical. He guided the point to the holy man's left shoulder, the top of his rib cage. Without hesitation, he adjusted the angle slightly and plunged. The blade tore through flesh and bone with sickening ease, slicing lung, heart, liver and bowel. Death was almost instantaneous. The legate had done that at least for his victim. The congregation let out a collective gasp as Bishop Eliodoro collapsed, his blood spurting out and flowing across the floor.

'With a grunt, the legate pulled his sword from his victim, wiping it on the crimson robes of the dead man and walked purposefully toward the door.

"Centurion, to me," he called. "Bring any wood that remains unburnt and bring it here place it on the wooden benches, and light it. Bar the doors let no one leave."

"But legate, the marble won't burn."

"No, but the wood and the heretics will. It will get them accustomed to the fires of hell."

'He walked out. His orders were followed. Screams filled the Basilica echoing around the acoustic walls. Lives were extinguished one by one but not the fire, the sacred space transformed into a slaughterhouse.

'Outside, the soldiers moved with mechanical precision, their blades striking down priests, men, women, and children alike. There was no mercy, no hesitation. Blood pooled on the ground, mingling with shattered relics and torn vestments. Desperate cries for mercy were silenced with brutal efficiency.

'In the end, silence reigned. The Basilica, once a sanctuary, was now a tomb. The Roman soldiers stood amidst the carnage, their task complete. The legate surveyed the scene without emotion. No citizen of Scylletium had been left alive. No-one to tell tales to children of Roman cruelty and destruction. There would be no attack by the Lombards from the south.

'The fires outside raged on, consuming the city, while inside the Basilica, only the lifeless, charred bodies remained, silent witnesses to the cruelty of war and the pitiless savagery of powerful men. By dawn, Scylletium was a smouldering ruin. The imperial forces had withdrawn, leaving behind a city gutted of its former glory. Thousands were dead, their bodies scattered among the ashes.'

The room was silent. Brother Eochaid saw Columba's tears. 'He is mourning the loss of another 3,000 souls, Camulus.' Cobthach said; 'Let us leave him to pray. He will join us to eat later.' He ushered everyone to leave, but Columba continued to hold onto Finn's shoulder.

When they were alone, Finn said, 'That's exactly like your vision uncle Colm.'

'Yes Finn. This is not the first time I have wished God did not bestow me with these foresights, but that would be to deny the will of God and therefore a sin. Another 3,000 souls lost, at Cúl Dreimhne they were pagan and denied the Kingdom of Heaven. I cannot state the fate of the citizens of Scylletium, for although they were heretics and blasphemers, they did worship the one true God in their own way.'

Finn frowned, 'If they worship the same God, why did they deserve to die?'

Columba was thoughtful. 'It is not for us to decide who deserves life or death, Finn. That is the lesson I learned at Cúl Dreimhne, too late.'

'Why do we still call them heretics? If they had been spared, could they not have repented? Why did they have to die?'

'Fear, Finn. Fear is more powerful than faith. And Rome fears nothing more than a challenge to its authority.'

Finn hesitated. 'But… they still worshipped Christ, didn't they? The same Christ we follow?'

Columba nodded. 'They did. But they denied His nature.'

'I don't understand.'

Columba gestured for Finn to sit. 'Arius of Alexandria taught that Christ was created by God, not equal to Him. He believed there is only one true God, and that Christ, while divine, was not part of Him.'

'But Christ said, 'I and the Father are one.'

Columba's smile was approving. 'Yes, Finn. And that is why Arianism is heresy. To separate Christ from God is to say that Christ was wrong. That is blasphemy.'

Finn frowned. 'So… the people of Scylletium died because of this single belief difference?'

'No, Finn.' Columba's voice was quiet. 'They died because of men who feared that belief.' He paused. 'Rome did not kill them for their souls, but for power, or the fear of losing power. That is why we must pray not only for the dead, but for the killers, too.'

Finn was silent for a long moment. Then, softly, he said, 'I will pray for them, Uncle Colm; but I'll never forget what they have done.'

Columba took Finn's hands in his and they prayed together for those who perished in that faraway place, they also prayed again for all the deaths at Cúl Dreimhne.

Finn and Columba joined their fellow monks for the prayers and the three Psalms of Sext then went to the dining room to share the midday meal with their guests. Columba invited all the guests to join him at the high table. Finn sat next to Camulus hoping, at the end of the total silence during eating, to hear stories of adventures on the sea and perhaps pirates, which Cormaic had told him of in the past. He had missed the storytelling of the old soldier.

'As instructed by St. Benedict,' Brother Eochaid began, we have prepared two dishes from which you can choose. Indeed, as a guest you may partake of both, whilst the brethren are restricted to only one, and only that, if they feel unable to abstain.' He looked around the room and all except Columba and the guests had their heads down as if in prayer, but Brother Eochaid knew better. These were hardworking men and boys who needed to fuel their bodies and maintain strength. Abstinence on non-fast days was optional and therefore not partaken.

'Brother Cellarer, please offer our guests their food and afterwards serve the Brothers in accordance with their choices.'

The following morning, Finn made his way along the path that curved around the monastery gardens and skirted the edge of the grazing fields beyond. With each step, the buildings of the monastery receded behind him, replaced by the rough, wind-stirred grasses and bleating of goats from the nearby slopes. Columba's words still echoed in his ears: 'You are to go to Finnian's house, where he and Máire will teach you, and you will write what they tell you and bring it back here.'

He had met the elderly goatherd Finnian many times before but had never spent more than an afternoon in his company. Now, he was to live with him and his wife for four weeks, learning the ways of healing, of herbs and plants, of tinctures and poultices. And, perhaps more difficult still, of patience and observation.

Finnian's home sat in a hollow between two grassy knolls, the house low and round, its walls made of rough stone and packed earth, its thatch darkened by rain and years. Smoke curled from the chimney hole, and the scent of herbs hung in the air, even before Finn reached the door.

He knocked once.

Máire opened it. Her eyes crinkled into a smile. Her hair, still mostly auburn despite her years, was tied back under a blue woollen wrap. 'You're late,' she said. 'But you've grown, and not just in height.'

Finn grinned and stepped inside.

The interior of the hut was dim, warm, and richly scented. Bundles of herbs hung from the rafters, their leaves drying slowly. Shelves lined the walls, stacked with clay pots, dried roots, and vials of liquid. In the centre, a long wooden table was spread with work, cuttings, a mortar and pestle, scraps of parchment covered in spidery writing.

Finnian stood at the table, bent over a bowl of crushed leaves, his long grey beard tucked into his shirt to keep it from the mixture.

'You're here,' he said, not looking up. 'Good. Grab that stool.'

Finn obeyed, sitting opposite the old man.

'We start now,' said Finnian. 'No rest. No stories. Only work. What do you know of kingsfoil?'

Finn blinked. 'It heals wounds.'

'All plants heal something,' Finnian grunted. 'Kingsfoil draws out infection, yes, but only if the leaves are fresh and crushed. Dry them, and they're little better than dust.' He pushed a sprig across the table. 'Smell it. Remember it. When we're done, you'll know fifty more like it.'

For the next hour, Finn was tested on scent alone. Finnian blindfolded him, handed him leaves, roots, crushed powders. He was to guess each one by touch, smell, sometimes taste.

Some were bitter, others fragrant. Some stung the tongue. One made him sneeze so violently he knocked over a pot.

Máire laughed softly as she refilled it. 'Better you sneeze now than on a patient later. That was elderflower, used wrongly, it causes swelling.'

By the end of the first day, Finn's head was spinning. His notes were clumsy, but he forced himself to copy them cleanly by the firelight. Máire helped, occasionally correcting a misnamed root or a confused preparation.

'Learning is not just remembering,' she said, watching him. 'It's recognising patterns. A good healer does not memorise a thousand cures. He learns what pain looks like, where it comes from, and listens. The plants will do the rest.'

Each morning began before sunrise. They walked the hills together, collecting herbs in woven baskets. Máire pointed out plants growing in the shade, while Finnian taught him which roots to dig, which berries to avoid.

'And this one?' Finn asked, holding a tall stalk with purple flowers.

'Foxglove,' said Finnian. 'Pretty. And deadly. It stops the heart if misused. But used rightly, it can slow a racing pulse.'

'How do you know how much to use?'

'That is why you write everything down. And why you test on yourself before you test on others.'

Finn blinked. 'Have you done that?'

Finnian held up a hand with two twisted fingers. 'Once, I didn't wait for Máire's approval. That was the last time.'

Máire snorted from further down the slope.

Some afternoons were spent treating villagers who came seeking help. Children with coughs, old men with aching joints, young women with swelling in their feet and faces.

Máire showed Finn how to wrap sprained ankles with willow bark poultices, how to boil meadowsweet for fevers, and how to distil valerian for sleep. The boy watched and mimicked, always writing, always asking questions.

One day, a child was carried in, his leg torn open from a fall on jagged rocks. Blood soaked the bandage wrapped hastily around the limb.

Máire took charge at once, laying the boy on the table, slicing away the cloth. 'Finn, yarrow and honey. Boiled water. Clean cloths.'

He moved fast, hands shaking only slightly. The scent of blood was sharp, but he forced it down.

Together, they cleaned the wound. Finnian applied pressure while Máire stitched. Finn crushed yarrow leaves with honey into a thick paste, then packed it into the wound. The child whimpered, his mother crying softly in the corner.

When it was done, and the boy was sleeping, Finn sat back, breathless.

'You did well,' Máire said.

He looked at the blood on his hands.

'You won't forget that,' said Finnian. 'You never forget your first patient.'

That evening, Finn walked to the hill above the cottage and watched the sea. He thought of the boy's face, pale and twisted in pain. He thought of his own hands, steady despite the fear.

He had once thought himself a warrior. Now, he saw there were battles fought with herbs and cloth, with care and courage. This too was strength.

By the end of the fourth week, he had a large number of annotated vellum pages. Pages covered with drawings of plants, measurements for tinctures, steps for boiling, steeping, drying, wrapping. There were notes on pain, on fever, on the strange ways sorrow could linger in the body.

When it came time to return, Máire handed him a small bundle.

'Your own healing pouch,' she said. 'For the road. Use it wisely.'

Finnian clapped his shoulder.

'You won't remember it all. But you'll remember what matters. Come back, when you're ready to learn more.'

Finn bowed his head.

As he walked back toward the monastery, the sun rising behind him, he felt older. Not in years, but in knowledge. And in responsibility.

Healing, he realised, was its own form of battle. And he would be ready for both.

Chapter 8

Mo lámh i lámh Dé.
(My hand in the hand of God)
— Old Irish expression denoting divine guidance in one's actions

By the time Finn reached his sixteenth birthday, he had become the equal of any of King Conall's guards in swordsmanship. His skill was matched only by his loyalty, to his King, his kin, and to God. His bond with Eochaid and Connad had grown stronger through the years; what had begun as a boyhood friendship forged in sweat and laughter had matured into something deeper, a brotherhood tested by steel, scripture, and silence.

The three of them stood together now, tall and proud on the windswept stone platform below the church on Hy. The sun glinted off the sea behind them as they awaited the arrival of King Conall and Queen Sabhdha. The two princes wore finely woven cloaks dyed in the royal hues of Dál Riata, gold and deep green, their brooches gleaming in the afternoon light. Finn, standing between them, wore the dove-embroidered grey mantle that marked him as one of Columba's acolytes, and yet the sword at his hip told another truth. He was both monk and warrior, and in that balance he had grown into himself.

The harbour bustled with movement. Monks and layfolk gathered along the paths, eager for the celebration. Word had spread quickly: today was not just Finn's birthday, it was his coming of age.

A grand feast had been prepared in the open air beside the priory. Over three hundred monks lived and worked here now, their lives shaped by prayer, labour, and learning. Today, they would pause for joy. The air was rich with the scent of roasted meat, freshly baked bread, and the wildflowers that grew along the edges of the monastery walls. Laughter rang out, children chased each other in the grass, and pipers played lively tunes as guests arrived from every part of the kingdom.

At the centre of it all sat a raised wooden platform. There, beneath a woven canopy bearing the crests of Dál Riata and Columba's dove, sat King Conall, Queen Sabhdha, and the Abbot himself. Their presence elevated the moment from a celebration to a moment of rare solemnity.

As the young men approached, a hush fell over the gathered crowd. Conall rose to his feet and gestured for Finn to come forward.

'So, Findlugán mac Cobthach,' said the King, his voice carrying clear across the assembly, 'you have come to the threshold of manhood. Today, you stand before us not as a boy of promise, but as a man of choice. Tomorrow, you will decide the path you will follow. Will you take your place among the warriors of my household, beside my son Connad and his cousin Eochaid? Or will you serve God fully, dedicating your life to the work of this holy place and to Columba, your cousin and Abbot?'

A murmur passed through the crowd. All eyes turned to Finn. He stepped forward, the breeze tugging gently at his mantle, his posture proud and steady.

'My lord,' Finn said, his voice firm and clear. 'For that is how I must address you now, not as Uncle Conall. I have no need nor wish to wait until tomorrow to speak my heart.'

The King tilted his head slightly, intrigued. Sabhdha leaned forward, her eyes bright with interest.

'I have known my answer for some time,' Finn continued. 'I have already spoken with Abbot Columba in private. He has guided me in prayer and counsel, and I believe I am ready to speak aloud what has long been settled within.'

Columba smiled gently. 'Finn, I hope you'll still call me Uncle Colm as you always have.'

'If that is your wish,' Finn said, allowing a brief smile. 'But today, I speak as a man, and I say this: my sword, my strength, and my faith belong to both my King and my God. I was raised among monks, and I will never forsake prayer. But I have lived among warriors. I have stood with Eochaid and Connad, shoulder to shoulder, in practice and in pain. I will not be parted from them.'

He took a steady breath and lifted his head.

'I cannot walk one path. I was never meant to. I believe I am meant to walk both. I will fight when called, but I will also serve in peace. I will defend this land and the innocent, and I will speak the truth of Christ to those who would hear it. If that is acceptable to you… and to God.'

For a long moment, silence followed.

Then the Queen stood. 'Well then,' she said with a smile, her voice filled with warmth, 'my little Finn, for such you will always be to me, you've given us your answer, and one well spoken. You have chosen not between the sword and the cross, but to hold both.'

Cobthach rose from his seat beside the dais, his voice full of pride. 'Then let it be so. I am witness to this choice. And I give thanks that my son has found his path, even if it is not a simple one.'

‘Then it is done,’ said Conall, nodding solemnly. ‘You have declared your heart before your King and your kin. We accept your oath.’

Applause broke out among the gathered monks and islanders, echoing against the stone walls and the sea beyond. Eochaid clapped Finn on the shoulder. Connad grinned and nodded in approval. Columba lowered his head briefly, a silent prayer on his lips.

For a moment, Finn stood motionless, letting the sounds and sunlight wash over him. He had made his choice, not to become someone else, but to fully embrace who he already was.

And so, the boy who had once run barefoot through the fields of Daire stood now on Hy as a man, known and claimed by both crown and cross.

King Conall stood and raised his hand for silence.

‘Now,’ he said, his voice ringing out across the gathered crowd, ‘it is time for you to receive our birthday gifts, the tokens of your manhood, and of our esteem.’

Finn stepped forward from among his friends, his movements steady despite the anticipation curling in his stomach. The sea breeze stirred the edges of his mantle as he climbed the steps to the dais. He bowed his head, first to the King, then to the Queen, and finally to Columba.

‘Findlugán mac Cobthach,’ the King said solemnly, ‘you have chosen your path. Now receive the tools that will help you walk it.’

Eochaid came forward first, bearing a large, cloth-covered object in both arms. With great care, he set it down and removed the cover, revealing a polished bronze shield. The light caught its surface and scattered golden reflections across the dais and down into the crowd. At its centre, a striking medallion of a Roman eagle spreading its wings wide, proud, sharp-eyed and defiant. Around it, expertly etched Celtic knotwork spiralled outward like vines, interlacing eternity with might.

'This shield,' said the King, 'is a marriage of worlds. The eagle, a remnant from an old legionary shield, speaks of the disciplined power of Rome. The knotwork is the unbroken line of our people. Together, they tell the story of who we are, and who you are. You stand at a crossing of paths. Let this shield remind you to hold firm when worlds collide. May it protect you, as you protect those who look to you for strength.'

Finn bowed and accepted the shield, feeling its solid weight settle comfortably against his side. His fingers brushed the eagle medallion, smooth, ancient, alive with history.

'I will carry it with honour,' he said quietly. 'And never let it fall.'

The Queen rose next, her movements graceful as ever, though her eyes were wet with emotion. In her hands she held a small carved box of alder wood, the lid inlaid with mother-of-pearl in the shape of a dove in flight. She opened it and lifted out a ring, slim and gold, woven in such intricate interlacing patterns it seemed almost alive. At its centre, a sapphire gleamed, deep blue, as if the sea had been captured and stilled.

'This,' she said, 'is a gift from a mother's heart.'

Finn blinked, startled by the tenderness in her voice.

'Not your mother by blood, but one by choice and love. This ring is a symbol of wisdom, clarity, and constancy. The sapphire's depth mirrors the sea, always moving, but always true. May it remind you, when the world turns chaotic, that calm and clarity will light the way. And know, dear one, that you are never alone. You are forever in our hearts.'

She slipped the ring onto Finn's finger herself. The warmth of her hands lingered even after she let go.

'I am deeply honoured,' Finn said, his voice low. 'May I be worthy of this trust, and of your love.'

Then came the moment everyone was waiting for.

The King turned to Connad, who advanced with a long velvet-wrapped bundle held reverently in both arms. He knelt and offered it to the King, who took it with ceremonial care. Slowly, before all present, Conall unwrapped the final gift.

A collective breath caught in the air.

The sword was unlike any Finn had ever seen. Its blade was long, straight, and impossibly bright, forged of fine steel, so polished it reflected the face of anyone who looked into it. Runes lined the fuller in twin scripts, Latin on one side, Gaelic on the other, prayers for strength, justice, and mercy.

But it was the hilt that stilled Finn's breath.

Shaped into the form of a crucifix, the cross guard extended like the arms of Christ, not in suffering, but in protection. Tiny, embossed figures of saints and angels adorned the guard and pommel, each rendered with breathtaking detail. The grip was wrapped in dark leather, soft but firm. The sword felt holy, not merely forged, as though it had been blessed at its making.

'This sword,' Conall said, lifting it high so all could see, 'was forged not just for war, but for purpose. It is named *Fidelis*, the Faithful. Not because it must serve, but because it reminds the bearer to be true. True to their faith. True to their people. True to themselves.'

The King stepped down from the dais. Silence fell as he held the sword out, offering it not as a weapon, but as a charge.

Finn knelt before him, hands raised.

'I name you servant of both crown and cross,' the King declared. 'Stand when you are ready to bear the burden.'

Finn closed his hands around *Fidelis*. It was heavy, heavier than it looked, but the weight was right. Not just steel, but duty … calling.

He rose slowly, the sword now at his side, the shield on his back, the ring gleaming on his hand.

Columba moved towards Finn. He placed one hand on the boy turned man's shoulder and the other on his head.

'We bless this child now grown,' he said, voice calm and clear. 'May he walk in light and not stumble in shadow. May his hands serve justice and his heart know peace. May he wield his strength not in pride but in mercy. And may *Fidelis* always remind him whose servant he truly is.'

The wind picked up as if in answer, stirring Finn's mantle and tousling his hair. Somewhere behind him, someone began to sing, a hymn from Daire, one Finn had known from his cradle. Others joined. The monks, the nobles, the farmers, the children, all raising their voices in unison.

Finn stood, sword in hand, tears gathering in his eyes, and knew without doubt that this was his beginning.

He was no longer a boy who promised much.

He was Findlugán mac Cobthach. Knight of Dál Riata, Columban monk of Hy and faithful to country and God and family.

Later, as the celebration waned and the stars pricked through the indigo sky, Finn found himself summoned to a quieter place. Within the wooden chapel, lit only by the flicker of oil lamps and the fading warmth of the hearth, Queen Sabhdha and Columba waited. The hush of the sacred space seemed to cradle the moment in reverence.

Finn entered slowly, still wearing the dove-embroidered mantle, *Fidelis* now sheathed and strapped across his back. He bowed his head respectfully.

Columba was the first to speak.

'Come, Finn. Sit beside us.'

The young man obeyed, kneeling on the thick wool rug laid

before the hearth. Queen Sabhdha offered him a gentle smile as Columba reached into a linen wrap resting on the bench beside him.

'Tonight, you became something new in the eyes of the world,' Columba said, his voice low and steady. 'But it is not only kings and warriors who bestow honour. We in God's service recognise a deeper calling.'

He unwrapped the cloth and held out a small, dark cross on a simple leather cord. It was worn smooth with care, its wood a rich, weathered brown.

'This,' Columba continued, 'was carved from the fallen branch of a great oak that once stood outside our church in Daire. The tree from which it came had watched over many generations before the winds took it down.'

Finn took the cross reverently, his thumb tracing the worn grain.

'It is a reminder,' said the Queen softly, 'that even things that fall can be shaped for purpose. That strength is not always in standing tall, but in how we rise when broken.'

Columba nodded. 'The sword you received today may protect your body. But this... this is for your soul. Wear it close. Let it rest on your heart.'

Finn looped the cord over his head. The wooden cross settled against his chest with quiet finality.

'Thank you,' he whispered.

The Queen reached over and tucked a strand of hair behind his ear as she had done when he was small. 'We love you, Finn. Never forget that.'

Columba placed a hand on his shoulder. 'And we trust you. Go forward in peace. In strength. In faith.'

And so, by firelight and quiet blessing, Findlugán mac Cobthach sealed his path, not just with steel, but with the humble weight of oak and the love of two who saw in him the hope of all their worlds.

*

The following morning, the Royal party prepared to set sail for Dalruadhain and their home built on stilts in the water. The palace crannog was a marvel of engineering. A heavily guarded pier led out onto the water with a series of interconnected buildings containing a vast dining hall, throne room and accommodation.

Queen Sabhdha approached him first. Her eyes shone, but she did not weep. Instead, she cupped Finn's face with both hands, her fingers cool against his skin. 'You walk a dangerous path, Finn,' she said softly. 'A warrior must kill without hesitation. A priest must forgive without condition. Can you truly do both?'

Finn could not answer.

'You have become a son to me and a true brother to Connad, A light in our house.' she continued; 'Our home will always be open to you and I hope that it will not be too long before you come to brighten all our lives again.'

'I cannot say a time, My Lady, but of course I will always regard your home as my home. I am very lucky to have two places that I can call my home. One here with my cousin, father and uncle and one with you, your husband and my brothers-in-arms, Connad and Eochaid.'

The Queen hugged Finn long and hard. 'Then go with God's blessing, my dearest boy.'

Connad and Eochaid were next, grinning to mask their sorrow at leaving their friend behind. Eochaid clapped Finn on the back, nearly knocking him off balance. 'Try not to get yourself killed by a Pict.'

Finn smirked. 'Only if you promise not to let Dál Riata fall apart in my absence.'

Connad grinned but his voice was quieter when he spoke. 'We'll miss you, Finn. You belong in Dún Att as much as we do.'

'And I will return,' Finn promised. 'Just make sure you both stay alive long enough to see it.'

The three clasped forearms in a warrior's embrace, not as boys, but as young men about to start an new phase in their lives.

King Conall had been spending time with Columba and was the last to board. He clasped Finn on both shoulders. 'I wish you well, Finn, you are an asset I would welcome amongst my Guard at any time. May your journeys bring you to our door from time to time.'

Finn bowed. 'Thank you, My Lord.'

As the Royal boat moved out of sight, Finn's thoughts moved to the preparations being made in the monastery for a different kind of visitor. One from Rome.

As he continued to look out to sea, his fingers brushed the hilt of *Fidelis.*

A visitor from Rome?

He imagined the city swallowed in fire, its people screaming for mercy and the vision of Columba. Christians whose beliefs differed from Rome. He thought of the differences between the Celtic Church and the Roman. Were these devout and honest monks now to be deemed heretics?

What did Rome want with them?

Chapter 9

Is cóir do gach duine seasamh go diongbháilte ar a chreideamh.
(Each person must stand firmly upon their faith.)
– Old Irish Saying

The Roman Bishop arrived two days later, accompanied by four horsemen who struggled to control their mounts as the ferry swayed beneath them. The horses snorted and stamped, their hooves clattering uneasily on the damp wooden planks.

As was tradition, Columba stood at the entrance of the church, a basin of water on the ground in front of him. Finn stood behind him, watching as his Abbot knelt before the Bishop, washing his dust-streaked feet with solemn reverence. The old Roman winced as the cold water met his skin but gave no comment.

All conversation was in Latin, the uniting tongue of the Church.

Columba said the words prescribed by St. Benedict. 'We have received Thy mercy, O God, in the midst of Thy temple.'

'Amen,' Bishop Adelmo responded, though his voice held no warmth.

'You are welcome to our humble priory, far from the Holy See,' Columba said, rising to his feet. 'It is an honour to receive a guest from the heart of our faith.'

Adelmo scanned the small island, lingering on the women and children in the fields. His lips pressed into a thin line.

'Holy Abbot, I do not come as an emissary of the Pope,' he said. 'Ioannes III is preoccupied with matters of graver concern. The Lombards press harder against Rome's walls. It is Abbot Gregorius Anicius, the Prefect of Rome, who sends me.'

Columba studied the Bishop for a moment, inclined his head and spoke. 'I must inform you, Bishop, that Pope Ioannes was taken by the Lord more than a year ago. Benedictus now sits upon the throne of St. Peter, though I fear his tenure will not be a long one.'

A flicker of something, disbelief? irritation? crossed Adelmo's face.

'Ioannes is dead? Benedictus is Pope?' His voice was tight. 'How do you know this, so far from Rome?'

Columba's expression did not change. 'The Lord has ways of keeping us informed.'

From behind, Finn caught the slight twitch of Columba's lips, the closest thing to amusement he would allow on such occasions.

Adelmo breathed in noisily through his nose. 'Whoever holds the papacy, my mission remains the same. Abbot Gregorius has commanded me to assess the churches of these distant lands, to ensure their adherence to the Law of Rome.' His gaze flickered once more to the families tending the fields. 'To test their loyalty.'

Columba's voice was soft but unwavering. 'You will not find us wanting in either, Bishop.'

'Are you certain?' Adelmo countered. 'I see women and children here. Your church is small. And what of Easter?'

The air seemed to change.

Columba's voice remained measured, calm, but there was steel beneath it. 'Do you doubt my faith?'

'You do not observe the Paschal date set by Rome.'

Columba's hands folded before him. 'We follow the tradition of St. John, as we always have. Victorius of Aquitaine was a man, and men are fallible. Easter must always follow the Jewish Passover, for the Scriptures tell us Christ Himself observed it before His crucifixion.'

Adelmo's nostrils flared. 'The Pope is infallible.' His voice rose, brittle with certainty. 'When he decrees Easter, it is God Himself who has spoken.'

A long pause.

Columba's reply came quietly, like a distant tide rolling in. 'Beware, Bishop, that in your pursuit of order, you do not fracture unity.'

Adelmo stiffened. 'Is that a warning?'

Columba's expression was unreadable. 'It is an observation.' He turned slightly, gesturing to Baithéne. 'You are welcome here as our guest, for as long as you wish. But tomorrow, I leave for Hinba. I will spend my days there in silence and prayer before continuing east.'

Adelmo scoffed. 'What could be more important than receiving an envoy of Rome?'

Columba finally met his gaze. 'God's work. You are not an envoy from the Holy See, but of an ambitious, fallible man who one day, hopes to be Pope. He didn't find favour with the Cardinals when Ioannes died and may never do so.'

A hush fell over the courtyard.

'We are not here for Rome, Bishop,' Columba continued, his voice low, but it carried, a ripple across still water. 'We are here for Christ and his works.'

The Bishop opened his mouth to reply, but Columba continued, his tone final.

'I will pray for you.'

And with that, he turned and walked away.

Chapter 10

Ní hionann bréag i gcroí na bhfear agus fírinne i súile Dé
(A lie in the heart of men is not the truth in the eyes of God.)
— Leabhar na hAbhann, Folklore Fragment,
8th century

The obscured sun rose in a grey sky over the restless sea. A biting wind rattled through the monastery, carrying the scent of salt and storm.

Columba, Finn, and two new acolytes, Colman and Fergus, stood at the water's edge, chanting Prime together. Their voices rose and fell in unison, barely audible above the crashing waves.

Columba's blue traveling cloak, the symbol of his abbacy, billowed in the wind. His grip tightened on his crozier, his weathered face unreadable. Finn, watching him closely, felt the burden of something unspoken was in his uncle's bearing.

'Is everything well, Abbot?' he asked, keeping his tone respectful before the others.

'A shadow lingers over us, Finn,' Columba said; 'Rome will not let this argument rest.'

'But surely they cannot force us to change our way of worship?'

A fleeting, knowing smile crossed Columba's lips. 'Force takes many forms. But it will not be in my lifetime. Perhaps not even in yours.'

The sea roared, indifferent to their words.

They boarded the small wooden boat, a vessel hardened by years of battling these waters. The hull groaned as they pushed off, the oars creaking in their hands.

The crossing to Hinba was never easy.

The small harbour was flanked by jagged cliffs, but the monks were seasoned rowers, their darkened faces streaked with salt and lichen. The boat's prow where Finn sat, turned seaward. Columba settled into the stern, gripping the side of the vessel as the first swells of the open sea lifted them. They recited a prayer in unison, their voices low and steady, calling upon God to guide their passage through the perilous waters.

As they left the shelter of the harbour, the waves grew rougher, their crests capped with white foam. The cold wind howled across the sea, driving sharp sprays of saltwater into their faces.

Columba gazed ahead, his keen eyes scanning the horizon. The destination lay somewhere beyond the jagged rocks that thrust out of the sea like the teeth of a great beast. These waters were infamous for their hidden dangers, where sudden storms could materialize and wreak havoc on even the most experienced mariners. The bishop's prayers grew more fervent as the boat pitched and rolled.

Finn looked at Columba, whose face showed signs of the burdens he bore of faith and responsibility. As time passed Finn grew concerned. A feeling of dread came over him, and fear for the safety of his cousin.

The open water swallowed them. The wind howled through the oarlocks, and the boat rocked violently beneath them.

Salt spray lashed Finn's face. The monks rowed tirelessly, the oars heavier with each pull, their hands raw beneath their sleeves.

Columba raised his voice, steady despite the wind. 'Hold fast. Keep your faith.'

A rogue wave crashed over the side. Brother Fergus cried out, scrambling for balance.

'Steady!' Columba's voice cut through the storm. 'The Lord watches over us and will protect us.'

Finn's pulse pounded in his ears. Something wasn't right. Not just the storm, but something deeper, a prickling at the base of his skull.

The closer they drew to Hinba, the more the wind seemed to fight them.

Then, land.

Through the mist, the island took shape. Cliffs, black and sharp against the sky.

'The inlet!' Columba pointed ahead. 'Row now!'

They pushed forward with the last of their strength.

The final wave hit like a hammer, flinging them toward shore. The boat struck the shallows with a bone-rattling thud.

They had arrived.

Exhausted and soaked, they pulled the boat onto the rocky beach. The rain still pelted down, but Finn didn't notice. His unease growing.

Columba gestured toward the cliffs. 'There's a cave ahead. We'll shelter there for the night.'

By the time they reached it, darkness had fallen. The cave mouth yawned before them, sheltering them from the wind. Fergus, shivering, hurried to light a fire with the dry wood left there for travellers.

Finn lingered at the entrance.

Something moved in the distance.

Or did it? A shadow, shifting in the moonlight, there and gone in a heartbeat.

Finn's hand closed around the hilt of *Fidelis*, his sword hidden beneath his cloak. His pulse thrummed in his ears.

Columba, still kneeling in prayer, opened his eyes. 'You feel it too.'

Finn nodded, voice low. 'Something isn't right.'

Columba studied him. 'You're learning to listen.'

A pause.

'Let's trade cloaks tonight,' Finn said.

Columba raised a brow. 'You wish to take my place?'

'Just for tonight. If I'm wrong, it's nothing. But if I'm right...'

Columba didn't argue.

Finn pulled the blue cloak over his shoulders, settling it around him. He lay by the fire, feigning sleep, his hand firmly on *Fidelis*.

The cave fell into silence, the only sound the distant crash of waves.

Two figures crept through the darkness.

Leather-clad, faces obscured by hoods. Knives gleamed in their hands, catching the flicker of firelight.

Finn lay motionless, his breathing slow.

They moved closer, closer, their steps whispering over the sand.

Steel flashed.

Finn rolled. *Fidelis* came up.

The first assassin struck, but Finn was faster. He deflected the dagger, steel scraping steel. Sparks scattered like fireflies.

The second lunged. Finn twisted, sidestepped, a glancing blow caught his shoulder, but not deep.

He countered. A sharp strike to the wrist, steel against flesh. The first assassin howled in pain, his dagger clattering against stone.

The second attacked wildly. Finn ducked, drove his knee up slamming into the man's ribs. A sickening crunch.

The cave erupted in chaos.

The monks rushed forward, blocking the entrance. The assassins turned to flee, only to find themselves trapped.

Columba's voice echoed through the struggle. 'Enough.'

Finn's breath heaved. His blade was steady, ready to strike again.

Columba stood resolute, his gaze calm but unyielding. 'Who sent you?'

A long silence.

Then, one of the men spat, 'You murdered our brother.'

Columba's expression did not change. 'And who was your brother?'

Silence again.

Columba sighed. 'Ioan, son of Conall mac Domnaill?'

A flicker of surprise crossed the assassins' faces.

'He was no innocent,' Columba continued. 'A thief, a plunderer. He raided a Christian home not once, but three times.'

'You cursed him!' one assassin snarled. 'You brought the storm that drowned him!'

Columba shook his head. 'It is only God who commands the sea. I have no such power.'

A beat of hesitation.

Columba stepped aside. 'Go. Leave your weapons, and do not return.'

The assassins hesitated before fleeing into the night.

Finn watched them go, his grip still tight on *Fidelis.*

The cave was silent once more.

Finn lowered his sword. His hands still thrummed with energy, but Columba simply turned back toward the fire.

'Come, Finn,' he said. 'It's time for Matins, then we will see to that shoulder.'

Finn stared at him. 'We were attacked, and your first thought is of prayer?'

Columba's eyes twinkled, the faintest smile playing at his lips. 'Did you think danger changes our duty?'

Finn shook his head, exasperated, and in awe.

He sheathed *Fidelis* and knelt beside Columba. Together, the four monks prayed.

Outside, the wind raged on, but inside, the fire burned steady and strong.

Part Two

PAGANS

Nabuid idir dé agus laochra acu.
Líonann cogarnaí na foraoise, agus cuimhníonn na cnoic ar fhuil.
— Athinsint ar Gildas, c. 6ú haois

They make no distinction between gods and heroes.
The forests are full of whispers, and the hills remember blood.
— Paraphrase of Gildas, c. 6th century

Chapter 11

An té nach bhfuil eagla air roimh Dhia,
beidh sé faoi smacht na ndall.
(He who does not fear God will fall under the rule of the blind.)
— Teachtaireachtaí na Seanórach, c. 650 AD

After a week of prayer and contemplation, Columba and his small entourage left Hinba and travelled to the mainland.

The journey north took them beyond the safety of Dál Riata and into Pictish lands, wild, untamed, and steeped in ancient beliefs.

Columba had not chosen an easy path: hoping to bring Christ's message to the most powerful ruler of the Picts, King Bruide. Convert their greatest leader, and his people would follow.

Finn walked beside him, the only one armed. Columba trusted in God's protection, but Finn kept *Fidelis* close at hand.

At the crest of a hill, a small village appeared in the valley below, a cluster of thatched huts beside a winding stream, smoke rising in thin grey ribbons. As they descended the narrow path, Finn's keen eyes took in the quiet industry of daily life, women stirring pots over open fires, men mending fences, children darting barefoot between homes. A distant hammer rang on iron, the heartbeat of a forge.

Columba's gaze settled on a woman kneeling by a clay pot, herbs in her hands, three children playing around her. He nodded toward her, and they approached.

'Peace be with you,' Columba greeted.

The woman looked up, startled by the sight of robed strangers. She wiped her hands on her dress, eyeing them cautiously.

'And with you,' she answered. 'What brings followers of the Christ-God to these parts?'

Columba folded his hands. 'We seek a place of quiet for prayer. A clearing, if such a place exists nearby.'

The woman hesitated, glancing toward the dark line of forest beyond the fields. 'There is such a place. A ring of ancient stones, but be wary, the druids hold their rites there.'

Finn felt a ripple of unease.

The woman lowered her voice. 'The stones are older than memory, some say blessed, others that they are cursed.'

Columba inclined his head. 'We mean no disrespect to your customs. We seek only to hold a simple service to spread the light of Christ. You and all the villagers are welcome.'

She studied him for a long moment. 'I'm curious. I'll bring my children and speak to others hereabouts. I cannot say if they will come.'

As they walked toward the forest, Finn cast a glance back. The woman returned to her work, her eyes still focused on them.

'Do you think they will come?' Finn asked.

Columba smiled. 'Faith is like a seed. It only needs a place to grow.'

The forest swallowed them in silence. Ancient oaks loomed above, their branches entwined like clasped hands. Shafts of light pierced the canopy, casting shifting patterns on mossy ground and weathered stone.

The clearing appeared suddenly, a perfect circle, ringed by colossal trees. At its heart stood a ring of standing stones, their surfaces etched with strange, time-worn symbols.

Finn's breath caught. 'It feels… ancient.'

Columba knelt in the grass, pressing his palm to the earth. 'It is,' he said; 'but no place is too ancient or wild for God's presence.'

As dusk fell, they prepared the clearing. Columba placed his travel altar upon a flat stone, while Finn, Fergus, and Colman built a small fire. Their prayers rose with the scent of pine and burning wood, a quiet challenge to the spirits of this place.

At first light, they stood ready.

The villagers came hesitantly, the woman with her children. Others followed, their faces marked with both curiosity and unease.

Columba's voice was strong yet gentle. 'Welcome. This is a place of peace. A place of hope.'

He spoke of God's love, of forgiveness, of new beginnings. His words were simple but rang true.

Finn, Fergus, and Colman sang a hymn in Pictish, a haunting, rhythmic melody that echoed through the trees. One by one, as the villagers learned the words they joined in, their voices tentative at first, then stronger.

Something was shifting.

The air turned cold.

A sudden hush fell over the clearing.

Heads turned toward the tree line.

They entered with thunderous faces. Five figures cloaked in darkness, their eyes burning with fury. They moved without sound, their presence a force as old as the stones themselves.

The leader stepped forward, a man of iron-grey hair and a wild, untrimmed beard. His voice was like distant thunder.

'You dare defile our sacred ground?'

The villagers shrank back. A child clutched his mother's skirts.

Another druid raised his hands. 'We call upon the gods of sky and stone! Let them strike down these intruders.'

Columba remained still, his hands folded before him.

'Peace be with you, brother,' he said. 'We are not here to defile this place, but to offer light. The God we serve is a God of peace, not destruction.'

The druid sneered. 'Your words are poison. Your god is weak, a god of broken men.'

The air thickened with tension.

Finn took a step forward.

His cloak fell back, revealing the sword at his hip. The polished hilt of *Fidelis* gleamed

The villagers gasped.

Finn did not draw the blade. But his hand rested on it, and his stance left no doubt that he knew how to use it.

'If you seek to harm this holy man,' he said, 'you will face me first.'

The druids hesitated.

Columba placed a gentle hand on Finn's shoulder.

'Violence is not the answer. This is not a battlefield.'

Turning back to the druids, his eyes full of sorrow, not anger.

'I understand your pain. This place is sacred to you. But we do not come to take anything from you or from this place you hold in reverence. We come to share something greater than stone and earth.'

The druid leader's gaze wavered.

'Words are easily spoken,' he said. 'What proof do you have that your god is real?'

Columba smiled faintly. 'Sometimes God speaks in stillness. But if it is a sign you seek, perhaps He will grant one.'

He raised his hands and closed his eyes.

A breeze stirred.

It grew stronger, swirling through the clearing. Leaves danced in the air, shimmering in the sunlight. A golden warmth settled over the gathered people, gentle, yet overwhelming.

The villagers gasped.

Even the druids stiffened, their expressions shifting from defiance to awe.

The druid leader lowered his hands.

'Perhaps we were too quick to judge.'

A silence stretched between them. He nodded. 'Let us speak more of this God of yours.'

Columba smiled. 'You are welcome among us, brother.'

Finn let his hand slip from *Fidelis's* hilt. The villagers let out a communal sigh, their shoulders relaxing.

The danger had passed, but the battle had only just begun.

Chapter 12

Bíonn an diabhal i bhfolach sa dorchadas,
ach seasann an creideamh ar uisce agus talamh.
(The devil hides in darkness,
but faith walks on water and earth alike.)
— Annála hÉireann, Fragment Archaic, 7th century

The journey continued along the verdant banks of Abhainn Nis. The river glistened beneath the rare warmth of a soft, golden sun, and goose-down clouds drifted lazily across the endless blue sky.

Finn strode ahead of the group, his mood as buoyant as the rippling current. The journey had been peaceful, the weather kind, and soon they would reach the stronghold of King Bruide.

Columba was more pensive.

His mission, forced upon him by the Bishops in Tailtin, to bring three thousand new souls to the Christian faith, was now truly beginning. His years of preparation, hardship, and exile had brought him to this moment. Though he had faced many challenges, the assassination attempt on Hinba had been a stark reminder.

He glanced at Finn, who had fallen back and into step beside him, moving with the easy grace of a young warrior.

Columba smiled. 'This land has seen the footsteps of countless souls,' he said, gesturing to the vast hills and thick forests beyond the river. 'Each stone, each tree, clings on to their memories.'

Finn nodded, his hand resting on *Fidelis*. 'I'm sure not all those memories are peaceful,' he mused. 'The people in the village spoke of creatures lurking in the dark places of the earth.'

Columba's expression softened. 'The old ways are full of stories, Finn. Some are meant to frighten, others to teach. Walk with God and you need be afraid of nothing.'

A shout shattered the quiet.

'There's trouble ahead,' Finn called, already running.

Columba quickened his pace, reaching Finn minutes later. He watched in silence, stopping short of the grim scene before him.

A group of men stood around a shallow grave, their expressions tight with sorrow. One of them, an elder with trembling hands, was already covering the body with earth.

'Who is this man?' Columba asked.

A younger man, his face pale, swallowed hard. 'Our friend. Slain by the beast.'

Columba's eyes darkened. 'What beast?'

The elder straightened, gripping his spade like a weapon. 'It lives in the loch but sometimes comes into the river to hunt. It tore him apart before we could reach him.'

Columba stepped closer. 'Why bury him in such haste?'

'His wife and children must never see him like this,' another man murmured. 'Better they believe the beast took him whole.'

Finn's fingers twitched toward *Fidelis*. 'Have you seen it?'

'Only shadows beneath the water,' said the elder, 'but its wake is like a wave. It is said the monster is as large as two horses, with teeth that cut through bone.'

Columba knelt beside the half-covered body and closed his

eyes. 'May God grant him peace and his family comfort.' Then, lifting his head, he said: 'God protects his servants from harm. We will cross this river in safety.'

The men exchanged wary glances.

A small boat bobbed gently on the far bank. It was the only means across.

Columba turned to Finn. 'Swim to the other side and bring it back.'

Finn hesitated, eyes flicking to the dark, still water. 'What if the beast is near?'

Columba's voice was calm, resolute. 'Have faith, my son. God is with us.'

Finn stripped off his sword belt and cloak. The water was icy, he pushed forward, strong arms cutting through the current.

Columba stood on the shore, watching, praying.

The river stirred.

A ripple. Another, larger.

Columba held his breath.

The water behind Finn swelled, something enormous moved beneath the surface.

'Finn!' he called, voice urgent. 'Swim faster.'

Finn turned his head, his blood ran cold.

The monster broke the surface, its serpentine neck rising like a black tide, eyes gleaming with hunger. Its maw opened, lined with jagged teeth.

The men on the shore cried out in terror.

Finn kicked harder, lungs burning as he closed the final distance to the boat.

The creature surged after him.

Columba stepped to the water's edge, lifting his wooden cross high. His voice rang out, bold as thunder:

'In the name of Almighty God and His Son Jesus Christ, I command you, halt!'

The beast froze.

For a long, breathless moment, it seemed to struggle against something unseen. The cross, catching the fading light, appeared to glow.

Then, with a deafening screech, the monster thrashed violently before plunging into the depths.

A single fin sliced through the surface, and it was gone, disappearing into the loch with a final, echoing ripple.

Finn, gasping, hauled himself into the boat and grabbed the oars. He rowed back, hands shaking.

Columba reached down, gripping Finn's arm and pulling him ashore.

'You were brave,' he said, eyes full of pride. 'God's grace protected you.'

Finn, still breathless, managed a grin. 'And your faith, Abbot. I've never swum so fast in my life.'

Laughter rippled through the gathered crowd. Even Columba chuckled.

The Picts stared at him.

'Your God is powerful,' one man said.

Columba let the wooden cross fall against his chest. 'He is not just my God, He is the only God. The same Supreme Being you worship in your ancient ways, now revealed through Christ.'

A hush settled. Some nodded. Others frowned.

Columba gestured to the grave. 'Come. Let us finish burying your friend and pray for his soul.'

One by one, the men came forward, each placing a stone on the grave, forming a cairn.

Finn watched in silence, thinking of Christ's words to Peter: 'Upon this rock, I will build my Church.'

Perhaps this was the first stone in a foundation for what was to come.

As the last stone was placed, a man approached Columba.

'Holy teacher, we ask a favour.'

Columba inclined his head. 'If it is within my power, you may ask anything.'

'Our noble lord, Emcath, lies gravely ill. It is his grandson we have buried here. News of the death will worsen his condition. Will you minister to him?'

Columba nodded. 'Of course.'

The man, Galan, smiled. 'It is on your path. He will give you shelter for the night.'

Another test awaited.

As they reached the great fortified hall of Emcath, the guards opened the gates without hesitation.

Inside, the old lord lay, his face drawn and pale.

Galan knelt beside him. 'My lord, Emcath, I come bearing sad news. The river monster has slain Oengus. I bring a holy man, who, with only strong words drove the beast away.'

Columba, moved to the bedside, his voice low. 'Sadly, I was too late to save your grandson. But the beast will trouble these waters no more.'

The dying man's eyes glistened with tears.

As Columba approached the bedside, a nurse wiped the tears from Emcath's cheeks. Columba took his frail hand. 'Let me pray with you, my lord. I will stay with you in prayer. Finn, Galan, can you please try and find some broth for the Lord Emcath. Finn, please place in the broth the herbs you keep in your pocket.'

'How do you know…?' Finn started to say but Columba cut him off.

'Nothing is hidden from God, Finn. You should have learned that by now.'

'Nor from him, it seems,' Finn murmured to Galan as they left the room.

In the kitchen, they found the cook.

'Of course I have broth it is ever on the fire, but my lord has not eaten anything these past three days.'

'Let's try him again, now he is with the holy man, and add some of these herbs,' said Galan.

'Are the strangers trying to murder him? My broth needs no addition of herbs or potions.'

'Please don't worry. This is not poisonous,' Finn said; 'it is just a mixture of wild garlic, heather, figwort and dried seaweed from the shores of our island, Hy. All are blessed by the Abbot and I will gladly eat some of the broth before serving Lord Emcath if you need to be assured it is not poison.'

'Very well. Here, give me the mixture.'

'Just a small pinch should be enough.' Finn said.

'Do not, I repeat, do not, ever try to tell me how to flavour my broth. It is the finest in Pictland. King Bruide has told me so himself.'

Finn dropped his head so she could not see his smile. 'Sorry,' was all he could say.

Chapter 13

Tá an cumhacht i lár an chrú,
ach is i gcroí na fírinne a thosaíonn gach réabhlóid.
Power lies at the heart of the fort,
but it is in the heart of truth that every revolution begins.
— Amhrán an Tiarna, ca. 675 AD

The wind cut across the rugged hills as Columba led his small band through pagan lands. Beside him walked Finn, the young warrior priest, no longer a boy, but not yet fully a man. Behind them, Brothers Fergus and Colman followed in silence, their robes billowing with each gust. The fire of Christ's teaching burned bright in Columba's heart. Their mission was clear: to bring the light of Christianity to those still bound to the old gods.

Far ahead, the outline of the fortress emerged like a dark crown upon the hills, the stronghold of King Bruide, a powerful and enigmatic chieftain whose reach extended across much of Pictland. Wreathed in mist and shadow, the hillfort stood encircled by ancient standing stones, their weathered surfaces etched with spirals, beasts, and symbols so old that even the druids had long ceased to speak their names aloud. This was a place where the breath of the old gods lingered, embedded in stone, in soil, in the wind.

Bruide's name was spoken with both reverence and fear. He was said to commune with the spirits of the land, to read the smoke of burning yew, and to speak in dreams with those long dead. His fortress, cradled between wooded ridges and a high ridge that overlooked a sacred loch, was not merely a seat of power, but a living temple of ancestral strength. It was also a symbol, a last bastion against the tides of Roman faith and Anglo-Saxon steel.

As Columba and Finn approached the gates, the air grew taut with tension. Fergus and Colman remained a respectful distance behind. The monks' plain robes and wooden crosses marked them as strangers in a land where tradition and blood bound men tighter than any scripture. The guards who met them were cloaked in wolf pelts, their faces painted with ochre and ash, spears gleaming in the cold northern light.

'Be gone,' one barked, stepping forward with the confident menace of a man used to being obeyed. He gripped his spear with both hands. 'We have no need for your foreign gods or soft prayers.'

With a heavy motion, the carved timber gates slammed shut. The iron locking bar fell into place with a final, echoing clang that seemed to shake the ground beneath their feet.

Columba called out, his voice calm but firm. 'Tell your king that I am Columba of Hy. I have travelled from the western isles with tidings of peace. I come not with swords, but with the Word. I am the one who tamed the beast of Abhainn Nis.'

A second guard narrowed his eyes. 'The king has heard of that tale. He does not believe in monsters. Nor does he believe in you.' He turned and disappeared into the shadows behind the gate. 'Go back to your island, priest of the Christ-God.'

Columba stood motionless for a moment, then turned away, retreating several paces down the hill. He planted his staff into the earth and raised his eyes to the sky, whispering a prayer that carried through the stillness like a breeze before a storm.

The wind stirred. First, a faint sigh among the trees. Then a gust that tugged at cloaks and hair. A creaking groan came from the fortress gate, timber straining, the iron bar rattling in its brackets. With a sudden crack, the gate lurched open of its own accord, its great doors yawning wide as if pulled by invisible hands.

Silence fell.

Columba did not move. Finn stood beside him, heart thudding.

Gasps erupted from the gathered warriors and courtiers. Some fell to their knees, eyes wide with fear, while others gripped their weapons as though uncertain whether to fight or flee. The guards, once so confident, now stood frozen, their sneers replaced by astonishment.

King Bruide himself stood at the threshold of his hall, his dark eyes fixed upon the robed figure standing unshaken at the gate. He was no stranger to magic and power, but this was something else. This was no warrior's trick or druid's incantation. This was a sign.

Slowly, the king raised a hand, calling for silence. 'Enter,' he commanded, his voice a mixture of curiosity and respect. 'Let us hear what you have to say.'

Columba stepped forward, his staff in hand, the whispers of his prayer still lingering in the wind like the last breath of a fading storm. With each step into the heart of the fortress, the air shifted, subtly, almost imperceptibly, as though something ancient had stirred and then withdrawn. The power of the old gods, once palpable in the standing stones and silence, seemed to recoil from the presence of the monk. Light broke through a high smoke vent above, a narrow beam catching the silver thread on Columba's cloak, illuminating him like a figure from vision or myth.

The three monks followed in his wake. The walls of the great hall loomed high around them, timber darkened by generations of fire and incense. Braziers cast flickering shadows across tapestries that depicted the deeds of kings and warriors, stags hunted in moonlight, great boars felled by spears, battles fought beneath crescent moons. Skulls of beasts hung between the rafters, adorned with feathers, carved runes and coloured threads. The air was thick with woodsmoke, roasted meat, peat fire, and the faint, bitter tang of burned herbs.

At the far end of the hall sat King Bruide, broad-shouldered and draped in a robe of white wolf fur. His throne was a raised seat of blackened oak, carved with twisting knotwork and the sigils of his gods, solar wheels, serpent spirals, and guardian beasts with eyes that never closed. His face was carved by weather and wisdom, his eyes sharp and cold as mountain lochs.

'So,' he said, voice like gravel shifting beneath a river, 'you are the man they call Columba.' He leaned forward, fingers tapping the arm of his throne. 'The one who speaks of a single god, foreign to our lands. What brings you here?'

Columba's voice was steady and resonant in the smoky hall. 'I bring you the word of the one true God, the Creator of all things, seen and unseen. He is the God of the sea and the stone, the stars and the soul. A God of love, of peace, and of salvation.'

He let the silence rest for a moment.

'The gods you worship are but shadows. Flickers of truth, perhaps, but powerless against the light of His glory.'

A murmur ran through the hall, druids shifting in their seats, warriors' hands twitching near axe handles, a ripple of disbelief and offence. But Bruide raised a hand, and silence returned.

Bruide's eyes narrowed, but he did not interrupt. His hawk-like gaze held Columba's without blinking. He was not a man quick to anger. He was a king raised among druids, a ruler who valued debate and understood that strength lay not only in arms, but in conviction. His voice, when it came, was calm and measured, but edged with iron.

'Your words are bold, monk. But boldness is not proof. My gods have served my people well for a thousand years. We call upon them and they answer, with rain for our crops, with strength in battle, with visions that guide us in the dark. They are as much a part of this land as the stones and the trees. Why should I abandon them for your unseen god?'

Columba's brow furrowed with a quiet intensity. He took a step forward, his staff echoing against the flagstones.

'Because your gods demand blood and fear,' he said. 'They are born of the earth, shaped by man's desires and the fickle turnings of season and storm. But the true God, the Creator, needs no sacrifice. He asks not for blood, but for faith. Not fear, but love. He gives freely, without barter, and offers eternal life not to kings alone, but to the lowliest of your people. Let me show you the truth of His power.'

One of the druids shuffled uncomfortably, lips pursed but said nothing. Warriors cast wary glances at their king. Bruide sat still.

He stroked his braided beard with slow fingers, the firelight catching in the copper rings threaded through it. 'You speak well, Columba,' he said at last. 'You are unlike the other holy men I've heard. They brought threats and riddles, fire and fury. You bring parables and promise. But still, you must know, words alone will not sway me. I've seen too many men of faith, each claiming their god is truth, each fading away as my gods remain.'

His gaze drifted then, to the boy standing just behind Columba. Finn, holding his wooden cross like a shield, met Bruide's stare with wide but unflinching eyes.

'The boy,' Bruide said, his voice changing slightly, curious now. 'He is your disciple?'

Columba nodded. 'He is Finn. A faithful servant of Christ, raised by me and his father from birth. He has stood with me in hardship and exile. And though he is young, he is brave. A warrior pledged to King Conall, and to God.'

A flicker of surprise passed over Bruide's face. 'A priest and a warrior?' he said. 'That is a strange mix. I know no druids who take up the sword in the name of their gods. You claim to bring peace and yet this boy wears the cross and the scars of battle both.'

Finn lifted his chin. 'Sometimes peace must be protected, my lord. And sometimes, even Christ's servants must bleed.'

The court fell into silence.

Bruide leaned back slowly, his expression unreadable.

Columba and Bruide paused mid-discussion, the soft rustling of a young woman's skirts drawing their attention. She stood at the threshold of the great hall, a radiant figure of about sixteen summers, her silhouette limned by the flickering torchlight. Her hair fell in coppery waves, catching the firelight like polished metal, and her eyes, wide and bright as a noon sky over still water, moved across the room with keen curiosity. She held herself with the grace of one raised in privilege but not pampered by it.

The hall itself was vast and heavy with the smell of old things, animal hides and peat smoke, iron and oak, sweat and honeyed mead. Shields lined the walls, bearing the painted sigils of various clans sworn to Bruide. Near the hearth, warriors drank from carved cups and laughed in low voices, but all stilled as the king's daughter entered.

Bruide, King of the Picts, watched with quiet amusement. His expression softened, his eyes following hers as they landed on a young figure standing beside Columba. The hall, for Finn, contracted suddenly into a single point of focus: her.

Finn stood rooted, caught between awe and confusion. He had faced spears, harsh weather, and exile, but never a presence like hers. His heart seemed to stumble in his chest. Something old and sacred stirred in him, though he lacked the words for it. Her gaze held his just long enough to scatter his thoughts like leaves in the wind.

Bruide let a small smile curve the corner of his mouth. 'This is my daughter, Morag,' he said. 'She is not one to make a quiet entrance.'

Her presence demanded attention, and Finn found himself utterly unprepared for it. The faintest smile touched her lips, half-curious, half-playful, and she moved with feline elegance into the light.

There was no gold or silver adorning her. Her gown was simple but finely made, deep blue wool, belted with a braided sash. Her only ornament was a pendant shaped like a triskele, three swirling arms carved in bone, resting against her breast. A Druidic symbol, Finn noted, though she bore it with neither shame nor explanation. She was her father's daughter, yes, but also her own woman.

'Come, my child,' Bruide said, his voice warmed by paternal affection. 'Do you have business that cannot wait?'

Her eyes flicked to him, a soft flush blooming on her cheeks, though she lifted her chin proudly. 'I heard voices raised in debate. I thought perhaps the hall might offer more challenge than my weaving.'

She spared a glance at Columba. 'Though perhaps not more wisdom.'

Bruide raised an amused brow. 'We speak of matters too tedious for young ears, though I suspect my daughter has always found ways to listen anyway.'

She answered with a mischievous glint and moved closer. The scent of wild herbs, heather, thyme, and perhaps crushed juniper, clung to her. Finn caught it in the air and it sent him reeling. It was not perfume, not something applied. It was simply her.

Columba inclined his head, welcoming her presence with a smile, then turned back to Bruide. 'With your leave, perhaps your daughter and Finn might walk the hall while we continue? Ours is a sacred conversation, yes, but not a dangerous one.'

'But Abbot,' Finn said quietly, his sense of duty flaring, 'I am here to guard and protect you.'

'I am in no danger, Finn,' Columba replied gently. 'And perhaps today, this hall is better guarded by kindness than by steel.'

Bruide studied them for a moment, the warrior monk and the girl whose name meant great one in the old tongue. 'Very well,' he said at last. 'But keep to the corridors. The wind howls tonight, and I would rather not lose my daughter to it or my guest to her charms.'

The comment was light, teasing, but Finn's ears burned. He managed a bow that was more respectful than practiced and offered Morag his arm.

She took it without hesitation.

Her fingers rested lightly on his sleeve, and they stepped away from the fire's warmth into the stone-lined corridor beyond. The torches there burned lower, their flames dancing as the wind whispered through unseen cracks in the walls.

Finn glanced sideways at her but said nothing at first. He didn't want to break the spell. Her presence calmed him but also kindled something, a thrill that ran deeper than curiosity. She looked ahead, unhurried, seemingly content to let silence do the talking.

Behind them, the voices of king and abbot receded into the thick air. Before them, only flickering shadows stretched along the corridor floor, as if ushering them onward. Each footstep was a quiet punctuation in a sentence neither yet knew how to finish.

And somewhere in the stillness of that short walk, in the meeting of two hearts shaped by very different worlds, the first threads of a bond began to form.

By the time Finn and Morag returned to the great hall, dusk had begun to settle outside, casting long shadows across the floor and deepening the golden glow of the firelight. Servants moved quickly but silently, through the scent of roasted meat and herbs, setting trenchers and jugs of mead at the long tables. Columba sat in quiet conversation with King Bruide, their postures relaxed yet alert, two powerful minds circling one another with the wariness of old wolves.

As the doors opened and the young pair stepped inside, the low murmur of the hall softened. Morag's hair caught the torchlight, a shimmer of copper-gold, and Finn walked beside her, his stride matching hers. Columba noted his flushed cheeks and the way his eyes lingered, and so did Bruide.

The King's eyes twinkled. He leaned forward, steepling his fingers, the smile on his face sly but not unkind.

'Your words intrigue me, Columba,' he said, his voice cutting clearly through the gathering noise. 'But they are not enough to move the mountain of my beliefs. Words are wind unless rooted in action.'

Columba met his gaze evenly. 'Faith is often tested in silence, not in noise.'

Bruide's smile deepened. 'Then let us put it to the test.'

He turned his gaze to Finn, eyes gleaming with an idea taking form. 'Leave the boy with me for a year. Let him dwell among my people, walk our woods and halls, speak our tongue, and learn the songs of our ancestors. Let him see our rituals, feast under our gods, feel the pull of our land. If, after one full turning of the seasons, his faith remains unshaken, then I will listen to you more closely. I will open my heart to your teachings, perhaps even kneel to your God.'

A silence fell.

Then, Bruide's voice turned cold. 'But if he strays… if his heart wavers, if he turns from your teachings, then you will leave my lands and never return.'

The air in the hall grew still. Even the crackle of the hearth seemed to quiet.

Columba's jaw tensed. The proposal was dangerous, not only for the mission, but for Finn himself. He glanced at the boy who had been raised among monks yet trained in the ways of warriors and kings. Columba thought of Queen Subhdha and her husband, who had taught Finn to straddle both the sacred and the secular. Still, temptation was no small thing, and Bruide's daughter was no minor part of the equation.

But this… this was an opportunity. A challenge wrapped in royal pride, yes, but also a door.

Columba placed a hand gently on Finn's shoulder. 'What do you say, little cousin?' he asked, his voice low but resolute. 'The choice is yours. Not mine, nor Bruide's.'

Finn stood straighter, his hand tightening instinctively around the carved wooden cross at his neck. He looked briefly to Morag, who returned his gaze with a questioning tilt of the head, not pleading, not pushing, only watching. Finn turned back to the men before him.

'I will stay,' he said, his voice clear. 'My faith will not break. I walk in both worlds. I do not fear yours, King Bruide, but I will not forsake mine.'

A hush hung over the hall. Then Bruide sat back with a satisfied nod, as though a piece of a greater puzzle had clicked into place.

'So be it,' he said. 'Then let the year begin.'

Columba bowed his head, more in acceptance than triumph. Inwardly, he prayed that this decision, made in firelight and silence, would shape not only the boy, but the kingdom.

As the great fire in Bruide's hall died down to glowing embers and the revelry began to slow, Columba stood and took Finn aside. The air between them was still, full of unspoken things. Outside, mist curled along the edges of the fortress like fingers reluctant to release them.

They walked together into the courtyard, away from the warmth of the torches and laughter of men. Finn could see the dim outline of the gates, open now, and beyond them, the forest, the hills, and the unseen roads back to Hy.

Columba stopped beside a low stone wall and turned to face him. The flickering light played across the lines of his weathered face, softening them.

'You know why I accepted his challenge,' Columba said gently.

'I do.' Finn nodded; 'because it was the only way forward.'

'And the most dangerous.' Columba studied him for a long moment, his eyes filled with both pride and worry. 'You are not here simply to survive temptation, Finn. You are here to understand it, not to become like them, but to see them clearly, to learn how hearts are changed.'

Finn glanced down at the wooden cross hanging at his belt. 'I am not afraid. I will not break.'

'Good,' said Columba, placing a hand on Finn's shoulder. 'But remember this: even Christ walked among sinners, not as a judge, but as a witness to love. Do not let pride harden your faith. Let compassion temper it.'

Finn nodded again, the words settling deep in him.

'I will return in a year as agreed,' Columba said; 'and when I do, I pray I find not only my cousin still standing tall, but hearts softened, soil tilled for something new to grow.'

They embraced briefly. No grand farewells, no weeping words. Just the quiet bond of two men who knew that true faith must often be proven in silence, and alone.

In the days that followed, Finn was given a small chamber within the eastern wing of the chieftain's longhouse, a room with a narrow window cut into the stone and a straw-stuffed mattress laid on wooden boards. Sparse, but not uncomfortable. Outside his door, the world of the Picts bustled with firewood, feasts, chanting, and war-honed laughter.

The people regarded him with guarded curiosity. A foreign boy who prayed without idols, who spoke with the King and would drink little at feasts. Some scoffed. Others watched. A few, surprisingly, began to speak with him not always kindly, but often.

Bruide, ever the strategist, took an active interest in the strange young guest left in his care. He called on Finn frequently, engaging him in long discussions beside the hearth or in the shadow of the standing stones. They debated the origins of the world, the nature of souls, and whether gods could die.

The Pictish court dazzled and unsettled Finn. At night, long tables groaned beneath roasted meat and sweet berry wine. Horns of mead passed from hand to hand. Songs filled with ancient battles and praises to gods like Taranis and Cernunnos rang through the rafters. The air always seemed full of woodsmoke and earth.

And then there were the druids. White-robed, solemn-eyed, always watching. Their rituals mostly took place under moonlight, in forests and around fires, their chants heavy with a strange beauty. Finn would sometimes stand at a distance, watching with a quiet ache in his chest. He prayed silently, not only for strength, but for understanding.

One night, Bruide summoned him to the edge of the forest where the stones stood like silent sentinels. A sacred ceremony was about to begin.

Torches lit the path. The scent of burning pine and crushed herbs clung to the air. The druids moved in slow circles, whispering chants older than memory. An enormous bonfire was lit, flames leaping and twisting like spirits set loose.

Bruide stood at the centre of the circle, tall and commanding, his arms raised to the heavens. 'Do you see their power, Finn?' he called out, his voice cutting through the low murmurs. 'These are the forces that sustain us. Our strength, our memory. These gods have watched over us for generations.'

Finn took two steps, the carved cross in his hand, cool and solid, a quiet counterpoint to the roaring fire.

'I see men reaching toward the shadows of creation,' he said evenly, his voice low but unwavering. 'But I do not see the Creator. These gods have power, yes, but it is borrowed, fading. Like flame without kindling. My God needs no ritual, no sacrifice but the heart. He gives what no other power can, eternity, not mere survival.'

The flames crackled. A log split with a pop. The druids fell silent.

Bruide did not answer immediately. His eyes lingered on Finn, as though trying to read something hidden behind the youth's face, a spark perhaps, a weakness, a truth. Whatever he found, he kept to himself.

'You speak boldly,' he said at last, and turned back to the fire.

But Finn's words stayed with him, haunting the silence long after the chants had faded.

Chapter 14

Ní bhíonn grá fíor gan trua, ná céile ceart gan comhfhios.
(There is no true love without compassion,
no true companion without shared understanding.)
— Seanchas na nGael, Oral Tradition

Finn's breath hung in the crisp morning air as he finished his run around the hills encircling King Bruide's fortress. Each sunrise painted the heather in soft gold, a quiet reminder of how much he still had to learn about war, about faith, about himself.

When he returned inside the high walls of Bruide's fortress, he headed straight for the training yard. There, straw-stuffed targets lined up against a stout wooden fence. Rows of battered shields and spears rested on wooden racks. Pictish warriors, men with braided hair and knot work tattoos swirling down their arms, sparred in pairs, shouting in the guttural tones of their language. They were tough men, close to the land and proud of their heritage. Their fierce loyalty to King Bruide matched their formidable skill in battle.

As Finn approached, he caught sight of the flame-haired Morag, standing near the centre of the yard. Her auburn locks tumbling about her shoulders. Her bearing was confident as she twirled a practice sword in one hand. Each movement was measured and precise, displaying the hours of martial training she had obviously dedicated to perfecting her craft. The morning light gleamed in her green eyes, bright with fierce determination and subtle curiosity.

Finn nodded in greeting. 'Good morning, Morag.' He could feel the warmth of her smile, though her lips hardly moved.

'And good morning, back to you, monk,' she answered. Her tone, teasing but friendly. Since his arrival, Morag had taken great pleasure in mocking Finn gently about his shaved head. Now his hair was growing, flame red like her own.

'Are you ready to spar?' Finn asked, taking up a training sword from the rack. Their daily training together had grown in intensity, turning from being timid into a fluid dance of strikes and parries. When they first crossed swords, Morag had been amused by his chivalrous caution. Now nothing was held back, Morag respected Finn's skill, and he admired her relentless spirit as well as everything else about her.

Morag nodded eagerly, stepping into the open space. The surrounding warriors paused, watching with interest. Seeing the king's daughter train was not unusual. Seeing her laughing while she trained with the ever-smiling monk was still cause for curious whispers. No one intervened; Bruide himself had encouraged their training together. Who better to sharpen Morag's sword arm than the outsider who trained as a knight in a foreign court?

Finn settled into a familiar stance, left foot forward, sword angled slightly downward, shield at the ready. The early sun cast shadows across the dirt. Morag mirrored him, her posture upright, shield braced. Then, almost at once, they surged toward each other. Their weapons clashed. Finn tested her defences, flicking his sword in swift arcs, but Morag was ready for him. She angled her shield deftly, deflecting his attempts with discipline and economy of movement.

Their breath came faster as they continued, step by step, blow by blow. Finn lunged; Morag twisted aside and aimed a quick counterstrike at his flank. He raised his shield in time, felt the jolt reverberate through his arm, followed with a strike at her shoulder. Morag ducked, dropping beneath his swing, her hair brushing the ground, and thrust at his exposed side. Only a frantic pivot saved him from a decisive tap.

Steel rang against steel, echoing through the training yard. Warriors watched as Morag danced around Finn, her movements light as wind over the heather. She laughed, taunting him with quick footwork, until Finn altered his grip. A sudden feint left, a sharp strike right. His blade tapped her ribs lightly.

A heartbeat later, her sword clipped his shoulder.

They stepped back, panting, eyes locking. Equal skill. Equal fire.

'She's good,' said one of the warriors, a gap-toothed grin splitting his tattooed face.

'Aye, she has her father's strength and wile,' another said.

Sweat dotted Finn's brow as he bowed to Morag. 'Shall we call it a draw?' he asked, fighting to keep his breath steady. Both had landed a touch at nearly the same moment - a testament to their equality of skill.

Morag nodded, cheeks flushed. 'Agreed.' A hint of a smile tugged her lips, and for a moment, she and Finn gazed at each other in silence. She cleared her throat, lowering her sword and exhaled loudly. 'I'll need a few moments to catch my breath.' she said

'Me too, you were amazing Morag, as good as any opponent I have ever practiced with, and that includes Darragh and Eochaid.'

Morag turned away, but not before Finn caught the flicker of colour in her cheeks. He busied himself returning his practice sword to the rack, but his mind lingered on her. It wasn't just admiration, though she had earned that. It was something deeper. A quiet, unspoken understanding. She carried duty with the same fierce stubbornness he did, balancing tradition with the pull of something more.

A commotion heralded the arrival of Bruide, flanked by two bodyguards. His thick beard, braided into a single plait framed his rugged face. Tattoos of swirling runes and ferocious beasts covered his arms. At his belt, he wore a short sword inlaid with silver. The entire courtyard hushed in respect.

Bruide surveyed them sternly. 'Finn, Morag, well fought. It does this father's heart good to see his daughter's skill tested and improved.' His voice rumbled through the crisp air. Turning his attention to Finn, he added, 'You look like you have more than monastic prayers in your bones, lad. Tell me', he glanced with a slight frown toward the gates, 'have you heard any word from my sentries?'

Finn shook his head. 'Not yet, my lord.'

Bruide's gaze hardened. 'A rival clan leader, Drosten of the Western Hills, threatens our borders. Scouts say Drosten's men are massing.' He paused, turning to look at Morag, who stood a little straighter under her father's gaze. 'We can't risk underestimating his ambition.'

Morag leaned on her sword. 'We must prepare and be ready.'

Bruide broke into a half-smile. 'That we shall. You've trained well today. We'll soon need you both.'

He turned and strode away, his guards trailing behind him. As soon as he was gone, the lively chatter resumed. Finn felt apprehension stirring in his chest. Conflict was coming; such was the way of the clans. He had grown up in a monastery where battles were more often fought with words of scripture than blades, and at the court of King Connall where he had become a member of his Guard but had never fought in a real battle. Now, in his time with the Picts, he had learned that life here was hard and not always secure.

He turned to Morag and touched her elbow lightly. 'Shall we walk?' He wanted to give her space away from the other warriors and their attentive ears.

She nodded wordlessly. They passed through the gates, stepping onto a winding path that went down the hillside to the stream. The sun had risen fully now, illuminating the swaths of purple heather and whispering grasses. They walked in companionable silence, it was a glorious day and they were enjoying their own company, alone.

'I worry for my father,' Morag said, breaking the silence. 'He's strong, but he always yearns to prove himself. This threat from Drosten, it's not the first, and it won't be the last.' She shot Finn a sidelong look, her expression uncertain. 'You will fight with us, won't you?'

'Yes,' he said, without hesitation. 'I've sworn to your father and Abbot Columba, that I would remain here for a year. To learn your ways. If warfare comes I cannot stand aside and just be an observer.'

Her shoulders relaxed. 'I hoped you'd say that. Our warriors have a growing respect for you. They perhaps think that your God has given you some magic and that you carry blessings in your sword arm.'

Finn chuckled, 'There is no magic, only discipline and faith.'

Morag bit her lower lip thoughtfully. 'Perhaps that's magic enough.' Flashing him a teasing grin, she said; 'Come on, monk. Let me show you something.'

She took his hand lightly, deliberately, and led him off the main path, boots crunching over dry needles and hidden roots. The late afternoon sun slanted through the canopy, setting the edges of the pine trees aglow in amber and gold. Birds called in distant pairs, and every now and then a squirrel, its coat the same colour as Morag's hair, dashed through the underbrush. Finn didn't ask where they were going. He let her lead.

Morag wove her way through the dense woodland, she belonged here, she knew how to listen to trees. Finn followed close behind, struck by the quiet determination in her gait, the way her copper hair caught glimmers of light as if kissed by flame.

Eventually, they broke into a small clearing, a circle of stillness held gently by the forest. At its centre stood a solitary silver birch, its bark gleaming white against the dark pines that loomed beyond. The tree was adorned with dozens of ribbons fluttering from its branches: faded scraps of linen, bright threads of wool, braids of horsehair, beads, feathers, and small painted stones tied with cord. Each one bore the quiet weight of longing, offerings, tokens, or silent pleas.

Morag stepped toward it, her movements suddenly reverent. The wind stirred softly, rustling the cloth and the leaves, making the whole tree whisper.

'This is where I pray,' she said, her voice a hush against the silence. She ran her fingers along a sun-bleached ribbon, its ends fraying in the breeze. 'When the world feels too heavy. When I need something to hear me. Sometimes… I pray to the old gods. Sometimes… to yours.'

Finn blinked. 'To Christ?'

She gave a half-smile, without looking at him. 'To your God. Yes. Quietly. I've no hymns or Latin words, but I believe he hears me anyway, if he's listening.'

There was no mockery in her tone, only honesty, layered with caution. She turned, meeting his gaze. 'I leave something when I'm troubled,' she continued. 'A token, a memory, a hope. It's not a temple, but it's sacred, to me. My own kind of church.'

Finn felt a stirring he hadn't expected, a warmth rising from somewhere deep in his chest. He looked around the clearing.

The ribbons were not just pretty scraps. They were stories. Some hung fresh and vivid. Others had faded nearly white with rain and sun, like ghosts. He saw carvings scratched into small stones, spirals and runes he didn't know how to read. One bore a crude image of a hand holding a flame.

'Does that make me a believer, monk?' Morag asked, tilting her head.

Finn didn't answer immediately. He took a few steps closer, gazing at the silver birch, and then at her. 'I didn't know you prayed to my God too.'

She shrugged, but her expression remained open. 'I believe in anything that might protect my father. My people. You…'

That final word hovered between them. Not a question. Not quite a confession. It was fragile, like the threads tied to the tree.

Morag glanced away first, brushing hair from her cheek. Then, her voice sharper, steadier: 'Don't think I've gone soft, monk.'

Finn grinned, the corners of his mouth tugging upward. 'I wouldn't dare.'

He reached into his belt and pulled free a thin leather cord he'd kept folded into a pouch, one of the prayer bands given to him on the day of his departure from Hy. The tiny knotwork cross sewn into its centre had been touched with holy water. He hesitated, then held it out to her.

'May I?'

She nodded. Together, they tied the strip of leather to one of the lower branches, near a faded red ribbon.

They stood there in silence, heads slightly bowed, the wind threading between. Finn didn't speak aloud, but he thought of his mother, of Columba, of Bruide's strange challenge, of the choice he was still learning how to make. And he thought of Morag, her voice steady in the clearing, her hand resting warm in his only moments before.

When they returned to the path, walking side by side toward the stronghold, the sun had slipped lower, painting the sky in bruised purples and molten gold. The trees grew tall and shadowed around them, but something in Finn's heart felt lighter. A sacred place, neither pagan nor Christian, but something older and perhaps deeper, had opened between them.

And though neither said it aloud, both knew they would return to the birch again.

That night, Finn lay awake, staring into the black stillness above him. The timber beams of the ceiling were hidden in shadow, but he knew their shape, just as he knew the rhythm of the wind pressing against the stone walls and the muffled sounds of the stronghold settling into sleep.

He had trained with many warriors, men of stature and renown, whose names carried weight. But none had unsettled him the way Morag did. Her presence lingered like firelight in his blood, warm, crackling, impossible to forget. She fought with precision, spoke with wit, carried the bearing of a queen and the heart of a wild deer unbroken by duty. Discipline. Skill. Fire. And something else. Something he dared not name.

He turned on his side, pulling the rough wool blanket tighter around him. The thatch above creaked with the breath of the wind. Still, sleep eluded him.

Would he leave when the year was done? Would she follow?

Or was this bond forged in glances and silences, this fragile spark in the dark, only a moment? A passing ember in the great bonfire of his life?

He pressed the heels of his hands against his brow.

'Lord,' he whispered into the darkness, 'guide my hand... and watch over Morag.'

There was no answer, only the rustling hush of the wind through ancient timbers, and the faint scent of peat smoke still lingering from the hearth.

Eventually, sleep took him, slow and reluctant. It came not as rest, but as a wandering haze. In dreams, the red of Morag's hair caught the sun like flame, and the ring of steel-on-steel echoed in a pattern not of violence, but of dance, blades moving not to wound, but to understand.

'Lord,' he murmured again in his half-sleep, 'watch over these people... and watch over her.'

Dawn crept quietly toward the stronghold, bringing with it a grey hush, the promise of sword drills, of druids whispering beneath standing stones, of messages yet to come and choices still unwritten. And perhaps, if the day allowed, another moment to walk beside her beneath the trees.

Finn breathed in deeply, as if trying to hold it all within him. Then he turned on his straw pallet and surrendered to whatever the morning would bring.

Chapter 15

Nuair a bhíonn na scáileanna ag fás, tagann an grian i ndiaidh.
(When the shadows grow long, the sun soon follows.)
— Ceachtanna an tSaoil, Monastic Saying

War drums had begun to beat, quietly at first, the rhythmic sound mixed with the shuffle of boots and whispered war plans. Over the next days, Bruide drew Finn and Morag deeper into his councils, his trust in them growing as the storm of battle neared.

Word was sent out to the tribes loyal to Bruide and they answered in their droves. It had been a while since there had been a battle of any note and some of the warriors had missed the excitement and danger.

'What do our spies say?' Bruide asked.

'Drosten is readying, he could march in seven or eight days,' a warrior replied.

'And his spies?'

A grin. 'Fed only the lies we pay them to repeat. Safer for them to mislead him than to say nothing at all.'

'Are we agreed?,' said Bruide; 'better to choose our own ground than wait for him to come to us?'

'It would make more sense. Meet him in the open. His

warriors are tough but ill-disciplined. Also, fewer than us in numbers, they have been relying on being able to surprise small groups of us and wearing us down.'

Bruide's gaze landed on Finn. 'Our young knight has trained my warriors in the Irish shield wall. Tomorrow, we test it in war.'

The following morning eight hundred Pictish warriors marched the one-day journey to the selected site.

King Bruide stood at the head of his forces. His deer-hide battle gear fitting loosely around his broad shoulders. Sword strapped to his side, shield across his back and spear in hand he looked formidable. A sharp wind blew across them, carrying with it the tang of pine and damp earth. All around him, a vast host of Pictish warriors, both men and women, marched towards Cernunnos Hill. Metal rings clinked on their leather armour, and a low chorus of voices rumbled through the ranks, a generous mingling of excitement and tension.

Finn walked near the front of the column alongside Morag. Her flame-red hair bound in a single braid. Green eyes gleamed with fierce determination, her posture a reflection of her father's proud bearing. Beside her, Finn clutched the hilt of *Fidelis*, a weapon as keen as his faith. Their footsteps beat a steady rhythm on the packed earth, merging with the marching tread of hundreds of pairs of feet behind them.

The rolling expanse of moorland and heather stretched out in front of them. A few banners fluttered overhead, long strips of cloth dyed in deep blues and vibrant reds, each bearing the swirling knots of their tribal symbols. Bruide's personal standard, a snarling boar's head in black, caught every gust of wind. Spirits were high. Drosten of the Western Hills would feel the might of Bruide's power.

The column wound through the ancient hills, their boots stirring dust on paths worn smooth by generations. Sunlight glinted off spearheads, the moorland stretching golden before them.

Behind him, laughter rippled through the ranks, young warriors masking nerves with bold boasts. Finn listened, the sound stirring memories: the creak of the boat from Daire, the shouts of friends in Dún Att's halls, the quiet hymns of Hy.

He had walked many paths, but today, this one felt different. Now, amongst these fierce Picts, he was relaxed, knowing that he could trust them as they knew they could trust him. He prayed quietly as he marched.

Morag broke the silence between them. 'I've never seen so many of my father's warriors assembled at once,' she murmured, glancing back over her shoulder at the undulating ranks.

'It's…impressive,' Finn agreed, not entirely hiding his awe. Indeed, the Pictish host stretched nearly as far as the eye could see, a living serpent of bristling spears and war-painted faces. He had grown used to the smaller war bands training within the fortress. But this was different, a grand mustering of forces, each man and woman fully aware they might soon be fighting for their lives and the safety of their families.

They marched across rolling hills, pine trees standing like sentinels dotted in assorted groups along the way. Now and then, a scout on horseback galloped up to Bruide, muttered some report, and sped off again. Finn noticed King Bruide's face break into a smile, each time he heard the news from ahead. His presence at the vanguard fuelled the warriors' confidence, reminding them that their king stood strong in defence of their tribes.

Around midday, they reached a ridge that overlooked a wide valley. From there, Cernunnos Hill rose in the distance, round-topped and cloaked in dense greenery at its summit. The land curved inward around the hill, forming a natural basin. On one side of that basin lay a small river snaking through the lowlands before feeding into a glassy lake at the valley's heart. Woodlands bordered each flank, thick with ancient oaks and lurking shadows. It was a prime location for the coming engagement.

Bruide raised his hand, signalling the column to halt. He and several chieftains surveyed the terrain, pointing out where Drosten's men might approach. From this vantage, they could see Cernunnos Hill flanked by the river on the east and the steep ridges on the west. If Drosten did as expected, he would have to navigate the narrow corridors of woodland or cross the river. In either case, Bruide intended to make him fight on ground that favoured the defenders.

With the decision made, the warriors descended carefully into the valley. The scale of their force was even more evident on the slopes below. Carts rumbled along, loaded with supplies, tent canvas, provisions, spare weapons. Morag and Finn took note of each vantage point, each patch of wooded cover. Already, Bruide's captains were shouting orders to set up camp in the woodland to the east.

In a flurry of activity, the warriors unpacked the tents. Bruide ordered them to be placed out of sight from the valley below.

A rider came up and Bruide called his chieftains, Finn and Morag to a meeting. Sitting around a small campfire they listened.

'Drosten seems completely unaware of our presence. He is still in his camp preparing.'

'Perhaps he is waiting for more warriors to accompany him?' asked one of the chieftains.

'That is possible, Lord, but from what I have been able to observe it appears to me he is nervous and reluctant to commit to a war.'

'Is it possible,' asked Finn; 'that he might change his mind and avoid battle altogether?'

Bruide laughed. 'You don't fully understand the ways of our people yet, Finn. He has raised the tribes with promise of death or glory. To not carry through means he is a coward and would lose the following of the others. They would probably execute him.' Turning his attention to his messenger he said, 'How much time do we have?'

'Even if he marched tomorrow we would have two days, maybe three. They have few horses so it would be a slow foot march.'

'What if he goes another way?' asked Finn.

'There is no other way other than going over the mountains and he is not so foolish as to do that,' replied Bruide. 'Good let us make our preparations.'

Dividing the warriors into sections aligned by tribal affiliations and warrior companies, the hidden camp was prepared. Smoke from hastily built cook-fires soon drifted skyward, carrying the scent of stewed meats and fresh bread.

Finn helped where he could, hauling water from the river alongside a trio of young Pictish warriors, their arms tattooed with swirling patterns that told of their lineage. Morag oversaw the placement of supply crates, ensuring that weapons and rations were stored where they could be easily accessed if battle erupted. Occasionally, father and daughter conferred, heads bent together over a rough map etched on a wide piece of hide.

As the sun descended, turning the sky a rich pink, the camp took shape. Torches flared to life at regular intervals, their flames dancing against the gathering dusk. The hum of conversation filled the air, punctuated by bursts of laughter. Despite the looming threat, there was a sense of unity and excitement among the Picts. They had come to defend their land, and under Bruide's leadership, they would do so fiercely.

Morag finished checking the lines of tents and joined Finn near a flickering fire pit, where two women were ladling out bowls of hearty stew. Accepting their portions gratefully, Finn and Morag withdrew to a quieter corner of the encampment, near a row of spears driven into the earth. A large oak tree, its boughs heavy with late-summer leaves, provided a measure of cover from the wind.

They ate in silence at first, gazing out at the endless rows of warriors. Finally, Morag spoke, her voice low. 'Will Drosten meet us here in open battle, do you think?'

Finn looked down at his bowl, pondering the question. 'He might have to. He doesn't know we are here but if he comes, and finds us all here... they say Drosten's pride is as great as his ambition, what choice will he have? If he truly wants to claim these lands, he'll have no choice. But...' He paused, choosing his words carefully. 'We cannot underestimate him. If he's cunning, he might try to draw us into the woods on his side of the valley or catch us off-guard near the river crossings.'

Morag nodded, absent-mindedly tapping her wooden spoon against the bowl's rim. 'Father says Drosten's men are bold but can be reckless. That might be our advantage.'

Finn pondered for a moment. 'I have an idea,' he said; 'let's go and speak to your father.'

Morag raised one eyebrow. 'What idea?'

'You'll have to wait and see. Come on.'

As they made their way to Bruide's tent, a stiff breeze snaked through the camp, sending sparks dancing from the fire pits. A group of warriors nearby struck up a war-chant, their voices blending in a deep, resonant bass that seemed to make the earth move in rhythm. They reached Bruide's command tent and ducked inside. The king glanced up, a formidable figure even amid the swirl of smoke from a brazier. He nodded in greeting. Around him sat half a dozen chieftains. On a low table lay a rough map of the valley, depicting the river's course, the wooded areas, and the slopes leading up to Cernunnos Hill.

Small wooden tokens marked the Pictish positions, while a few stones indicated where Drosten might approach.

When Finn and Morag arrived, Bruide gestured for them to be seated.

'We're discussing various possibilities for our battle plan,' said Bruide.

'Finn has a plan,' Morag said.

Bruide arched a brow. 'A warrior monk schooling my chieftains? Bold.'

Laughter rumbled through the tent.

'Well go on then,' continued Bruide; 'Let's hear it.'

Finn stood, his voice a little shaky. 'Well, are we sure that Drosten doesn't know we are here?'

'As sure as we can be,' replied Bruide.

'My plan might just work,' Finn said. He continued to speak and the chieftains listened. The more Finn spoke the more interested Bruide's seasoned warriors became.

'Risky. You'd be walking into Drosten's blade before we could lift a spear.'

Finn met their eyes. 'Not if he thinks it's his only chance of victory. He needs to believe we're vulnerable. If we bait him and he reacts quickly, before he sees the full field, he won't have time to turn back.'

The chieftains exchanged glances. One grunted in approval. Another frowned, stroking his beard.

Finally, Bruide exhaled through his nose. 'A bold plan.' A slow smile crept across his face. 'Very well. Let's see if Drosten is as predictable as you think.'

As the sun rose, campfires were rekindled. Warriors sharpened blades on whetstones, sparks flying through the morning air. Others checked arrow fletchings. Everywhere, there was an undercurrent of readiness; occasional lulls in conversation hinted that the following days might bring bloodshed.

Bruide, Finn and Morag walked to the lake in the valley. You'll need to be ready by the morning,' Bruide said. 'If he's sensible, he'll bring scouts there,' he pointed to a partially hidden area at the top of the valley. 'It's essential that he is convinced.'

Morag inclined her head. 'We'll make sure he is, father.'

As they walked back to the camp, Morag squeezed Finn's arm lightly.

Long into the night, Finn and Morag talked, of gods and warriors, of childhood and duty, of futures neither dared name aloud.

The moon had climbed high when they finally fell silent, listening to the hush of the camp. Outside, warriors murmured prayers to gods old and new. Beneath the calm, the ground itself seemed to hum with the weight of what was to come.

Chapter 16

Ní shaorann claíomh gan croí.
(No sword saves without a heart behind it.)
— Scríbhinní Cholm Cille

Dawn broke cold and silent. Frost clung to the earth, crunching beneath boots as Finn, Morag, and fifty seasoned warriors struck camp. Their voices rose, deliberately loud and careless, echoing across the still lake. In the shadowed woods behind them, the rest of Bruide's army crouched unseen, holding their breath like wolves before a kill.

Word had arrived: Drosten was on the move. If he had any sense for war, his scouts would already be near.

Finn directed the men to build camp at the river's mouth, where it fed into the lake. The waters here ran deep and fast, difficult to ford, but not impossible. He chose the spot carefully, daring Drosten to come. As the tents went up and fires were lit, Morag led them in song, an old warrior's hymn, passed to her from her father, down from generations long past. Its melody raw, its rhythm ancient, the words shaped by prayer and defiance.

Up, sons of stone! Cry aloud,
With blood and woad our skin is proud.
Call ye gods of hill and heath,
Wake the winds and loose the wreath!

Cromm of the Crooked Mound, arise,
With breath of iron and stormy skies!
Break their blades, blind their sight,
Let none withstand thy shadowed might.

Bride of flame, O burning maid,
Stride the smoke with sword unstaid.
Shriek in wind, and blaze in foe,
Let fire through their war-hosts go.

Dark things dwell in loch and fen,
Ancient beasts that rend all men.
We summon thee with chant and cry.
Drag them down who dare not die!

The hills do moan, the forests speak,
The ravens fly, the cairns do creak.
Stones remember, bones do stir,
What man shall face the wrath of Her?

O Father Oak, and Night-bound Queen,
Guide our hands, keep our spirits keen.
Lend us tusk and talon true,
That we may strike and slay and hew!

Drums like thunder, hearts aflame,
We ride for blood, for kin, for name.
O gods of glen and barrow deep,
With us walk, and none shall sleep!

Their voices carried far across the valley, a warning and a challenge. Spirits ran high. Bruide had supplied meat and mead, enough to warm the blood, not dull it. That afternoon, a lone rider was spotted in the distance. He lingered a moment too long, before turning and vanishing into the woods.

Finn's stomach tightened. 'We must be ready at first light,' he said, though he spoke mostly to himself. His pulse had begun to race.

As dusk approached, torches flared and firelight danced on steel. The warriors gathered, their faces cast in flickering gold, eyes reflecting a grim resolve. Finn posted sentries, ordering them rotated every two hours. He wanted no one exhausted come morning.

Low murmurs drifted through the camp, snatches of prayer, quiet jokes, the rustle of mail. Inside his tent, Finn sat cross-legged on a bedroll of animal skin. The earth beneath him smelled of damp wool, leather, and ash. A single candle burned low. *Fidelis* lay across his lap, and he drew a whetstone along its edge, habit more than need. The motion calmed him.

He tried to steady his breath, listening to the scrape, scrape, scrape of stone on iron. His face still had the softness of youth, but his eyes, sharp and green, seemed older than his years. He had trained for this. He had prayed. He found the waiting to be a kind of slow death in itself.

The flap stirred. Finn's heart leapt. A figure stepped inside.

Morag.

She looked otherworldly in the candle's flicker, her red hair falling in fiery waves, freckled skin glowing soft and golden. Her leather armour hugged her frame, supple and battle-worn, the tension in her shoulders betraying nerves she didn't voice. Her eyes met his, steady and unreadable.

'You're awake,' she said, stepping fully inside and letting the flap fall.

Finn nodded, setting the whetstone aside. 'Couldn't sleep. Too much circling in my head.'

Morag smiled faintly and knelt across from him. Her movements fluid, assured.

'The night before battle is always like this,' she said. 'The gods test our courage by filling our heads with doubt.'

Finn swallowed. 'Do you think they'll favour us tomorrow?'

She studied him for a long moment. 'That depends. Are you ready to face them, body and soul?'

The question struck deeper than he expected. He hesitated. 'I've trained. I've tried to prepare. But I don't know if anyone's ever truly ready to face death.'

Morag leaned closer, her voice lowering. 'There is one thing we can do to gain their favour. Something they value above all else.'

He frowned. 'What's that?'

She reached for his hand. Her touch was light but steady, her fingers cool. 'Life, Finn. The gods protect those who've truly lived. They don't waste their blessings on those who die untouched, untested.'

Confusion flickered across his face.

She spoke even softer. 'The gods won't shield virgins, Finn. Not in battle. They want warriors who've known love, pleasure, fire. Those who have tasted the world, even for a moment.'

His breath caught. 'I… I've never,'

'Neither have I,' she admitted. 'But if we die tomorrow… I'd rather go having lived. Even if only tonight.'

She leaned in, and her lips brushed his. It was a soft kiss, hesitant, searching, but it ignited something in him, something warmer than fear. They broke apart briefly, eyes locking on each other, and kissed again, deeper, surer.

The world narrowed to the quiet hush of breath and skin. Finn's hands trembled, unsure, but Morag guided him gently.

Together, they shed their armour, piece by piece, until nothing stood between them.

Their bodies came together with a mix of awkwardness and wonder. There was no rush, only discovery. No desperation, only the raw need to feel something more than fear. Outside, the night deepened. Inside the tent, time paused.

Later, they lay side by side, fingers intertwined. Morag's head rested on his shoulder, her breath warm against his skin. Finn stared at the canvas ceiling above them, emotions churning in ways he couldn't name.

'That was… thank you,' he whispered.

Morag smiled. 'Thank the gods. They'll protect us now.'

Sleep found them quickly after that, born of exhaustion, nerves, and the strange calm that follows surrender.

The camp stirred fitfully through the night, whispers and armour clinks carried on the cold air. But inside the tent, there was peace. Fleeting, fragile, but real.

A horn blast shattered the dawn. It cut through the mist like a knife, mournful and sharp. Finn sat up at once, heart hammering. Morag was already moving, pulling on her armour with swift precision. Her face was calm, but her eyes sparked with the clarity of purpose.

He rose, fumbling with his battledress, adrenaline sweeping away the fog of sleep.

As he strapped *Fidelis* to his side, he looked at her, searching.

'I swear to you,' he said, voice low. 'Whether I am a warrior or a priest, I will love you always. I will take no other woman.'

Morag paused, smiling wryly. 'Oh, my handsome monk. You're too young to make promises the wind could carry off.'

'I mean it. My God gives free will. I swear, whatever fate or god may come, I'll stay true to you.'

She laughed gently. 'And maybe, in a year, you'll leave with your Abbot and forget all about me.'

'I won't.'

Her eyes softened, but she said nothing more. She only reached for her sword and shouldered her shield.

'Come,' she said. 'We've done what we could. Now we see who the gods favour.'

They stepped into the cold morning air, where the world was already waking for war. Fires burned low, warriors tightened straps and sharpened blades. The dawn sky, delicate and golden, seemed almost cruel, too serene for the blood it would soon bear witness to.

Finn and Morag exchanged a final glance. There were no more words left to say.

As they walked toward the waiting warriors, a hush fell over the camp. Somewhere above, God or gods looked down, silent, inscrutable. Their favour uncertain. But their presence undeniable.

Chapter 17

Fuil ar an bhféar, ach glóir sna spéartha.
(Blood on the grass, but glory in the heavens.)
– Annála na Catha, c. 680 AD

The morning silence shattered. A hundred voices roared from the trees, shaking the hillside. Finn's pulse hammered as he turned toward the sound. They were coming

'Shield wall! Hold the line!' Finn's voice rang out.

'Shield wall! Shields tight!' Morag echoed, her tone steel sharp.

Each warrior moved calmly to stand in rows, shoulder to shoulder. Finn and Morag in the centre of the front row. They watched as the larger attacking force emerged from the treeline and readied at the top of the incline, shouting abuse. Finn began singing the pagan war song and the others joined in.

The first rank of Drosten's warriors started to move forward. Drosten seemed to think that would be enough to destroy the small band in front of him. When they broke into a run Finn shouted.

'Shields!'

The men overlapped the edges of their shields, creating an impenetrable barrier of wood and iron. The front rank leant forward, knees bent, weight balanced, bracing for impact. Behind them, a second row held their spears, poised to thrust over, around or under the shields at the enemy. Grim and silent the warriors stood, adrenaline and nerves coursing through them. The cries of the attackers drew closer and closer.

Drosten's warriors erupted from the treeline, a storm of steel and fury. They came in a wave, shields up, axes raised, feet pounding down the slope, surging over the uneven ground with reckless haste, their mismatched armour clanking. Some wore boiled leather tunics, others long yellow tunics, dyed with urine, many bore the scars of previous battles. A more disciplined army might have approached the river in careful ranks, but Drosten's men spread themselves wide, streaming down in a broad wave, each determined to be the first to make contact.

Finn had chosen the position of the shield wall well. He was ready, his shield with its Roman emblem, was gripped in his left hand, held close to his body forming part of the interlocking barrier. In his right, he held *Fidelis*, he could taste the metallic tang of anticipation on his tongue. Next to him, Morag's tall figure stood resolute, her own shield lacquered with a simple red swirl that caught the light, and her expression was as grim as Finn's.

Behind the front line, stood two deep ranks of warriors, every man and woman with shields raised and spears angled upward to catch any attacker who managed to force their way through the first row. They had practiced these formations countless times under Finn's exacting drills, training in the muddy fields behind the fort to ensure their line would not buckle under pressure. Even so, the tension before battle was always a living, breathing thing. Each heartbeat seemed to echo in the cage of Finn's ribs, and he could sense the same tension rippling through the warriors around him. Quiet words of encouragement passed up and down the line, and a few last-minute prayers were murmured to the old gods in trembling voices.

'Lock shields! Steady' cried Morag. She struck the rim of her shield with her sword. The thud of steel against wood echoed through the defenders, a drumbeat of defiance that spread confidence along the line. Finn added his own call, short, sharp, and emphatic, to keep the men and women on his side from breaking formation.

They hit the river like charging bulls, water exploding around them. War cries mixed with the clash of steel, curses snapping in the cold air. Axes brandished, broadswords flashed, their fury crashing against the shield wall like a breaking tide. A few archers, further up the slope, loosed arrows sporadically, hoping to sow panic among Finn's defenders. The arrows fell in an erratic volley, their arcs uncertain and badly aimed due to the rush of the charge. Most clattered harmlessly off shields or buried themselves in the mud, though one or two found lodging in the upper edges of wooden bulwarks. Still, the shield wall held firm. Nobody broke ranks to yank out an arrow or cry in alarm. They had trained for this.

The first real clash occurred as a trio of Drosten's men charged headlong into the front of the shield wall, water flying from their boots. The defenders braced, and the collision rang out in a cacophony of metal on metal and the thick thud of leather-bound wood. The axe came down, a blur of steel and death. Finn barely got his shield up. The impact slammed into his forearm, sending a shockwave through his bones. Sparks flashed, wood splintered, but the shield held.

Before the warrior could raise his axe again, Finn lunged. His shield bashed into the man's ribs with a brutal crack. The attacker staggered, feet slipping in the river mud, just as a spear lanced through his shoulder. His scream ripped through the air, cutting off as he collapsed into the water, blood swirling around him.

To Finn's left, Morag fought ferociously. Whenever an attacker's sword or axe rose above the wooden barrier, she struck swiftly with her own blade, pushing the weapon aside or splitting flesh if they came too close. Her shield was a constant block, never wavering from its place beside Finn, and he took reassurance in her unyielding presence. Occasionally, her voice rose above the clamour, shouting for the line to 'Push!' or 'Hold!' as the wave of attackers ebbed and flowed at the foot of the bank.

Drosten's troops, for all their zeal, had never clashed against such a rigid defensive formation. A shield wall was not glorious; it was not about single combat or flashy swordplay. It was methodical, disciplined, and structured, each man and woman defending their neighbour as much as themselves. The defenders stepped in tandem to keep their formation, ensuring no gap opened wide enough for an enemy to exploit. Even as fresh attackers leapt into the river, the combined weight of the shield wall held them at bay. Swords and axes crashed on shields, but the well-timed thrusts of spears found openings between gaps in Drosten's line, drawing out cries of pain and frustration.

Finn felt the slippery stones beneath his feet shift with every step, forcing him to be mindful of his balance. The water itself was ankle-high here, but the mud, churned by dozens of boots, created a mire that threatened to trip any warrior who grew careless. Sweat poured down his temples and stung his eyes. Yet no matter how loud the attackers roared, no matter how many weapons crashed into the shields, the line held. This was the art of the shield wall: endure.

A momentary lull fell as Drosten's men pulled back slightly, regrouping just beyond the river. Some of their warriors glanced around, uncertain, perhaps expecting an easy rout that had not come. Others knelt to catch their breath, slapping mud and water from their legs. The archers, straggling further behind, tried again to send a volley of arrows across, but their vantage was poor, and the defenders raised their shields overhead. A few missiles found the ground in front of the wall, quivering in the mud.

That was the cue for the next wave. With a guttural shout, the remainder of Drosten's men poured down the slope, determined to overwhelm the shield wall with renewed force. Among them, Finn could see taller figures, perhaps more seasoned fighters, who began shouting for some semblance of order. Their voices cut through the din, trying to coordinate the assault rather than letting it devolve into chaos. But in the heat of battle, so many men were deafened, by the roaring in their ears, that any true coordination faltered.

This was the moment. Bruide's hidden contingent waited silently in the surrounding woods. Camouflaged by thick underbrush and pine trunks, they watched Drosten's men concentrate on the shield wall. Bruide, stood at their head, his dark eyes fixed on the unfolding melee. With a quick hand signal, he beckoned one of his scouts, who reported that Drosten's warriors were fully engaged. Satisfied, Bruide placed one calloused palm on the hilt of his broadsword and steeled himself for the coming onslaught.

Drosten's army ferociously battered the shield wall, axes and swords thudding heavily against interlocked shields. The noise was deafening, making it impossible for the defenders to hear orders. The defensive line groaned under the pressure, their discipline and training ensuring they were able to absorb wave after wave of attacks and sustained pressure. Mud and water sloshed around their feet, and the acrid stench of sweat, fear induced urine and excrement, and blood assailed the senses.

Drosten himself stood behind his pressing warriors, bellowing orders and urging them to break through. All the while, he remained oblivious to the greater danger stalking behind him beyond the tree line.

Over a hundred seasoned fighters were ordered by Bruide to circle quietly through dense woodland. While Drosten fixated on smashing the shield wall, Bruide's warriors flanked him from the rear. There would be no escape from this trap. Bruide wanted Drosten contained. Taking a deep breath, he nodded to his second-in-command, an older woman named Tressa, who signalled the rest of their ranks. Feet tensed, weapons raised, and hearts pounding, they prepared to unleash havoc. Three strong blasts of the war horn and Drosten's men were surrounded by angry, fierce and determined yet disciplined warriors.

The war horn blasts lifted the spirits of those in the shield wall, brought extra reserves of strength to tired limbs and bodies. Finn, braced in the front rank, he sensed a change. The pressure from the attackers waned slightly. The first piercing war cries erupting from Bruide's forces obviously distracted Drosten's men. Though his vision was limited, Finn saw Drosten's forces twist around, startled, their confidence faltering. They were no longer the attackers but the attacked. Morag, beside Finn, barked a command to hold the line. Silhouettes emerging from the tree line brandishing swords, spears, and axes. Their pace, which began as a measured jog, quickly exploded into a charge, aimed straight at Drosten and his army.

The trap snapped shut.

Drosten's warriors turned, too late.

From the trees, Bruide's forces struck like wolves descending on wounded prey. The first screams of panic rose as steel found flesh. Warriors whirled to face the ambush, their backs momentarily unguarded, just long enough for Finn's shield wall to lurch forward, hacking into exposed flanks.

The tide had turned.

Bruide led the charge, his broadsword swinging in a sweeping arc cutting down two of Drosten's men before they had time to raise their shields in defence. Tressa followed, her spear lashing out to skewer a third soldier who tried to lunge at Bruide's flank. Bruide's warriors moved cohesively, expertly hacking and thrusting. Drosten's disorganized formation were no match for the battle-hardened hordes bearing down on them.

It was clear Drosten's forces had little hope of escaping. They lacked discipline and leadership. The shield wall, once forced on the defensive, now advanced step by step, driving Drosten's men backward into the whirling blades of Bruide's force. The rear ranks of the shield wall moved to the sides, a single line was sufficient for this task. Screams of the wounded mingled with the ringing of steel. Blood spattered the grass, the riverbank, and the smooth rocks. The river ran red.

Morag, her face streaked with sweat and grime, led a surge from the left flank of the shield wall. She struck a warrior on the temple with her shield rim, toppling him into the muddy water. She drove her short sword into another man's gut before he could pivot away. Around her, Finn's warriors punished anyone who lingered within striking distance. Their line, reinforced by adrenaline and Bruide's well-timed arrival, held. Drosten's fighters were being butchered on every side.

Amid the chaos, Drosten roared in frustration, swinging a broad-bladed axe and trying to rally the men nearest him. His face, contorted with fury, veins in his neck bulging as he screamed curses. Drosten lashed out, with threats of death for any man who attempted to retreat or surrender. Neither of these were options available to them. They were hemmed in by walls of steel and merciless eyes. Death awaited them.

Seeking out Drosten, Bruide's sword, coated with blood and entrails, dripped onto the grass. He stepped closer to the defeated chieftain. The two leaders locked eyes across the dead and dying laying between them. Drosten spat on the ground. Bruide smiled.

Beyond them, Finn's shield wall pressed forward, ruthlessly dispatching any who came within sword or spear length. Drosten raised his sword, determined to end Bruide's life. With a roar, he sprang at Bruide, weapon arcing downward. Bruide parried the blow, pain running up the arms of both men. They moved apart, circling, their eyes locked. Drosten swung. Bruide sidestepped. Sensing an opening, Bruide lunged in close, slamming the pommel of his sword into Drosten's temple. The other man reeled, blood trickling from a fresh gash above his eye.

Drosten lifted his sword, but his strength was gone. His grip faltered.

Bruide struck.

The blade punched through flesh and bone, a wet, grating sound tearing through the air. Drosten's eyes widened, shock, pain, the realization that he had lost. Blood bubbled from his lips as he staggered back.

Bruide wrenched his sword free. Drosten collapsed, falling among the dead he had led to slaughter.

Those of Drosten's warriors who had not already fled or been cut down collapsed to their knees in surrender, some dropping their weapons, others clasping their heads in horror. Many were too wounded to move, lying in the blood-soaked grass groaning. Bruide's exhausted, but ebullient, fighters corralled the survivors. The noise of battle was replaced by the caws and cries of ravens and crows amassing above.

Bruide took an axe from a warrior beside him and in one swoop decapitated the lifeless rebel. He grabbed Drosten's head by its matted hair and lifted it high. The battlefield fell silent.

Wordlessly, he strode forward, his boots squelching in the blood-soaked grass. A spear jutted from a fallen warrior's chest, he yanked it free.

With a single, brutal motion, he drove Drosten's head onto the spike.

His sightless eyes gaped at the carnage.

Bruide's voice thundered:

'Let this be a warning.'

Among the handful of Drosten's surviving soldiers, fear etched their every movement. One man, barely more than a youth, trembled so violently that he dropped his sword twice as Bruide approached. Bruide regarded him with measured contempt before hooking a finger beneath the lad's chin, forcing him to look up. The soldier whimpered but dared not resist.

'You,' Bruide said to the youthful, white-faced soldier, 'will carry a message to Drosten's family. Go back to his home, tell them we have no mercy for those who threaten our lands. Do you understand?' The young man swallowed hard, nodding as tears poured from the corners of his eyes.

Bruide handed the boy the gruesome trophy, he stumbled away, scrambling over the fallen in his desperation to escape. Those who survived watched in silence as he vanished into the trees.

The King's voice reached him through a haze, but Finn barely registered the words. He had done what was necessary. He had led them well. The shield wall had held. He had survived.

But at what cost?

He thought of Columba, of the gentle voice that had taught him that every life, even a pagan's, was precious in the eyes of God. He thought of Cobthach, his father, who had placed a Bible in his hands before he could hold a sword. He thought of Christ, who had taught love over war, forgiveness over vengeance.

And yet, today, Finn had killed men.

He forced himself to look up at Bruide. 'Yes, My Lord,' he murmured. 'We held.'

The king clasped Finn's shoulder, grinning, unaware of the war raging inside him. 'And you fought well. The gods will honour your bravery, and my warriors will remember your leadership.'

The gods.

Finn nodded absently, but he felt hollow.

'I'll set the healers to work,' Morag said.

'Shall I help?'

'No, not today Finn, you're exhausted. Better leave it to the fresh minded.'

Chapter 18

Tar éis an bhua, tagann an uaigneas
(After victory, comes loneliness.)
— Amhrán na Marbh, Anonymous Monk of Hy

The fight against the forces of Drosten had ended. Casualties amongst Bruide's had been light, five deaths and fifty injured. The same could not be said for the warriors from the Western Hills. They had been annihilated. More than three hundred had left their homes full of hope for glory and wealth, only one returned, a young soldier charged with bringing Drosten's head home to his family on a pike.

In good spirits Bruide led his forces back to the fortress. Some were clutching wounds others supporting their injured comrades. The able bodied, sang of victory and laughed, as they approached, before the gates swung open in welcome, sounds of commotion came from within. Frantic calls drifted over the walls: the fortress population, alerted by messengers, was already scrambling to set up additional healing stations. Those who had not joined the battle, boys just old enough to wield daggers, women with aprons stuffed with herbs bustled in all directions, carrying bundles of cloth for the wounded or distributing cups of water. Anxious faces greeted the warriors as they returned, searching for a loved one. Most of the wounded bore shallow cuts or broken bones.

A warrior Finn recognized, Muirgheas, clutched his stomach, blood oozing between his fingers. Finn knelt beside him, pressing a linen cloth over the wound. Muirgheas hissed in pain but managed a weak grin.

'You fight like a madman, priest,' he rasped. 'Yet you mend wounds with the hands of a priest.'

Finn forced a smile, though his chest ached with something nameless. What was he now? Warrior or monk? A part of King Connall's guard, or a servant of Christ?

Morag knelt beside a man with an arrow lodged deep in his thigh, murmuring reassurances as she worked to remove it. Finn watched her hands, steady, sure, unflinching. She belonged here, in battle, in healing, in command. But where did he belong?

Amid the chaos, Finn and Morag entered the great hall, shoulders drooping from exertion but their hands intertwined, drawing on each other's strength.

'We survived,' Morag whispered, as though saying it aloud might make it more real.

Finn nodded. 'Your plan worked. We were protected.' He hesitated. 'By your gods. Or mine.'

Morag's lips quirked in a wry smile, but her eyes were serious. 'Does it matter?'

Finn didn't answer. He wasn't sure he could.

Morag blushed and squeezed his hand tightly. 'We should go back outside and help with the wounded.'

'They are being well cared for,' Finn replied; 'You should get some rest.'

They walked through the Great Hall and out of the back, through the animal enclosure, to Morag's part of the Royal residence There, with the din having receded, they sat by the light of a single torch, the flickering light shining across their faces. The silence of that small room was a sanctuary from the chaos outside.

For a time, neither spoke. Their gazes locked their hands interlocked. Two souls trembling in the aftermath of battle. Then, Morag threw her arms around his neck, pressing her cheek to his. He smelled, as she did, of sweat, blood and leather, of mud and grime. She felt his pulse beneath her fingertips, and she was grateful to be alive.

'There will be a feast,' Morag said, her voice low, almost reluctant. 'My father will want to drink to the victory.' She paused. 'I don't think I can stomach it.'

Finn slid his hands around her waist. 'Neither can I,' he said. 'But a feast is also a way to thank those who risked their lives. To bind us together and blur the horrors. We must attend, at least for a while until most are so drunk they won't feel our absence.'

Morag's fingers brushed his. 'If we must, we will. But not for long.' She leaned back and met his eyes. 'We should be grateful. We're alive. We survived, you and I. And the casualties were far fewer than we feared.'

'Yes, Morag, and we must show those who were prepared to die beside us, that we love and appreciate them.'

'You're right,' she said. Her voice wavering, a tear running from the side of an eye. The memory of the night before the battle burned bright in her mind. She was grateful to the gods that they had both surrendered to their love and were protected in battle.

Finn also remembered. Her giving herself in his arms, the sweetness of her breath, the low whispered words. In those stolen moments, they had joined their Christian and Pagan worlds together.

'I'm grateful,' Finn said quietly. He cupped her cheek, gently brushing away a stray strand of hair. 'More than I can ever say.' He kissed her.

Morag gave in to his kiss, but steadying herself, she said, 'Come, We must see to the wounded, give what help we can. We'll speak again, later.' She stood, linked his arm and they walked back through the Great Hall and out into the tumult.

Word of Bruide's success spread quickly throughout the heather strewn hills and valleys. Riders were sent to all settlements to ensure Drosten's defeat was heard by all.

Over the following days, the fortress was consumed by the tasks of healing. Warriors nursed bruised bodies, huntsmen scoured the forest for fresh game, and Finn and Morag grew closer. Music drifted through the halls in the evening, minstrels plucking lyres to accompany the telling of heroic deeds. At night, minstrels wove their names into song. The warrior-monk, the foreign knight who fought like a pagan, prayed like a saint and won the heart of a princess.

From monastic hall and royal command,
A warrior came, with sword in hand
Young Finn, the priest, obeyed the call
To guard this hallowed land.
His Christian blade shone in the night,
A vow seared on his heart,
To fight for Bruide's ancient throne,
And ne'er from honour part.

Sing of Morag, with flaming hair,
Who led true and loyal men;
Her spirit as fierce as a summer storm,
Her armour donned again.
They battled on the heathered moor,
Midst swirling mist and dew,
And bound by oath to King and cause,
Their might and faith grew true.

The Picts had never seen a holy man like Finn.

Druids whispered their prayers to the wind and carved symbols into stone, but they had never stood in the shield wall, blood on their hands, steel in their grip. Finn had.

He spoke of Christ, of salvation, of peace, but they had seen him kill for them, stand beside them in the chaos of battle. They listened because he had fought for them.

Finn was self-assured but also burdened by self-doubt. He prayed often, offered blessings for the sick and wounded, and used his healing skills where he could. Still, every spare moment was filled with thoughts of Morag.

Finn and Morag enjoyed the peace of the clearing where she had set up her 'church.' One bright afternoon they walked down to the copse and sat on a fallen pine tree. The towering pines surrounded them. A rustling disturbed their conversation. Shapes began to emerge, men and women clad in robes of pale linen. He recognised some of them as being from the fortress, one in particular, Taran the leader of Bruide's religious men. Others he had never seen. Morag reached out her hand and touched his. He felt her nervousness. The Druids bore expressions that flickered between caution and disgust. These, keepers of the old faith rooted in the land and guided by unseen powers from nature, assembled in front of the young couple.

Finn stood slowly, inclining his head. 'I am Finn, of the Holy Island of Hy.' His voice remained steady, though the weight of many watching eyes pressed against him.

Taran's gaze was like flint. 'We know who you are, monk. Word of you spreads like wildfire, of your foreign god, your foreign ways. That you whisper of love and peace but kill like any other warrior.'

Finn met his gaze without flinching. 'I fight for those I love. For those who cannot fight for themselves. Is that not what your warriors do?'

Murmurs rippled through the gathered Druids.

Taran's scowl deepened, but before he could speak, an older druidess stepped forward.

'Enough, Taran,' she said, 'I am Rhosyn. And I would hear what the monk has to say.'

Her tone held weight. Finn saw how the other Druids deferred to her, although Taran still looked hostile.

'I am not here to judge your faith or force you from your ways,' Finn said. 'I only wish to learn. I only speak of my God to show there is an alternative way to look at the world. We believe in free will and believe that men and women should choose the path that is right for them. When I was young, I heard tales that you and your brethren, were to be feared as dark sorcerers who twist nature. However, in the few months I have been here among Bruide's people. Morag has taught me of your wisdom and kindnesses and how to appreciate the old ways.'

'Morag has taught you more than that,' Taran said.

Morag rose. 'Taran, do you insult the King's daughter? Your position in my father's house is granted by him. Do you wish me to inform him of your words?'

'He already knows what I think, but he seems to approve. It's an abomination. Your father should be ashamed, you should be ashamed.'

'Taran, enough,' Roshyn said, and Taran seemed to shrink from her words. 'Finn, you are welcome here among us. You are right, we are accused of many things, some are only unkind, others are completely untrue. And we hear stories about your God's followers. How you drink blood and offer human sacrifice, but we do not believe this.' She glanced at Taran, 'Well, most of us give it no credence.'

She invited the group to gather around in a circle surrounding the log where Finn and Morag had been sitting. Please Finn,

Morag, sit. Roshyn sat on the ground in the middle of the circle, confirming her place as leader. 'Taran, stay where I can see you.'

As they all settled down and made themselves comfortable on the grass, Roshyn continued. 'We have rarely met with monks and priests of the new faith,' she said; 'but you appear to have come with earnest heart and no thirst for violence. So, we shall share a part of our truth with you.'

Finn inclined his head again. 'Thank you Roshyn.'

A young druid, about the same age as Finn, spoke next. 'You say you worship Christ. He is your Redeemer, yes? You believe He died to free humankind from sin.'

Finn nodded. 'We hold that He is the Son of the one true God, incarnate among us, who sacrificed Himself so that we might be saved and rise to new life.'

Several druids turned to one another, exchanging thoughtful looks. Rhosyn rested her hands on her knees. 'We find our spiritual anchor in nature itself. The forest, the stones, the rivers, the sky they are all divine in their different ways. We do not believe in a single God, but in the power of the earth. Our gods are an extension of nature. The changing of the seasons, the cycles of life and death, these are our sacred mysteries.'

Finn considered her words carefully. 'In truth,' he said, 'our beliefs are not entirely different. We say, God's work is written in the wonders of nature. Yet the difference is that we believe God created these earthly wonders but remains separate from them and not an integral part of them.'

Rhosyn tilted her head. 'That is the heart of it, isn't it? You seek a God beyond this world. We find divinity in the world itself.'

Finn ran his thumb over the worn wood of his cross. 'But what of the soul?' he asked. 'What of what comes after?'

A younger druid spoke. 'Do the leaves vanish when they fall in autumn? No. They nourish the earth, and new life rises.

Death is not an end. It is a return.'

Finn thought of the Pictish dead, lying beneath the sky. Of Drosten, of the blood-soaked battlefield. Were their spirits drifting now in the wind, as the Druids believed? Or standing before Christ, as he had always been taught?

For the first time, he wasn't certain. He reached for the cross around his neck and ran his fingers over its worn surface as he spoke. 'When my heart was once darkened by hatred for my enemies, I found hope in Christ's sacrifice. I learned I could surrender my anger at the foot of the cross, trusting that there is a higher grace. Do your rites help you find such peace, or do they serve another purpose?'

Taran answered: 'Our rites help us attune ourselves to the rhythms of the earth. Peace is found in understanding that we, like the trees, must grow and shed, weather storms and bask in sunlight, and in time, return to the ground. We do not speak of original sin or the need for redemption. We speak of honouring the balance of life. That is the true way.'

Finn could feel his pulse quicken. 'Balance,' he said. 'We often speak of the battle between darkness and light, with Christ as the victor over sin and death. Do you not believe that evil rises to challenge the good in this world?'

Rhosyn sighed, as though she had grappled with such questions many times. 'We have eyes and we can see suffering. We are not blind to the cruelty that exists among men, or storms that destroy crops, or indiscriminate illnesses that claim both the young and old. Yet evil is not a separate power warring against good. We believe misfortunes occur when the delicate equilibrium of nature is disturbed. Greed, hatred, and hurricanes can bring harm. But for us, the remedy is to restore harmony, not to cast out some malevolent being.'

Finn pressed his lips together, recalling the stories of demons being exorcised by saints, Christ's own encounter with, and victory over, the devil in the desert. It appeared strange that druids did not conceive of evil in the same manner. He recognized that there was wisdom in their words and beliefs but could not accept they were correct. 'So, you seek alignment with nature's flow, while we seek grace from a God who loves us beyond measure.'

Nodding, Rhosyn said, 'And in demonstrating your devotion to your god, you perform sacraments. Am I right? Baptism, communion, confession, and so on? Our devotion is demonstrated in our rituals of sowing, harvest, solstice, and equinox. We gather when the veil between us and Mother Earth is thin, when the changing of the seasons allows us to commune more deeply with the forces and gods of nature that govern our lives.'

Softly, Finn said, 'Yet are you not concerned about what lies beyond this life? We believe in eternal salvation through good works and deeds. We believe that death is not the end.'

A hush fell. The young druid spoke once more: 'We believe that death is merely a transition; an opening to the next life. We hear our ancestors voices in the wind, and the rustling of trees and this is how we will communicate with our descendants in the future, after our mortal forms are taken back into the cycle of nature. You have hopes of heaven and resurrection, we have cycles of rebirth.'

Finn breathed deeply. He could feel neither hostility nor condemnation. They spoke with calm conviction. They talked for hours. Each respectful of the other's opinion. Each asking questions and given honest answers which, in many ways, showed they had more in common than there were differences. These Druids, or at least most of them, for Taran continued to scowl and look on Morag with hatred, were as honest and devout as the monks at home on Hy.

As dusk approached, mellow dappled light shone through

the branches overhead, and Rhosyn stood. Lifting her staff she looked at Finn. 'Thank you for teaching us a little about your God, You have shown that the fears we grew up with were based more on myth than reality. We both revere the sacred and wish the world to remain in balance.'

Finn bowed. He had been touched by her words. 'And I thank you. So many misunderstandings come from ignorance or fear. You cherish life and hold reverence for mystery, those are qualities I understand and respect.'

The druids began to disperse in silence among the trees. Rhosyn bowed her head in farewell, and Finn and Morag turned to make their way back along the forest path. Ahead of them walked Taran and the Druids from the fortress, they could hear his angry tones ahead of them.

As Finn walked, the Druids' words lingered. He had come to this land certain of his faith. But now?

He would pray. He would share his thoughts with Morag. He would seek counsel from Columba when he returned.

For the first time in his life, Finn had some misgivings about his faith. He was unsure if prayer alone would give him answers.

Chapter 19

Is i ngrá a thagann beatha,
agus is i mbeatha a mhúineann grá dúinn.
(It is through love that life comes,
and through life that love teaches us.)
— Briathra na gCríoch, 7th Century Hymnal

The days and weeks following the meeting with the druids, passed calmly. Finn trained, prayed, and spoke of Christ's love, but fewer than he had hoped came to pray with him. Faith, he had learned, could not be forced, but he could not ignore the sting of rejection.

'It's Taran,' Morag told him one morning. 'He sends spies among the people. Anyone showing interest in your God receives a warning, what he will do to them if they stray too far from the old ways.'

Finn's fists clenched. This was no simple reluctance, it was fear. 'What can I do?'

Morag's lips curved into a knowing smile. 'Leave it to me. Just tell them you're holding a feast tomorrow.'

He frowned. 'A feast? How does that…? '

She kissed his cheek and dashed off, laughing. 'Trust me, monk.'

He wandered back to his rooms. It was almost time for Sext. The fortress had returned to calm normality. As he walked, blacksmiths, forging new weapons, greeted him. Seamstresses, repairing garments, gossiped and joked with the farmers and bread makers passing by. He was happy in this world Columba had allowed him to be a part of.

The next morning Finn and Morag trained hard. When the time came for them to hang up their training swords he called the warriors together. 'This afternoon, in the great field I invite you all to join me for a great feast with roasted boar, to celebrate the saint's day of St. Patrick. He is said to have been born in these very hills but was taken into slavery across the water. I will tell you his story and much more. Come, bring your families, all are invited.'

He caught a flash of a smile from Morag. She gave a slight nod and dashed off to prepare. Finn returned to his rooms, wondering how this would help curtail Taran's intimidation. Morag's plan remained a mystery, but his faith was in both God and her.

Servants set up trestle tables as three wild boar roasted over open fires. The smell of roast meat competed with the smell of freshly baked bread. Barrels of ale and mead were rolled towards the celebrations. Soldiers and villagers, hungry for distraction and enticed by the smells, gathered in small clusters. Morag supervised every detail.

Finn stood at the head of the feast, watching as Bruide approached. The warriors and villagers fell silent, parting like the sea for their king. Bruide's presence was more than approval. This was a direct challenge to Taran. With the king at Finn's side, no whispered threat from the druid could silence those who wished to listen.

The scene in front of Bruide pleased him. Whole boars crackled on spits, on laden tables mead sloshed into cups, and fresh-baked bread filled the air with warmth. His gaze flicked to his daughter.

'This looks more like your work than the monk's,' he said.

Morag gave a playful shrug. 'The best hosts know when to remain unseen.'

Bruide chuckled. 'A rare quality in my house.'

Laughter rippled through the gathering, loosening tension. Even Taran, lingering at the edges, could not stop the tide turning against him.

As they ate, a minstrel, playing a lute, sang a song Finn had taught him.

O come ye people, gather nigh,
And heed a wondrous tale of old,
Of Padraig from this Pictish land,
Whose faith did shine more bright than gold.

He was a youth in his father's hall,
When Irish raiders crossed the bay,
They seized him from his loving kin,
And bound his hands that fateful day.

In foreign fields he toiled in dread,
Yet God's voice stirred his soul so deep,
He prayed at dawn and prayed at eve,
And found the strength his faith to keep.

At last, one night the Spirit led
His footsteps to a ship astray,
He fled the land that bound him fast,
And found safe passage on the way.

Home he returned to Pictish shore,
His kin rejoiced to see his face,
But in a dream God called him forth,
To Erin once again with grace.

No fear of chains could break his vow,
With staff in hand he braved the sea,
To teach the Cross 'mid pagan groves,
And set the isle from darkness free.

He preached the word of Christ the Lord,
And many souls the truth did hold,
Till from the land all serpents fled
Before the staff of Padraig bold.

So soared his name in Erin's fields,
A shepherd once in bonds of fear,
Yet called by God to banish sin,
And show the Light that all might hear.

From Pictish land his tale began,
And unto Ireland's holy shore,
He forged a path with humble faith,
To serve the Lord forevermore.

O people, keep this story nigh,
Where'er the storms of life may blow,
For Padraig stands a beacon bright,
A guiding lamp all souls may know.

People were enthralled by the ballad never heard before. A fellow countryman converting Irish warriors and farmers to the Christian faith. They were enthralled. Taran stood with a few of his followers on the edge of the crowd.

'Come, Taran,' Bruide's voice rang out, rich with command. 'Join us. Eat as these warriors, farmers, and servants do.'

All eyes turned to the druid. His jaw tightened. He had no choice. Refusing a king's offer, a public invitation, no less, would be seen as an act of rebellion. Slowly, stiffly, he moved forward.

The warriors made room, but their gazes held something different now. Not fear. Not reverence. Curiosity.

Morag's lips moved only slightly as she whispered to Finn, 'Look around you. Taran is losing control.'

And Finn saw it, too.

When the sun dipped lower, King Bruide rose from his seat. Silence fell. He gestured for Finn to stand at his side.

'Morag tells me many of you hesitate to hear Finn's teachings, fearing certain threats,' he said; 'I am here to say that you have no cause to be afraid. If Finn wishes you to join him in prayer and you wish to do so, you must do it. I command none of you to do so, for it is your choice, but I shall not permit intimidation, from Taran or anyone else.'

Surprise swept the audience. Morag squeezed Finn's hand. Buoyed by such clear Royal endorsement, Finn led them at sundown in Christian prayer, unafraid to speak his faith before all who wished to listen.

Taran stormed away.

At first, Morag dismissed the fatigue. She was no stranger to hard days. Then came the nausea, the aching limbs, the breathless moments when simply standing felt like a battle.

And then, the absence. The rhythm of her body had changed.

One morning, she woke with her palm pressed against her belly, an ache deep inside her, not of sickness, but of knowing.

She was carrying Finn's child.

The realization sent a shiver through her, not of fear, but something heavier. A shift in her soul, the world rearranging itself around her.

Alone in her private chamber, taking measured breaths to quell the feeling in her belly, she dressed hurriedly in a simple wool tunic, and slipped out into the corridor. The fortress was quiet as she made her way to the courtyard, searching for Finn.

She found him in his quarters kneeling in prayer. A faint candle glow fell across his face, illuminating the gentle curve of his brow. Morag watched him in silence for a moment, tenderness washing over her. Then, she approached and laid a hand on his shoulder. He looked up, surprise flashing in his eyes, followed by a warm smile.

'I have news,' she whispered. 'Come with me.'

They walked away, past the courtyard and through a small gate that led to a herb garden. Dew sparkled on the grass, and the scent of mint and rosemary clung to the air. Morag led Finn beneath the drooping branches of a willow. There, in the quiet dawn, she turned to face him, her hands cradling his.

'Finn,' she said. 'I believe I'm carrying your child.'

Finn's chest tightened. Everything else faded. 'Morag…' His voice wavered, heavy with something he couldn't quite name. 'Are you sure?'

She nodded, tears shimmering in her green eyes. 'It's been weeks. My body feels… different. I know it's true.'

For a moment, he could only stare at her, at the woman he loved, at the life they had created. Then, with a breathless laugh, he pulled her into his arms.

'God has blessed us,' he whispered against her hair. 'A child...' He swallowed hard. 'I never imagined... but I, I am so happy, Morag.'

She clung to him, her fingers digging into his back. 'So am I. But my father will have much to say.'

His joy dimmed slightly. Yes. Bruide's approval would mean everything.

Finn's heart pounded. He feared King Bruide's reaction. 'Let's go and see him together.'

She smiled through tears. 'Yes. Together.'

Bruide's reaction was immediate and unexpected. He laughed. 'I thought nobody would be able to tame my Morag. Congratulations, Finn, and thank you.'

'Thank me? Thank me for what?'

'For helping my daughter make me a grandfather. This is something to be rejoiced and celebrated.' Bruide placed a hand on Finn's shoulder. 'I have seen your courage on the battlefield, Finn, let us hope that your courage extends to fatherhood.' He frowned; 'But be aware. Taran and his followers will not condone this union. They will claim the gods are insulted. We'll have to be watchful.'

'King Bruide, I promise I will protect Morag and our child with my life.'

'Father, will you shield us from their anger?' Morag said.

The king grimaced. 'I will do what must be done. For now, let them mutter in their circles. You are my daughter, Morag. That alone is enough to protect you. And you, Finn, stay steadfast. I suspect there may be trouble.'

Finn nodded.

A ripple of excitement ran through the fortress as word spread that Morag was with child and the father was the foreign monk. A royal baby was a cause for great celebration. Morag was well-loved. Approachable, generous, and brave. Most were eager to welcome the baby, the birth should signal a time of good fortune.

Yet from Taran, came undiluted hostility. He clustered with other druids at the fortress edges, chanting at dusk and offering sacrifices to ancient gods. Their glances at Finn and Morag, did not go unnoticed. Tension lingered.

Time passed quickly. The first flushes of pregnancy gave way to more obvious changes. Morag's belly grew, her appetite changed, and her energy waned. Through it all, Finn stayed close, offering his love and support. At night, Morag was restless. Finn would recite the psalms or cradle her in his arms until she slept. Occasionally, she asked him about the Christian teachings particularly anything that offered comfort or hope. He would speak of the compassion of Christ, and the promise of eternal life. Morag would listen thoughtfully.

King Bruide, for his part, revelled in the approach of grand fatherhood. He declared hunts in celebration, laid aside casks of ale for the baby's naming ceremony, and boasted to the warriors about the strong child to come.

It was not an easy pregnancy. Morag's health deteriorated alarmingly in the final weeks. She struggled to keep food down, and nights were plagued by feverish dreams. The midwives were experienced and wise. They brewed potions of chamomile and elderflower to soothe her. Lavender-scented oils were rubbed on swollen feet and ankles. She bathed in warm baths laced with rosemary. Finn would kneel by her side, praying, hoping to call upon both heaven's grace and any healing presence the earth itself could give. Some nights, he feared he might lose her. But her spirit, forged by the rugged hills, refused to break.

When her labour finally started, it arrived in a wave of pain so intense that Morag nearly collapsed. The midwives guided her to a prepared birthing room, an airy chamber with thick tapestries and a crackling hearth. They cleared away all but essential items: clean linens, basins of water, carefully blended potions. No men were allowed within, not even King Bruide. Finn paced outside in the corridor, heart pounding, hearing Morag's cries. Time stood still.

Near midnight, a child was born with a piercing cry heard throughout the fortress halls. A flushed-faced midwife rushed out, calling to Finn. He returned with her, his breath catching in his throat as he saw Morag, pale and exhausted, propped on cushions, a tiny, wriggling bundle in her arms. Tears running down her cheeks glistened in the candlelight.

'It's a boy,' she whispered; 'you have a son.'

Finn approached, 'A son,' he repeated, kneeling at her side. He brushed his finger over the infant's cheek, small, pink, and perfect. The child fussed, opening tiny fists and kicking tiny feet.

Morag's expression glowed with joy. 'I want to name him Colm-Bruide,' she said softly. 'Columba… and Bruide, to honour my father and your holy man.'

Finn's eyes misted. He glanced at the midwives, who nodded approvingly. 'It's beautiful,' he managed. 'Thank you, Morag.'

'Thank me?' She laughed weakly. 'I only carried him for nine moons and bore him through hours of agony.' Her laugh turned to a smile, letting him see how delighted she was. 'But yes. Let him bridge both worlds, yours and mine.'

Word soon reached Bruide. He entered the birthing room. The daughter he loved without measure held his grandson in her arms.

'Have you chosen a name?' Bruide asked.

'Colm-Bruide,' replied Morag.

'Colm-Bruide… Colm-Bruide,' said the king, 'Colm-Bruide, may you bring blessings upon our realm.'

Finn was unable to speak.

The fortress was filled with celebration. Morag rested, a steady stream of well-wishers left gifts: cloth, carved toys, and protective amulets. The midwives allowed Finn a place by Morag's side, though they were mindful of her need for rest. Occasionally, King Bruide appeared, pride shining in his eyes. Soldiers gave up portions of their rations for an impromptu feast in the courtyard. The storyteller sang a song of welcome, praising the child who mingled Christian and pagan heritage.

Morag slowly regained strength walking around her chamber, cradling Colm-Bruide. Finn marvelled at her resilience. Two weeks passed. Morag still tired easily, but she insisted on a few short strolls beyond her chamber. She missed the open air. One afternoon, as the sun cast a warm glow through the fortress yard, Morag decided to visit her special clearing in the woods. She told no one but Finn, who was momentarily preoccupied by a summons from Bruide regarding boundary disputes. Rather than wait, Morag set out alone, confident that her father's victory had made the surrounding area safe once more.

She left Colm-Bruide in the care of the midwives. Stepping through the fortress gate, she inhaled the heady scent of pine. Autumn's approach touched the leaves with gold along the edges of the forest. This clearing had long been a refuge. Here, she sometimes felt the presence of her mother. She felt at peace with the shifting balance of her own faith, torn between ancient beliefs and the glimpses of Christianity that Finn had shared.

Entering that familiar clearing brought a sense of calm. The breeze stirred the ribbons. Morag closed her eyes, letting the rustle of leaves lull her into prayerful reflection. She prayed for her son's health, for Finn's continued devotion, for her father's realm to know peace. Thoughts of the future drifted through her mind: perhaps she could reconcile the old ways and the new faith. Perhaps Colm-Bruide might grow up in a world where Christian chants harmonized with the beat of the druidic drum, each tradition illuminating the other rather than tearing them apart.

She was so lost in reverie that she did not notice the faint crunch of leaves behind her. Only when a chill prickled the back of her neck did she open her eyes and sense someone else was there. Turning, her gaze snagged on a figure half-hidden in the shadows.

'Hello?' she called, her voice tentative. She took an instinctive step backward, alarm stinging her gut.

The cloaked figure advanced, face half-obscured by the hood's shadow. Morag recognized him. Taran. His posture menacing, shoulders stiff with purpose, a dagger in his hand.

Morag realized instantly that she had no weapon, no defence. Her chest tightened. 'What do you want, Taran?' she said.

The druid spat on the ground. 'You have defiled our bloodline. A bastard child by that Christian monk? You are spreading false worship among our people. Your ancestors are crying out in pain.'

Morag's mind raced. She recalled some of the druids voicing discontent, even threatening ill omens. She had tried to ignore their rancour, trusting her father's authority would shield her. But here, alone in the forest, she saw how misplaced that trust was. Speaking calmly, she said, 'My father has decreed otherwise,' she said. 'He celebrates my child, his grandson. Finn and I will be wed, Taran. 'You have no right,'

He stepped closer, forcing her to move back.

'Your father does not rule the gods, and neither do you.'

The dagger glinted in the dappled light. She moved to run,

Too late.

A flash of silver, a burst of pain. She staggered, hands pressing to her side. The world blurred as she sank to the forest floor. 'You have no right...' she repeated.

A blur of silver. Fire lanced through her side.

She gasped, hands clutching at the sudden, searing pain. Warmth, too much warmth, spilled through her fingers.

Taran's breath was a growl above her. 'You have defiled our bloodline,' he repeated.

She tried to scream. His blade plunged into her again.

The clearing swayed. Her legs refused to obey. The world blurred, trees, sky, ribbons snapping in the wind.

Colm-Bruide.

Her lips formed his name, but no sound came.

The dagger struck once more. White-hot pain. Numbness.

Her body lay crumpled on the earth.

She saw his shadow retreating, fading into the forest. The wind stirred the branches, whispering the prayers she could no longer say.

And then, darkness.

Chapter 20

Is mó pian an fhírinne ná bréag chompordach.
(Truth wounds more than a comforting lie.)
— Tuar na nDéithe, Lost Texts of Dál Riata

Afternoon faded to dusk, Morag did not return. A growing dread enveloped Finn. He searched everywhere. He asked the midwives, every guard, anyone he came across. No one had seen her since she walked out earlier.

Dread turned to panic.

Panic spread to Bruide when Finn told him. Rallying a group of guards, father and husband raced into the woods, torches flaring in the darkening evening.

A shout slashed through the night.

'Here! Over here!'

Finn ran, stumbling over roots, torches bobbing wildly around him. His breath came in ragged gasps.

He saw her.

Morag lay beneath the trees, her tunic, dark with blood, unnaturally still, the ribbons she once tied with care now mourning her.

Finn's knees hit the earth. 'No.'

His hands trembled as he reached for her pulse, his fingers

pressing against cold skin. No warmth. No flickering of life beneath her eyelids.

'Morag…' His voice cracked.

Bruide stood frozen, his face pale, his body trembling. Then, in a voice almost a whisper but raw and guttural, he said, 'Who did this?'

A heavy silence before rage exploded.

'Find them!' Bruide roared, his voice a storm in the night. 'Find them and drag them before me!'

Finn barely heard him. His world had collapsed. the woman he loved, growing colder and colder, her skin paler and paler, as she lay motionless in his arms.

Word spread swiftly. The gates bristled with guards, scouring the perimeter in case the murderer tried to sneak in. Within the fortress, shock mingled with sudden outbursts of weeping.

Morag's body was carried inside the great hall and laid upon a cloak. Bruide himself, eyes blazing with grief, demanded revenge.

The druids arrived, drawn by the commotion. Taran stooped over Morag's body, his expression unreadable. Others murmured among themselves. Snatches of words reached Finn's ears.

'She offended the old gods.'

'The spirits demanded a price.'

'Punishment for lying with the Christian.'

Serpent-like a suspicion coiled in Finn's gut. One of them had done this.

Bruide's face darkened. 'Seize the druids. All of them.'

Guards moved swiftly, forcing the robed figures into confinement. Finn, numb with grief, sank to his knees beside Morag's still form. He prayed, but he didn't know to whom he was praying his God or her gods, both had let her down.

That night, the soldiers searched the druids' quarters. In Taran's chamber, they found it. A blood-soaked cloak.

Taran was dragged before Bruide's throne. He did not struggle, nor did he flinch. His eyes glinted with twisted conviction.

'Your daughter betrayed the old ways,' he spat. 'The gods demanded she pay.'

Finn stood at Bruide's side, hands shaking. His fingers twitched toward *Fidelis*. This man should die by his hand. Now, this instant. But Bruide's presence stayed his fury.

Bruide turned to the guards, his voice cold. 'Call for Roshyn, the High Druidess. She must witness this man's execution. She must be here tomorrow by dawn, for he may not see the noon of another day.'

A red sky heralded the rising sun.

The courtyard was silent, thick with anticipation and unease. The entire garrison had assembled, torches flickering in the early dawn light. The air was cold, but the fury simmering in Bruide's veins burned hotter than any flame.

Taran was hauled into the Great Hall, his feet dragging through the dirt, his face bruised but impassive. No fear in his eyes.

Bruide stood at the dais, flanked by Finn, his face carved from stone, and Roshyn, her head covered. Silence weighed heavy. No one spoke. No one breathed.

The guards threw Taran to his knees.

'Confess,' Bruide demanded.

Taran smiled. Not a smile of joy, but one of unfettered evil.

'She betrayed the old ways,' he said, his voice ringing through the hall. 'She lay with the Christian. She bore his child. The gods demanded a price.'

Finn lunged.

He scarcely registered the arms restraining him. He barely

heard the gasps of the gathered crowd. All he saw was the man who had stolen everything.

'I'll kill you myself,' he snarled.

Bruide's voice stopped him. 'No. He will die, but not by your hand.'

Taran sneered, blood dripping from his mouth. 'You think this ends with me? You think your false god will save you?'

He turned his gaze to Finn, his voice edged with malicious hatred. 'Your bastard will not live to sit on the throne.'

A ripple of unease spread through the crowd. Some muttered superstitiously. Finn's hands clenched.

Roshyn spoke. 'Taran, you have betrayed yourself, the ancients and all who have listened to your poison. You are not being guided by the earth, or the stars, but by your own blind stupidity.'

'I am not an unfair man,' Bruide said. 'I told you, you would not see another noon. But I want you to reflect on what you have done. You will not be executed at noon.'

Taran's eyes flickered.

'You will die at dawn, after a day chained dangling from the fortress walls. By dawn you will be begging to die.'

Taran didn't beg. He didn't flinch. He smiled. He believed that death would be nothing more than another step in a plan far greater than himself.

That thought unsettled Finn. Bruide had not been generous to Taran. Roshyn disagreed with the condemned Druid's view. She wanted the extra time to commune with the ancients in the forest. Taran deserved to end his life or lives here and after death, travel into nothingness. She knew the spells, and the ancients knew her heart. They would assist her.

The dawn sky was obliterated by dark storm clouds.

The entire fortress had gathered, the air thick with tension.

Roshyn stood beside Bruide and Finn, murmuring a quiet incantation, dispersing whatever curses the condemned man might attempt.

Taran was forced to his knees, his arms bound, his head pressed against the execution block.

He did not fight. He did not plead.

'You are sentenced to die for the murder of my daughter,' Bruide declared. 'Let the gods you serve carry your soul away.'

Taran laughed.

A low, rasping sound that sent a chill through those gathered. 'The gods do not forget. They do not forgive.' His gaze locked onto Finn. 'You will suffer, monk. You will pray to your powerless God, pleading for death. The ancients have marked you.'

Finn gritted his teeth. He would not give Taran the satisfaction of seeing fear.

The executioner steadied himself, axe rising above his head.

Taran looked to the ground waiting for Mother Earth to take him and his life force.

The axe fell.

A sickening thud.

Blood splattered the ground. The severed head rolled onto the dirt, eyes wide, lips parted in mid-curse.

No one moved. Breath and time stood still.

Bruide turned on his heel. 'Burn the body. No ceremony, just burn it and quickly.'

The gathered warriors murmured in agreement. Some turned away, but Finn remained frozen. Roshyn approached and placed an arm around Finn's shoulders.

'Pay no heed to his words, Finn. The gods were not listening. He took a life for no reason and our gods abhor such actions.'

She then ordered her druids to build a pyre and supervised as they dug up the ground where his blood had spilled and threw it onto the firewood. 'The blood will be burned with his body to prevent it soiling our precious earth,' she continued. 'He will be forgotten and he will not join the ancients. His voice will never be heard in the wind or babbling water. A being no more, a fading memory time will forget, even though you, Finn, will never forgive. If, as you believe, there is a hell, then he will be there.'

The days blurred into one another. The fortress was hushed, as though Morag's absence had left a wound upon the very stones. The people grieved, yet life pressed forward, one step, one breath at a time.

Finn did not sleep. When exhaustion finally claimed him, it came in snatches, filled with dreams of red hair tangled in blood, of Morag's voice calling his name only to vanish like mist.

He knelt in his chamber, hands clasped so tightly in prayer that his knuckles ached. He spoke the words, but they felt hollow.

Why, God?

Silence.

No answer came. No vision. No peace. Only the weight of grief pressing against his ribs, making it hard to breathe.

Finn could not look at Colm-Bruide.

The cradle was set by the fire, small and silent. A tuft of red hair peeked from the blankets. So much like Morag.

He reached out once, his fingers hovering over the baby's cheek, but pulled back.

She should be here.

Morag's sweet and tender tones should be singing to him, her soft arms, cradling him. Instead, her ashes were scattered in the winds, and their son would never know her voice. Finn had never known his mother and now that same fate had befallen his son.

The pain was unbearable. He turned away.

Nights melded, one into another. He prayed, but it felt as worthless as screaming at the stars.

Why did You let this happen, God? Why must the innocent suffer?

Silence. No answer. No comfort. Only emptiness.

A knock at the door made Finn turn. His body aching from kneeling too long. A guard stood there, hesitant.

'My lord Finn… there is someone at the gates. He asks for you and the king.'

'Who?'

The guard hesitated. Then, 'A holy man. He calls himself Columba.'

Finn's breath stopped.

For a moment, he thought he had misheard. Then, hope, faint but real, pierced through the darkness.

He didn't register he was moving. His legs carried him through the halls, past the silent warriors, past the remnants of grief that clung to the fortress.

The gates creaked open.

There, standing with the same steady strength that Finn had known all his life, was Columba. His robes were dusty from travel. His eyes appeared older, more troubled, but still with that same quiet aura of faith.

And when he spoke, it was not with grandeur, but with the gentle certainty of a man who had come because he knew he was needed.

For the first time since Morag's death, the crushing weight on Finn's chest faded, if only slightly.

Perhaps he was not lost forever.

Chapter 21

Focail an duine, ach guth Dé iontu.
(A man's words, but the voice of God in them.)
— Scríbhinní Colm Cille

Columba stretched out his arms, Finn rushed into them; 'My son,' Columba said; 'I have come.'

Finn released Columba from the long embrace. Always close, their bond had strengthened on the journey here a year ago. He also greeted Colman and Fergus with great joy. That long, fateful journey from Hy and Hinba had changed Finn and his life forever.

Bruide arrived hurriedly at the gate. 'Good day Abbot Columba. Your return is most welcome.' They clenched arms. 'You have arrived at a very dark time. It is not only Finn who is pleased to see you. You must be tired. Finn, show Columba and the others to the guest quarters. Columba whenever you are rested please come and meet me in the quiet audience chamber. Much has happened since the day you left Finn with us.'

Columba lowered his head and voice. 'I have felt things, seen images… but I need to hear everything from you and Finn.' His gaze swept from Bruide's grief-stricken face to Finn's haunted eyes. 'Come Finn, show me the way. We can speak as we walk, if you are able.'

As they walked, Finn glanced at Columba's familiar face, at the steady presence that had guided him his whole life. A pang of longing flickered through him, memories of quiet dawn prayers, of evenings spent in study and reflection. Life at Conall's court had been a world apart, loud and restless. Here, was different again. Duty to Bruide and the people bound him. Part of him missed the simple certainty of the monastery. The youthful friendship with Eochaid and Connad. He shook the thoughts away. His place was here. *Wasn't it?*

With a mixed cloud of joy and sorrow above them, Finn led Columba through the fortress. He realized how much had changed since the last time his old mentor walked these halls.

The once-crowded alcoves where druids whispered their incantations stood empty. The great hall, once alive with feasts and revelry, felt hushed; it was in mourning.

He looked at Columba's steady face, the face of his past, the monastery, the hymns carried on the wind, the rhythmic lapping of the sea against Hy's shores. It felt so far away. And yet… a part of him yearned for it.

Could he truly leave this place?

The thought clawed at him.

Columba's voice pulled him back. 'You have been tested here, Finn. Tell me, what have you learned?'

Finn swallowed hard. 'That faith is not as simple as I once believed. That love and duty can divide a man's soul. And that God…' His voice faltered. 'God remains, even in grief. Even in doubt if you look hard enough.'

A small smile touched Columba's lips. 'Finn, you have learned more than many men twice your age.'

When Columba arrived at the audience chamber he found Bruide and Finn in deep conversation. On seeing the tall slender figure of the Abbot arrive, Bruide rose. 'Columba, your arrival is like seeing the first flowers of spring break through after a long, bitter winter. Can I offer you something to eat?'

Servants brought bread and mead, 'Bless you Bruide. I am not sure that I am inclined to eat at the moment. Fasting is a way of life for me and I often think better and receive God's guidance better after a period of abstinence.

Bruide sank into his chair at the head of the table, motioning for Columba and Finn to sit. The three of them formed a triangle of unspoken heartbreak. Finn's voice quavered as he told the story: victory in battle at Morag's side, the joy of his love for Morag, the fear and excitement of her pregnancy, the birth, and finally the devastating murder.

Each word spilled out like blood from a fresh wound. Bruide remained silent, occasionally clenching and unclenching his hands. Columba listened, his face conveying profound sympathy, tears glistening in his eyes as Finn described the discovery of Morag's body.

When the tale ended, silence filled the room.

Outside, the wind whistled. Columba put a hand on Finn's shoulder. 'I grieve with you,' he said quietly. 'Morag was dear to you… and you to her. I can only imagine the depths of your sorrow.'

Words caught in Finn's throat. He bowed his head. 'I have prayed, Uncle Colm, I have prayed day and night… but all I feel is emptiness. I do not understand God's will in this.'

Columba nodded. 'Our Lord's plan is often hidden. Suffering weighs upon our hearts, and answers are sometimes not easily found. But fear not, my son. Love is never lost and sooner or later God's purpose will be revealed.'

Bruide's voice cut in. 'If your Christian God is so merciful, why did He not spare my daughter?'

Columba met the king's gaze steadily. 'I can't offer easy comfort, Bruide. I only know that God shares in our sorrow and does not abandon us to darkness. The same question has been asked by kings and paupers alike since the dawn of time. I myself have asked it after I caused a battle where three thousand souls were lost. No man can fully understand the plans of the Almighty.'

Bruide ground his teeth, his anger somewhat subdued by grief. He exhaled heavily, covering his face with one hand. 'I banished many of the druids,' he said after a moment,

I realised that when I saw so many on the road as I arrived here.

'They took my daughter's life. And now...the realm is left with a shortage of its ancient guardians. My people do not know where to turn. Some cling to the old ways in secret, others claim the Christian God must punish us further. Chaos brews, Columba. We are in turmoil.'

Columba nodded slowly. 'Perhaps that is why God has ordained that I be here at this time. To offer counsel, if you accept it. If you wish for peace, for healing, we must talk openly. Let no fear or bitterness remain hidden.'

Finn listened, waiting for the right time to interject. 'Morag embraced Christ, in her own special way, yet never abandoned her people's traditions. She taught me that faith and heritage need not be enemies. But now, Bruide's people are lost. They fear abandoning the gods they've always known, yet they look to me for answers I cannot always give.'

Columba studied Finn carefully. 'And what answer do you wish to give them?'

Finn though for a moment. 'That Christ's light does not erase the past, that the land itself carries the whispers of God's creation. That we can honour the old ways without bowing to superstition.'

Bruide nodded. 'If such a path is possible, I would welcome it. But some will resist, Finn. The old faith still grips many hearts, and men like Taran, ' his voice caught, thick with grief; 'would rather spill blood than allow such a union.'

Columba sighed. 'It is a fine line to walk. But Finn… perhaps this is your calling. Your time here has not been wasted,' Columba said; 'You have had an insight into the ancient ways that few followers of Christ will ever have. This is a gift for you. I would like you to teach Colman and Fergus, for I have asked them to remain here as my emissaries.'

'And what of me?'

'Finn, your destiny has already been written. The decisions will be yours, but no doubt they will be guided by God. Colman and Fergus can learn much from you. When you believe they are ready they can start their work and we shall talk of your future.'

Finn closed his eyes, imagining Morag's face, her smile. He would not let her memory fade in vengeance or despair.

Bruide inhaled. 'We shall speak further on this Columba,' he said. 'But first, I must see my grandson. The boy is all I have left of my daughter. I cherish the time I can spend with him. and it will soon be time for him to sleep.'

'May I come with you?' Columba asked. 'I wish to bless the child, Colm-Bruide. Finn, I wish I had known your Morag. I believe she is a special soul.'

Bruide rose. 'Of course, Columba. Follow me. The midwives keep him warm in the old nursery. Finn, are you coming?'

'Yes, Columba's presence has given me strength and I would wish to hold him whilst he is being blessed.'

As they neared the nursery, a faint cry sounded, Colm-Bruide, stirred in his cradle. Tears slipped down Finn's cheeks. His son would grow up knowing of his mother's courage, her kindness, her deep love, but not her.

Over the following days, Columba spent many hours with Finn, Colman and Fergus. They discussed at length Finn's new views of faith and conversion. Frequently their walks took them to Morag's church in the wood. Fresh ribbons hanging from the branches.

'I have not turned from Christ,' Finn said. 'In truth, the loss of Morag, drove me to prayer even more than the rites we follow on Hy. I feel the presence of God constantly, giving me strength. At the same time, Holy Abbot, I cannot deny that part of me resonates with Morag's old ways.' Finn had returned to using Columba's title in the presence of Colman and Fergus. 'I have supported Bruide as he offered gifts to the spirits of the land, hoping to ensure a good harvest, to keep away ill fortune and to honour Morag's memory in the traditions she, too, valued. I do not see why these two beliefs must be at war.'

Columba listened intently.

Finn continued. 'Is it a sin to acknowledge that the old ways have some worth? Does it anger God if I attend the lighting of a candle to honour the spirit of the river? I know the Holy Scriptures speak against idolatry, but I also know that all creation is from God. Is it not possible that these old customs, stripped of superstition and fear, might simply be man's attempt to commune with the divine presence in nature?'

Columba pressed his lips together, considering how best to answer. 'Brother Finn,' he began; 'your questions are not new. The worship of the old gods often includes devotions we cannot in good conscience uphold, for example, human sacrifice, or incantations calling upon lesser spirits with bad intentions.'

'There is no history of human sacrifice here,' interrupted Finn. 'You should speak to Roshyn she can explain so much.'

'I have spoken with Roshyn and will continue to do so. She is a deeply religious woman and we agree on so many things. But please Finn, let me continue. Many older customs, such as blessings for harvest and offerings of gratitude, are not evil. They can be forms of reverence for God's creation, if a Christian heart guides them.'

'Is that truly permissible? I fear condemnation from the monks who do not see any nuance in the old ways. Yet I cannot deny that something in these hills, these streams, and these ancient rites calls to my spirit. Morag felt it, too, even as she embraced Christ. She believed the two ways could exist in harmony, one does not have to extinguish the other.'

Columba nodded. 'I have met men of many beliefs, Finn. Faith in Christ can transform hearts, but it need not always eradicate every cultural expression of reverence. Are we in the Irish Church sinning by not complying with every edict of Rome? It is the intention of the heart that matters. Remember also, that we celebrate Christmas in December. The gospels do not tell us what month Jesus was born, but the Church decided that the date of a pre-Christian Roman pagan festival just after the winter equinox, that of Saturnalia, would be the date for honouring the birth of Our Saviour.

A fragile hope lit Finn's eyes. 'You do not think me heretical for my respect toward the old ways?'

'I do not,' Columba said firmly, 'so long as Christ remains for you the true path of salvation, and you refrain from any practice that leads to harm or denies the truth of the Gospel. Remember: The Word became flesh and dwelt among us. God's love can reach into every culture and every language. It's the worship of demons and the cruelty of some dark practices that we must refuse. Celebrating the changing seasons or honouring the memory of loved ones with solemn respect, are not wicked if one's heart is in the light.'

A small smile tugged at Finn's mouth. He bowed his head, relief washing over him. 'Thank you, Columba. I needed to hear those words. Too often, I fear condemnation from both sides: from those Picts who cling to the old gods and see me as a betrayer, and from the Christians who see me as wavering in my faith.'

Columba placed a comforting hand on Finn's shoulder. 'You are not alone, Finn. We all walk a path through doubts and complexities. What matters is that we seek the truth with humility and love.'

In the king's chamber, the walls hung with old trophies of war, shields, ornate swords, spears, and golden neckwear that had once graced rival chieftains. In a corner a newly carved cross had been erected. Tall and unadorned, it stood next to an ancient stone, intricately chiselled with spirals and beasts. Lying across the stone, a sword and battered shield, last used in a shield wall beside a river. This was Bruide's memorial for Morag.

'Columba,' the king began, leaning forward in his chair. 'I don't know if I shall ever recover from Morag's death. Yet I must remain strong for my people, and for her son. Are you able to give your blessing to my daughter's memorial, remembering her life?'

'I can, Bruide, but I would like to do something a little different. With your permission, I have invited someone here today.' Before we begin can I ask that you and Finn stand either side of the memorial, one of you holding Colm-Bruide.'

Finn walked in, the child in his arms. He walked to the memorial and stood next to the cross. Bruide stood beside the rune stone. Finn handed Colm-Bruide to his grandfather, who took him carefully and tenderly.

Columba, nodded to Fergus who left the room, returning immediately with a hooded figure. Roshyn walked in. She and Columba greeted each other reverently.

Columba and Roshyn stood together before Morag's memorial, a monk and a druidess, a bridge between the worlds she had loved.

Roshyn's voice wove through the air first, chanting the names of the ancient gods, the earth, the rivers, the sky. The language was old. A blessing of the land, for the daughter it had lost.

Columba raised his voice, a prayer to Christ, the Redeemer, the Shepherd.

The two voices entwined, neither drowning the other, neither bending in submission. A harmony, not a battle.

Bruide handed his grandson to his father who, cradling his son, felt a deep stillness. He held Morag's legacy. A child born of two faiths, standing at the edge of a new world.

Bruide knelt before Roshyn and Columba. Not as a king, but as a father.

'Thank you,' he whispered. 'For showing me there is another way.'

Roshyn took one of Bruide's hands, Columba the other and helped him rise.

'You do not need to kneel before us,' said Columba.

Roshyn smiled. 'Your family is a beacon to us Bruide. I have learned much in the past few months, first from Finn and Morag and lately from Abbot Columba. There need be no war of faith in these lands.'

Finn joined the small group with Colm-Bruide. The King placed a hand on the child's brow, as though blessing him with fatherly affection.

'This child is precious to me,' Bruide said quietly. 'He is all I have left of Morag, apart from memories. And he is the future of this kingdom.' He looked back at Columba, eyes bright with unshed tears. 'I want him to grow up in a land free of these conflicts. Let him inherit not a legacy of war, but one of unity.'

'With God's grace, it can be done,' said Columba; 'patience and forgiveness, will be necessary but it is achievable.'

Bruide nodded, continuing to watch his grandson. 'You have shown me a way forward, old friend,' he murmured. 'I may yet place all my trust in your God without disdaining the heritage of my people.'

Finn spent many hours speaking with Columba. They talked not only of faith and tradition but of the future. Finn's gaze often strayed to his infant son, who was growing stronger each day, his cries becoming more robust, his eyes more alert. Yet a restlessness crept into Finn's expression whenever he and Columba spoke of returning to Hy.

One afternoon, as they sat overlooking the river, Finn voiced what had been pressing on his heart.

'Morag filled my world, I never thought I'd ever want to leave her or here,' he said. 'Now something in me misses my previous life, on Hy with you and my father and in Dál Riata with Eochaid and Connad.'

Columba nodded. 'Hy is a place of peace, Dún Att a place of comradeship. But Finn you are no longer the same young man who left. You have loved and fought, you have killed. Your path is not simple.'

'That troubles me,' Finn confessed. 'I know I have responsibilities here. I cannot abandon my son.'

'No,' Columba agreed. 'Nor should you make this choice lightly. But I have seen men ignore the stirrings of their soul, and it leaves them hollow. Pray on it, Finn. Do not fear the weight of the decision.'

As the days passed, Finn. sought solace in the quietest corners of the fortress, looking out over the hills, letting the wind carry his thoughts. He prayed as he had on Hy, but here, the silence felt different, weighted, expectant. At times, he imagined himself back on the island, walking along the rocky shore, the sea's endless rhythm guiding his contemplation.

When Columba spoke of returning, Finn found himself listening intently. The words stirred something within him. The decision had gnawed at him for weeks.

He stood atop the fortress walls, the wind whipping through his hair. Below, the land stretched toward the horizon, the land of Morag, of their son. His home.

And yet…

He closed his eyes. He could hear the waves on Hy's shore, the calls of the seabirds, the echoes of prayers at dawn.

'I think I will return with you,' Finn finally admitted to Columba. The words, heavy yet light, hard yet easy, depressing yet uplifting, had taken all his courage to say out loud.

Columba nodded, his gaze thoughtful. 'And the child?'

Finn's throat tightened. He turned toward the courtyard, where Bruide cradled Colm-Bruide, the fierce warrior reduced to a grandfather's tenderness.

'I cannot take him from this. It is his home. Here, surrounded by love, the boy will know both the strength of his grandfather's people and the lessons of his mother's spirit.' Finn said. 'I will not deprive him of that.' He swallowed hard, steadying his voice. 'But I will come back.'

As Finn and Columba met with the King, Bruide asked 'What have you decided?' Columba stood beside Finn in silent support.

Finn knelt before Bruide, not as monk or warrior, as a son.

'Father,' he said, 'I must go.'

Bruide's jaw tightened, his hands clenched at his sides. 'To Hy.' It was not a question.

Finn nodded. 'Yes, and beyond. But Colm-Bruide… his place is here. His home, his bloodline. Will you raise him? As your own?'

For a long moment, Bruide said nothing.

Then, slowly, knelt before Finn.

Finn startled. Kings did not kneel. Not before monks, warriors or even sons.

Now at the same level, Bruide's hands gripped Finn's shoulders, his voice hoarse. 'You are my son, Finn. And this child, this child is Morag's gift to the world. I cannot raise him as my own as you ask, for he is more than a child of mine could ever be. He will be raised as Morag would have wished. Your son, made of love and respect.' He pulled Finn into a rough embrace. 'Go. But come back to us. He must know his father.'

Finn pressed his forehead to Bruide's shoulder, fighting tears. 'I will.'

They rose. Finn stepped back, forcing himself not to look at the cradle again. If he did, he might break.

Columba placed a steadying hand on his back. 'Come, my son. The hills await.'

And so, as the sun dipped beyond the hills, Finn walked away from all he had built, all he had lost, towards a future he had yet to understand.

Chapter 22

Is i ndorchadas na hintinne a dhéantar corónú an chroí.
(In the mind's darkness, the heart is crowned.)
— Sean-Rún na hÉireann, 6th Century Meditation

Words travel faster than an abbot and his sword wielding young acolyte. Words don't stop for prayer, or to offer blessings to people on the road. By the time Columba and Finn arrived at An t-Òban, to begin the sea part of their journey, Cobthach was waiting for them.

As Finn leapt from the boat, he had just touched the ground when his father's arms wrapped around him.

'My son,' Cobthach murmured, gripping him tightly. 'You seem… changed.'

Finn swallowed hard, a lump in his throat. How could he explain?

'I am, father,' he said softly. Then, unable to hold it back, he smiled through the grief. 'And you're a grandfather.'

Cobthach pulled back, eyes widening. 'What?'

Finn nodded. A moment of joy, in the midst of so much loss. But there was no time to dwell, Cobthach's face was grave.

'There's trouble on Hy,' he said. 'Áedán is there. He threatens to execute us all unless Columba gives him a Coronation blessing.'

'Let's set sail Cobthach, tell me on the way.'

The island of Hy was no stranger to fierce winds, but the storm that Columba was facing came not from the sea. Áedán mac Gabráin, paced like a caged wolf within the monastery's halls. The moment Áedán set foot on Hy, peace shattered like glass. The quiet, orderly life of the monks had been replaced by the clatter of armed boots on sacred ground. Their routine of prayer, study and working in the fields or scriptorium disrupted by his restless energy and unpredictable temper. Warriors lounged near the chapel, their swords untouched but present, a silent, unsheathed threat.

The monastery, once a refuge, now felt like a fortress

'When did he arrive?' asked Columba.

'Five days ago, he came with a group of warriors, he refused to instruct them to remove their weapons when they entered the religious compound and ordered them to make camp in the grounds. We treated him with all due respect but he would not be placated. Our holy island, a place of peace, and sanctuary of learning and prayer, has become like a military camp.'

'Áedán has ever been difficult, but this?' Columba was growing anxious.

'He demands to know where you are. Refusing to believe that you were not on the island. His warriors have searched our quarters constantly. We told him you were in the land of the Picts and would return soon, but he did not accept that as the truth.' Cobthach was struggling to find the right words. 'We attempted to carry on with our work, but Áedán's presence has disrupted our sacred order. He has not awaited your return in quiet anticipation, but prowls the length and breadth of the monastery, wielding his sword, threatening those he comes across.'

As their boat touched the shore, Columba wasted no time. 'Not a moment to lose,' he said. 'Take me to him at once.'

The monastery, usually a place of solemn devotion, felt different. A charged silence hung in the air, broken by hurried footsteps and whispers of anxious monks. Soldiers armed and armoured strolled around. As Columba and his companions passed through the courtyard, a distant shout reached their ears, angry and commanding.

Then, from within the small wooden church, came the unmistakable sound of a struggle. Columba quickened his pace. He pushed open the door and stepped inside.

Áedán's fingers tightened around a novice's throat, his face inches away, breath hot with fury.

'You cower behind your prayers,' he snarled. 'Does Columba think himself too holy to bless his own king?'

The novice gasped, eyes bulging.

'Áedán!' Columba's voice rang through the chamber.

The king's head snapped up. He blinked, as if waking from a dream. 'Columba,' he spat. 'You kept me waiting.'

'Please be calm, dearest cousin,' Columba said; 'I am now here, let us sit and talk about what you desire of me.'

'Columba, where have you been hiding?' Áedán said. He released his grip on the young novice's throat. The boy stumbled backward, clutching at his neck, but Áedán didn't notice. 'I searched everywhere for you.'

'Áedán, I was carrying out missionary work amongst the Picts and look, I have returned with Finn, who has been absent for, more than a year.'

Áedán looked at the young acolyte. Finn wasn't sure Áedán recognised him.

'Conall is dead,' he said; 'Some seek to deprive me of my throne. I demand your blessing.'

Áedán's son, Eochaid, entered the church, he had clearly been running. The concern on his face lightened when he saw Finn and Columba. He touched Finn on the shoulder as he moved passed him. 'Father, please stop. Everything is good. Columba is back now, he will see you crowned. You cannot keep threatening the monks who do nothing but wish you well. If you continue, you will make an enemy where you already have a friend.'

Áedán turned on him, 'You think me a fool?

'I think you are not yourself.'

'What do you know of it, boy? Have you borne the weight of a kingdom on your shoulders? No, you haven't nor ever will. Your brothers will have to bear that burden.'

'Columba said nothing. Áedán had obviously forgotten the vision the Abbot had had on first meeting the young Eochaid in Dún Att.

Áedán continued. 'You think I should remain in silence while rivals conspire against me?' He gestured towards the monastery. 'These men claim to be servants of God, they know nothing of war, or the struggle for power, but conspire to block me. Columba if you refuse me, you may as well cast me out naked into the winter mountains.'

'Áedán, you know that I spend much time away from here, carrying the Word to the Picts. You should have sent word ahead. I was not aware of the death of Conall and it saddens me deeply. How is Queen Sabhdha? '

'What care I of her? She is one of those who conspires against me, wanting her son to be King.'

'Father, that is not true.' Eochaid remained calm. 'The Queen believes only that you should have a small group of Counsellors around you.'

'She believes me incapable.'

The situation needed diffusing. 'Come Áedán,' Columba said; 'let us go and sit and discuss these things. If I am to give you my blessing, there are many things to organise.'

Áedán didn't move. His chest rose and fell in quick, shallow breaths. His eyes, shadowed and wild, darted between Columba, Finn, Eochaid and the monks gathered near the door, their faces filled with a mixture of fear and silent prayer. His gaze finally settled fully on Columba, searching his face, trying to read something beyond mere words.

'You will bless me then?' he asked, his voice still taut with anger and desperation.

Columba gave a slow nod. 'But first, we must talk. You're in distress, cousin. A coronation blessing is not a simple ceremony. Let us go somewhere private and speak as men, not as king and abbot.'

Áedán let out a sharp laugh. 'Private? You think privacy exists for a king? Every word I utter is heard and spread, every move I make, questioned and debated. If I so much as hesitate in my decisions, a thousand whispers rise in the halls of Dún Att and beyond.' He turned to Finn. 'And you, boy, do you now serve Columba as a priest in place of the sword? The last I saw of you, you were still untested.'

Finn held Áedán's gaze steadily. 'Much has changed, my lord.'

Áedán gave a bitter smile. 'So, it seems.'

'Father, you cannot go on like this,' Eochaid said; 'You say everyone conspires against you, but I see only friends before you.'

Áedán staggered back, running a trembling hand through his hair. His eyes, wild and sunken darted around the chapel, unfocused.

For a moment, he looked lost.

Then, with an abrupt laugh, too sharp, too hollow, he turned to Columba. 'Very well, let's talk. But if I don't like what I hear…' His fingers drummed the hilt of his sword.

Columba met his gaze, unwavering. 'Then you must listen carefully.'

Columba led him from the church, stepping into the cool, salt-tinged air. A hush had fallen over the monastery. The other monks, sensing a fragile truce, dispersed in pairs, glancing back at the departing king.

Áedán walked stiffly, his breathing still uneven, his hands clenching and unclenching at his sides. Finn followed at a respectful distance, his fingers unconsciously reaching for *Fidelis*, only to remember he had surrendered it to the monastery armourer upon arrival. He had known men with eyes like Áedán's: men who were unpredictable, on the edge of losing control.

They crossed the compound in silence. Inside Columba's chamber, a fire flickered low in the hearth. Áedán sank into a chair opposite the abbots seat; his body tense, his hands gripping the chair arms.

Columba regarded him carefully before speaking. 'Tell me of Conall's death.'

Áedán's jaw clenched. 'He fell ill. Some say it was natural, I don't believe it. There were too many wanting him gone. I wasn't there. Before I could claim my right as his successor, the whispers began.'

Columba leaned forward. 'So, you fear treachery?'

'I do not fear it, I know it is there.' Áedán raked his fingers over his beard. 'There are those who would see Conall's son on the throne, with Sabhdha ruling in his name. And if not him, it would be another. The nobles are divided.'

'I do not believe that everyone is against you, Áedán,' Columba replied

Áedán let out a sharp breath. 'And yet, I find myself sitting here, demanding what should have been given freely.'

Columba remained calm. 'You cannot demand a blessing, Áedán. It is something sought in humility. If you wish me to anoint you as King of Dál Riata, I must know that you are ready to bear that burden, not as a warrior who takes and divides, but as a leader who serves and unites.'

Áedán rubbed his temples. 'I can't sleep, Colm.' His voice dropped. 'I hear whispers where there are none. I see shadows move when no one is there.' His fists clenched. 'Everyone lies. Everyone conspires. I trust no one.'

Columba saw not a king, but a man unravelling. 'Your greatest battle,' the Abbot said, 'is not with your rivals, Áedán. It is with yourself.'

A dry, bitter laugh as Áedán said. 'Wise words, Columba. But wisdom won't keep my throat from being slit in the night.'

Columba studied him carefully. 'And yet, you have come to me. Not to your warriors, but to a man of God. That tells me something.'

Áedán's eyes flickered with something like uncertainty. 'Perhaps, it tells you that I am in a state of desperation.'

'It tells me that you seek more than just power,' Columba countered. 'You seek peace.'

As the sun rose, the following day, casting an orange hue over the eastern sky, Columba gathered the monks and Áedán's, now unarmed, warriors in the courtyard of the monastery. Áedán stood at the centre, dressed not as a warrior but as a man humbled before God.

Monks chanted, their voices rising into the cool morning air. Columba stepped forward with a vial of sacred oil. He raised it above his head, letting the golden liquid catch the morning light.

'A king does not rule by might alone,' he intoned. 'He rules by wisdom, by justice, by mercy.'

Áedán stood rigid.

'Áedán mac Gabráin,' Columba continued, tracing the cross onto his forehead, 'do you swear to uphold these things?'

Áedán's held his breath, not moving.

Then, slowly, he dropped to one knee.

'I swear it.'

The oil gleamed against his brow, but no triumph flickered in his eyes. Only wariness.

Columba placed a hand on his head. 'Rise, Áedán, King of Dál Riata.'

A hush fell over the gathering.

Even in victory, Áedán looked gaunt, More like a man facing execution than a newly crowned king.

Eochaid called out, 'All kneel to swear allegiance to the king!'

All obeyed, even Columba.

Eochaid met his father's gaze and nodded in quiet approval. Finn knelt next to him. 'Is this now settled or should we expect another storm?'

'He remains unpredictable. There are uncertain times ahead.'

The day stretched out, filled with prayers, feasting, and quiet conversations among the warriors and monks. Despite the formal blessing, there was an undercurrent of uncertainty, whispers exchanged in corners, cautious glances toward the newly anointed king.

As the sun dipped below the horizon, Finn stepped away from the torchlight of the courtyard. He walked past the monastery walls, following a familiar path to the cliffs. There, silhouetted against the darkening sky, stood Áedán and Eochaid. The wind whipped at their cloaks, but neither man moved, their gazes fixed on the restless black sea beyond.

'You've left the celebrations early,' Finn said.

Áedán did not turn. 'What is there to celebrate?'

'You have won God's blessing.'

Áedán let out a bitter laugh. 'And yet, I feel no different.' He turned, looking at Finn for a long moment.

'And you, boy, ' he sneered. 'Have you traded your sword for a prayer book?'

Finn met his stare, unflinching.

'I have fought beside kings,' he said evenly. 'And I have prayed beside saints. The difference between them is whether they rule by fear or wisdom.'

Áedán's lips curled. 'And which do you think I am?'

Finn did not answer. Sometimes silence can convey more than words ever can.

'Tell me then, Finn,' Áedán said; 'do you believe men can change?'

Finn hesitated. He thought of Bruide, of his own journey between two faiths of the many who had struggled between the past and the future.

'Yes,' he said at last. 'It takes time, it cannot be achieved in an instant.'

Áedán looked away again. 'I suppose the passing time will reveal what kind of king I become.'

Chapter 23

Is é cailliúint mac an ualach is mó ar choróin.
(The loss of a son is the heaviest burden of a crown.)
— Litir go hÁedán, Unknown Author
Fourteen years later

The horizon trembled, a haze of mist and rolling clouds blurring the edges of land and sky.

Eochaid inhaled the scent of damp earth, thick with the promise of rain and war.

Around him, the warriors of Dál Riata were like restless wolves, adjusting grips on spears, whispering oaths, some to Christ, others to the land and their ancestors.

Few voices rose above a murmur. Here and there, hushed conversation melded with the rustle of standard-bearers struggling to keep their banners upright in the stiffening wind. Eochaid, took a deep, nasal breath, calming himself, before war's thunder drowned all else.

King Áedán remained in Dún Att, He sent his eldest sons, Domangart and Eochaid Find at the head of a small army to quell a Pictish uprising in the north. His three sons and the warrior monk marched to defend Dál Riata's fertile glens and rocky coasts from a band of Picts emboldened by a clan chieftain who promised them rich spoils if they could crush Áedán's men. Other clans seemed to be stirring up trouble, or perhaps they were warriors with no clan at all, merely rallying around that big braggart of a chieftain. Whispers said this 'king' boasted of pagan pacts, stirring dread with stories of savage warlike devotions. Rumour was rife in these lands. Finn mistrusted rumour.

The army had come prepared but not wholeheartedly eager for bloodshed. Eochaid found comfort in the closeness of his siblings, though Domangart was always quick with a firm admonition if younger men faltered, while Eochaid Find offered gentler reassurances to those trembling at the thought of battle. The three siblings had grown up hearing battle legends. Now, they stood side-by-side, about to write their own.

'Look,' Domangart said, nodding toward the tree line beyond the slope. 'Movement.'

Eochaid followed his brother's gaze. Dark shapes, half-seen through the morning mist, flitted from behind pine trunks and clusters of gorse. The enemy was stirring. At Domangart's shoulder, Eochaid Find closed his eyes for a moment, perhaps offering a prayer that this day would spare them. Eochaid himself said nothing, his heart pounding in his chest. He merely hefted his spear and placed his fingers on the brim of his shield.

Behind them, Finn paced along the line, silent, steady, unshaken.

In his hand, *Fidelis* glinted, its blade baptized in past battles. Around his neck, a small wooden cross, stark and simple, swayed.

Some men touched their own crosses in quiet reverence; others glanced at him with unease.

A warrior with a sword and a blessing.

A monk who had shed blood.

*

As Domangart signalled the men to form lines, the morning hush broke. A clamour erupted from the far side of the field: horns, shrieks, wild laughter. The enemy was nearly upon them.

'Shield wall,' shouted Finn.

Around Eochaid, warriors bristled with weapons: spears lowered, swords drawn, shields locked. 'Stand firm,' he called, his heart quickening.

Eochaid tried to focus on the details swirling around him. Domangart led a small vanguard on the left flank, Eochaid Find took position on the right with an agile force of swordsmen. Eochaid himself remained in the centre, near Finn and a cluster of younger men. The plan was simple: hold the line, let the enemy charge in confusion, striking back once their momentum stalls.

A shadow loomed through the mist, huge, broad-shouldered, wrapped in an eagle-emblazoned tunic. The bronze torque at his throat gleamed like a war trophy. He raised his axe and bellowed a challenge, a guttural sound ripping through the battlefield.

Axes thundered against shields. Iron clashed with iron. The Picts surged like a tide of bodies and blades, their war cries drowned beneath the brutal percussion of battle. Whatever strategy they'd formed was lost in the melee, now it was blood and instinct. Limbs thrashed. Blades flashed. Shields cracked under the weight of blows. Shouts twisted into screams, and the air reeked of sweat, blood, and churned earth.

Eochaid drove his spear forward. He felt it bite deep into flesh or bone, he couldn't tell. A scream tore through the din. He ripped the weapon free, slick and warm.

Beside him, Finn swung *Fidelis* in a clean arc, the steel humming as it sliced through the throat of a Pict who had lunged at Eochaid's exposed flank. Blood sprayed. The man dropped without a sound.

Domangart's voice rose from somewhere, over to their right. His roar, typically strong and booming, was lost in the madness. In the swirl of bodies, Eochaid could not see either brother. He prayed they were still safe. Another wave of enemies surged forward. Eochaid and Finn stepped back, shields raised. A cry rang out; a shield-bearer crumpled beside them. Then, from behind the melee, a new band of foes crashed through the weakened line.

In the midst of the violence, the chieftain reappeared like a surging tide, eyes wild with lust for blood. He cut down several of the Dál Riata warriors, swinging a great sword, sunlight flashing off its gilded hilt. Eochaid found himself face-to-face with the beast. With little time to react, Finn interposed, raising his weapon. The big man battered it aside, forcing Finn down onto one knee. Eochaid lunged, hoping to save the priest, but the champion's backhand blow smashed Eochaid's shield, forcing him to stumble away. The world spun as Eochaid hit the ground, the breath knocked from his lungs. Mud splattered his face, the roar of clashing swords momentarily muffled by the ringing in his ears. Blinking through the downpour, he glimpsed Finn, alone, exposed. Panic surged through him. Finn was left behind, at the mercy of that monstrous fighter.

All around them, men struggled, hammering at shields, jabbing with spear points. Eochaid jumped backward, narrowly evading a downward slash from an axe. Steel rang against his sword's edge. He twisted free and thrust once, twice, landing blows that sent his dying opponent sprawling. Another wave of the enemy pressed forward. The lines parted and folded, creating pockets of swirling duels. Rain fell and soaked the combatants. Thunder rolled. Eochaid looked for Domangart or Eochaid Find or Finn, but there was only confusion, figures slipping on muddy ground and colliding in violent tangles.

Far on the left flank, Domangart was rallying men to keep form. A tight cluster of his warriors had broken through a smaller band of the enemy and were on the verge of scattering them. Domangart's sword, a battered relic inherited from an uncle, cleaved through an attacker's shield and struck flesh. Behind him, one of his men cried out as a spear found its way through unprotected flesh. Domangart whipped around, face twisting with anger, and ran another enemy through. The man collapsed. The ground was dark with pooling blood.

Domangart's rain-drenched hair, reddened with the gore of others, clung to his forehead. A stench of sweat and death clotted the air. Domangart, strong and relentless, pressed on, Victory glimmered just within reach if only the men held their nerve.

From his right, two enemy warriors lunged at Domangart in quick succession. He parried the first blow with his sword, turning aside a spiked club, but missed the second man's blade. It slid in, swift and merciless.

He drew a breath, shallow and tight, chest lifting just enough to fake composure before the tremor betrayed him. He blinked as though in disbelief.

Not here.

Not now.

The Pict ripped the sword free, and Domangart staggered. His knees buckled, hands clutching at the wound that would never heal.

Above him, the storm churned, grey clouds rolling like the sea.

A breath, a whisper, stillness.

The men of Dál Riata around him roared. Domangart fell to his knees. Blood trickled between his fingers. He tried to rise, to swing his sword, but his strength was gone. The battle seemed to close in around him.

Domangart raised his eyes to the sky, grey clouds swirled overhead, faint lances of sunlight broke through. He breathed in once more, then toppled face-down to the ground. Dirt and blood stained his cheeks. His heart thundered one last time. Domangart, son of Áedán, future king, lay motionless.

Meanwhile, Eochaid Find led a swift charge against another group of Picts. He always carried a slight smile when going into battle, confident that victory would soon be his. A nimble swordsman, he darted between foes, guiding younger warriors in a dance of steel. For a while, the momentum favoured him. The enemy reeled under Dál Riata's disciplined surge.

Lightning crackled overhead as the rain turned into a thunderous downpour. The ground slickened. Mud sucked at the boots of the fighting men, Eochaid Find, spattered with rivulets of filth and blood, saw a cluster of the enemy gathering. They formed a wedge, intending to punch through his line. Quickly, Eochaid Find shouted a command, urging his men to tighten the wall, but the din of thunder swallowed his words. A deafening crack startled everyone. The enemy wedge slammed forward.

Swords, clubs, and spears tangled. Eochaid Find fought with the grace of a man who trusted both his skill and his cause. He disarmed one attacker and slashed his chest. Twisting around, he deflected another blow and stabbed deep into a third man's side. For a moment, hope glimmered in his chest. The wedge faltered. If they could hold another minute, if they could keep the line, victory would be assured.

War is cruel. Eochaid Find turned to call for an advance, an arrow whistled out of the gloom. It caught him beneath his ribs. The shock struck him first, like an icy spike lodging in his chest. He staggered, nearly dropping his sword. One of his men cried, 'Eochaid Find!' and grabbed at his shoulder to support him. A second arrow whistled, grazing Eochaid Find's arm. He hissed, pressing a hand to the blossoming stain on his tunic. The world dimmed around the edges of his vision.

'I'm… fine,' he rasped, swallowing a mouthful of iron-tasting spit. He tried to force a smile.

More of the foe rushed forward. The lines wavered. Desperate, Eochaid Find's men fought to shield him, but the enemy pressed onward. Eochaid Find coughed, lips flecked with crimson. He braced himself, summoning what strength he had left, and lunged forward to drive his blade into an oncoming attacker. The man fell, but Eochaid Find's balance slipped. Enemy boots thundered by. Rainwater and blood ran in small rivers around him. He inhaled, feeling the agony of the arrow shaft lodged beneath his rib cage.

The arrow had struck deep. Eochaid Find staggered. Pain through his ribs, but it was the cold that spread faster. His sword slipped from trembling fingers. Through the haze of battle, he saw more than warriors, more than death and carnage. He saw the meadows of his childhood, golden summer sun, Domangart laughing as they raced through tall grass. Their father, Áedán, watching, strong and smiling. He wanted to call out to them, his lips wouldn't move.

A second arrow whispered through the rain, finding his side. His heartbeat once, twice…

Darkness.

Elsewhere on the battlefield, Eochaid held his own, though exhaustion weighed on him. His lungs burned, and each breath rattled in his chest. When lightning flared, he glimpsed the big chieftain again, a mighty shape among the throng, wearing that distinctive eagle tunic. Eochaid spotted Finn, battered and drenched, staggering but still on his feet. The priest advanced with grim determination, wielding a makeshift sword, a crude metal cross riveted onto a pointed shank.

Eochaid tried to push closer to them, but a cohort of desperate enemies, seeing their chieftain still alive and savage, blocked his way. Many of them had realized the tide was turning in Dál Riata's favour, and their only hope was to rally behind that monstrous leader or flee. For long moments, Eochaid was forced to fend off frantic strikes. He shouted commands, trying to regroup the men. His mind flickered with worry over Domangart and Eochaid Find. Where were they? Were they still safe? One fleeting thought stung him: Columba's prophecy. He tried to push it aside.

The downpour intensified. Rain lashed the faces of the living and the dying alike. Sheets of water poured from the sky, turning the ground into a swamp of clay. Weapons slipped from slick hands, and mud claimed the fallen. Thunder rolled again.

At last, Eochaid managed to fight his way near Finn. The priest was locked in a deadly dance with the big man, their blades crossing in jarring clangs. Eochaid lunged toward the champion's flank, hoping to distract him. But the chieftain was no fool. He twisted, smashing the pommel of his gilded sword against Eochaid's shield, driving him backward. Eochaid skidded in the mud, losing his footing.

The champion roared, turning back to Finn. The priest muttered a prayer. The battle raged on, but in Finn's ears, there was only silence. The giant loomed, his tunic slick with rain and blood.

Finn tightened his grip. Not yet.

The Pict swung his blade, Finn ducked, pivoted, and drove his sword upward.

The iron pierced flesh, sinking deep beneath the ribs.

The warrior shuddered, breath catching. His sword clattered to the earth. He swayed, his stance unsteady and faltering, For a moment, he was a man, not a beast. No sound came from his moving lips. His body collapsed, the rain washing his blood into the saturated ground around him.

Finn breathed heavily, his pulse hammering, he looked down at the dying man, murmured a prayer, for both of them and turned away.

For an instant, the battlefield fell silent for Eochaid, all the chaotic noise of war had been stripped away. With the death of their self-proclaimed king, the enemy's will broke. Some men froze, wide-eyed, weapons half-lowered. Others turned and fled. The men of Dál Riata shouted in triumph. Eochaid, breathing hard, locked eyes with Finn. The priest clutched his bloodied sword. Rain pounded their shoulders.

The hush vanished. The air filled again with the sound of men screaming, some from mortal wounds, others in celebration or relief. Many of the enemy fled towards the hills and forests, leaving behind the broken bodies of friends, foes, and even the big man they had called king. They had no spoils to claim, only the chance to save their own lives.

'Finn!' Eochaid shouted, stepping over a lifeless form to grab the priest's shoulder. 'Are you hurt?'

Finn shook his head, water streaming from his hair. 'Not badly,' he answered. His voice sounded thick. He wiped a mixture of rain and blood from his face.

Eochaid stared at the big man's corpse, disturbed by the lingering expression of bewilderment in those once-ferocious eyes. He felt no joy in this. He looked around, wondering at the toll. More than anything, he needed to know where Domangart and Eochaid Find were.

'Come with me,' Eochaid said to Finn. 'We need to find my brothers. Are they…?'

Finn's grim gaze hardened. 'We'll look. Keep an eye open for *Fidelis*.'

They moved through the field, stepping over the injured and the dying, offering what mercy they could when a man groaned in agony. The pounding rain made recognition difficult.

Eochaid squinted, scanning collapsed bodies in the mud. Men bled from arrow wounds, sword slashes, the ragged tears of axes. Broken weapons lay half-buried in the softened earth.

They found Domangart first, lying where he fell, not far from a cluster of fallen foes. One of his loyal soldiers knelt beside him, his forehead pressed to Domangart's chest. As Eochaid drew near, the soldier looked up, eyes brimming with tears. He shook his head. Eochaid knelt, swallowing a surge of grief. Domangart's eyes were open but unseeing. Blood congealed around his abdomen. His sword hand was still curled around the hilt, as though refusing to surrender even in death.

Eochaid laid a trembling hand on his brother's cold cheek. The prophecy was coming true. Eochaid still clung to hope that Eochaid Find might live.

With Finn's help, Eochaid gently closed Domangart's eyes, tears mingling with rain on his face. Men around them paused. No words were needed; all recognized the heartbreak of losing a comrade and, worse for Eochaid, the heightened grief of a brother.

'I… I must find Eochaid Find,' Eochaid managed.

Finn placed a hand on Eochaid's shoulder. 'I'll help you.'

They trudged on, fear gnawing at their hearts. More bodies. Enemy warriors, Dál Riata men, tangled in death's embrace. They forced themselves not to look too closely, terrified that each pale face might be his brother. Then, near a trampled stand of grass, he saw a small knot of survivors huddled around a body.

Eochaid sprinted forward. The men parted, revealing Eochaid Find sprawled in the mud, an arrow still jutting from his side. His eyes were shut, his breath absent. One of the men had tried and failed to staunch the bleeding. A hush gripped them as Eochaid sank to his knees, looking upon his brother's face. Eochaid Find's lips were parted slightly, as though he had tried to speak some final word or prayer before darkness swallowed him.

Grief speared Eochaid's heart. He pressed his palm to his brother's motionless chest, the sticky blood seeping through his fingers. Tears traced paths down his cheeks. The prophecy, Columba's words, came back to him. The heartbreak was real, Eochaid could only imagine the sorrow that would strike his father's core when the news arrived.

Finn knelt beside him, silent. The men surrounding them bowed their heads. The rain, unrelenting, hammered the earth, washing away the blood that pooled around Eochaid Find's lifeless body, as though cleansing the land of the horrors wrought this day.

Later, when the battle's roar had faded to distant echoes and the last enemy stragglers had vanished into the hills, Eochaid, Finn, and the surviving warriors of Dál Riata gathered near a struggling fire. Though the rain had lessened, cold droplets still fell from the pine branches above, and damp smoke curled into the air, carrying the acrid scent of scorched wood.

Eochaid sat on a fallen log, his shoulders heavy with exhaustion. Across from him, several men passed around a flask of honeyed spirits, tearing hunks from a shared loaf of bread. Finn had discarded his soaked cloak, but whether from the chill or the weight of the day, he still shivered. He forced himself to take a bite of bread, though his stomach twisted. Water trickled from his hair down the back of his neck. Without a word, the priest handed Eochaid the flask. He took a sip; the liquor burned, momentarily chasing away the cold that had seeped into his bones.

One of the older warriors, his face lined with scars, and his crooked nose broken years ago said, 'You cannot outrun death, priest. It finds a way.'

'Or it comes screaming from the hills,' a younger man added, 'or crashing out of the woods, as it did today.'

A rough chuckle passed through the group. Another soldier wordlessly walked up to Finn and handed him *Fidelis*. Finn smiled, nodding his thanks. The warrior wiped his mouth with the back of his hand before muttering, 'Even without *Fidelis*, death didn't come for you today, Finn.'

Finn met the man's gaze. 'No. It did not. I have work yet to do in this world. My Father in heaven has not called me home.' He hesitated, his grip tightening around his cup. 'Though I fear I've added to the sins I must confess.'

Eochaid's stare remained fixed on the flames, his hands joined as if in prayer. The weight of his loss a physical pain in his chest.

Finn broke the silence with a weary sigh. 'Those heathens we cut down today, I didn't have time to convert them.' He shrugged. 'Perhaps I'll leave that task to the saints and angels.'

A quiet pause. A smirking soldier added, 'You didn't convert their king either, I take it?'

Eochaid found the faintest flicker of humour against the grief gnawing at him. 'You certainly got your point across,' he murmured to Finn.

'Please don't,' Finn said, shaking his head. 'Not now.'

Eochaid tried to summon a grin, remembering how, only hours ago, he and his brothers might have joked in just this way. But the silence of Domangart and Eochaid Find stole the moment from him. 'Perhaps,' he said softly, 'it is always time for some semblance of humour. We must find light where we can. We survived another day.'

But in his heart, there was no relief, only sorrow.

As the hours stretched on, Eochaid rose and walked away from the fire, toward where the fallen lay in grim stillness. Some had already begun the solemn task of covering the dead with cloaks, though nothing could keep out the damp. The remnants of battle, shattered weapons, torn banners, and the broken shields of friend and foe alike, were scattered across the field, sinking into the sodden earth.

Lightning flashed in the distance. The storm had begun to roll toward the mountains, but the occasional murmur of thunder still haunted the sky. Eochaid drew closer to where his brothers rested. He knelt beside them, brushing damp strands of hair from Eochaid Find's brow. He turned to Domangart, whose hands were still folded over his chest, his sword at his side. Even in death, their faces were peaceful.

Eochaid knelt between his brothers' bodies, the rain drumming against their still faces.

Domangart, the strong one.

Eochaid Find, the hopeful one.

Now both were gone.

His hands trembled as he traced a thumb across Eochaid Find's brow, and clasped Domangart's lifeless fingers. He should pray, but the words would not come.

His mind was swamped with the memory of his father's laughter, echoing from the ramparts of Dún Att as his army marched to war, and now a terrible, terrible certainty that Áedán would never laugh again.

Chapter 24

Ní fheiceann an croí briste an fhírinne soiléir.
(The broken heart sees not the clear truth.)
— Amhrán na gCaorach Fhiáin

A wave of sorrow threatened to choke Eochaid. There was still so much more to do and he could not allow himself to give in to his grief. The battle dead needed to be buried. Word needed to be sent to his father. The spoils of victory needed to be distributed amongst the men, not that this blood-soaked field would yield much of value. He wondered if the cost had been worth it.

Later that night, once the wounded had been tended and the gravely injured eased into their final rest, Eochaid joined a small gathering. Finn oversaw a quiet vigil. The monk's voice, raspy and low, recited passages of scripture, asking God for peace and rest for the dead, and for mercy upon all survivors.

Eochaid sat on a rock, face in his hands, as Finn concluded the prayer. The men bowed their heads. Some wept openly. Others, too fatigued, stared at the ground. Eochaid's eyes burned, but no tears came.

The service ended. Men filtered away to find what rest they could. Some sought quiet corners to sleep; others kept watch.

Eochaid remained by the wavering torchlight. Finn approached.

'You should rest, Eochaid, my dear friend,' he said.

Eochaid sighed, rubbing his hands over his face. 'I'll rest soon.' His voice was hollow.

A pause.

Then, almost reluctantly, he murmured, 'Thank you, Finn. If you hadn't been there… I'd be in the ground with them.'

Finn studied him. 'You lived. That's what matters.'

Eochaid's laughter was tinged with bitterness. 'Does it?' His gaze flickered to the dark horizon. 'Domangart was the eldest. Eochaid Find was… steady, wise. I was always the least of us. And yet I'm the one who remains.'

Finn shrugged. 'We all do what we must. I've known enough death. Perhaps that was my purpose today: to strike down that man, so that you might live to lead.'

'Lead?' Eochaid asked with a hollow laugh. 'Is that truly my fate? My father, he is still king, yet I know these losses will devastate him. Domangart was the eldest; Eochaid Find had the better temperament. Now I'm left to carry… everything.' He shook his head. 'I don't feel ready.'

Finn laid a firm hand on Eochaid's shoulder. 'I don't think any man can be fully ready to bear the weight of so much sorrow. The Lord, in His wisdom, has placed you here. Trust that He will guide your path, if you let Him.'

Eochaid lowered his eyes. The warmth of the priest's hand seemed to stir a faint spark of comfort, though the ache of loss remained. 'My faith is not as strong as yours, Finn.'

Dawn came grey and sullen. A swirl of crows circled over the ravaged field. Eochaid woke from a brief, fitful rest to find many of the men already at work tending to the dead and wounded. The stench was pungent and thick. Clouds pressed low, but the wind had calmed.

Eochaid nodded to the men who passed. He busied himself helping to move the fallen from Dál Riata's ranks onto carts. Their bodies would be buried on the field. He recognized faces as he worked: men he had chatted with by the fire just two nights ago. One by one, they joined the procession of the dead. When he found the enemy corpses, jumbled in pitiful heaps, he felt a tug of pity for them as well. They were nameless to him, but they had been men. They followed their leader's promise. At one point, seeing a young warrior whose unlined face suggested a mere boy, Eochaid closed the lad's eyes with gentle respect, recalling how easily they might have been on the same side in some other life.

He paused by the place where Domangart and Eochaid Find lay under a makeshift shelter. Their bodies had been lifted from the mud. Someone had cleaned their faces, though the pallor of death clung to them. He found himself wanting to talk to them, hoping they might stir, open their eyes, and grin at him.

Once the dead were buried, and Finn had said prayers for their eternal souls, wagons were loaded and the victorious host began the slow march back toward home. The bodies of Domangart and Eochaid Find lay wrapped in woollen shrouds, their swords lying on their chests, their fingers curled around the hilts. Evergreen wreaths crowned their brows, symbols of endurance, though they had not endured. Eochaid placed his father's crest over Domangart's heart. 'For him, not you, beloved brother. I know you understand,' he muttered under his breath, thinking of Áedán's absence.

The journey was sombre. Eochaid took little solace in the battered standard they carried, the emblem of Dál Riata still fluttering. His father's crest might have symbolized majesty and power in life, but now the image only reminded him of his dead brothers, lying in their own blood.

They stopped at a clearing near a small river for the night. The wagons were drawn up in a circle, fires lit for warmth. The men ate sparingly, offering more to the wounded who needed strength to endure. Eochaid found no appetite, though, picking distractedly at a strip of dried meat and a crust of bread. He turned to Finn, who sat close by.

'Finn,' he said, voice hushed so as not to disturb the tired men. 'What do I tell my father? How can I possibly explain that Domangart and Eochaid Find… are gone?'

Finn looked him directly in the eye. 'You tell him the truth, Eochaid. That they died bravely, serving their people. You share how they fought to protect Dál Riata. You do not hide your sorrow or your anger. Áedán may be king, but he is also a father. He will need your comfort as much as you need his.'

The young man bowed his head, tears threatening again. 'I am afraid that as soon as I see him, I'll lose my ability to speak.'

Finn smiled. 'Let yourself mourn, son of Áedán. It is your right.'

It took several days of travel before they reached the outskirts of the royal stronghold. Word of the victory, and its cost, had travelled ahead, borne by swift riders. By the time Eochaid and the warriors arrived, the gates were open, and a solemn crowd stood waiting.

A hush swept over the gathering as the funeral wagons creaked into view. Women wailed as they found no sign of their loved ones. Eochaid walked at the head of the procession, eyes downcast. He heard whispers, 'Domangart? Eochaid Find? Both?'

No sign of the King.

Áedán Mac Gabráin stood alone in the gloom of the Great Hall, the walls of stone and rough timber pressing in on him. The fortress, once a sanctuary, perched high on its rocky outcrop above the winding river, now felt like a tomb. Everything felt tight, suffocating. The burning torches cast trembling shadows, shapes bending, curling at the corners of his vision, conspiring to assault him with the ghosts he could not acknowledge.

His hands trembled; he pressed them to his temples. Footsteps echoed in the corridor outside, slow, ominous.

Eochaid pushed open the tall wooden doors of the hall with a loud groan. Behind him strode Finn. The two men carried the raw exhaustion of battle upon them. Dust, mud and dried blood coated their cloaks and boots. Eochaid's gaze was harrowing, a mixture of sorrow and duty. Beside him, Finn's eyes showed compassion.

The men bowed their heads, an unspoken apology, a tacit communion of grief. Áedán stared at them. They must be apparitions. Their presence threatening to confirm his darkest fears. He did not speak, a shallow, trembling breath left his lips. His eyes slid past Eochaid, searching for Domangart's broad shoulders or Eochaid Find's quicksilver grin, anything to dispel the notion of their deaths.

The hall's silence was broken only by the crackle of burning pitch on the torches and wood on the fire.

Finally, Eochaid spoke, 'Father, I,...I have brought them home.' He paused, collecting himself, tears welling at the edges of his eyes. 'Domangart and Eochaid Find. They fought... valiantly.'

'Valiantly.' The word tumbled in his mind, falling like a stone into a pond, ripples of disbelief and anguish spreading outwards. His beloved sons...gone. The knowledge dangled just out of reach, a truth he both knew and refused to accept. He felt as though acknowledging it would crystallize the pain, turn it into fixed reality. Áedán was not prepared to face that reality. Not as a king. Not as a father.

He could not ask. The words clawed at his throat, but if he gave them voice, if he let them loose into the world, they would become real. He needed to believe this was some terrible mistake. His sons weren't gone. They were late. Delayed. Even now, they were riding home, their laughter echoing through the valleys or at home. Their voices raucous in a drinking song. He listened. He strained his ears, Dún Att was silent. He clasped his head in his hands. He could hold the truth at bay, force it backwards, into the shadows until it disappeared into the night.

'My King,' Finn said. 'We bring Domangart and Eochaid Find for a royal funeral, that their spirits may rest with our ancestors and the saints alike. Let us prepare them according to your wishes.'

Áedán's eyes hardened. 'See to them with honour,' he said, looking away. 'That is my wish.' Inky shadows spread across the walls. 'Do whatever you must. I will not see them.'

Finn and Eochaid exchanged glances. Both had hoped that Áedán might at least try to close this wound with a proper farewell to his sons. The slope of his shoulders and the glassy fix of his stare, told them that his fragile mind had recoiled from the blow, seeking a refuge of denial.

Eochaid moved uneasily from foot to foot. 'Father,' he tried, gently, 'the people wish to see you. They're waiting outside the gates. They want to celebrate the land we have gained, the victory. We want you to lead the ceremonies.'

A sudden storm of anger twisted inside Áedán, A shapeless rage that threatened to spill out on any who forced him to accept this heartbreak. 'There will be no ceremonies,' he said. The finality in his tone made Eochaid's shoulders drop. 'Let them mourn their dead,' Áedán went on, struggling to keep his voice steady. 'Burn torches and say prayers for the fallen. I will not be disturbed with it. I have no place there.'

'Father,' Eochaid pressed. 'You must.'

Áedán's head snapped up, his eyes fierce. 'Must I?' The torches flickered, as though reacting to the heat of his anger. 'All my life, I have done what is expected. Worn crowns, led armies, forged alliances, buried friends. Am I not permitted,' His chest heaved; 'one moment of peace from burying my own children?'

Outside, Domangart and Eochaid Find wrapped in fresh linen, their shields laid above their swords upon their still forms, were carried to the centre of the courtyard. A hush of sorrow and respect had settled over the fortress. Soldiers who had battled alongside them surrounded the bodies. A few villagers and clan members who had followed the funeral procession from the battlefield watched from the periphery, their eyes wet with tears. The cloudless night sky above Dún Att was strewn with stars.

Eochaid led the approach to the chapel. Under Finn's quiet instruction, the bodies were placed upon stone platforms, ready for the rites and final farewell. Those who had known the princes best came forward, one by one, to whisper words of goodbye. Some shed tears; others remained quiet, their hands gripping sword hilts or wooden crosses.

But Áedán did not come.

Eochaid lingered near the threshold, casting repeated looks toward the great hall, hoping against hope that his father would emerge. The door remained firmly closed. Eochaid felt an ache that threatened to tear him in two. He was now the only surviving heir, charged with a destiny he had not asked for. His father was the King, the great leader, the one who should guide them through this heartbreak. But the King was lost in his own storm, leaving Eochaid to navigate the swirling currents of mourning and duty alone.

Within the hall's upper chamber, Áedán paced. His breath came in ragged bursts. Silence had given way to a brutal pounding in his ears, his own heartbeat, relentless and heavy. The walls seemed to close in with every turn he made. At times, he thought he heard Domangart and Eochaid Find. He would freeze, heart thundering, listening. But the voices never returned. Grief was mocking him, hollow echoes reminding him again and again that they were no longer among the living.

His mind had always been prone to 'dark hours.' Even before he ascended to the throne of Dál Riata, even before fatherhood, he had wrestled with an unquiet spirit. At times, he had confided in Columba, his only true friend, hoping for rituals or prayers that might cast out the darkness. It always returned, a relentless tide that threatened to drown him if he lost vigilance for even a moment. And now this. The greatest blow of all. Two sons, two bright sparks of life, extinguished.

He pressed his palms to the cold stone wall, bending his head forward until his forehead touched the smooth surface. He tried to focus on the chill that seeped from the stone into his skin, hoping to numb the chaos within. The torment would not relent: Domangart as a toddler, reaching out to him; Eochaid Find learning to ride his first pony, full of glee and pride. Ghostly laughter of children.

A knock at the door startled him. He whirled. 'Who is it?' he demanded, voice cracking.

'It's Finn,' came the reply. 'I come only to speak. May I enter?'

Áedán's lips parted in silent protest. The last thing he wanted was more talk of funerals, or more pity. But part of him remembered that Finn was not just a distant holy man. He was family, a cousin to his children and Columba, a friend to Eochaid, an honest heart who had known battle and sorrow. Slowly, grudgingly, Áedán crossed the cramped chamber and lifted the bar, allowing Finn to enter.

Finn stepped inside, his presence calm and reassuring. He offered a subtle bow of respect, familial courtesy.

'Áedán,' he began softly, 'forgive my intrusion. But Eochaid is worried. He asked me to… to see if you might accept any comfort.'

Áedán's hands curled into fists. He turned his back to Finn, his chest heaving. 'There is no comfort.'

The words burned his throat. They barely made a sound.

Finn did not step back. He did not leave. 'Even so,' he said gently; 'you must face your grief. If not for yourself, then for them.'

Áedán spun on him. 'For them?' His voice cracked, raw, a wound torn open.

Finn held his ground. 'Yes. Because if you do not grieve them, who will?'

Áedán's breath hitched. The fury in his chest warred with his sorrow.

Finn softened his voice. 'You must let them go, Áedán. If you do not… '

'If I do not, Finn, what will happen?' Áedán said. 'Will the heavens smite me? Will the old gods come for my bones?'

Finn met his gaze without flinching. 'No, my lord. Grief will consume you from the inside. And you will watch your last living son slip away from you, too.'

The words struck like a thunderbolt. Áedán staggered, his body trembling. His mind reached for rage, but it shattered into something else.

Silence fell. A terrible, heavy silence.

His shoulders sagged. His arms hung limp.

He was breaking. There was no stopping it now.

Finn took a measured step forward. 'Sometimes we must face our pain with others, rather than alone.'

Áedán's grief flared, twisting into anger at the suggestion. 'Who else can feel what I feel?' His voice broke. 'Who among you lost two sons this day? It's easy enough to speak of solace, to offer well-meaning words. But it is I,' his fist pounded his chest; 'who stands alone in this darkness.'

Finn bowed his head. 'I do not pretend to know the depth of your anguish. But I have seen what befalls those who shut themselves away from all kindness. The despair becomes a poison that clouds the mind, until…' He paused, as though searching for the right words. '…until the soul can be lost in its own shadows.'

Áedán barked a hollow laugh. 'My soul was lost long ago, Finn.' His breath rattled in his throat. He stared at his hands, splaying his fingers, looking for the blood he could feel on them, but there was none. 'If I step into that chapel, if I lay eyes on my dead sons, I fear I shall never stand again. I fear it will break me.'

Finn's voice grew gentler still. 'I have no illusions that it will be easy. But you must let them go, Áedán, in the way our faith and the old ways both teach. By refusing to see them, to say goodbye, you condemn yourself, and them, to roam in torment.'

Áedán turned, eyes ablaze with tears. 'You speak of faith. You speak of mercy. Where was God's mercy when Domangart and Eochaid Find were struck down? Why did He not shield them with His mighty hand? They were innocents, my flesh and blood. And yet they died, while old men who have killed and sinned remain standing. Is that the "justice" you want me to trust in?'

Finn closed his eyes, a silent lament of his own. 'The ways of the world are often cruel and beyond our understanding. Yet I have seen men find a measure of peace, even amid devastation. All I ask is that you not lock your heart from those who love you now, lest that cruelty claim you as well.'

Áedán staggered back, collapsing onto the edge of his cot. His hands rose, not in anger, but in surrender. The walls pressed in, thick with whispers of the dead. He could hear Domangart's laugh, sharp and confident. He could see Eochaid Find's eager grin, his boyhood smile. His fingers trembled as they touched the empty space beside him.

'Domangart…' he whispered. 'Eochaid Find…'

But only silence answered.

Outside, the funeral torches flickered. Áedán did not rise to meet them.

'Leave me,' he said at last, his voice muffled. 'I cannot hear these words. Not now, probably not ever.'

Finn remained motionless, torn between the call of compassion and the King's command. He bowed and stepped back. 'I will be near, should you find the strength to speak again.' He retreated, leaving Áedán in the hush of the dimly lit chamber, alone with his despair.

Chapter 25

Caithfidh an leoin é féin a chosaint ó na sionnaigh freisin.
(Even the lion must guard himself against foxes)
— Focail na nAmadán
Two Years Later

The wind howled like a wrathful spirit as Eochaid and Finn sat on the cliffs of Hy, staring across the angry sea in the bay. Clouds, heavy with rain, the air thick with the scent of damp earth and salt.

Finn pulled his cloak tighter against the biting wind.

'War is not the answer to all problems, Eochaid.' His voice almost lost in the gale. 'I wish Abbot Columba could make your father see that.'

Eochaid's breath curled in the cold air. His gaze remained fixed on the distant horizon. 'I'm afraid not even Columba can help him now.'

'Since Domangart and Eochaid Find died,' Eochaid continued, 'it's as if my father's only purpose is vengeance. He speaks of it even in his sleep. He sees enemies everywhere. The Picts, the Welsh, and now Bernicia. He hungers for blood, perhaps he thinks it will make him whole again.'

Finn's expression darkened. 'But Bernicia? Why? Northumbria

has never threatened him.'

Eochaid laughed, hollow and sad. 'Must there be a reason? Whatever is left of his mind is rotting from the inside out, Finn. Some days, he forgets that Domangart and Eochaid Find are gone. Other times, he calls for my mother, believing she still lives. But his fury never fades. He is drowning in shadows and doesn't know how to swim.'

'Let's speak with Columba, he'll give us good advice,' said Finn

'He has become known as Áedán 'The Treacherous' by his neighbours. He's constantly breaking treaties claiming they never existed. Something must be done.'

With a sigh, Eochaid turned and followed Finn towards the church.

They spotted Brother Baithéne, waiting near the abbey's gate. His face creased with concern. 'Eochaid, Finn,' he said, 'Abbott Columba has returned safely. He bade me call you to his quarters'

'This is not a meeting I'm looking forward to, Finn,' said Eochaid.

Finn placed his hand on Eochaid's shoulder. 'Neither of us are, but we must trust in God's guidance, and in Columba's wisdom.'

Columba sat alone in his study, surrounded by scrolls, quills, pots of ink, and scraps of parchment. His hands were folded in prayer. For a long time, no one spoke. Columba turned.

'Dearest Eochaid, son of Áedán,' Columba began, 'and you, Finn, sit with me. Take comfort for a moment, if you can.'

The two men seated themselves on stools near the table. Columba was resting his elbows on the worn wood. Outside, the wind rattled the shutters. His fingers tracing the edge of a parchment, 'I do not bring joyful news from Dún Att,' Columba said. 'Your father's condition is worse, Eochaid. His mind flits like a sparrow from branch to branch, unpredictable, anxious. He is consumed by the stories of Bernicia's new king, Æthelfrith. I fear that all reason might soon flee him. He still has the presence to rule, but that presence is overshadowed by suspicion and rage.'

Eochaid felt his throat constricting. 'And... is it true that he's preparing for war?'

'He speaks of it constantly,' Columba replied, nodding. 'Yet the time is not ripe. Far from it. If Áedán pursues a campaign against Bernicia now, he marches to disaster, dragging the men of Dál Riata with him. To face Æthelfrith prematurely would be the undoing of many souls.'

'Has Áedán's reason vanished completely?' Finn said

A sad, gentle smile pulled at Columba's lips. 'Not completely. But he is not as he once was. Listen to me: I saw something in him. A deep sorrow, a fear. He thinks perhaps the house of Bernicia, is a mortal threat not just to him but to the future of Dál Riata. He is not aided by certain counsel he is receiving.' Columba's eyes narrowed. 'The world is shifting. Old alliances are fading, new alliances forming. Peace is always fragile in these isles. Áedán's war might one day be inevitable. Indeed, I sense it will be. But not yet. We must delay. Delay as long as possible, until the Lord reveals the way.'

Silence held the room. The only sounds were the distant shuffle of monks outside and the tapping of the shutters in the wind. Eochaid's mind swam, picturing his father lashing out in blind anger, the armies of Dál Riata on forced marches across the moors, perhaps confronting Bernician shield walls in the gloom. His breath came unevenly.

'But how?' Finn's voice broke the stillness. 'If Áedán's determination is so fierce, how do we convince him to wait?'

'I spoke for many hours with him before returning. When his mind is clear, he listens to you, Eochaid. There is still the love of father for son, even if overshadowed by madness. His counsel may be closed to many, but you might yet reach him. Finn, too, is known for reason and a certain… skill when it comes to persuasion.' Columba offered Finn a smile. 'You both must go to Dún Att, to the royal fortress. Speak with Áedán, calm him if you can, show him how much more time is needed to gather strength and alliances. Remove the influence he now favours and try to calm him.'

'What influence?' Eochaid asked.

'One who is not who Áedán believes him to be. You'll see when you're there. Once you have done this, I want Finn to travel to Bernicia, to Dun Gaurie and Æthelfrith, as a missionary of peace.'

'The fortress has now been renamed, it's now Bebbanburg after Æthelfrith's dead Pictish wife, the mother of his eldest son.'

'Then go to Bebbanburg. Attempt to form a relationship that can buy time. Goodwill and patience may yet avert immediate bloodshed. It may be dangerous Finn, but it's necessary.'

Finn's eyes widened. 'Travel to Bebbanburg as a cousin of the King of Dál Riata? I would be regarded as a potential enemy.'

'No,' Columba said. His voice softened, but the gravitas did not. 'You will go not as an enemy, but as an emissary of peace. You will carry the Word of God.'

Finn drew a deep breath. He had faced warriors before, but this… this was different. He would be walking willingly into the heart of the greatest fighting force in England.

'Alone?' he asked, quieter now.

'Yes, mostly.' Columba held his gaze. 'It is your destiny.'

A silence stretched between them. The fire cast shadows on the walls. Eochaid sensed the tension in Finn's posture, the faint flicker of uncertainty in his eyes. Neither man desired to leave the safety of Hy only to rush into a storm.

Finn clenched his jaw. 'A mission of peace, among war-hungry men.'

Columba nodded. 'A dangerous road, yes. But you have always walked between worlds, Finn. You are the only one who can do this.'

The call was clear. Dál Riata, Eochaid's father and even Northumbria needed them, though they didn't realise it yet.

'Are you both willing?' Columba asked.

'Do we have a choice?' asked Eochaid, not expecting an answer.

As the shutters rattled, Finn heard whispered warnings in the wind. Eochaid looked at him, hesitant determination in his cousin's eyes, and nodded. 'We will do it. For Áedán, for Dál Riata, for the future of the land.'

'And for God,' said Finn.

Columba bowed his head. 'May the Lord guide your steps. Gather your belongings and be swift. You should leave before sunrise.'

Chapter 26

Bíonn na fuilcheangail níos láidre ná an fhuil féin.
(Blood bonds are stronger than blood alone.)
— Seanchas an Teaghlaigh

Finn and Eochaid crossed the sea and rugged terrain of Dál Riata. They walked and rode at a steady pace. The late spring weather offered occasional rains, but the air was warming. After leaving the coastal region, they cut through gentle slopes dotted with sheep, occasionally glimpsing villages built of wattle and daub. Everywhere they stopped, word of Áedán's troubles preceded them, carried by merchants and wandering bards.

'What do they say exactly?' Eochaid asked a local reeve one evening when they were enjoying a simple meal of oatcakes and stew.

The reeve shrugged. 'They say your father has lost his senses, that he sees enemies in every corner. He's fortifying Dún Att. Men whisper about the Bernician threat, how they might sail up the coast or come across the hills. But others blame Áedán for stirring the hornets' nest. Hard to tell what's true, my lord.'

By the time they were nearing Dún Att , the sense of impending conflict was palpable in every settlement. Women lamented the possibility that their sons might be mustered. Men sharpened weapons with a grim sense of duty.

Finn tried to bolster Eochaid's spirits whenever possible, reminding him that not everything whispered by travellers was true. 'Do not despair, We have time yet. Columba believes it can be delayed, so let us trust him. I've never known him to be wrong.'

Eochaid tried to cling to that hope, not entirely successfully.

They arrived at Dún Att on the eve of a high feast day. Trails of smoke curled into the sky, and from beyond the gate came a dull roar of activity, a blend of voices, animals, metal on metal.

At the main gate, two guards bowed respectfully as Eochaid and Finn entered. They lifted the heavy crossbar and ushered the pair inside. Immediately, Eochaid noticed that more warriors than usual crowded the courtyard. Armed men in tight clusters, was not usual.

A stable hand rushed up, offering to take their horses, Eochaid dismounted and the stable boy guided the beasts away.

A steward approached them, bowing. 'My lord Eochaid, your father awaits. But… I must warn you, he has not been well these days. Tread lightly, if I may say so. I suggest you visit him alone. He glanced at Finn.'

'Thank you,' Eochaid murmured, exchanging a worried glance with Finn.

'Go my friend,' Finn said; 'I'll go to my quarters, send word if you need me.'

Eochaid paused on the threshold of the great hall, trying to steady his breathing. His heart hammering as he stared beyond the open doors. Smoke from torches and the large hearth drifted thick in the air, the chamber hazy and pungent. He was nervous.

Áedán, was speaking with a stranger in the hall. Eochaid's hand tightened around the leather-wrapped hilt of his sword.

Grief and the pressures of kingship had weighed heavily upon Áedán, and often he would fall into moments of confusion and anger.

Taking a breath, Eochaid passed through the doors. Torches cast flickering pools of light on the rushes covering the floor. Laughter rang out. Not the familiar rich, hearty laugh of his father of old, but something brittle, more fragile. Áedán sat between two long oak tables, The crown of Dál Riata, beaten bronze, set with a single stone, rested crookedly upon his dishevelled grey hair. Standing beside him, looking every inch the warrior in a cloak of dark wool pinned with a heavy, gilded brooch, was a man Eochaid had never seen before.

The stranger was tall, with broad shoulders and a short, neatly trimmed beard. Across his left cheek was a shallow scar that tugged at the corner of his mouth, giving him a permanent, sinister half-smile. Cold, hawk-like eyes watched Eochaid approach. Áedán's eyes gleamed. he stretched out a hand.

'Eochaid! Come, come, my son. Look. A miracle has been granted us.' His voice on the edge of desperation and triumph. 'Look who has returned to us. Domangart lives. The saints have blessed us.'

The words, spoken with such conviction, shook Eochaid. His spine chilled. Turning his gaze toward the stranger, his stomach tightened.

The man's expression was neutral, his posture poised. If he had meant to impersonate Domangart, he hadn't troubled to disguise his features. Domangart had been younger than this, slimmer build and bearing different scars. Yet Áedán seemed entirely convinced.

A storm roared in Eochaid's chest, grief, fury, disbelief.

'I…' His voice struggled to escape. His father's hopeful, burning gaze was unbearable. He looked at the imposter, at the cold calculation behind his eyes, and his hands clenched.

'Father, please listen to me. Domangart…' He forced the words out, each one like a blade to his tongue. 'Domangart is dead.'

No reaction. Had Áedán heard?.

The stranger extended an arm, inviting Eochaid closer. 'Eochaid,' he said in a low voice, 'it's been a long time, brother.'

Before Eochaid could move, a voice whispered in his ear from just behind him. Connad leaned in close. 'Cousin,' he whispered; 'that man is Hering, son of Hussa. He's from Bernicia.'

Eochaid stiffened. Bernicia? 'Hering, son of Hussa?' Eochaid repeated, he was not familiar with the name.

'He's the son of the old king. He claims the crown of Bernicia is rightfully his, that Æthelfrith is a usurper. He's using your father's… confusion. He intends to draw Dál Riata's armies into conflict with Northumbria. If Áedán truly believes he's Domangart, he might march us to war on this man's whim.'

Eochaid's heart pounded. He recalled hearing that several exiles from Bernicia, believing they had stronger claims to the throne than Æthelfrith, were seeking alliances to challenge him. None to his knowledge had come to Dál Riata. Hering must have learned of Áedán's problems, how easily the king might be swayed by the reappearance of a beloved son.

Áedán saw Eochaid's hesitation and frowned. 'Well, boy, are you not gladdened by the sight of your brother? Have you no words for him? No brotherly greeting?'

Eochaid bowed his head, contemplating his options. His father had never responded well to contradiction, and in recent months, any challenge had caused violent outbursts. Yet Eochaid could not let this continue uncontested. He lifted his head, tried to meet his father's eyes with gentleness.

'Father,' he began quietly, 'I am overjoyed at your happiness. But if you would only…'

Áedán's brow furrowed. 'Only what? Embrace your brother and do it now.'

Hering kept his eyes fixed on Eochaid. 'Yes, my dearest brother,' he said; 'Let us not sour our father's mood, especially when he has so long awaited my return.'

Eochaid with fists clenched, forced a thin, polite smile and inclined his head toward Hering. 'If Father wishes, I will greet you, but we have all changed since the last time we met fighting side by side on the battlefield.'

Hering smirked as he leaned forward. 'War changes a man. Far more than you can imagine, Eochaid.'

The tension in the hall was palpable; the warriors and servants who witnessed the scene seemed uncertain whether to cheer or remain silent. Some of them were perplexed, recognizing that this man was not Domangart. Others, seeing Áedán's excitement, were relieved to see their king happy for once. Confusion and hope intermingled.

'Father,' Eochaid ventured again, 'might we speak in private for a moment? I would like to… to share in your joy but also to hear the tale of Domangart's miraculous return.'

'Hah! What need for privacy? Everyone should rejoice to see my son returned to me. And you, Eochaid, always so cautious, so sceptical. Domangart is bolder. He fought the Picts without fear. Perhaps I let you grow too soft.'

'Majesty,' Hering interrupted softly, 'I fear Eochaid may have changed in my absence. Perhaps the lad is no longer certain of his father's will. We cannot blame him. So many tragedies have befallen us in these last years.'

The words were carefully chosen, laced with just enough sympathy to suggest that Eochaid was a timid, uncertain child.

Eochaid's pride flared. 'Father, I've stood at your side through campaigns and raids,' he said, 'I have led your army and bled for Dál Riata. My loyalty has never been questioned.'

'Until now. You sound defensive, Eochaid,' Hering replied.

Eochaid bristled but steadied himself. An outburst now would serve no good. 'Father, I only wish for clarity…'

Suddenly, Áedán lurched upright. The king's eyes were wild. He jabbed a finger towards Eochaid. 'Enough! You doubt me? You dare question my word? You think I don't know my own son? Who are you? You, who claim to be my son, but cannot trust my judgment. Where is your loyalty?' His voice rose to a furious bellow. Dogs in the corner of the hall whimpered.

Eochaid swallowed, shock making him mute for a moment. 'Father, I do not question your authority. I fear only that…'

Áedán cut him off. 'You fear everything. Always have. Where is my real son, the one who never hesitated, who never balked at my word? If you refuse to greet your brother, Eochaid, you are not the son I remember.'

Silence enveloped the hall. Connad, standing beside Eochaid, looked down, his stance one of helpless rage. Áedán's outburst stung Eochaid. Although he knew it was the ravages of his failing mind speaking, it hurt to be disavowed.

Before Eochaid could utter another plea, the doors to the hall swung open. A gust of evening wind fluttered the torch flames. A flurry of sparks sputtered across the flagstones. Finn stepped through the threshold, dressed in the robes of a monk, but bearing *Fidelis* his warrior's sword. As he entered, he bowed his head in reverence, though his eyes took in the whole scene.

'King Áedán,' Finn said; 'may the blessings of our Lord be upon you.' His eyes shone with an inner tranquillity.

Áedán blinked, perplexity momentarily dulling his anger. He stared hard at Finn, squinting. 'Columba?' he asked, confusion thick in his voice.

Finn shook his head. 'No, my king. I am your cousin, Finn, humble servant of Christ and a warrior in your guard. I come at Eochaid's behest, as well as for the forthcoming feast.' He glanced at Eochaid, who nodded in silent gratitude.

Áedán's face went through a series of subtle contortions, as though he was trying to place this new arrival. 'Finn,' he repeated. 'Finn… You serve Columba, do you not?'

'I do, Majesty,' Finn said quietly, stepping closer but making no sudden movements. 'You and I have spoken before, many times since I came here as a child. I was appointed to the king's guard by King Connall and I swore my sword and allegiance to you and Dál Riata at your coronation on Hy. Do you remember?'

Áedán's brow drew together again. 'Yes, yes, of course.'

Confusion filled the king's eyes, and the tinge of fear that sometimes came when he tried to reconcile the present with his jumbled memory. 'Finn… yes, yes, Finn'.

Finn continued with calm compassion, 'The sorrow of losing Domangart wounded you greatly, my king. It weighs heavily on you. But we must be wary of illusions. God blesses us in many ways, but He does not often return the dead to this realm.'

Áedán opened his mouth to shout, perhaps to object, but Finn raised his hands in a placating gesture. 'My Lord,' the young monk said; 'take no offense. I but speak from the heart. Let us not rush to quarrel when we are so near to the feast you yourself decreed. Let the feast be a time of gratitude, of unity. If this is indeed Domangart, you have been granted an exceptional blessing. Perhaps you would wish to rest now, gather your strength, and allow your sons to reconcile, together with me, for I too fought by Domangart's side.

Áedán's gaze flitted between Finn and Hering, then Eochaid, back to Finn. His anger seemed to abate, replaced by a strange exhaustion. His shoulders drooped, and he sagged back into his chair. 'I… yes, I should rest. The feast is soon. My head… everything seems so bright.'

Finn bowed deeply. 'The brightness is your joy. Come, let your servants accompany you to your chambers so that you might lie down. This day has brought many surprises.'

'Whilst you rest, Eochaid and I will reacquaint ourselves with Domangart.'

Áedán turned his bleary gaze toward Eochaid. His expression softened briefly, before confusion reasserted itself. 'Yes, yes, rest.'

Finn placed a hand on the king's arm, guiding him up from the chair. 'Come, my king. Let your mind be eased. The feast will be one of great celebration. We will gather your sons and your loyal knights. Dál Riata will celebrate with you.'

Áedán allowed himself to be guided away, pliable in his confusion. Several attendants hurried to offer their shoulders for support. Áedán's steps were unsteady. His once-powerful frame frail and stooped. Connad hung back, reluctant to leave Eochaid's side in the presence of the imposter but eventually trailed after the king to ensure his safety. Finn slapped him as he walked past and smiled broadly at his old friend.

Eochaid, Finn, and Hering, stood alone in the middle of the great hall, eyes locked. The dancing flames highlighting the tension in their faces.

Hering folded his arms. No need for further pretence. 'A cunning monk you have there,' he remarked. 'Calmed the old king. Is that what the mighty Columba teaches you? How to twist men's minds with words.'

Finn's expression remained tranquil, though Eochaid sensed his friend's disapproval of Hering's mocking tone. 'Columba teaches compassion, reflection, and brotherly love. Our aim is peace, not manipulation,' Finn replied softly. 'It is no fault of the king that age and grief have weakened his grasp on reality.'

Hering snorted. 'Peace is well enough if one is content to remain under the thumb of Æthelfrith. But your father…' he turned his eyes to Eochaid, '… commands respect. Áedán mac Gabráin was never shy of war. If he were in full command of his faculties, he might leap at the chance to topple the Bernician usurper. I simply… offer him impetus.'

Eochaid's jaw tightened. 'You've used a father's grief to pretend to be his dead son.'

'How better to spur him to action?' Hering said. 'If Áedán is mad, that is not my doing. Yet I still see cunning in his gaze. Part of him must know Domangart is dead, and yet… he clings to hope, and hope, my friend, is the spark that lights fires.'

Finn said nothing. He let Eochaid speak, perhaps understanding that Eochaid's personal stake in this charade was immense.

'A spark that could consume Dál Riata in a pointless war,' Eochaid said. 'My father is ailing. I will not let you manipulate him so that you can gather soldiers to kill them in a pointless war, to try and claim a throne you never had.'

'Pointless?' Hering's voice, smooth, laced with steel. He tilted his head slightly, amused. 'Tell me, Eochaid, what is more pointless, letting Æthelfrith rule unchallenged, or seizing what is rightfully mine? My father was King of Bernicia. That title should have passed to me.' His smile didn't reach his eyes. 'Instead, Æthelfrith sits on my throne, while you play at keeping an old man's dreams intact. You think that is nobler?'

Eochaid regarded him darkly. 'You speak as though you have an open claim, but I hear no mention of loyalty among the Bernicians. Would they truly rally to you?'

The cold gaze did not waver. 'If you help me dethrone Æthelfrith, Bernicia will have no choice but to accept me or descend into chaos. And in that chaos, I would still find my place. I have enough kin there loyal to my father.'

Finn finally interjected, voice calm but firm. 'Regardless of the politics, you have chosen a foul method to gain Áedán's support. Lies cannot yield a lasting peace. You will earn no trust this way.'

Teeth bared, one hand drifting to the pommel of his sword. 'Peace,' Hering said. You think that is what we live for in these wild lands? Power is our strength, and war is always near. A man must grasp at advantage wherever he can. If Áedán's illusions serve me, I will use them. The question is: what will you do about it?' He looked pointedly at Eochaid. 'If you denounce me, you risk plunging your father into madness, for I suspect he does not want to hear that Domangart is gone. Perhaps you can shield him from the truth for only so long. Or you can let him keep his illusions and march forth to war. Or, better yet, you might help me quietly achieve my goal: the removal of Æthelfrith. Then, once I sit on Bernicia's throne, I will no longer need to pretend to be your brother. The old man can be eased gently into the knowledge that Domangart has died gloriously in battle after all. I will relinquish the masquerade, and he can cling to whatever story you weave. He need never see me again.'

Eochaid stood rooted in place, appalled. Equally, he knew the reality. If Eochaid unmasked Hering abruptly, Áedán would be thrust into such shock it might crush him completely.

Finn, sensing Eochaid's turmoil, said. 'Let us think carefully. We must also consider that truth, in the end, is a gentler medicine than living a lie forever.'

Eochaid eyed the empty throne where his father had sat, recalling the proud and vigorous king Áedán had once been. 'Hering,' he said finally, 'I cannot abide this deception. Domangart was my brother. He died a warrior's death. To see his memory twisted sickens me.' He drew a slow breath. 'Yet my father is in a precarious state. If I am forced to choose between protecting him and letting you dance around him with your illusions, I choose to protect him. But know this: I will not lead Dál Riata into a war for your sake.'

Hering's jaw tightened. 'You think you can stop me if I choose to stoke his madness? I have a hundred men at arms standing in your courtyard awaiting my signal.'

'Many of the King's guard know you are an imposter,' Eochaid said. 'They fought alongside me, Finn and Domangart. They helped me bring my brothers' bodies home and buried them. They are doing nothing now, as they await my orders. Do you think your hundred men at arms are a match for the Dál Riatan army? These men will never follow you.'

'You risk undermining the king,' Hering said, shrugging. 'He needs confidence if he is to keep the throne from any who would challenge him in Dál Riata. Be careful, Eochaid. You have more enemies than just me.'

Finn had heard enough. He took a single step forward, calm, immovable. His hand rested lightly on *Fidelis*, an anchor, not a threat.

'Hering of Bernicia,' he said, voice quiet but firm, 'you know nothing of faith, nor of loyalty. You wear another man's name like a stolen cloak, yet you expect warriors to follow you into war? Deception may serve you today, but it will not buy you a kingdom.'

Hering's scarred cheek twitched, his fingers flexing near his sword hilt.

Finn didn't blink. 'But let us not be hasty. There is a feast tonight. And feasts are for conversation, not bloodshed. Perhaps we can find a path forward that preserves King Áedán's dignity and spares Dál Riata from a needless war. Hering, if you try to force Eochaid's hand, you may find yourself undone. Now let us enjoy the celebration, Eochaid and I will seek counsel and will inform you in due course of our decision.'

Hering's scarred cheek twitched again . 'Your decision?'.

Eochaid's eyes hardened, his stance hardened. His bearing authoritative. 'Hering of Bernicia,' he said, a quiet, lethal edge to his voice. 'For the sake of my father's failing mind, and for the memory of Domangart, we will play along… for now.' He took a step closer. 'But make no mistake, you breathe here only by my consent. If you so much as whisper war to my father again, I will see your headless corpse cast into the sea, for the gulls to pick apart.'

The Angle met his gaze but said nothing. Torchlight dancing between them.

'Now,' Eochaid continued; 'shall we go to feast like brothers? Or shall we end this now?'

Chapter 27

Is sa tsíochháin a ullmhaítear an cogadh is fearr.
(It is in peace that the best wars are prepared.)
– Cnuasach na gCeannairí, Dál Riata Proverbs

As autumn days drew shorter, and the strong green pines stood out against the bronzing, falling leaves of other trees, Finn, Eochaid and Connad stood together, at dawn, at the top of the fortress.

'I must leave for Bernicia,' Finn said; 'before the winter snows make my journey nigh impossible.'

'Are we agreed what is to be done about Hering?' Eochaid said.

'Yes, the plan should work,' Connad replied.

Finn laughed. 'I am not in favour of deception as you know…' Now it was the turn of Connad and Eochaid to burst into laughter.

'Please, gentlemen,' Finn said, his broad smile brightening his face. 'Let me continue. It is up to you, Eochaid, to convince Hering this is his best chance of getting what he wants. He cannot rely just on the forces of Dál Riata, Æthelfrith is too strong. Connad, as head of the King's guard you need to ensure that Hering's men are in no position to aid in any resistance.'

'The guard is ready, Finn. The visit from your son is also well timed.'

'Ha! He is coming of age, it is only fitting that he be here to receive my birthday gift.'

'But did he need to bring 300 Pictish warriors with him?' Eochaid said.

'No, that was not strictly necessary,' replied Finn; 'but they are marching under a joint Christian and Pagan flag and they are accompanied by a Dál Riata escort, and led by two monks, so no-one need feel threatened.'

'No-one?' asked Connad.

'Well, no-one of peace and goodwill,' Finn replied.

The clouds that hung over Dún Att promised rain. The townspeople had been up since before dawn. Some cleaned the great hall of scattered rushes, spilled ale, and half-eaten bread and bones; already cleaned of meat by grateful hounds. Others tended to animals or sharpened blades. Dál Riata's peace could be broken at any moment and the fortress's inhabitants had a strict routine to ensure readiness. The fortress walls were manned constantly.

Eochaid, scanned the courtyard below, where some of Hering's men gathered in small groups. They were watched by Dál Riata's own warriors mingling similarly, an air of uneasiness palpable. Leaning over a parapet Eochaid scanned the eastern horizon. Behind a ridge, faint sunlight began to colour the clouds with pale gold. Today would see their plans come to fruition, he hoped.

Below, he spotted Finn entering the courtyard, hood drawn up against the chill. Connad was checking the guard at the gate. Everything was proceeding as planned, Still no sign of Hering. A cold gust of wind ruffled Eochaid's hair, reminding him it was time to act.

As he climbed down and into the courtyard, a guard ran

in from the gate. 'My lord Connad bids me inform you,' the guard said, 'a fast messenger has arrived bearing an urgent message. A sizable company approaches from the north, along the main road. About half a day's march away. Hundreds, it seems.'

Connad smiled, 'Hundreds, you say?' he said, feigning surprise.

'Aye, more than three hundred, maybe five. They bear Pictish and Cenél Loairn standards. Two monks accompany them, also on horseback.'

'Please, go and inform Domangart of this and request that he join me in the Great Hall. Oh, don't mention the banners. Also fetch Finn and Connad.'

Finn and Connad arrived first. Áedán was seated on his throne looking refreshed and alert. Eochaid was standing beside him.

'Good day, Finn and Connad,' Áedán greeted. 'Have you heard the news?'

'Yes, my lord,' replied Connad. 'May I say you seem in good spirits.'

'Now, young cousin, let's just say, the day has started bright. I'm not sure how long it will last.'

Hering entered. Áedán's face darkened a little.

'Have you heard? A large force approaches from the north. Is it Æthelfrith?'

'Domangart, welcome. Bernicia is to the south and east, why would Æthelfrith approach from the north?' Eochaid said.

'He is devious and cannot be trusted. He is capable of anything. Should I raise the guard?'

Finn laughed. 'Heri… sorry, Domangart, you are well aware that Connad commands the army and if there is to be a call to arms, it will be done by him, At such a time your own men would be subject also to his command.'

Hering was about to speak, when Eochaid stopped him. 'Worry not brother, these are friendly visitors. They are from the Cenél Loairn, the clan that oversees Hy. They come with two monks from the Abbey there and a special guest, Finn's son, whom he has invited for a surprise celebration. Our father knows of this and is content.'

Hering stayed silent, he had no idea what Cenél Loairn meant but to say so, would be proof he was not Domangart.

'Come now,' said Áedán, 'Let us prepare another feast.'

'And I'll go and greet our guests,' said Finn.

Hering stood by Finn's side. 'Your son? How old is he?'

'Sixteen.'

'Sixteen? Traveling with an entire war band?' replied Hering.

'A war band implies war, Hering. My son comes in peace. He must have gathered Picts from the north, veterans and kin-lords seeking amusement in these uncertain times, to celebrate his becoming a man.'

'He can command the Pictish tribes?'

'He is their next king, and they listen to him, yes. But, as Domangart, you know the story already. Áedán does. Shall I tell him you don't?' replied Finn.

Hering was silent.

The long column of riders and footmen wound up the slope toward Dún Att's gates. At the head, flanked by two monks wearing grey cowls, an embroidered dove on one sleeve, rode an impressive youth. Tall, muscular, braided red hair, and clad in a polished leather cuirass studded with bronze. Behind them, fearsome warriors marched in disciplined rows.

As the column neared the gates, the youth signalled a halt. Eochaid ordered the gate opened and descended the steps to join Finn, Connad and a very disgruntled Hering, to greet the newcomers.

Colm-Bruide passed through the open gates and dismounted. Standing on the muddy ground, he gave a broad grin as he spotted Finn. They ran towards each other and wrapped arms.

'Father,' the lad said, 'I bring you a gift.' One of the monks behind took a step and lowered his hood. Cobthach, proud father and grandfather joined them. Finn was overjoyed.

Eochaid and Connad approached, 'Friends, cousins, greet my son, Colm-Bruide mac Findlugán, Prince of the Picts and a man his mother would be proud of.'

Hering and a knot of his men stood motionless, startled by the sudden influx of heavily armed newcomers. Hering's eyes narrowed, his stance tense. The pretender moved to approach, but a handful of Dál Riatan guards blocked his immediate path, forcing him to circle around.

Colm-Bruide signalled and the Pictish contingent fanned out in a semicircle, their broad swords clashing in unison against their shields. The Cenél Loairn warriors kept ranks just behind. Hering halted, recognizing the demonstration as a calm, statement of power.

Eochaid stepped forward. 'So Domangart, you now see how Dál Riata welcomes its allies. My father, King Áedán, has no shortage of friends, Pictish or otherwise. If war comes, we shall not be found wanting in arms.'

Hering's lips pressed together. 'So, I see. These forces arrive unexpectedly.'

'Unexpected only to you,' Connad put in. 'We have had relations with Pictish clans for decades. And Finn, well… he is no mere monk, as you once mocked. He has stood in a shield wall with these men and killed their enemies. They respect him and these men answer to his son.'

Finn advanced with Colm-Bruide at his side. 'Hering of Bernicia, allow me to officially present my son, Colm-Bruide mac Findlugán. He commands the Pictish clans. You may consider them my family, and by extension, Eochaid's allies. They stand ready to protect King Áedán.'

Hering studied Colm-Bruide, who stood half a head taller than might be expected for someone his age. The youth's calm, confident bearing, and the lethal competence of the men behind him, left no doubt that Hering had been outflanked. His position weakened. Hering dipped his head in an approximation of courtesy.

'I see that Dál Riata has many friends I was unaware of,' Hering said. 'Be assured, I meant no disrespect.'

Eochaid seized the opening. 'Whatever your intent, you have acted with dishonour. King Áedán's health is not to be taken advantage of. However, he, and we,' he motioned towards Finn and Connad, 'also believe that war with Æthelfrith may be inevitable. Therefore, here is what you are going to do.'

Connad stepped up, 'It is Áedán's order that you journey south, east and west. Gather support among the Britons and Bernicians who support your cause. Spend the winter forging those alliances. In the spring, or the following spring, if you are able to raise a substantial army, we will match your numbers. Man for man.'

An uneasy silence followed. Hering's men looked for a reaction. Hering's cheek twitched. He had one last attempt to salvage something from his predicament. 'I hear your words. However, I came to stand by Áedán's side, to protect him from the threats that swirl around him. He believes me to be Domangart. We have a... bond.'

Finn's shoulders stiffened. Eochaid raised a hand to stop him speaking.

'A bond that exists only in the sick mind of my father. Threats that exist only in your warped imagination. Your only chance of protecting him, is by defeating Æthelfrith. If you succeed in raising an army, my father's forces shall join you.'

Connad's tone went frostier. 'Do not mistake the king's confusion for a genuine claim to our throne. If you persist in exploiting his grief, you will find your hold here is tenuous at best. The presence of these warriors only clarifies that you have no path to seizing Dál Riata. Your best chance for power is to go south. Raise an army against Æthelfrith. Return in the spring with allies. That is the only path you have left.'

Hering's expression soured. The tension ready to explode. He considered his options. *Accept?* That prospect galled him. *Fight?* His one hundred against near a thousand? That was unrealistic and foolish. He was no fool. He exhaled, shoulders relaxing. 'Very well. If your father desires me to prepare for war, I shall do so. Upon my return, I expect Dál Riata to honour its promise.'

'A word of caution, do not attempt to enter our kingdom with an army. Inform us of your readiness and our army will join you. Now you must leave Dún Att.'

Hering bowed his head. 'I will gather my retinue. We will depart within a week.'

'No' Finn said; 'you will leave today. Your horses and supplies are prepared, we've seen to that. Leave whilst we still feel some goodwill toward you.'

Hering turned on his heel and strode off, his men hurriedly following behind. As they disappeared into the guest quarters, Eochaid felt relief course through him. The confrontation had ended without violence. Hering was leaving.

Later that afternoon, drizzle settled over Dún Att in a misty curtain. Eochaid and Connad stood at the main gate. Finn and Colm-Bruide looked on. Around them, a cluster of Dál Riatan soldiers and all of Colm-Bruide's Pictish contingent, formed a line of silent watchers. Beneath their gaze, Hering and his 100 men marched out of the fortress, heading south.

Eochaid couldn't help a wry remark as Hering passed. 'Farewell, brother. May your quest for Bernicia's throne keep you warm on the long winter nights.'

In response, Hering nudged his horse into a gallop, men trailing in his wake. One of his captains spat on the ground but no one dared more. In a few minutes, they were gone, swallowed by the grey horizon.

That evening, in Finn's private rooms, he tended a small brazier. The peat sods glowed as they burned, warming the dimly lit space. Colm-Bruide, sat warming his hands, Cobthach beside him.

'I have something for you,' Finn said to his son. 'A gift for your sixteenth birthday. I intended to deliver it sooner but matters grew complicated here.'

Colm-Bruide smiled, curiosity lighting his eyes. 'You owe me no gifts, father. You have already given me so much: A heritage among both Picts and Christians, training in arms and faith.'

Finn motioned him closer. On a sturdy wooden table rested a long bundle wrapped in thick, oiled cloth. Carefully, Finn peeled back the layers to reveal a sword. The blade, the finest steel, broad and bright. Its cross-guard bore Celtic knots, and the pommel glinted with a single polished carnelian stone. Two words were also etched on the hilt. He extended it to his son.

'This sword is named *Droichead,* meaning bridge,' Finn explained. 'It was made on Hy and blessed by Columba. May it serve you as a symbol of what you are: the door between the old ways and the new, between the Picts and Dál Riata, between the old religion and Christian faith. It is also a tribute to your mother. She looked upon you as a bridge between her culture and mine. Wear this with pride and think of your mother, every time you strap it to your waist.'

Holding the weapon, Colm-Bruide's caught his breath. It was perfectly balanced, lighter than it appeared. He held it upright, turning the blade so the firelight danced along its steel. A hush lingered in the room, broken only by the soft crackle of the burning peat. He looked at the words written on the hilt. Tears welled up as he read them. 'Morag, Finn,' he said. 'Thank you, father. It's even better than *Fidelis*. I will keep this close and use it wisely. May it never spill innocent blood.'

Finn placed a hand on his son's shoulder. 'May God and your own honour guide you. Colm-Bruide, you are at a threshold, as I was at your age. You have responsibilities beyond yourself. The Picts look to you as a future leader, one who might unite clans long divided. The descendants of Ireland see you as a link to their northern neighbours. And the Church sees in you a soul drawn to Christ but sympathetic to the older beliefs that persist.'

Colm-Bruide lowered the blade, nodding solemnly. 'I feel that weight. Some nights, I wonder if I can shoulder it.'

'You can,' Cobthach assured. 'You must. Sadly, I did not know your mother, but Finn believes she was the finest of warriors. Her blood is inside you as is mine and Finn's. We have faith in you.'

Finn cleared his throat. 'I also have a request. An invitation.'

'Name it,' Colm-Bruide said.

'Will you come with me on a journey to Bernicia?' Finn asked. 'I am requested by Columba to meet Æthelfrith. He hopes we can forestall bloodshed. We have greatly delayed Hering, now we need to act quickly. You hold a unique power to negotiate or at least impress upon the Bernicians that the Picts are potential friends but a formidable enemy. If we can cultivate some relationship with him, then if war threatens, we might have a voice that will be listened to.'

Colm-Bruide's eyes widened. 'Meet Æthelfrith? The very man Hering wants to destroy?'

'Æthelfrith is formidable,' Finn agreed. 'He has expanded Bernicia's power. But sometimes, it's wiser to deal openly and honestly with a strong neighbour than to wait for war. King Áedán is… less capable of diplomacy now, and Eochaid has enough burdens at home. We go there in peace. Your presence will remind them that the Picts stand behind Dál Riata. And you might glean insights that will shape your future rule.'

Colm-Bruide set *Droichead* gently back on the cloth. 'I… I am honoured you trust me with such a mission. But is this not dangerous?'

'Dangerous, yes. But less so if we travel as envoys of goodwill, with the blessings of the Church. Æthelfrith is not known for piety, but he respects strength, and he might fear provoking the wrath of the Picts and Dál Riata if he kills messengers.'

Colm-Bruide took a steadying breath. 'Very well. If you think it wise, I will go. On one condition.'

'Name it.'

'We ensure Eochaid is safe from Hering and our strategies are aligned,' Colm-Bruide said. 'We must coordinate. Also, we'll take a strong enough escort to deter any bandits or unscrupulous Bernician lords who might see an opportunity.'

Finn nodded. 'Agreed. We shall speak to Eochaid and Connad. I believe we can gather a small retinue: some of your Picts, a few men of Dál Riata. That might suffice. The rest of your force can return home.

Finn clasped his son's forearm. 'We'll discuss details soon. Now rest. You and your men have travelled far, and there is a feast to attend.'

Colm-Bruide, tucking the newly gifted sword under his arm, bowed respectfully. 'Thank you, Father. I'll pray for guidance, and for success in forging peace. I prefer words to bloodshed, though I won't shy from defending us if forced.'

'I know,' Finn said with a soft smile. 'And I'm proud of you.'

*

Preparations were completed. Finn and his son sat with Eochaid, Connad and Cobthach.

'So, you'll head along the coastal route?' said Eochaid.

'That's the plan,' Finn said. 'We'll follow the coast south, avoiding the high passes that may soon be choked with snow. The storms might still hamper our journey, but it's more reliable than crossing the mountains.'

'Very well. We'll provide you letters bearing the king's seal, and you have the message from Columba. When do you intend to depart?'

Colm-Bruide's hand unconsciously brushed the pommel of *Droichead* at his belt. 'Tomorrow'

A short silence followed. Eochaid nodded. 'I pray for your safe journey. If all goes well, we gain knowledge and possibly stave off a war we aren't ready to fight. If trouble arises, dispatch a messenger, if you are able. We'll do what we can to aid you.'

Finn managed a half-smile. 'Thank you. We'll do all in our power to keep the warlord talking rather than fighting.'

'Æthelfrith is no mere warlord,' Eochaid said. 'He thinks like a hunter, one who sees kingdoms as prey.'

Connad laid a hand on Finn's shoulder. 'Take care, friend. And watch over the lad. He's as tall as me and stronger by the day, but sixteen is young to stand in a serpent's den.'

Colm-Bruide straightened, a steely resolve flickering in his eyes. 'I will not let my youth make me a fool, cousin Connad. I've faced Pictish warlords in counsel and in battle. Æthelfrith is just another man.'

Connad chuckled. 'Spoken like a warrior. You are indeed Finn's son. May God and the old gods keep you both safe.'

As dawn broke , the courtyard bustled with activity as the small delegation prepared to ride out. Finn emerged from the chapel, wearing his monk's robes beneath a stout traveling cloak, *Fidelis* strapped at his waist. Colm-Bruide wore a similar cloak, *Droichead* slung across his back.

Eochaid and Connad came to bid them farewell. King Áedán had tried to attend, but a wave of dizziness confined him to his chambers. Instead, Eochaid carried a small carved wooden token from Áedán, a stylized boar.

'My father sends his blessing,' Eochaid said, pressing the token into Colm-Bruide's hands. 'Return with good news if you can. If there is no good news to be found, return safely.'

Connad clasped Finn's arm. 'May God keep you. If you find Æthelfrith hostile, get out swiftly. We cannot afford to lose either of you.'

Finn offered a confident smile. Colm-Bruide turned, vaulted onto his horse. Finn walked his horse out of the gates before mounting. With a final wave to Eochaid and Connad, the party moved out and were quickly lost to sight.

Chapter 28

Se ðe beorhtest beacen byrð, hæfde moncynn mæst truwan.
(He who bears the brightest banner
held the greatest trust of men.)
— Fragmentum Bebbanburgensis, ca. 7th century

Finn and Colm-Bruide rode along the road toward Bebbanburg. The cold sea winds howled as they swept across the vast open expanse of water, broken only by the occasional small island. The fortress loomed ahead, its formidable palisade stark against the grey sky. Sitting high on its rocky perch it was visible from miles around. Wrapped in furs, and their hoods pulled up, Finn whispered a prayer of gratitude that their destination was in sight.

As they approached the gates, Finn studied the looming defences with a soldier's eye. Bebbanburg was unlike the rounded hillforts of Dál Riata or the scattered stone holds of the Picts. This was a fortress bred for siege, carved into the land, a warning to all.

With a groan of timber and iron, the gates creaked open. Fifty riders thundered out in disciplined formation, their presence more declaration than greeting.

At their head rode a young warrior, imposing despite his youth, his fur cloak pinned with an intricate bronze brooch.

'Who approaches Bebbanburg?' he said.

Finn pulled back his hood. 'I am Findlugán mac Cobthach, monk from the holy island of Hy, emissary of Abbot Columba and a messenger from King Áedán of Dál Riata. I travel with my son, Colm-Bruide,' he said ushering his son forward. We seek an audience with King Æthelfrith.'

The Angle looked at Colm-Bruide, his braided red hair, and the men behind him, swirling tattoos and bearded faces. 'Why have you brought Pictish warriors to these lands?'

'There is no cause for concern,' Finn replied. 'We come in peace. My son was visiting me and offered to escort me to ensure safe passage. Once our meeting with the king is concluded, he and his men will return north for the winter.'

'His warriors? He seems little more than a child.'

'I am to be the next king of the Eastern Pictish tribes,' Colm-Bruide said; Please do not confuse age with station or ability. Now if it is convenient we have travelled far, our horses need rest and my men need to eat. Can you please seek permission for us to enter?'

The Angle leaned back in his saddle and laughed. He turned to look at his men. 'Well, what do you think? Shall we seek permission?'

His question was greeted with smiles.

'So be it,' he said. 'You and your warriors must leave all weapons at the gate but you may rest here. Meeting the king is a matter for him alone to decide. Come, boy, ride beside me, you too priest. Convince me that you are worthy of an audience with King Æthelfrith.'

The Angle warriors parted to let the three riders through, positioning themselves all around the Pictish men, not taking any chances, and accompanied them to the gates.

As Finn and Colm-Bruide unsheathed their weapons at the gate, the Angle warrior took hold of them. 'These are exceptionally fine weapons for a Christian priest and a young Prince.'

'This is *Droichead*,' Colm-Bruide said, handing over his blade. 'A gift from my father.'

'And this,' Finn added, relinquishing his sword, 'is *Fidelis*, given to me by King Conall on the day I was made a warrior in the King's guard.'

The Angle raised an eyebrow. 'Warrior? Then you're not truly a monk?'

Finn smiled. 'I am a monk. But faith alone does not always shield a nation. I was raised by Columba, yes, but also at the court of King Conall, my cousin. I walk between two worlds, the sacred and the secular and both demand strength. The name *Fidelis* means faith. I trust both in God, and in my sword arm.'

The Angle chuckled, handing the blade to a guard.

'And mine means bridge,' Colm-Bruide said. 'My father is one, and so am I, between faith and tradition, Christian and Pict. We fight only when peace cannot be maintained.'

The Angle also handed Colm-Bruide's sword over to the guard. 'I think the King would like to hear your stories. These guards will show you to your quarters. Your men will be barracked and fed and your horses well looked after. Go, bathe and rest. You will be called for.'

The great hall was warm, its walls hung with woven tapestries, its beams darkened with years of smoke from the peaty hearths. Finn and Colm-Bruide stood before a dais on which two thrones were placed. They were of equal size. A guard announced the arrival of the King and Queen and the guests bowed their heads as they took their seats.

When they raised their heads, the King and Queen were seated. The King was instantly recognisable as the warrior who had accompanied them into the castle. His broad smile was reciprocated by his guests and reflected in the Queen's young and beautiful face.

Æthelfrith, a man in his prime, broad-shouldered, with thick dark hair and piercing blue eyes, bade his guests to sit. There was an aura of power around him. His hand rested idly on the hilt of his sword. At his side Queen Acha, her dark eyes watchful, her expression, kind and welcoming.

'Dál Riata sends envoys at last,' Æthelfrith said. 'I expected men bearing shields, not words.'

Finn inclined his head. 'Words, when wielded well, can shape the course of battle as surely as swords.'

Æthelfrith chuckled. 'So, I've heard. And what words do you bring, Findlugán mac Cobthach and Colm-Bruide mac Findlugán?

'We bring no threats, no demands, only a simple request. Peace between our lands remains unbroken.'

Æthelfrith studied the young man, 'A Pict speaks for Dál Riata?'

Colm-Bruide met his gaze evenly. 'A son may speak for his father. Although my mother was Pictish, my blood is tied to Dál Riata and to my family there. I was raised among warriors, as you were. I know what you desire, and I know what you fear.'

Æthelfrith's brow lifted, his interest piqued. 'Fear? Do you think I fear?'

Colm-Bruide met his gaze without flinching. 'You fear weakness. You fear betrayal. But you also value strength, not just in arms, but in words. We have not come to deceive or beg, but to build something that might endure longer than any sword's reach.'

Acha, who had remained silent until now, leaned forward. 'You speak well for one so young.'

Colm-Bruide turned to her and bowed slightly. 'A wise ruler

listens to all voices, whether they come from the mouths of warriors or the wisdom of queens.'

Acha's lips curled in a faint smile. Æthelfrith, however, laughed outright. 'You have courage, lad. That much I respect, but courage alone does not shape kingdoms.'

Finn stepped in. 'Neither, my lord, does reckless conquest. Your people are strong, Æthelfrith, but war on too many fronts can break even the mightiest of kings. You have enemies to the west, to the south, and now, Hering, seeks war against you.'

Æthelfrith's smile faded slightly. 'You believe I should spare Dál Riata out of convenience?'

'I believe,' Finn said, his voice measured, 'that a strong king knows when peace is the greater victory.'

Æthelfrith leaned back, considering. 'And what does Dál Riata offer in return for this peace?'

Colm-Bruide lifted his chin. 'We offer no gold, no feigned allegiance, only an understanding. If you hold to peace with us, the Eastern Picts and Dál Riata will not move against you. If you are attacked from the south or west, we will not sharpen our blades against your borders.'

Æthelfrith studied him, then turned to Acha. 'What do you think, my queen?'

'They speak wisely,' she said; 'and the boy is one to watch. If he lives to see his reign, he may be a greater threat.'

Colm-Bruide smirked. 'Or a greater ally.'

Æthelfrith grinned. 'Very well. We shall consider peace.'

Days passed in discussion and feasting. Finn and Æthelfrith spoke at length of politics, of war, of the shifting power in the isles. But it was Colm-Bruide who truly held Æthelfrith's interest. His first wife, Bebba, after whom he named his fortress, came from a Pictish tribe, but not the same one as Colm-Bruide.

The Bernician king tested the young warrior's mind as well as his mettle. They sparred in the courtyard, debated military tactics over cups of mead, and exchanged stories.

One evening, as they sat by the fire, Æthelfrith finally leaned back and regarded Colm-Bruide with something akin to respect.

'You are not the boy I expected on first seeing you,' he admitted. 'You are not soft, nor easily swayed. If the Picts ever unite behind one man, and that man is you, the north will change.'

Colm-Bruide met his gaze steadily. 'And if Bernicia holds peace with us, you may find a friend rather than a foe when that day comes.'

Æthelfrith grunted. 'Time will tell.'

At dawn, Colm-Bruide and his warriors prepared to depart. Æthelfrith met them at the gate. 'Go then. I give you my word that Bernicia will not march against Dál Riata, so long as Dál Riata does not march against me.'

'Thank you,' Colm-Bruide replied; 'now father, it is up to you and Eochaid to ensure Hering is thwarted.'

Acha stood nearby, watching Colm-Bruide. She hoped her own sons, as yet just beginning to walk would turn out like such a man. She turned to Finn, 'He is a boy to be proud of,' she said.

'He is his mother's son,' Finn replied. 'A force that will achieve much, through love and war. Using the first carefully and the second, only when necessary.'

Later that evening, Finn was invited to dine in the Great Hall with the King and Queen. This was more informal than the feasts of the last days and the royal princes played whilst their parents ate.

'These last days, we have concentrated on your son,' Æthelfrith said. 'Now tell us what the famous Columba has sent you here for. To bring me the words of a foreign god?'

'No, my lord, at least, not only that. Columba is like a second father to me, he has taught me so much. He's a very wise and perceptive man, who has a gift for seeing things that will happen in the future.'

Finn saw the look on Æthelfrith's face.

'My lord Æthelfrith, I know you doubt me and I understand that doubt, but believe me when I say, I do not doubt, for I have seen the proof. However, you need not concern yourself with that. What you do need to concern yourself with is that he believes a battle between your forces and those of Dál Riata is inevitable.'

Æthelfrith's tone sharpened. 'So, you and your son have lied to me?'

Acha laid a calming hand on his arm.

'No, my lord,' Finn said calmly. 'We spoke no lie. I did not say there *will* be war, only that a battle is likely. Columba has foreseen it. Hering is stirring unrest, twisting King Áedán's grief into delusion. The king believes Hering is his lost son, and that belief will draw blades.'

Æthelfrith's jaw clenched. 'Hering is a serpent. That's why I exiled him.'

'Yes,' Finn said. 'But even in exile, he whispers poison. Eochaid, Áedán's true son, works to expose him, aided now by Colm-Bruide and his warriors. Together, they gather strength.'

'So, I must prepare,' Æthelfrith muttered.

'Prepare, yes, but not strike first. That is all we ask.'

Æthelfrith studied him. 'Will you ask me to bow before your Christ?'

Finn shook his head. 'That is another matter, and one for another time. I ask you only to listen and show wisdom.'

The king's mouth curled into something like a smile. 'You speak like a warrior, not a priest.'

Finn did not answer.

Æthelfrith turned to his wife.

'My sons,' she said, 'should not grow up in endless war.' She turned to Æthelfrith. 'There is sense in what he says.'

Æthelfrith looked determined. 'I will not strike first,' he said; 'But if Áedán brings war to my lands, I will end it.'

Winter passed, Finn had become an accepted part of Bebbanburg life, spending time with warriors and king, farmers and bakers, Queen Acha frequently sought out his company and he spent many hours talking with her and her children. He continued to practice his fighting skills gaining respect amongst the fighting men. He no longer walked solely in the modest garb of a monk. At times he would dress as a warrior, A deep blue tunic, trimmed with silver, a heavy leather belt cinched around his waist, a cloak of dark green reminiscent of the highlands, Finn embodied the spirit of a man with a foot in two worlds.

The first days of spring brought increased activity. Æthelfrith called to him one day on the practice field. In his hand he held *Fidelis*. 'The chief of my guard is impressed with your fighting skills. I have something I would like you to do for me, if you are willing.'

'Of course, my lord, work would make me feel I'm earning my keep.'

'You eat little and drink less, your keep will not destroy my wealth. No this is a job of trust and not a small honour. It is also one which allows you to wear a sword in my presence.

'I must admit I have missed the comfort of *Fidelis* by my side.'

'We leave soon for my new Palace at Ad Gefrin, the place of the goats.' Finn smiled remembering the favourite animal of his youth. 'I need a man I can trust to travel at the vanguard of my retinue. One who signifies the passing by of the royal household and one who carries my standard. It needs to be someone I can trust for if danger lurks unseen…'

'But surely you will have riders going ahead of you to scout for trouble?' Finn asked.

'Yes but they may not see everything. Don't worry, Finn, the role is more ceremonial, but I need a trusted warrior and Acha and I believe you to be that man.'

'It will be my honour.' Finn bowed as Æthelfrith passed *Fidelis* to him.

Later, as Finn mounted a horse gifted to him by Queen Acha, a magnificent, black-coated, battle-worn charger he felt honoured. He had come to Bebbanburg with some fear for his life, now he was a trusted member of the King's household. Finn understood his presence here in Bernicia. The potential for harmony between pagans and Christians, warriors and priests, tradition and transformation, war and peace were now on his shoulders. He relished the challenges ahead.

The procession began as dawn broke. The crisp air filled with the sound of clanging armour, and the steady beat of drums. Finn led the column, his figure an imposing silhouette against the light of a rising sun. He rode with measured confidence, each step of his horse deliberate and resonant, echoing the heartbeat of the land itself. He recited a quiet prayer. A plea for unity, peace and understanding, for the courage to walk the narrow path between old hatreds and new hope.

The banner Finn carried was of red and gold. It fluttered in the wind as he held it aloft, a symbol of power and unity. Despite being a son of Ireland, and a man of the Picts, Finn felt no unease leading the march of an Angle king.

Æthelfrith rode up beside him. 'You seem deep in thought, Finn. Is anything troubling you?'

Finn smiled. 'No, quite the opposite, my lord. I feel today I am starting a new adventure. God has called me here, to your side, for a greater purpose that I do not yet understand.'

Æthelfrith chuckled. 'We are pleased you are here, Finn. Acha and I also feel the gods smiling on you.'

The road wound through the hills, where the land rose in great undulating swells. The further they travelled from the coast, the scent of salt disappeared, replaced by the smell of damp soil, trampled grass and the ever-present hint of manure.

Finn found himself riding easily. Though the men around him were warriors of Bernicia, their movements, their habits, their laughter, were much the same as those of the men he had fought beside many times. The world of kings and warlords was not so different, whether in the north or here among the Angles and Saxons.

Æthelfrith rode with his chief warriors at the heart of the column, his eyes ever watchful. Though this was his land, he moved with the wariness of a man who knew peace was never certain. Britons from the west, raiders from Mercia, there were always dangers lurking in the wild places between strongholds.

By late afternoon, as they crested a ridge, Ad Gefrin spread before them. The settlement was newly built, its great timber hall rising like a king's crown amid the farmland and grazing enclosures. The hills that encircled the valley seemed to shelter it, standing like ancient sentinels against the northern winds.

Finn slowed his horse, drinking in the sight.

Beyond the hall, herds of wild goats moved across the high ridges, their nimble bodies picking their way over rocky outcrops. Below, within the enclosures of the palace farms, sheep and domesticated goats clustered together, their woolly coats shifting in waves as they moved. Further still, in a grand enclosure, cattle grazed in their hundreds, their breath steaming in the crisp air.

Something stirred in Finn's heart.

Goats, wild ones, roaming freely in the hills called to Finn. His mind drifted back to Daire, and the goats that were his closest childhood friends. To Hy, where Finnian's goats had run away from him on that first day. For a moment, he was neither in Bernicia nor Dál Riata. He was a boy again, playing amongst the goats, the scent of brine and grass filling his lungs, the sound of the wind, carrying whispers of old prayers and forgotten songs. Roshyn had taught him to listen.

He had not thought of home in this way for years. Here, beneath the shadow of a foreign king's new palace, he felt at home.

Acha rode up beside him, following his gaze. 'You look upon this land as if you have seen it before.'

Finn let out a quiet breath. 'No, not this land, but land very like it. The sight of goats brings back memories of childhood and uncomplicated life.'

Acha smiled. 'So, wherever there are goats, you are content.'

Finn laughed, shaking his head. 'Perhaps.'

The company pressed onward. Warriors and servants gathered to receive their king. The air was filled with the mingled scents of roasting meat and damp thatch, the sounds of hounds barking and children laughing as they ran between the legs of the gathered warriors.

Acha dismounted with grace, her attendants hurrying to her side. Æthelfrith swung down from his horse, stretching his broad shoulders before turning to Finn.

'Come, my friend,' he said. 'Tonight, we feast. Tomorrow, we speak of things to come.'

Finn inclined his head, casting a final glance to the high ridges. The goats moved like shadows against the setting sun.

For this one night, he allowed himself peace.

Tomorrow would bring new roads, harder choices, and the shaping of futures yet unwritten.

But tonight, in the shelter of Ad Gefrin, with the banner raised and the fires burning, he belonged. Not just between two worlds, but to both.

To be continued…

Epilogue

Nestled between the sea and the rolling hills beyond, the church was a quiet sanctuary. Its beams creaked gently bowing to the evening breeze. The scent of burning candles and old wood filled the interior. Tapestries, depicting saints and the suffering of Christ, lined the walls. The air was thick with the incense of the day's prayers, though now the church was empty, save for one lone figure sitting in a pew near the front.

An old woman sat hunched, her frame wrapped in a heavy woollen cloak, the hood drawn low over her face. Her gnarled hands rested upon her lap, fingers curled around a small tree branch, its leaves beginning to wither. Her breath was steady, but there was a heaviness in it, a burden carried silently. She had walked many miles to sit in this place, though she did not belong.

She was not of the Christian faith. Not yet, and perhaps not ever.

She was a Druid, one of the last of her kind in this land that no longer welcomed the old ways. Once, she had lived freely in the depths of the great forests, where oaks stretched high and the rivers whispered secrets to those who knew how to listen. She had spoken with the trees, read the language of birds, and called upon the power of the earth beneath her feet. She had seen the world in ways others could not.

But time had changed things. The gods of the forest were

growing silent, harder to find. Or perhaps, they were no longer listening. The villages that once sought her wisdom in matters of healing and fate had turned to the men in robes who carried books instead of staffs, who spoke of a single god rather than many. The old paths were fading, lost beneath the weight of a new faith.

And so, she had come here. Not as a convert, but as a seeker.

She did not fear the Christian god, she had no quarrel with him, nor he with her. She suspected. If he was truly the only god, perhaps she would know it in time. If he was one among many, as she had always believed, she wished to understand his place among the others. Either way, she needed guidance. She needed to hear something, anything, in this silence that had grown within her soul.

She sighed, shifting slightly as she gazed toward the altar. The great wooden cross loomed before her, its surface carved with careful hands. Christ hung upon it, his face serene despite the pain carved into his features. She had heard the stories, the sacrifice, the suffering, the promise of redemption. It was not so different from the old tales of gods who bled to bring life to the land, who died and were reborn with the changing seasons.

Yet, there was something about this god that unsettled her. He was not bound to the earth as the others were. He was not of the rivers or the stones, not of the trees or the sky. He was beyond them all, outside the world she had always known.

A creaking noise broke the stillness.

The Druid stiffened, her fingers tightening around the edge of her cloak. The sound had come from the far side of the church, near the entrance. She did not turn immediately, waiting instead, listening. The candlelight flickered as a breeze entered through an open door.

Then, a voice, familiar and soft.

'You have been sitting here for some time.'

She turned her head slightly, just enough to see the man. He stood a few paces away, his robes simple, his face marked with age and quiet patience. His eyes, though tired, held no suspicion. This was the man she sought.

She said nothing, she didn't want to reveal herself just yet. Finally, she spoke, her voice dry as autumn leaves.

'I am waiting.'

The priest stepped closer, his movements careful.

'For what?'

She sighed. 'A sign, perhaps. Maybe an answer.'

The priest nodded, glancing toward the altar. 'Many come here for the same reason. Some find what they seek. Others do not.'

She turned fully now, lowering her hood.

'And you, Columba?' she asked. 'Have you found your answer?'

'Roshyn, my old friend,' he said.

'You have not answered my question.'

'Answers do not come at once. Faith is like the wind. You cannot hold it, but you can feel it if you are still enough.'

Roshyn's lips pressed together. She had once believed in signs, the flight of birds, the shape of clouds, the murmurs of the river. But stillness? Silence? That was harder to trust.

She looked back to the cross. 'Your god… does he still speak?'

The priest tilted his head. 'To those willing to listen.'

She scoffed, without malice. 'My gods have grown quiet.'

'Perhaps they have said all they needed to say.'

She frowned. The thought unsettled her more than she cared to admit. If the gods of the land had spoken their last, what was left for those who still clung to their ways? Were they to wander, lost in the echoes of old prayers? Or was there truly something new waiting in the silence?

Columba stepped back, nodding toward the door. 'The night is long, Roshyn. You are welcome to stay, in one of our guest rooms, if you wish.'

'She hesitated. Then, slowly, she pulled her hood back over her head. 'Not yet, Columba, though I thank you for your kindness.'

The Abbot did not stop her as she made her way toward the door. The floor creaked beneath her boots. Cold air swept in as she stepped outside. The moon hung low in the inky sky, casting a silver light across the rooftops of the monastery. In the distance, the forest waited, dark and familiar.

'Roshyn, I'm here and would enjoy your company,'

She smiled and touched his arm as she passed him. She didn't know if she would return. She trusted Columba, so perhaps she would come again. If she found her answers, maybe she would never set foot inside these walls again after this night. As she made her way down the worn path, one thought remained in her mind, turning over like leaves in the wind.

Maybe silence is not the absence of answers.

Maybe silence is the place where answers begin.

Historical Note

This novel is rooted in the vibrant, violent and complex history of sixth- and seventh-century Ireland and Britain. This was a time of shifting powers, spiritual awakening, and cultural transformation. Many of the figures and events portrayed are based on historical record, while others are fictionalised to bring greater depth to the untold stories of the period.

Columba (Colm Cille) was a real Irish abbot, missionary, and scholar. Born in 521 AD into the powerful Uí Néill clan in what is now Northern Ireland, he left his homeland following the Battle of Cúl Dreimhne and sailed with twelve companions to the island of Hy (modern-day Iona), where he founded a monastic community in 563 AD. His role possibly converting the Pictish king, Bruide mac Maelchon, and spreading Christianity in what is now Scotland, is drawn from early sources such as *Adomnán's Life of Columba*. The use of the word exile to describe Columba's departure from Ireland to Iona has long been a matter of debate among scholars. Some describe it as a voluntary act, a *peregrinatio pro Christo* (pilgrimage for Christ, undertaken out of spiritual conviction or penitence). Others, however, suggest that it may have been imposed as a form of ecclesiastical penance following the Synod of Tailtiu in 561 or 562 AD, where Columba may have been censured by fellow church leaders. While no definitive evidence exists to prove that Columba was formally exiled, it is important to note that the early Irish Church did use *peregrinatio pro Christo* as a disciplinary measure for clergy who had erred or caused scandal.

In this context, Columba's departure to Iona, may be viewed as both a spiritual journey and a form of penance. Although Columba's case is the most famous, there are references in early Irish texts suggesting that *peregrinatio* was at times used as a corrective measure, even if few specific examples survive with the clarity of Columba's story.

NB:

- The Tailtin/Tailtiu Synod is referenced in tradition but not firmly established in contemporary sources. I acknowledge the event carefully, it may just have been a meeting of senior Bishops which would have been much easier to call than a full synod.
- Other examples of *peregrinatio* as penance are scarce in hard evidence, but the practice was known and discussed. There are mentions of it in Canon Law collections and hagiographies, although names are rarely given.
- The idea that *peregrinatio* was sometimes involuntary or imposed isn't controversial among scholars, but documentation is patchy.

The Miracles of Columba

Much of what we know about Columba's life, including the many miracles attributed to him, comes from the *Vita Columbae* (Life of Columba) written by Adomnán, one of his successors as abbot of Iona, in the late 7th century. Adomnán's work is both hagiographical and historical, capturing the spiritual legacy of Columba and the growing influence of the Iona monastery.

Among these miracle accounts is the famous episode often cited as the first written reference to the Loch Ness Monster. In this story, Columba confronts a "water beast" in the River Ness that has already attacked and killed a man. As it moves to attack again, Columba makes the sign of the cross and commands the creature to depart. It does so immediately, retreating into the depths. This tale, while clearly shaped by the hagiographic traditions of the time, remains a key part of both Columba's legacy and the folklore of Scotland.

While modern readers may view such miracles with scepticism, they served a theological and political purpose in their time, demonstrating the saint's divine authority and the power of Christian faith in a land still influenced by older, pre-Christian traditions.

Áedán mac Gabráin, king of Dál Riata, was a historical ruler who reigned from approximately 574 to the early 600s. He was indeed inaugurated by Columba and is remembered for his military campaigns and the tragic loss of his sons in battle, events recorded in the Annals of Tigernach and other early chronicles. He was succeeded as king by his youngest son Eochaid.

The novel explores the tensions between the Celtic and Roman branches of Christianity, a real and divisive issue during this time. These tensions would culminate in the Synod of Whitby in 664 AD, decades after Columba's death, but the seeds of disagreement, over practices such as monastic tonsure, the date of Easter, and ecclesiastical authority, were already taking root. In the second and third books of this trilogy these conflicts will become more apparent as the Roman influence moves further north during the reign of King Edwin.

Alongside the spread of Christianity, there was growing conflict with the traditional Druidic and animistic belief systems.

Though the historical record of the druids is fragmentary (largely shaped by Roman and later Christian sources), it is clear that early Christian missionaries encountered, and often clashed with older spiritual authorities, especially in the rural and northern regions. This novel imagines some of that tension, dramatized in the encounters between Columba's followers and the druids of Alba.

Daily life in this period was governed by kinship, land, and seasonal rhythms. Farming, herding, and fishing sustained most communities. Settlements were often simple — clusters of roundhouses enclosed by timber palisades or earthworks. The fortress at Dún Att, the royal seat at Dál Riata and the monastic compound at Hy, reflect both archaeological evidence and the imagined scale of such early medieval centres of power.

Monasteries like Iona became beacons of learning, literacy, and craftsmanship. Monks followed strict daily routines of prayer, manual labour, and copying texts. They were also healers, teachers, and advisors to kings — serving both the spiritual and practical needs of their communities. Their libraries preserved not only Christian scripture but also classical learning, and their scriptoria would one day produce masterpieces like the Book of Kells.

Finn, the novel's protagonist, is entirely fictional. His story is inspired by a real archaeological discovery led by Brian Hope Taylor in the 1950s, at Ad Gefrin (Yeavering), the royal hall of Northumbrian kings. There, at the threshold of a great timber hall believed to be King Edwin's, archaeologists unearthed a grave containing a wooden standard and the skull of a goat — powerful symbols left unexplained. This novel offers an imagined history for that unnamed figure: a life spanning kingdoms, faiths, and battles. His title, Tācnbora, is Old

English for "Standard Bearer" — a role of honour, loyalty, and burden.

While this tale blends fact with fiction, it remains grounded in the spiritual and political landscape of the time: a world where prophecy and war, kings and monks, love and grief, all shaped the paths of those who walked between the fires of old gods and the rising light of a new faith.

A Note on Place Names

In this novel, I have chosen to use some modern place names such as "Ireland" for clarity, although these terms were not in use in the 6th and 7th centuries in the way we understand them today.

During this period:

- The name "Scotia" referred exclusively to Ireland, and its people were called the *Scotti*.
- The country now called Scotland was known by several names, depending on the region and who was speaking. To the Gaels of Dál Riata and Irish analysts, it was sometimes referred to as "Albion", while the Romanised world used "Caledonia".
- The lands north of the Forth and Clyde rivers — especially those ruled by the Picts — were often known as "Pictland", though this was a cultural rather than political designation.

The shift of the name *Scotia* from Ireland to what is now Scotland did not take place until several centuries later, following the expansion of Gaelic kingdoms like Dál Riata and the eventual unification of the Picts and Gaels.

Whilst striving for historical accuracy in other areas, I've also sometimes used modern place names to help contemporary readers and avoid confusion. There is a list of names and their modern equivalent at the front of this book.

A Note on Anachronisms

Historical accuracy has been a guiding principle throughout the writing of this novel. I have taken great care to represent the period as faithfully as possible, drawing on early medieval sources, archaeology, and scholarly research. However, I also recognise that some elements may appear anachronistic at first glance.

One such example is the inclusion of carrots in the diet of the monks at Iona. It has been suggested that this is historically inaccurate, as the modern orange carrot was developed in Asia during the 9th century. While that is true of the orange variety, it is not accurate to say that carrots were unknown in 7th-century Europe. Earlier forms of carrots — typically purple, yellow, or white — were cultivated in the Roman world and remained in use throughout Europe well before the 7th century. These early varieties were likely known to monastic communities with agricultural knowledge inherited from both Roman and Celtic traditions.

While I strive for historical precision, I apologise sincerely if any unintentional anachronisms remain however, the humble carrot is not among them.

The Prologue to this novel foreshadows the death of Finn, his life story will continue in Book 2 (TÁCNBORA *The King's Shadow*) and Book 3 (TÁCNBORA *The Final Crossing*) of this trilogy.

Acknowledgements

Novel writing is often described as being a lonely profession. It's true that many hours are spent poring over books and a computer, locked away from loved ones and friends. But no book is ever published without enormous support from fellow writers and friends.

The same is true of this novel and there are many people I wish to thank:

Dr. Chris Ferguson and Paula Constantine from the *AD GEFRIN* Anglo-Saxon Museum and whisky distillery in Wooler. Your help has been invaluable.

The KBOers, which little group includes a number of terrific writers both published and not, for their encouragement, constructive (and other!) criticism and support. Remember what doesn't kill us makes us stronger.

All of the wonderful and talented writers in the South Shields Fiction Writers' Group, for support and encouragement.

My old school friends from St. Mary's, Lugwardine, Hereford. The passing years have not diminished the friendship and humour of this fabulous group.

Friends from my days at Leicester University, still drinking and laughing together.

Finally, and above all, my wife, Alison, without whom this book would not have been possible.

Printed in Dunstable, United Kingdom

79821869R00188